As the warlord Rhita Gawr prepares his final assault against Avalon, three heroes must surmount enormous obstacles—both in the world around them and deep inside themselves—to defeat him. Tamwyn, the wilderness guide, must walk the secret pathway to the stars, a journey that will take him to the true source of magic. Elli, the brave young priestess, must confront a deadly sorcerer in a realm of utter darkness. And Scree, the eagleman haunted by tragedy, must inspire his people to do the impossible.

These three separate quests come together in three mighty battles—one deep underground, one on the muddy plains, and one high among the stars—that will decide the fate of Avalon . . .

"A fitting finale . . . Barron leaves himself an opening to revisit his Arthurian realm yet another time."
—*Booklist*

Praise for

The Great Tree of Avalon novels

Book II: Shadows on the Stars

"In the tradition of high classic fantasy, this is a lengthy novel of the battle between good and evil . . . Barron touches on many worthy themes: the power of one person to make a difference, trusting in one's abilities, the fragility of our environment, the need to honor all forms of life."
—*School Library Journal*

"Aficionados of Arthuriana and T. A. Barron get a double treat in the form of *Shadows on the Stars*." —*Publishers Weekly*

"Adventure and mystery. [A] riveting tale."
—*The Jackson (MS) Clarion-Ledger*

continued . . .

"An elaborate, richly detailed world . . . This sequel to *Child of the Dark Prophecy* continues the saga in a fine and multi-layered fashion . . . Barron infuses the story with humor as he shares both the wonders of his lovingly created world and his appreciation of nature . . . This dynamic fantasy adventure will leave readers wanting more." —*Booklist* (starred review)

Book I: Child of the Dark Prophecy

"A brilliant epic tale with memorable and glowing characters. T. A. Barron writes about ecology, compassion, feminism, and peace with a light touch and a sense of adventure—a real gift. I smiled, shed tears, and was thoroughly entertained. The story stayed with me and renewed my hope for humanity."
—Isabel Allende, author of *The House of the Spirits* and *Daughter of Fortune*

"*The Great Tree of Avalon* takes us on an extraordinary adventure through a damaged but magical world and reminds us of the fragility and wonder of our own natural surroundings."
—Robert Redford

"*The Great Tree of Avalon* opens a door into a mythical, magical world. I was transported and I was enthralled. Barron's heroic characters came vividly to life as they battled the evil forces threatening their world. I shall not forget them. And what an appropriate tale for our troubled times, with its message of hope—that wickedness, however mighty, can be vanquished by the true of heart and staunch of spirit."
—Dr. Jane Goodall, U.N. Messenger of Peace, founder of the Jane Goodall Institute

"Barron once again combines an intricate, rich story, complex characters, and breathtaking magical worlds with underlying themes of conservation and environmentalism—themes about which he is most passionate." —*San Antonio Express-News*

"T. A. Barron writes majestic tales, penned in an eloquent and dignified voice. *The Great Tree of Avalon* is sure to please any lover of fantasy or fan of J. R. R. Tolkien or J. K. Rowling."
—*The Allentown Morning Call*

"The thickening plot and the three key characters, along with a captivating supporting cast of sprites, fairies, and assorted changelings, will keep the pages turning . . . [Readers] will also delight in Barron's bonus revelations." —*Publishers Weekly*

"A tale of mythic proportions." —*The Huntsville (AL) Times*

"Reading *The Great Tree of Avalon*, I am again reminded why we so love [Barron's] work. Where else can you find books that so delicately combine mythology, care for the environment, great adventure, and most importantly, an experience of the fears and joys of growing up? A childhood with T. A. Barron's books is truly enhanced." —*Chinaberry Book Review*

"*The Great Tree of Avalon* takes its readers on an extraordinary journey—a vivid story of adventure, chance and fate, and moral exploration. This lively, entrancing tale is truly a parable for us today, as we pursue our own lives, our own search for purpose and understanding." —Robert Coles, M.D., Pulitzer Prize–winning author of *Children of Crisis*

"With its mixture of high fantasy and slapstick humor, the tale resembles Barron's The Lost Years of Merlin series and Lloyd Alexander's Chronicles of Prydain." —*School Library Journal*

"A landmark fantasy, built on a scale both epic and intimate. Here the island of Arthurian myth becomes a giant tree, each of its seven roots a richly imagined realm. Whether this world lives or dies depends on three young heroes, whose quests prove that the secrets of nature and love are the strongest magic of all." —William Howarth, Professor of English, Princeton University, and author of *Walking with Thoreau*

"Rarely does a book with its own magic and idealism have such a message for the world today: to respect and revere all life, to protect our fragile environment, and to end the divisiveness that is escalating between individuals, families, communities, and nations. Once again, T. A. Barron has produced a new volume in which readers, young and old, will see the battle lines drawn between the forces of greed, arrogance, and evil, and those of sharing, of compassion, and of the will to do good." —*The Vermont Country Sampler*

Titles by T. A. Barron

Tree Girl
Heartlight
The Ancient One
The Merlin Effect

THE LOST YEARS OF MERLIN EPIC
The Lost Years of Merlin
The Seven Songs of Merlin
The Fires of Merlin
The Mirror of Merlin
The Wings of Merlin

THE GREAT TREE OF AVALON
Child of the Dark Prophecy
Shadows on the Stars
The Eternal Flame

Visit **T. A. Barron's** website:
www.tabarron.com

The Great Tree of
AVALON

Book Three:
The Eternal
Flame

T. A. BARRON

ACE BOOKS, NEW YORK

THE BERKLEY PUBLISHING GROUP
Published by the Penguin Group
Penguin Group (USA) Inc.
375 Hudson Street, New York, New York 10014, USA

Penguin Group (Canada), 90 Eglinton Avenue East, Suite 700, Toronto, Ontario M4P 2Y3, Canada
(a division of Pearson Penguin Canada Inc.)
Penguin Books Ltd., 80 Strand, London WC2R 0RL, England
Penguin Group Ireland, 25 St. Stephen's Green, Dublin 2, Ireland (a division of Penguin Books Ltd.)
Penguin Group (Australia), 250 Camberwell Road, Camberwell, Victoria 3124, Australia
(a division of Pearson Australia Group Pty. Ltd.)
Penguin Books India Pvt. Ltd., 11 Community Centre, Panchsheel Park, New Delhi—110 017, India
Penguin Group (NZ), 67 Apollo Drive, Rosedale, North Shore 0632, New Zealand
(a division of Pearson New Zealand Ltd.)
Penguin Books (South Africa) (Pty.) Ltd., 24 Sturdee Avenue, Rosebank, Johannesburg 2196,
South Africa

Penguin Books Ltd., Registered Offices: 80 Strand, London WC2R 0RL, England

This is a work of fiction. Names, characters, places, and incidents either are the product of the author's imagination or are used fictitiously, and any resemblance to actual persons, living or dead, business establishments, events, or locales is entirely coincidental. The publisher does not have any control over and does not assume any responsibility for author or third-party websites or their content.

THE GREAT TREE OF AVALON: THE ETERNAL FLAME

An Ace Book / published by arrangement with the author

PRINTING HISTORY
Philomel Books hardcover edition / October 2006
Ace mass-market edition / October 2007

Copyright © 2006 by Thomas A. Barron.
Cover art by David Elliot. Cover design by Annette Fiore DeFex.
Interior illustrations copyright © 2006 by David Elliot.
Maps copyright © 2004, 2005, 2006 by Thomas A. Barron.

ISBN: 978-0-441-01535-1

ACE
Ace Books are published by The Berkley Publishing Group,
a division of Penguin Group (USA) Inc.,
375 Hudson Street, New York, New York 10014.
ACE and the "A" design are trademarks belonging to Penguin Group (USA) Inc.

PRINTED IN THE UNITED STATES OF AMERICA

10 9 8 7 6 5 4 3 2 1

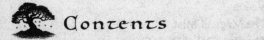

Contents

Part I

Part II

Part III

The Seven Root-Realms
of the GREAT TREE of

Avalon

BORN of MERLIN'S MAGICAL SEED PLANTED in LOST FINCAYRA

T.A.B. 69 2003

GOBSKEN
FORTRESS

EVERNIGHT PEAKS
Beware of Night Dreamers Land

Vale of
Echoes

LASTRAEL
(SHADOWROOT)

CAVERNS of the FLAMING JEWELS

DARK ELVES
Be here

VOLCANO
LANDS

LOST CITY
of LIGHT

RAHNAWYN
(FIREROOT)

EAGLE FOLK BE HERE

CAVERN of the
CROOKED TEETH

RIVER of FIRE

HIDDEN CITY

CLOUD
GARDENS
of the FAERIES

BURNT HILLS of the FIRE DRAGONS

FLAMELON
FORGES

HOOLAHOME

DANCING GROUNDS
of MIST MAIDENS

ANCESTRAL
HOME of
MUSEOS

PALACES
of the
FLAMELONS

MALÓCH
(MUDROOT)

MAALSEROW the Sorcerer's TOWER

Y SWYLARNA
(AIRROOT)

the HARPLANDS

MUD HILL

PLAINS of ISENWY

mud makers
BE HERE?

MISTY
BRIDGE

Isle of the Bards

the SOUNDSWELLS

VEILS
of
ILLUSION

SHORE of FLOTSAM

CLIFFS PERILOUS

SECRET SPRING
of HALAAD?

HALL of the WINDS

AIRFALLS of SILMONA

GNOME
LANDS
of the
LOWER
MALÓCH

BEWARE of BINKLES

BIRTHPLACE of
SYLPHS

CRAFTED
FROM THE BEST
AVAILABLE SOURCES
YEAR of AVALON
1 002
By the
GOBIA COLLEGE
of MAPMAKERS

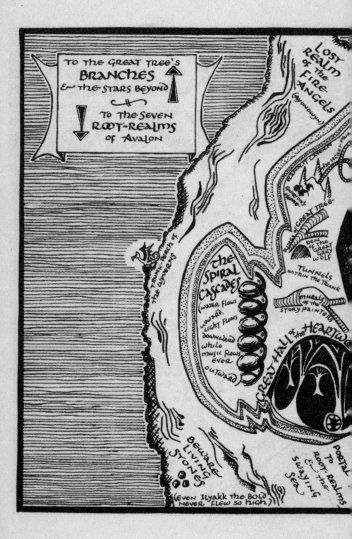

LAST REFUGE OF ETHAIN

A PRISM BIRDS SOAR HERE

MERLIN'S KNOTHOLE KNOWN BY THE AYONOWYN AS NUADA ILBRÍA WINDOW TO THE STARS

OF AMON HOLM

THE MIDDLE REALM of THE GREAT TREE of

Avalon

BORN OF MERLIN'S MAGICAL SEED PLANTED IN LOST FINCAYRA

WHERE BE THE HIDDEN PASSAGE KRYSTALLUS?

STARWARD

N

W

E

S

ROOTWARD

CRAFTED BY THE EOPIA COLLEGE of MAPMAKERS FROM THE ANCIENT ANNALS of the AYONOWYN EXPLORERS

T.A.B. 2004

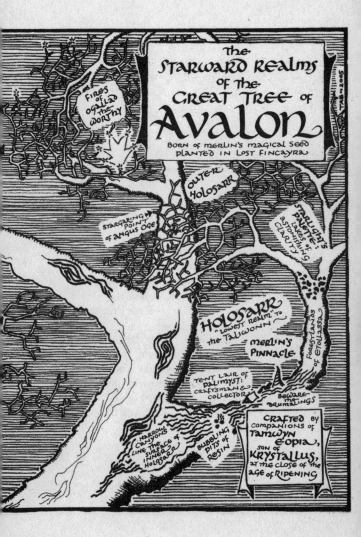

The
STARWARD REALMS
OF THE
GREAT TREE OF
Avalon
BORN OF MERLIN'S MAGICAL SEED
PLANTED IN LOST FINCAYRA

FIRES OF OGALLAD THE WORTHY

OUTER HOLOSARR

STARGAZING POINT OF ANGUS OGE

DRAUGHT'S LAKES OF ASTONISHING CLARITY

HOLOSARR
"LOWEST REALM" TO
THE TALIWONN

MERLIN'S PINNACLE

FORESTLANDS OF ETOLIASSA

TENT LAIR OF PALIMYST: CRAFTSMAN & COLLECTOR

BEWARE THE DRUMALINGS

NARROW CANYONS LINE THE SURFACE OF INNER HOLGARR

BUBBLING PITS OF RESIN

CRAFTED BY COMPANIONS OF
TAMWYN EOPIA,
SON OF
KRYSTALLUS,
AT THE CLOSE OF THE
AGE OF RIPENING

Two Sparks, Two Flames, of Avalon

> *Listen to Creation's morning,*
> *Waking all around you.*
> *Feel the spark of dawn within,*
> *Breaking day has found you.*
> —High Priestess Rhiannon

> *Vengélano, power dark,*
> *Fill this vessel with thy spark.*
> *Let it wield Unmaking Knife:*
> *Slashing, piercing, sowing strife.*
> *Carving out the heart of life!*
> —Kulwych of the Pale Hands

A Half-Remembered Song

Fair Avalon, I cry farewell,
A death within me waking;
So many seasons did I dwell
In wondrous realms forsaking.
You are my home! My highest goal,
Kept firm beyond all shaking.
Your mist shall ever stir my soul,
A distant music making.

Prologue:
The Unmaking Knife

KULWYCH'S CHORTLE, WHILE NO LOUDER than the thin stream of water trickling down the cavern wall, was unmistakably mirthful. He rubbed his pale white hands together. In the throbbing light of the crystal beside him—the only light in this cavern far beneath the surface of Shadowroot—his scarred face glowed with anticipation.

"Soon," he whispered to himself. "Mmmyesss, very soon."

Spying a small beetle crawling across the dank stone wall, he reached up and snatched it. Slowly, he crushed its body between his thumb and forefinger, savoring each and every crack of its shell and gush of its organs.

"This is how I will deal with you, Deth Macoll." He whispered the words with relish, imagining his long-awaited chance to kill the assassin. For he knew that Deth Macoll would soon return, seeking payment for the pure élano that he'd been sent to steal.

The sorcerer wiped the remains of the beetle on his cloak. Then, inspecting the smooth flesh of his fingers, he nodded confidently. "And that is how, mmmyesss, I will deal with anyone who dares to challenge me—the new ruler of Avalon."

The crystal, resting on the stone pedestal by his side, pulsed with reddish light. Rays shimmered in the jagged scar that cleaved his face; within his hollow eye socket, scabs and swollen veins glistened. And once again, he cackled with mirth.

He knew that his master, the spirit warlord Rhita Gawr, had promised him such power, and had even used that phrase, *the ruler of Avalon*. In less than one week's time, Rhita Gawr, now in the form of an immense dragon, would extinguish the pulsing star called the Heart of Pegasus—a star that was really much more than it appeared. And then, in a great moment of triumph, Rhita Gawr would lead an army of deathless warriors down from the sky. They would destroy the ragtag alliance of mortal creatures—elves, eaglefolk, giants, and any foolish humans still loyal to the Society of the Whole—who were now gathering on the Plains of Isenwy. Unless, of course, Kulwych's own army had already crushed the mortals by then.

Having secured Avalon, the precious world between all worlds, Rhita Gawr would then turn to his next conquest: mortal Earth. That would leave Kulwych alone to dominate Avalon. To rid it forever of the foul stench of Merlin. And to remake it however he chose.

His lone eye studied the crystal on the pedestal. Small as it was, this crystal of corrupted élano—vengélano, as Rhita Gawr had named it—held unfathomable power. It could destroy any flesh, poison any water, crumble any stone. More important, it could guide the spirit warriors of Rhita Gawr, for the warlord had called to them through the crystal, even as he had bound them to its power.

"And now," whispered the sorcerer, "you shall do one thing more."

Reaching into the pocket of his cloak, he pulled out a

savage-looking claw, the parting gift of Rhita Gawr before
he'd flown off to the stars. Black and shiny as the dragon's
own scales, it was, in fact, only the tip of a claw, though it
was still as big as Kulwych's whole hand. Its curled tip narrowed to a point sharper than a dagger; its base showed the
gouges of teeth, since Rhita Gawr had bitten it off his own
foreleg.

Deftly, Kulwych tied a leather cord around the claw,
making a simple necklace. He fixed the knot with a sturdy
spell of binding. Then, recalling the words that his master
had taught him, he concentrated all his will on the corrupted crystal, lifted the claw, and began to chant:

> *Vengélano, power dark,*
> *Fill this vessel with thy spark.*
> *Let it wield Unmaking Knife:*
> *Slashing, piercing, sowing strife.*
> *Carving out the heart of life!*

A faint crackling sound started to come from the claw,
as if something smoldered deep inside. Louder the sound
grew, and louder, swelling steadily until it echoed throughout the cavern. Abruptly, all the noise ceased—just as a
small red spark appeared on the claw's surface. It spread
swiftly, like molten lava, replacing the black sheen with a
dull red glow.

"Excellent," gloated the sorcerer. He examined the
glowing claw, twirling it in the throbbing light. "Here is a
weapon fit for a great warrior. Mmmyesss, and a great
ruler."

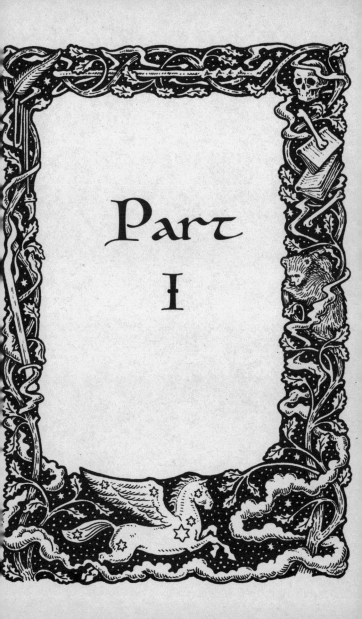

Part
I

1 · To Ride the Wind

JUMP? THOUGHT ELLI, INCREDULOUS AT HER own folly. *Am I really about to jump off a cloud?*

A sharp gust of wind suddenly rocked her forward, making her swing her arms wildly just to keep her balance. Her feet—submerged in the moist, spongy cloud where she and Nuic had rested—dug in more firmly. For a breathless moment, she teetered there on the edge, before finally managing to stand still again. Yet her heart kept pounding.

For she had glimpsed what lay below her: a bottomless swirl of mist, vapors, and nothingness. She was, indeed, about to leap off a cloud. And there were only shreds of mist to break the unending plunge.

"Well, Elliryanna?" snapped the pinnacle sprite at her feet, his liquid purple eyes squinting with doubt. "Are you ever going to do it? Or are you just going to wait here until we both sprout wings?"

"I'll do it, Nuic." With difficulty, she swallowed. "Just not yet."

"Hmmmpff," he replied. Slowly, his skin color darkened to leaden gray. "Maybe I should try to plant an herb garden while we wait."

Elli didn't answer. She merely gazed out at the misty realm of Y Swylarna, commonly called Airroot, that seemed to stretch forever before them. One hand clasped her belt, touching the silken strip torn from High Priestess Coerria's gown. The strip fluttered in the breeze, along with the hem of Elli's simple Drumadian robe and her thick brown curls.

Although made of mist, the airscape before her held as many shapes and colors as any realm of land. Green, gold, and lavender ribbons of vapor wrapped around the denser clouds. In the distance, scores of spiraling forms rose higher, twirling endlessly: the Dancing Ground of the Mist Maidens. Beyond these airy figures, an enormous flock of birds—joined by a few vaporous sylphs—flew toward a brilliant blue patch of sky that glowed like a starlit sapphire.

And as she watched, she listened. To the steady swish of winds all around; to the deep whooshing of the Air Falls of Silmannon; to the eerie, sucking sound of a distant maelstrom; and to the long, rippling notes of aeolian harps—music that always reminded her of Tamwyn. Thinking of their brief meeting in her dream, and their even briefer kiss, she blew a long sigh.

But the sound she heard more clearly than any other was the fearful pounding within her chest. *Jump? Into that?* she thought, shaking her head.

Suddenly she remembered the shrill scream of Deth Macoll, when the assassin had fallen off a cloud much like this one—and plummeted to his death. Instinctively, her feet crept back from the edge. She had only moved a tiny bit, but Nuic had noticed. Though he said nothing, his skin darkened to the color of a storm cloud.

Just then the wind slackened. Now, instead of the ceaseless rush of air, she felt just a gentle tickle on her brow, almost a caress. In that instant, she recalled the old bard who had appeared so unexpectedly—and his soulful song about *what wind that blows.* Those eyes of his, so old and yet so young, had made her want to trust him, although his notion of leaping off a cloud and riding the wind had seemed utterly preposterous.

And still seemed that way.

The breeze tickled her chin. To her surprise, she heard in her mind the bard's very words, almost as if he were whispering into her ear.

It's quite simple, really. You just stand at the edge of a cloud, hold tight to your magic crystal, and think hard about where you want the wind to carry you.

Quite simple! Elli shook her head. It really was preposterous.

And yet . . . the old bard's words had reached her somehow. They had even convinced crusty old Nuic. On top of all that, there didn't seem to be any other explanation for how the bard himself got around, moving so quickly from one realm to another.

She twisted one of her curls, wondering. Even though her common sense—and all her better judgment—told her that this whole idea was idiotic, it just might work. After all, the crystals that she and Nuic wore held enormous power. In the opinion of Rhia, the Lady of the Lake, they possessed more magic than anything else in Avalon—save perhaps Merlin's staff, the legendary Ohnyalei.

Or perhaps, she thought with a shudder, the crystal of élano that was now in the hands of that murderer Kulwych, who served Rhita Gawr. For that crystal, unlike the pure one that she carried, had been turned into a terrible weapon. Who could say whether the person who wielded it could ever be stopped?

Yet that, she knew, was her task. To find Kulwych, who was hiding somewhere down in the deepest mine of the darkest realm. And to use whatever powers she and her crystal could muster to prevent him from destroying Avalon.

But she had too little time to do all this! Less than a week, if she had figured correctly. Just as Tamwyn had far too little time to find his way to the stars and stop Rhita Gawr.

In the distance, the music of the harps' vaporthread strings swelled louder. Their tones seemed more clear now, as well as more urgent. As Elli listened, the strings rose to a high, warbling pitch that sounded like a desperate plea.

A memory of Tamwyn flashed across her mind: He was showing her the partly carved harp that he'd been working on, hoping to give it to Elli if they actually made it through all this alive. More than ever, she felt sure that destroying Kulwych's crystal would also help Tamwyn succeed. After all, the corrupted crystal was the tool of Kulwych, who was himself the tool of Rhita Gawr. Somehow, in a way she couldn't begin to guess, succeeding in her quest could possibly help Tamwyn succeed in his.

She drew a deep breath and stepped closer to the edge. Grimly, she glanced down at Nuic, who nodded impatiently. And then—

She jumped.

For an instant she hovered in the air, just long enough to see Nuic also leap off the cloud. Then she began to fall! Tumbling, twirling head over feet, she plunged downward faster and faster. Air whooshed past, flapping her gown and yanking her hair. Tears streamed from her eyes. Panic suddenly flooded her mind, obscuring all her thoughts.

Except one. A voice broke through, a voice she recognized as the bard's. *Think hard,* he had said. *Think hard about where you want the wind to carry you.*

Calling on every bit of will she possessed, she fought back her panic and concentrated on Shadowroot, that realm of eternal night. No one but dark elves and death dreamers—and now the sorcerer she sought—chose to live there; very few had even dared to explore its terrain since the fighting that had closed its only portal and destroyed the City of Light. Darkness was the soul of this realm, hiding its mysteries forever.

Still falling! For an instant Elli's concentration shattered, and the air tore at her as she plummeted down, down, down. Without thinking, she grasped the amulet of leaves that held her crystal. With all her remaining strength, she bent her thoughts again toward Shadowroot, and the task she wanted so badly to accomplish.

With a sharp jolt, her falling ceased. The wind seemed to stop, to vanish completely. Then she felt herself lifting, floating like a feather in an updraft.

All at once, she realized the truth. The wind hadn't vanished. It was simply supporting her, bearing her body in its invisible arms. Though she could feel it no longer, it was all around her, carrying her with ease.

She was riding the wind.

Not far above her, Nuic floated. His own tiny hand clutched the green jewel of the Galator, while his color had changed to a contented shade of blue. Turning toward Elli, he gave a wry grin. She could almost hear his gruff voice saying, *Took you long enough, Elliryanna.*

The wind swelled beneath them like a rolling wave. Swiftly it bore them, through airy avenues between clouds, and through shimmering veils of mist that burst into circular rainbows as soon as they approached. They rode over clouds and under them, rising upward at times and swooping downward at others, always moving steadily northward.

Over the Harplands they flew, listening to notes that now seemed as lilting as a child's laughter. To the east, Elli could see the massive, curling cloud that Nuic called Windwhistle Point. And on the horizon, a splash of violet and scarlet made her wonder whether she had glimpsed the famous Cloud Gardens of the faeries.

Slowly, the shreds of mist around them began to thin. The air grew clearer, as well as drier. Elli caught a faint whiff of sulfur, like eggs gone terribly bad. The wind carried them over a huge, lumbering cloud—and all of a sudden she saw volcanoes below.

Fireroot! Now, as far as she could see, marched the ridges of Rahnawyn's fire-blackened peaks. Their cliffs glowed with streaks of orange lava, while their summits swirled with clouds of red and gray ash. Noxious fumes poured out of flame vents, billowing as they rose skyward. All across this scorched landscape, fires flickered on the cliffs and heavy smoke poured out of deep crevasses.

Onward the wind carried them, through red-tinted clouds that dusted them with ash. At one point, as they passed above a desolate, charred ridge, Elli spied a crater surrounded by crooked spires of rock. Could that be, she wondered, the place that Scree had once described? The crater that had been his childhood home, and also Tamwyn's? She cringed, thinking of Tamwyn, who so loved the forests of El Urien, living in this place without any greenery at all. And she cringed again, recalling her own years without any trees or vines or flowers—the years she'd spent as a slave to those gnomes who had killed her parents and then kept her captive underground.

She coughed, trying to rid her throat of its bitter taste, even as a sulfurous cloud made her eyes water. She turned away from Nuic, not sure why she didn't want him to see.

Then, beyond the crater's rim, she caught sight of the molten River of Fire, and beyond that, several enormous towers. Conical in shape, they resembled perfectly formed volcanoes, crowned with turrets that arched skyward like erupting lava. Made of polished red stone, the towers gleamed in the light of the huge, intense fires that roared beneath them. Were they the forges of the flamelons, the war-like people who made such elaborate weaponry and building materials? Or were they, perhaps, the famous flamelon palaces—buildings that held, if the bards' tales were true, many marvelous inventions found nowhere else in Avalon?

All at once, the sky started to darken. Starlight faded from the sky, while the air grew swiftly colder. Below, the landscape disappeared, and even the bright fires of Rahnawyn soon flickered and vanished. Elli turned her head toward Nuic, but she could no longer see him. She called out, but heard no reply.

Into the deepening darkness she sailed, borne by the unbroken wind. Unable to see any landmarks below, nor even any clouds, Elli felt increasingly disoriented. Was she still moving at all? Was Nuic still with her?

A vague feeling of terror swelled inside her chest. If she was, indeed, entering Shadowroot, how would she ever find her way? How would she even survive?

Suddenly the wind sputtered. A fierce blast of air jolted her sideways; another slapped her face so hard that she tumbled backward through the blackness. Just then she heard air whooshing wildly around her, and she realized that she was falling. Falling fast! Before she could scream, or even squeeze her crystal more tightly, she hit the ground with a brutal thud.

She lay there, motionless, in the darkness—the darkness of eternal night.

2 · Whispers in the Dark

IN THE DARKNESS, ELLI ROLLED OVER. SHE straightened her back, which felt like one enormous bruise, and worked her sore limbs. Everything around her was black: the air; the ground, which was covered with some sort of stubbly moss that she could feel but not see; and even her own hand, when she raised it to touch her face.

"Am I blind?" she asked herself. "Or just in Shadowroot?" She spoke in the barest of whispers, for something about this impenetrable darkness made her want to be as quiet as possible.

Not far away, something moved on the rough moss. Then came a gruff whisper. "You're not blind, you dolt."

"Nuic," she breathed. "I'm so glad you made it, too. Are you still in one piece?"

"One broken piece. Though I suppose I'll walk again someday."

Understanding that this was the sprite's way of telling her that he hadn't been badly injured, Elli sighed gratefully. Despite how sore she felt, she sat up. Then, turning back to her companion, she whispered wryly, "At least we don't have to look at each other."

"Hmmmpff."

"And I can tell what color you are without even seeing you. Pitch black."

"Nonsense. I'm a glowing shade of pink, in keeping with my mood."

Elli chuckled, then clapped her hands in appreciation. "Nuic, you—"

She stopped midsentence, listening to the reverberating sound of her clap. The sound went on and on, without fading. Then it seemed to break apart and multiply, as dozens and then hundreds of claps filled the darkness.

That was when she realized that the sound had shifted to something deeper, more like a thud. Pounding and thumping, it also grew in volume, swelling steadily louder. Almost, it seemed to be drawing closer by the second.

Footsteps! Elli leaned forward on the moss, even as Nuic wriggled to her side. Both of them tensed, not knowing what to do. It sounded as if an entire army was striding toward them. An army of giants.

"What do we do?" she asked frantically, yelling to be heard above the growing din of footsteps. "We can't even see them to fight!"

Voices suddenly rose up all around them. They called back and forth to each other, shouting what sounded like battle cries. Over and over she heard the word *fight*. Elli wrapped one arm around Nuic. If he had answered her question, she wouldn't have been able to hear the reply.

I must see, she thought, her mind racing. *If only to know where to run.*

The footsteps grew louder than ever, drowning out the voices. Elli's ears ached from all the pounding. She could barely even think.

The crystal. Suddenly remembering the first time she'd

met the Lady of the Lake, when the crystal had shone brilliantly, Elli grasped her amulet of oak, ash, and hawthorn leaves. *Shine for me, please! Give me some light.*

A frail spark appeared in the crystal. It wavered feebly for a few seconds, as if uncertain whether to grow or die. But grow it did, as she kept willing. Slowly, the crystal's power expanded, until it radiated a soft, white light with subtle tones of blue and green.

Elli's fingers opened, allowing the light to spread. Although the crystal wasn't shining nearly as strongly as it had done for the Lady, it was bright enough to illuminate the companions and their immediate surroundings. And what they saw made them gasp. Not in terror—but in surprise.

Striding toward them, across the mossy field where they sat, was not an army. Nor a garrison. Nor even a small band of soldiers. In fact, it wasn't anything that resembled soldiers at all.

It was a lone bear cub.

Or it was, at least, something that looked rather like a chubby, round-bellied bear with thick, dark blue fur. Though not much bigger than Nuic, the creature shuffled toward them heavily. His wide paws seemed to stamp hard against the ground—although whatever sound they might have made was obscured by the continuing din of footsteps all around.

As the spreading light from the crystal reached the cub, he stopped abruptly. With a painful whimper, he raised one furry paw to his face, clearly trying to shield his eyes.

Elli covered the amulet more fully, dimming the light. The cub slowly lowered his paw. Although his blue eyes gazed at them fearfully, he didn't turn and run.

Bewildered, Elli looked down at Nuic. Before she could begin to ask him what this furry creature could be—and what was making those pounding footsteps—he put his finger to his lips. She could see by his expression that he was listening intently to the footsteps themselves.

They were fading! Gradually, over the next few minutes, the sound diminished. The field grew quieter, until at last it returned to silence.

Elli started to speak, but Nuic raised his little hand. In a quiet but insistent whisper, he said, "Welcome to the Vale of Echoes, my good priestess. Having not been to the dark realm of Lastrael for several centuries, I'd almost forgotten about this place. But hmmmpff, there's no doubt about it. So mind your voice: Anything here that's louder than rustling grass will sound like an avalanche."

"And so," whispered Elli, "those footsteps—"

"Were just that ball of blue fur over there." The sprite's skin, also dark blue, showed a few veins of silver. "And if he's as brainless as he looks, he probably scares himself with every step he takes."

Elli grinned. Eyeing the cub, she said, "I like him, though." An idea struck her. "Say, do you think he could possibly help us find our way from here to the Lost City of Light?"

"Unlikely," grumbled the pinnacle sprite. "He looks stupider than a bubble-headed buffoon. Besides, for that kind of help you'd need to talk with him. That won't be easy, unless he happens to know the Common Tongue. Or unless, like your friend Tamwyn, you can speak to other creatures through your thoughts."

At the mention of Tamwyn, her grin vanished. She glanced down at the bracelet that he'd made for her. Woven from the stems of yellow astral flowers, it now looked brown and brittle.

"Well, all right," whispered Nuic ruefully. "You could try, I suppose. Just don't expect any miracles."

Elli turned back to the cub. She covered the radiant amulet almost completely, so that only a small circle of light pushed back the encroaching darkness. With her free hand, she beckoned to the little beast.

For a long moment, he studied her. He cocked his head

to one side, while he sniffed the air uncertainly. At last, he took one small step toward Elli and Nuic—although the sound of his paw hitting the ground started a whole new round of pounding echoes.

Slowly, he shuffled toward them, always sniffing cautiously. Finally he stood beside Elli. For some time they just looked at each other, neither one moving. Then, very carefully, she reached out her hand and scratched behind his ear. Although his whole body cringed, he didn't withdraw. And over the fading echoes, she heard him make a sound much like a sigh of pleasure.

To Elli's delight, the cub lay down beside her, his furry back rubbing against her leg. He then yawned, wagging his tongue, and curled up for a nap. In seconds, he was breathing slowly and rhythmically.

"See what I mean?" asked Nuic in a grumpy whisper. "He probably thinks about nothing besides munching berries and napping."

Elli replied with a big yawn of her own. "Well, maybe a little nap isn't such a bad . . ."

Before she could finish her sentence, she had drifted off into a deep slumber. Unnaturally deep. Nuic, for his part, made no protest. For the sprite, too, had been lulled into enchanted sleep.

Elli dreamed that she lay curled on her side, resting upon a wide blue sea. Tranquil water surrounded her; the ocean stretched without interruption all the way to the encircling horizon. No boat supported her, however. She was floating right on top of the water.

Strange as that was, she didn't feel troubled. In fact, she had never felt so relaxed, so wholly contented. She simply lay there, eyes open, watching the gentle waves around her gather and recede, gather and recede.

Much like the Rainbow Seas, where she had gone swimming with her friend Brionna, these waters glowed with subtle colors that flowed amidst the bottomless blue.

Far beneath the surface, currents of iridescent purple, gold, and green swirled and gathered, mixing together like liquid starlight.

It's all so beautiful, she thought dreamily. *And so very restful. I wish with all my heart that I could swim in this sea . . . really swim, to be completely one with these waters.*

And then, to her amazement, she saw that her longing was actually coming true. With every caress of a wave, some of her own body washed away, melting into the sparkling sea. Far from upsetting her, this filled her with delight. She was joining with the endless ocean, the most peaceful place she had ever known.

Slowly, bit by bit, the waves washed away her toes, then her feet, her ankles, her knees. Another wave came, larger than before, and swallowed her shoulder and one of her arms.

She smiled tranquilly. Already she felt so much better. Her sore and tired body, her worries, her doubts, even her need to breathe—all were disappearing. Soon there would be nothing left of her but a hint of color within the waves.

Another wave approached, larger than all the others. It gathered from afar, rolling toward her at great speed. This wave, she knew, would take all that remained.

Swiftly the wave rushed toward her, lifting into a crest that towered high above her face. Placidly, she gazed up at it, watching its luminous spray gleam like thousands of prisms. Brighter the wave grew, and brighter still—

Disturbingly bright. She squirmed, trying to block out the light. But she just couldn't do it.

The great wave crested, roaring loudly. Just before it fell over her, washing everything away, the light within it suddenly blazed brighter than ever, like an exploding star.

Elli awoke. She was lying on her side—not on water, but on the field of stubbly moss. The crystal on her neck flamed brilliantly. And her legs, shoulder, and arm felt as stiff as slabs of flatrock.

Disoriented, she sat up, blinking. Where was the sea? Where was the wave that she could still hear roaring?

Then she saw the furry cub bounding away from the light, growling angrily—and all at once, she understood. Dreaming! She'd been dreaming. The light had come from the crystal. And the cub's growl, magnified by the Vale of Echoes, had been the sound of the wave.

She turned to face Nuic. And caught her breath. For he was chalk white, a color she'd never seen on him before. His skin seemed frosted with ice. She scooped him up, despite her stiffness, sensing that this was his color for something truly dreadful.

His eyes blinked, then focused on her. "The crystal . . ." he whispered hoarsely, barely loud enough to be heard over the cub's receding echoes.

"It woke us," she finished.

"No, no. It *saved* us."

Puzzled, she stared at him. "Saved us?" she whispered. "How?"

The little sprite shook himself. "Its powers are all about life—creating or protecting life. At some level, it must have sensed our peril." He stared at her grimly. "That cute little creature must have been . . . a death dreamer."

Her eyes widened.

"That's how they kill, you know. Death dreamers come in all shapes and sizes, but their only desire is to get near enough to their prey to cast a sleeping spell. Hmmmpff, foolish old dunce that I am, I never suspected until it was too late!"

Elli wriggled uneasily on the moss, trying her best to bend her legs. "And when the victims fall asleep? Are they eaten alive?"

"No, Elliryanna." His color darkened to that of the shadows beyond the crystal's rays. "Those creatures have a quieter way of preparing their meals. They give you a dream so deadly, yet so alluring, that you will your own life to end."

She swallowed hard, remembering her dream. "So . . . you kill yourself."

Nuic, thinking of his own dream, perhaps, didn't respond.

Working her stiff shoulder, Elli peered at the blackness that loomed outside their little circle of light. It seemed darker than night out there—thicker somehow, and heavier, like some sort of poisonous stew. And somewhere out there lived that innocent-looking creature who had almost made her destroy herself! She recalled Brionna's parting words of encouragement, that there may still be a sliver of light left somewhere in Shadowroot, but the thought only made her shudder.

What folly to think there could be anything good in this forsaken place! And what utter folly to think they could find their way across this realm to the Lost City of Light, and then to Kulwych's cave.

The sprite twisted free of her grip. He planted his feet on the ground, then bent over to inspect the black moss closely. After a few seconds, he straightened himself and announced in a satisfied whisper, "At least there's *something* about this realm I haven't forgotten."

Elli raised a quizzical eyebrow.

He bent down again, grabbed a tuft of black moss, and popped it into his mouth. After a vigorous chew, his color lightened a shade. "Night's blanket," he explained. "Tastes almost like peppermint. Come on, try some."

"Must I?"

"Only if you'd like to feel stronger. This variety is full of nutrients, you see."

She shook her head. "Nuic, you're amazing. One minute you're at the very edge of death, and the next minute you're giving me a lesson in local edible plants."

"Hmmmpff," he whispered gruffly. "Only because I

don't want to have to carry you all the way to the Lost City of Light." He gave her a wink. "That's still where we're going, isn't it?"

Despite everything, she almost grinned. And then she reached down and grabbed a handful of moss.

3 · Daffodils

FINGERING HER LONG, HONEY-COLORED braid, Brionna stopped to survey the lush forest. Just above her head, a pair of watercloak butterflies cavorted in the lower branches of an immense beech tree, whose bright green buds hinted at the return of spring. The butterflies' silvery blue wings flashed in the shafts of starlight, as did the yellow-speckled back of the snake curled around one bough. Not far away, she could tell by the sound of their hooves, a doe and fawn trotted through the unfurling ferns. She drew a deep breath of the richly scented air.

Yet even the familiar smells of young daffodils, baby toadstools, and nests made of fresh clover gave her no joy. For she knew that this springtime could well be her last.

Like all elves, she could stand completely motionless, joining with the forest as fully as a sapling joins with the soil. And here in the deepest forest of Woodroot, known by her people as El Urien, she had always felt as much at home as the trees themselves. Until she'd been violently uprooted not long ago.

Reaching into her robe, she pulled out a square of elvish

waybread, took a bite, and chewed thoughtfully. Her expression darkened, and her hand moved to the cedar longbow that she'd strung with thread from her barkcloth robe. She tapped the bow's handle. The past several weeks had seemed like a series of plagues: her enslavement by that wicked sorcerer White Hands; her beloved grandfather's death; and now the looming threat of a battle on the Plains of Isenwy, a battle that would decide the fate of Avalon.

She sighed. For even now, forces were gathering that seemed to make that battle unavoidable. She had heard from other elves, as recently as this morning, that the enemies of Avalon were already massing at Isenwy. And that those enemies were expecting to be joined, in just a few more days, by some superior force—White Hands himself, perhaps. For that reason, the elves and their allies were planning to attack first, to dispose of their foes as quickly as possible. If successful, they could have already won an initial victory on the battlefield by the time any help for their foes could arrive. Then, if necessary, they would fight a second battle—and win a second victory. But having listened to her grandfather's many woeful tales of battle plans gone awry, Brionna felt no surge of hope. Instead, she felt a deep emptiness down inside her chest: a gnawing fear for her people and her world.

And also for her friend Elli, who had become something akin to a sister. How she'd ever grown so attached to someone of the human race, Brionna couldn't explain. Just as she couldn't explain whatever it was that drew her to that ox-brained eagleman, Scree. In any case, she worried about them—more than she wanted to admit.

By now Elli should be nearing Shadowroot, thought Brionna, cringing at the thought of her friend in that darkened realm where she herself had almost died. *That's about the only place in Avalon I'd like to go even less than the place I'm going now—Belamir's village.*

The crackle of twigs underfoot told her that Lleu was

approaching. She turned just as the tall, gangly priest emerged from a thick stand of spruce trees. On his shoulder sat his maryth, Catha, the silver-winged falcon whose eyes were even sharper than her talons.

"Good of you to wait for us," panted Lleu. "I've never walked so fast through a forest."

Brionna's deep green eyes bored into him. "I've rarely walked so slow."

He stepped to her side under the beech tree. For a moment, he studied her. "You're regretting your decision to come with me to Belamir's?"

She sighed, tossing her braid over her shoulder. "I'm regretting a great deal these days. And every step I take reminds me of something."

She nodded at the old beech, whose smooth gray bark glistened, both on the immense trunk and on the boughs above. "Even that tree reminds me of Elna Lebram—*deep roots, long memories* in the elvish tongue—where we buried my grandfather."

Lleu watched her kindly. "Tressimir was a great scholar, and a great man."

Straightening her shoulders, she could still feel the scar from a whip, which always made her think of Granda's final days. And her part in his death. Facing Lleu, she said somberly, "He should still be alive."

"Maybe it's better that he didn't have to see what's happening now. His whole world threatened, his people going to war—"

"And his granddaughter groveling before Belamir, whose Humanity First movement considers the elves an inferior race."

"We're not groveling, Brionna. We're just going to his village to try to talk some sense into him. Make him understand that by encouraging his followers to fight against the old order at Isenwy, he's inadvertently helping Kulwych— and the greater horror, Rhita Gawr." His eyebrows lifted hopefully. "If we succeed, we could save a lot of lives—and maybe, if we can keep enough of Belamir's forces from going to Isenwy, we could prevent this whole battle from ever happening."

She sniffed. "That's the only reason I'm willing to try this scheme. But just going to see that despicable man still feels like groveling."

On Lleu's shoulder, Catha released a sharp whistle of agreement.

"Look here," said the priest, kicking a bunch of spruce needles. "Belamir's not evil. Just woefully misguided. He's basically just an old gardener who's been seduced by some ideas of human superiority."

The elf maiden's eyes narrowed. "You can say that after what his people did at the Drumadian compound? And to Coerria?"

Lleu's gaze faltered. In a low voice, nearly a growl, he said, "What happened at the compound will never be forgotten. Or forgiven. I'm just not convinced that Belamir knew anything about it. Llynia, who now seems to be his closest aide, hadn't even heard about it until we told her."

Brionna's own voice lowered. "Some elves believe, as you do, that he's not truly evil. But they also believe that he's under the influence of someone else, someone who may only *appear* to be human."

"You don't mean . . ."

"Yes. A changeling."

Just the mention of that word made Catha screech angrily. She ruffled her wings, pacing back and forth.

Brionna nodded gravely. "There aren't many changelings left in El Urien. But those who still remain are even more dangerous—and more bloodthirsty—than their ancestors, the shifting wraiths of Lost Fincayra."

Frowning, Lleu added, "Those beasts nearly killed both Merlin and Rhia when they were young."

"Right. So while I'm willing to go with you to meet Belamir and his advisors, my bow and arrows will be close at hand. Changelings always have some sort of telltale physical flaw, you know, something quite unnatural. And I'll be looking for it."

"With my blessing. Just be sure you're right before you shoot."

"Wood elves never kill anything unless we must," she answered. "Which is why it's worth trying to turn Belamir around." She tapped her bow again. "But if we fail, I am going straight to Isenwy."

"As am I."

A loud crash came from the spruces. Then, in rapid succession, came a shout of pain, the sound of someone tripping over some roots, the *thhhwack* of a bent branch springing back and smacking someone very hard, a mumbled string of curses, and yet another crash.

Brionna and Lleu traded knowing glances, while the falcon released a glum whistle.

"Sounds like Shim has caught up with us," said Lleu.

Shaking her head, the elf remarked, "How anyone so small can make so much noise is totally beyond me."

Just then a dwarf-size fellow burst out of the branches. From his white mop of hair down to the bottom of his baggy leggings, he was covered with broken twigs, cones, needles, leaves, fern fronds, and at least one spiderweb. Wiping a clump of wet leaves off his potato-shaped nose, he started toward his companions—but suddenly tripped on a sapling and fell into a patch of daffodils growing under the beech tree.

"Not fairly!" he groused. "Back in the olden daylies, I could walk anywheres at all with no problem. Bigsy I was, as bigsy as the highliest tree, and no little daffodilly could trip me up."

Brionna strode over and helped him stand again. "Thanks, Rowanna," he told her, his eyes shining. "You're a goodsy lass. As well as me favorite niece."

Though she scowled at his old joke, she wasn't offended. "I'm just glad you're not hurt."

"Sad for hot dirt?" He scrunched his nose at her. "That's a confudoozedly thing to say! But I'll tells you one nicely thing. At least I'm not hurt."

"And your hearing's still great," she added wryly.

"Earrings will skate?" He studied her with concern. "Rowanna, you is speaking most funnily today. Maybily your hearing isn't rightly?"

Before she could try again to speak, he shook his white head, spraying twigs and needles all around. "No, no, I'm sure it's old Shim who isn't rightly. Why did that giantly miss, Bonlog Mountain-Mouth, ever make me so smallsy and shrunkelled? Just because I ran away when she tries to give me a kiss, so disgustingly slobberly."

Brionna placed her hand upon his shoulder and gave him a gentle squeeze.

But Shim merely scowled and muttered, "That was a meanly thing for her to do! Certainly, definitely, absolutely."

Just then Brionna heard something that sounded like the nearby hoot of an owl. She tensed, because no owl would be hunting at this time of day. Catha, too, seemed agitated, ruffling her wings.

At that instant, eight green-clad men, with bowstrings drawn and arrows nocked, stepped out of the trees. Brionna and her companions were surrounded! Scanning the deadly arrows aimed at their chests, the elf maiden cursed herself for letting down her guard, even for an instant.

"We come in peace," protested Lleu.

"No, ye don't," growled the voice of one of the men. He stood directly behind Brionna and Lleu, so they couldn't see him, nor could they risk turning around to face him.

"It's true," Lleu declared. "We have come to visit Hanwan Belamir."

"To kill him, more likely," replied the man. "We trust nobody who comes this close to the village o' Prosperity, 'specially in times like this." Behind them, he spat. "And most 'specially if they're travelin' with a dirty elf and a dwarf."

Brionna, her body as tight as one of their bowstrings, quivered with rage.

"Ye think yer kind is the best at woodland trackin' and huntin', don't ye?" taunted her captor. "Well, looks like yer mistaken, elf-girl! Now take off yer bow and quiver, real slow and careful. I'd hate to have to carry ye back with yer body full o' arrows."

The thought flashed through Brionna's mind that she could, perhaps, get off one shot before she died—maybe in the throat of this arrogant human. But she fought back the desire, since that rash move would probably mean her friends' deaths as well. Reluctantly, she pulled off her bow and cast it aside, then did the same with her quiver of arrows.

"Good elf. Now if ye jest do as Morrigon says, ye might even live another day er two." The man chortled at his joke. "Now turn around," he commanded. "And start followin' me. We have a lovely welcome for ye back at the village."

When Brionna turned to face him, she caught her breath. What surprised her wasn't that he was so elderly, with scraggly white hair sprouting from his chin as well as the sides of his head above his ears. Nor that he looked so frail, as thin as a twisted old tree.

No, what surprised her was his right eye, so bloodshot that it looked pink. *Unnaturally* pink.

4 · The Strength of Wings

SLOWLY, SCREE ROSE TO HIS FEET. HE GRImaced from the painful gash in his side, and also from the sight of this village surrounded by the lava-belching volcanoes of Fireroot. It was the village of the Bram Kaie eaglefolk, whose leader Scree had just killed—before discovering that the leader had also been his only son.

Tall and grim, Scree stood before the villagers crowding around him. They were young and old, male and female, slim and stout. Some, like Scree, stood in human form; others bore talons and great wings whose feathers shone with the reddish glow of the clouds above. And the crowd continued to swell. Eaglefolk were climbing down from their fortified nests, hurrying down the obsidian-paved streets, climbing the bejeweled statues of soaring eagles and poles bearing silken flags—all to view the warrior who had so boldly challenged their leader. And won.

A sulfurous wind blew over the fire-blackened ridge, dusting the villagers with black ash and bits of pumice. But they didn't seem to notice. They pressed closer together, jostling each other, craning their necks and ruffling their wings, all the while keeping some distance from Scree. Then, as one, they fell silent, waiting for him to speak.

He scowled, rubbing his hands on his bloodstained leggings. Despite the gash in his side, he straightened up to his full height. The rust-red light of the Volcano Lands tinted his bare, muscular chest.

"I am Scree," he declared. "And I am your new leader."

Hushed whispers, exclamations, and hurried conversations bubbled up around him like molten lava. Wings opened and closed again anxiously, while talons scraped against the ground. Scree waited before speaking again, knowing that his bid to lead the clan was no less risky than the battle he'd just survived. Some of these villagers were bound to resist him, an outsider, trying to lead them at all—let alone in an entirely different direction from the raiding and pillaging of their past.

Yet that was his goal. Nothing less. That was the only way he could possibly help Tamwyn, Elli, and Brionna— as well as Avalon. For he knew that the fate of their world now rested on what happened in two distant places: somewhere in the stars, if Tamwyn had actually managed to stay alive; and on the Plains of Isenwy, where a great battle would soon be fought. And if Scree had his way, there would be eaglefolk from this clan at Isenwy.

He scanned the villagers surrounding him, as they slowly quieted again. Yet even as he looked at their faces, he thought about some other faces—ones he knew that he would never see again. There was Tamwyn, the brother he had finally found, only to lose once more. There was Brionna, whose strange elfish ways attracted him so strongly, even as he seemed bent on pushing her away. And there was Arc-kaya, the eaglewoman whose loving generosity hadn't spared her from a brutal death.

And there was one more face he couldn't forget—that

of a young, golden-eyed eagleboy named Hawkeen. Although they had truly bonded in the midst of their grief, Scree wished that he could have spent more time with this lad who reminded him so much of his younger self. But he had been forced to depart straightaway, leaving Hawkeen behind.

Suddenly a burly eagleman pushed his way out of the crowd. "What makes you think you can lead us?" he demanded.

Scree gazed sternly at his questioner. Although this eagleman stood in human form, he looked ready to sprout wings and take flight at an instant's notice. And from the many scars on his chest and the red leg band that identified him as a warrior, it was clear that he'd flown into combat several times.

The warrior thumped the end of his upright spear on the charred ground, sending up a puff of ash. "What makes you think so?" With a sneer, he added, "You're not even a member of this clan."

Scree's yellow-rimmed eyes narrowed. "That is true. But I *am* born of this same realm of fire and rock. And I also belong to this same people—your people, the eaglefolk of Avalon."

The warrior looked at him skeptically, rubbing his angular jaw. "Still, what do you know of the Bram Kaie clan?"

"I know that you have lost more than your leadership. You have lost your way as eaglefolk. By your murderous actions, you have disgraced yourselves—and the rest of your kind."

The warrior stiffened, his shoulders flexed. Behind him, villagers stirred, murmuring and arguing among themselves. Someone shouted, "Kill him for that!" while a woman's voice called out, "He's right. We have flown astray."

Just then a pair of young eaglemen near Scree started

shoving each other roughly. "You're a traitor to side with him!" shouted one.

"And you're just a thieving coward," retorted the other.

All at once, they transformed into their winged forms. One of them suddenly whirled, striking the other's face with the bony edge of his wing. Blood flowed from a gash in the youth's cheek. They raised their talons, just about to tear into each other—when Scree stepped boldly between them. He grabbed each of them by the shoulder and held them apart.

"Wait," he commanded. His voice rang with such authority, echoing over the fire-blackened ridge, that the young men slowly lowered their talons. Although they remained in their eagle forms, glaring at each other angrily, they did not try to break free.

"Fighting among yourselves isn't the answer," he intoned. "I ask you, can two wings of the same bird fly in opposite directions? No! And two clans of the same people are no different. If they try to fly in opposite ways, they will succeed only in tearing themselves apart. For we are all, every one of us, part of the same body, borne by the same wings."

As several eaglefolk nodded their heads, Scree released the young men. After pausing to make sure they wouldn't attack each other again, he continued speaking. "This clan, under Quenaykha, has gained great wealth."

He turned, waving at the obsidian avenues between the nests, the gilded statues, the spiraling stairways of oak and mahogany, and all the spoils of plunder that lay strewn about like discarded feathers. "But you have also gained," he declared, "far greater shame."

There were angry murmurs again. Yet now it seemed as if more people were listening, cocking their heads thoughtfully as he continued.

"You are eaglefolk, after all. The fiercest, proudest people in all of Avalon! Does it make you feel true to your glorious traditions—and to your ancestors, who have flown higher than any creatures in the Seven Realms—to stoop to murder and thievery? To soar not on the strength of your own wings, but on the wings of those you have robbed?"

He lowered his voice. "I said that you were lost. But I also say to you, people of the Bram Kaie, that you can find your way again."

He glanced at the scarred warrior, whose expression was now graver than ever. Then he announced, "Very soon a battle will erupt in Mudroot, on the Plains of Isenwy. If the army of sorcery, gobsken, and wicked men prevails, then free Avalon will be lost. But if the other side—the side of eaglefolk—prevails, then Avalon will be saved."

Scree lifted his arms over his head as if they were great wings. "I myself am going there to fight. And yes, to die, if I must. Will you join me? Will you fight alongside the rest of your people? Will you do your part to redeem your clan, and save our world?"

Hushed silence enveloped the crowd. An eaglefeather, blown out of one of the nests, drifted lazily over the people's heads. But no one answered Scree. Not a single person answered his call.

At that moment, a lone eagleboy stepped through the villagers and strode to his side. Scree turned toward the lad, then gasped. It was Hawkeen, the golden-eyed boy from Arc-kaya's home!

Hawkeen's bright eyes glinted. "I followed you here," he declared. "And I will follow you into battle for Avalon."

Scree spoke no words, but gazed at the eagleboy.

"Enough foolishness," bellowed the gruff voice of the scarred warrior. He tossed aside his spear, which clattered on the blackened ridge. At the same time, he changed into eagle form, stretching his mighty wings. He advanced toward Scree, feathers bristling.

Seeing this, Scree also transformed. His wings sprouted, and he opened them wide, ready to leap skyward at any instant. He clenched his jaw, wondering whether he had enough strength to prevail in yet another battle to the death. As he dragged his sharp talons across the ground, he said, "Fight me if you will. But I have spoken only the truth."

The warrior advanced another step, eyeing him coldly. When he stood barely a spear's length away, he stopped and folded his wings. "I am Cuttayka, first among the Clan Sentries. And I have not come to fight you. I have come to join you."

Even as Scree's eyes widened, Cuttayka turned to the crowd. "Enough foolishness, I say! Did you not hear the call of this bold warrior? Did you not feel the rightness of his plan? Come on, all of you. Join him."

He glanced at Scree, then added: "For he is our leader."

5 · The Climb

TAMWYN GLANCED, ONE LAST TIME, AT THE simple earthen mound that was a grave. And at the words he had carved there, using his newly reforged dagger—words that began, *Here lies the body of my father, Krystallus Eopia.*

As he stood there alone, the wind of Merlin's Knothole gusted around him, flapping the sleeves of his torn tunic. "You never made it to the stars," he whispered into the swelling wind. "But maybe your son will."

He reached behind his back to check the wooden pole that he'd tied to his pack strap. Finding it secure, he nodded with determination. "And I'll carry your torch with me."

Spinning around, Tamwyn turned toward the rocky brown cliffs that rose steeply higher, disappearing into shreds of mist. Above, the stars shone brightly—except, of course, the seven darkened stars of the Wizard's Staff constellation. Besides that gaping hole in the sky, another prominent feature caught his attention: the wide, dark streaks that ran between him and the stars. He didn't need to consult the special compass in his pack to know that he was gazing starward, into the heights of the Great Tree, and that those streaks were actually its vast, unexplored branches.

Where I'm going now.

He drew a deep breath, wondering whether he would ever succeed in his ultimate goal: to climb up to those branches, and the stars beyond. And not just any stars, either. He needed to reach those seven darkened stars of the Wizard's Staff, which were now open doors to the Other-world of the Spirits. Through those doorways on high, he knew, Rhita Gawr's army of immortal warriors had already begun to pour. They were massing up there, even now, waiting for Rhita Gawr's command to attack Avalon . . . a command that would come in no more than one week's time. And so, Tamwyn's task—so difficult that it seemed impossible—was to chase that army back through the doorways, and somehow defeat Rhita Gawr himself.

Then comes the really hard part, Tamwyn thought grimly. *I'll need to relight those stars, closing those doorways—something that no one but Merlin has ever done.*

He worked his shoulders, shifting the position of the torch on his back. It was far more than an ordinary torch, he felt certain. When lit, it would not be merely a source of fire, but also of magic. He sensed, somehow, that if he could grow powerful enough—or wise enough—to light it, then he might truly have the strength to close those door-ways. And to confront Rhita Gawr.

He swallowed, knowing that there was one more reason he had decided to carry the torch of his father. For as long as Krystallus had been alive, it had burned as bright as his very soul. So maybe, just maybe, if Tamwyn could find the way to light it . . .

I'd be a little closer to him.

With that, he started walking toward the cliffs that rose so steeply skyward. His bare feet, toughened by calluses, crunched on the hardpacked soil. Every step he took, gradually gaining altitude, he felt the ground hardening into rock, rough brown rock that felt appropriately like the bark of an enormous tree.

This would be, he knew, an arduous climb. Even merely to reach the lowest branch. To have any chance at all of reaching the stars before it was too late, he'd have to find some faster way to ascend—something like the Secret Stairway that had carried him all the way from Gwirion's village of the fire angels to this hidden valley high on the trunk of the Tree. Yet what way could that be?

He started to clamber across a jumble of loose boulders, debris that had broken off from the cliffs above. Often he needed to use his hands to keep his balance—and once, when a sharp-edged boulder shifted under his weight, to keep from falling. Moving as swiftly as he could, he was soon sweating and panting from exertion. But he knew that he still wasn't moving fast enough.

For he had very little time to do everything he must. Before long, Rhita Gawr would extinguish another star, the one known as the Heart of Pegasus. When that happened, *the great horse will die,* as the warlord himself had put it. And whatever else it would mean when that star's fires went out, it would also be the signal for Rhita Gawr's deathless warriors to attack Avalon.

Unless I can stop them somehow, Tamwyn told himself. Yet even as that thought formed in his mind, he sighed. *That's an awfully tall order for a lone wilderness guide, even one who dabbles in magic.*

The boulder beneath him suddenly slid sideways. Tamwyn lurched, then managed to leap over to another one. Fortunately, the new boulder held steady. But his ankle scraped as he landed, and blood dribbled down his foot.

Too busy even to notice, he continued to clamber. At last, he reached the end of the boulder field—and the beginning of the cliffs. He checked the torch again, as well as the staff he had placed in the sheath that he'd woven of willow bark. Allowing himself one swig of the sweet, nourishing water from the Great Hall of the Heartwood, he stowed his flask. And then he started to climb.

Hand over hand he hoisted himself higher, moving like a lopsided spider up the cliffs. He grabbed whatever handholds he could find, while his feet wedged into niches or cracks no wider than his little toe. Whenever crumbled bits of rock rained down on his face, which was often, he couldn't release his grip to brush himself off.

Tamwyn moved slowly upward, edging higher and higher. Yet more rocky cliffs always towered above him.

Hours later, they still towered. Though his arms and legs now felt as heavy as rock themselves, he continued to climb. Sweat from his brow dribbled into his eyes as he reached his hand up to a knob, one more handhold on one more ledge. Quaking, he pulled himself onto the lip of stone. When at last he lifted his chest, then one leg, then the other, over the edge—he collapsed there, flat on his back, breathing hard.

He closed his eyes, which were still stinging from perspiration. But he knew that it would only make them worse to wipe them with his dirty hands or tunic. Besides, what was there to see? For quite some time now, he'd been ascending through thick, swirling mist that obscured any view in any direction. Even the stars themselves were only visible as pale, ghostly spots within the vapors.

It's really a good thing, he thought glumly as he lay on the ledge, panting. *If I could see what's ahead, it would only be cliffs stretching up forever. And stars too high to reach.*

He rolled a bit to the side in order to stretch his back. The movement shook the small quartz bell on his hip. As it jingled in the misty air, he thought of Stoneroot, the land of bells. How he missed that familiar terrain! Now that the terrible drought had ended, spring should be just emerging there now, filling the air with the scent of honeygrass sprin-

kled with dew, moonberries plump and juicy, and those
first pungent shafts of skunkweed that made a surprisingly
tasty brew of tea.

Would he ever experience those aromas and flavors
again? There was no way to tell.

Feeling the handle of his dagger digging into his hip, he
shifted again, this time jostling his pack. From inside it
came a new sound, softer and deeper than that of his bell.
He knew well that sound. It came from his slab of harmóna
wood, partly carved into the shape of a harp.

The harp he was making for Elli. As he listened to the
low, quivering note, it seemed to vibrate within every bone
of his body . . . along with the memory of their shared
dream, and their one brief kiss.

Would they see each other again? Without quests to survive, or worlds to save? Again, there was no way to tell.

Just as he could only wonder about his other friends. As
he sat up, blinking his sore eyes in the mist, he thought
about Scree, whose wounds from Hallia's Peak would
surely have healed by now. And Gwirion, who must have
found the Golden Wreath that Tamwyn had left for him.
But had Gwirion also found his people's true destiny, and
the courage to lead them there?

Then he thought of Henni and Batty Lad, the two companions he had lost when they plunged into the upward-
flowing Spiral Cascades. Did that footprint near his
father's grave mean that Henni, the wacky hoolah, had
somehow survived? And was it possible that Batty Lad's
mindless chatter really meant more than Tamwyn had ever
understood? Did that chatter provide some sort of clue to
the nagging mystery of what sort of creature Batty Lad really was?

Tamwyn exhaled slowly, scattering the mist before him.
All those people—and others, such as Rhia—had proven
themselves to be true friends. They had stayed by his side,
despite all his foolishness and clumsiness. And despite his

bizarre fate to be the person who might actually save Avalon—and also the person who would bring its ultimate ruin. How could he be both at once? No one, not even Rhia herself, had been able to explain that to him.

In some distant part of his mind, he heard again the ringing words of the Dark Prophecy. They had haunted him all through the seventeen years of his life. Yet they had first truly come alive for him when he'd heard them sung by that strange old bard with the sideways-growing beard:

> *A year shall come when stars go dark,*
> *And faith will fail anon—*
> *For born shall be a child who spells*
> *The end of Avalon.*
>
> *The only hope beneath the stars*
> *To save that world so fair*
> *Will be the Merlin then alive:*
> *The wizard's own true heir.*
>
> *What shall become of Avalon,*
> *Our dream, our deepest need?*
> *What glory or despair shall sprout*
> *From Merlin's magic seed?*

Exhausted in spirit as well as in body, Tamwyn forced himself to stand upright on the ledge. Yet another rocky cliff rose above him, though not quite as steeply as some that he had climbed. The pervasive mist seemed to thin a bit, shredding itself like morning haze in the day's first light.

That was when he saw something new—something that made him rock backward, so much that he nearly fell right off the ledge. A splash of green, as well as a hint of lavender, gleamed through the vapors. And even more striking than the colors themselves was their position: They seemed to stretch not so much upward, like the formidable cliffs, but more outward, reaching to the side for a great distance, as far as he could see.

Tamwyn licked his salty, dirty lips. Could it be? He might actually have made it to the first branch.

6 · Wood Chips

TAMWYN SCALED THE CLIFF, CLIMBING hand over hand with renewed vigor. Sweat dribbled down his brow, streaking his face with dirt, but he didn't mind. He was thinking about just one thing: topping this rise.

As he pulled himself up the final ledge, a new landscape opened up before him. His grimy lips lifted in a grin, for he could see enough beyond the shredding mist to know that he had, indeed, reached the first branch.

And what a landscape it was! Sharp, steeply cut valleys, running right beside each other, stretched in long green rows as far as he could see. From where he stood now, atop one of the parallel ridges that divided the valleys, he could make out three or four of the green swaths on each side. And each of those valleys, like the ridges that divided them, ran straight to the hazy horizon. The look of these slim ridges reminded him of something, though he wasn't sure what.

Tamwyn peered down into one of the valleys below. Thick, lush grasses rippled in the buffeting breeze like the hides of galloping horses. It almost seemed as if the land itself were loping.

Adjusting the pack strap on his shoulder, he walked down from the ridge to explore the upper rim of the valley. Soft grasses soon replaced rough rock under his feet. Ahead, he could see several deep gullies that ribbed the slope. Within them, dense rows of lavender-colored bushes lined cascading streams where water sparkled in the starlight.

He smacked his dry lips. *A drink from a fresh water stream would taste wonderful right now.*

As he reached the first gulley, he pushed his way through the bushes toward the stream. A sharp chirp from a nest hidden in the shrubbery made him halt. Seeing a sudden flash of brilliance from the nest, he realized that it held a fledgling prism bird, whose wingfeathers would someday catch the light as it soared, painting the clouds with radiant color.

He sat down on the muddy bank of the stream, peeled off his pack and the torch, and plunged his whole head into the water. He lifted his head, black locks dripping wet— and then plunged his head back into the stream again. Finally, cooled and rinsed, he cupped his hands and took several long, lovely sips.

At last, he sat cross-legged on the bank. Curious, he broke off a lavender leaf and chewed it to see if it had any flavor. Instantly he spat it out on the mud. For it had a flavor, all right, one that came perilously close to goat dung.

Scanning the ridgeline above him, he followed it down the full length of the valley. He spied several steaming pits, deep green in color, that dotted the rim. Sniffing the air, he caught the sharp, sweet aroma of resins, much like he would have found in a forest of pine and spruce. Could those be boiling pits of sap, bubbling up from below?

Then, near a jagged outcropping of stone that resembled an uplifted hand with fingerlike spires, he noticed some movement. Creatures! Gigantic in size, with hunched, hairy backs, they looked almost as gnarled and weathered as the rocks themselves. Brawny arms hung from their massive shoulders, while their heads tapered into long snouts. And, if he was seeing accurately, each creature stood on just one leg. Then, to his amazement, the creatures clasped hands and started circling the stone, hopping in unison.

They are dancing, he thought, blinking his eyes in disbelief. Each one of them must have stood twice his height, yet they moved with the fluidity of blowing clouds, hopping and bowing in their strange, silent dance.

For an instant, he wondered whether he should use his last drop of Dagda's dew, Gwirion's parting gift, to study them more closely. But no—better to save that magical drop for later, when it might be more needed.

Watching the ring of huge, hunchbacked creatures, he reminded himself they could be dangerous. *Better stay right here in the bushes until they're gone. Just in case.*

Then he noticed a stand of tall, gangly trees just beyond the hunchbacked creatures. Drumalings! He shuddered, thinking of those walking trees that had nearly crushed the life out of him back in Merlin's Knothole. Were it not for Ethaun, the affable blacksmith who stood as broad as a bear, they would have surely killed him.

Tamwyn shook his head, spraying the bushes with water droplets. No, he did not want to encounter drumalings again. When it came time to climb back up the slope, and to find the best route higher on the Tree, he would take extra care to avoid whatever beasts might live among these parallel ridges.

All at once, he realized why these ridges, with their steep-sided valleys, had reminded him of something. They looked like rows of bark! More than that, they *were* rows of bark, running the length of this enormous branch.

This is a whole new realm, he reflected. *And to think that it is only one of many! Every single branch of the Great*

Tree is an unexplored region. And they could be as different from each other as Fireroot is from Airroot or Waterroot.

He lowered his gaze. *Or Shadowroot, where Elli is heading now.*

Feeling a pang of worry, and maybe something more, he pulled out the slab of harmóna wood. He unsheathed his dagger, grateful that Ethaun had reforged it. But he didn't take time to examine the ancient, mysterious words engraved on the side of the blade—words that spoke of Merlin's heir . . . and Rhita Gawr. He just placed the slab on his lap and started to carve.

As the first curling chip of wood fell to the ground, it hummed ever so subtly. Meanwhile, the magical slab itself made a soft, breathy music, its orange-streaked grain helping to guide Tamwyn's every slice. Slowly, the sound box grew more clearly defined, and the instrument began to take shape.

Something about whittling wood always consoled Tamwyn. The gentle sweep of a blade, the warmth of wood in his hands, made him feel more firmly planted in the present moment. And also more confident about the future. Yet today he couldn't seem to banish his doubts. Why, he didn't even know where he was going to find the strings for this harp! So how could he possibly hope to do his part to save Avalon?

He continued to carve. Wood chips piled up on the muddy bank, accumulating with his concerns. *I am, after all, just one person—and certainly no great wizard.* Then, unexpectedly, he remembered Ethaun's words, spoken in the blacksmith's rough whisper:

Ye know, the legends from Old Fincayra are mighty strange at times. But one o' the strangest says that a young wizard only came into power when he carved his first musical instrument.

For a brief moment, Tamwyn believed. Or wanted so much to believe that it felt like conviction itself. Then the knife blade slipped, nicking his thigh. He groaned, cursing his own clumsiness.

Full of doubts again, he raised his gaze toward the sky. It blazed with stars so bright that he needed to shield his eyes from the most radiant clusters. *What am I thinking? I don't even know how to begin to get up there!*

Then, for the first time, he noticed something odd. Very odd. A vague line of light, so dim that he could only barely perceive it, ran across the middle of the sky. Like a luminous crack, or a seam in the fabric of day, it ran through the realm of the stars.

Tamwyn stared at the line of light, blinking. What was it? Maybe just a trick of the remaining wisps of mist. Yet it seemed more real than that. Perhaps it had always been there, but he needed to have climbed this high on the Great Tree before he could actually see it.

Flipping fire dragons, what could that be?

A dark shadow fell over him. At the same instant, he felt a powerful rush of two emotions—fear and rage. But the emotions weren't his own. Tamwyn sensed, before he'd even turned around, that they were coming from whoever had cast the shadow.

He spun around.

Drumalings! Tall and treelike, two of the creatures towered over him, the barkless skin of their knobby, many-limbed bodies glinting in the starlight. Like the drumalings who had nearly killed him before, this pair had faces midway up their scraggly bodies. Each had a ragged slit for a mouth, as well as a lone, vertical eye almost as narrow as a twig.

The unblinking eye of each drumaling stared down at Tamwyn. He held their gaze. As with the drumalings he'd met in Merlin's Knothole, he sensed no thoughts from them—only simple, raw feelings. Right now he detected a steady undercurrent of anxiety, mixed with a hint of anger. Making no sudden movements, he quickly sheathed his dagger, stuffed the harmóna wood into his pack, and slipped the leather strap over his shoulder.

At the very instant he finished, he sensed a new flood of wrath—and the drumalings charged. Swinging their long arms studded with thick tufts of grass, they surged through the bushes, slamming down their heavy roots. Just as Tamwyn fled, those roots smacked against the stream bank where he'd been sitting, spraying mud and wood chips everywhere.

He bolted, leaping over the stream and hurdling the dense shrubbery on the other side. Hearing the crash of broken branches right behind him, he didn't have to glance back to know that they were pursuing. Whether they considered him prey or a vile intruder, they clearly wanted to crush his every bone.

He dashed through the waving grasses, which swished against his leggings. For a second he considered transforming himself into a bounding deer, as he'd done once to save Elli's life. But he knew that wasn't possible, even to save his own. The bulkiness of his load, especially the torch across his back, kept him from striding freely enough to release the magic. All he could do was sprint as best he could on two legs.

They were gaining! Not far behind, the slamming of roots grew louder. Now he could hear the whoosh of air from the drumalings' waving limbs, a sound that chilled him more than any winter wind.

Spying one of the steaming pools of sap, he veered higher on the slope to run toward it. With the drumalings' limbs practically brushing against the back of his neck, he took a desperate chance—and hurled himself straight over the bubbling pool. The smell of resins overwhelmed him, searing his throat and burning his eyes. He landed on the other side, barely clearing the rim of the pool, and rolled to a stop in the grass.

Anxiously, he looked up, peering into the greenish

steam over the pit. Had he lost them? Slow-witted creatures that they were, they might just think he'd vanished, and give up their chase. Or maybe they, too, had tried to jump, and fallen into the resiny cauldron.

No such luck. He saw the pair of drumalings charging around the pit. On each of them, the lone eye had reddened with rage. Their roots slapped the pit's edge, splattering hot sap onto the grass.

Tamwyn leaped to his feet. How could he ever escape these vicious beasts? He glanced around, then spied the outcropping of stone where the strange, hunchbacked giants had been dancing. Seeing no sign of them, he realized that they must have left while he was working on the harp. He took off, sprinting toward the outcropping, hoping to climb up into its fingerlike spires before the drumalings could get him. There was at least a chance that those spires might shield him from their battering limbs.

Even as he approached the outcropping, he could feel his pursuers just behind him. But now that he was nearly there, he realized that the stone would be nearly impossible to climb. Unlike the rougher rocks on top of the ridge, it was polished as smooth as a river boulder, up to a height well above his head.

Nothing to grab. Nothing to hold his weight.

A drumaling's limb swatted his shoulder, nearly knocking him to the ground. Stumbling, he dodged another blow. Madly, hoping to find some way to climb, he ran around the outcropping to check the other side. He hurtled around the corner—

And slammed straight into a giant, hairy mass. As he hit the ground, a wrathful roar shook the air. Tamwyn found himself staring up into the eyes of a huge, hunchbacked monster.

7 · A Terrible Weapon

THE HEAVY DOOR TO KULWYCH'S UNDER-
ground cavern swung slowly open. Meanwhile, the
sorcerer stood inside, waiting, feeling rather pleased with
himself. For he could sense, even now, the fear in the sturdy
warrior who was about to enter the cavern—could smell it,
as easily as if it were the pungent odor of a rotting carcass.

The big man strode inside, doing his best to look
brashly unafraid. As broad as a boulder he stood, his face
looking even more threatening than usual in the throbbing
red glow of the crystal, which sat on a stone pedestal in the
center of the cavern. His hands, as big as bear paws,
clasped his wide leather belt that bore a broadsword, a
rapier, two daggers, and a spiked club.

For a second he paused, peering into the gloom. Then,
noticing Kulwych standing motionless by the dank stone
wall, he tensed. "Ye called, Master?"

"Mmmyesss, my Harlech," spat the sorcerer's voice. "I
have news for you."

"Good news, Master?" The warrior licked a bead of
perspiration off his upper lip.

"Good, mmmyesss. Better than you can possibly comprehend."

Harlech bristled at the insult, but said nothing.

Pressing together the palms of his pale hands, Kulwych took a moment to examine his fingernails. Then, with the barest hint of a grin, he turned his lone eye toward the warrior. "You see, my Harlech, I will now show you why your victory in the coming battle at Isenwy is absolutely assured."

"Assured?" Harlech's usual grimace lessened, while his big fingers toyed with the handle of his broadsword. This was, indeed, good news. "Show me, Master."

"In a moment. But first, remember your goal. You shall crush that pitiful alliance of elves, aging priests, and eaglemen. Do you understand, Harlech? *Crush* them. And you shall do it even before my lord Rhita Gawr descends from the sky! Why? Because I want him to see that my army is powerful—immensely powerful. And that I am unquestionably ready to rule Avalon."

"Yes, Master." Harlech nodded expectantly. "Yer right to have such confidence in me troops o' gobsken. Many o' them are already marchin' on Isenwy. Garr, I was jest—"

"Silence!" The sorcerer's harsh command echoed inside the chamber, finally melting into the sound of water trickling down the walls. "I have *no* confidence whatsoever in your troops, or even in my pet ghoulacas, who will fly into battle on your side."

Visibly, Harlech winced at the mention of those deadly, nearly transparent birds whose bloodred talons had ripped apart his flesh more than once. Only thanks to his experience as a fighter, and his array of weapons, had he survived their attacks. While they might be useful allies in battle, there was no way to control them—or to ensure that they attacked only the opposing forces.

"Nor," Kulwych continued, "am I willing to rely on the help you will get from Belamir's people." He chortled quietly. "Although we have infiltrated his Humanity First movement at the very top."

"An' so, yer good news?"

"Is *this*." Kulwych stepped closer to the throbbing crystal, and at the same time, pulled from his cloak an object that glowed with the same malefic light. Holding it by its leather cord, he dangled it before Harlech's face.

"B-b-but," protested the warrior, "it's jest a claw."

Instantly, a bolt of bright red light shot out from the claw. It struck Harlech's rapier with an explosive *craaaaack!* so loud that chips of stone fell from the ceiling. The blade itself burst into intense flames, which burned fiercely for a few seconds and then vanished. Along with—

"Me sword!" In a panic, Harlech searched all around to find the rapier. He checked the loop where it had hung, the rest of his weapons belt, and the cavern floor. But it was nowhere at all.

Kulwych's throaty cackle filled the chamber. "I could have taken off one of your ears, my Harlech, but I decided you might need that in battle."

The warrior could only gape at him, unable to speak. His large hand continued to grope at the spot where his rapier had hung only a moment before.

"So you see, my Harlech, this is much more than just a claw." He twirled the necklace in the flickering rays of the crystal. "It is a weapon. Mmmyesss, a terrible weapon."

Managing to swallow, the warrior asked, "How . . . does it work, Master?"

"It draws from the power of the vengélano crystal, you see. It is connected to the crystal, and bound to that power—just as Rhita Gawr's warriors, who were called from the Otherworld by the crystal, are also bound to that power."

Kulwych studied the claw with admiration. "To use it, all you need to do is concentrate on whatever object—or whatever person—you'd like to destroy. Then let the power go to work! After each bolt, you must wait a few seconds before using it again, so that its strength can gather anew."

"That's all?"

"That is all, my warrior." Handing the necklace to Harlech, he smirked. "Now even you and your unruly gobsken cannot fail."

Cautiously fingering the glowing claw, Harlech hung it around his neck. Slowly, he nodded. "Methinks I'm goin' to like this new weapon."

"You will indeed. Just wait until after the parley before you start to use it."

"Parley?" Harlech almost spat the word. "Yer askin' me to parley wid me enemies afore the fightin' starts? Only a coward does that."

Kulwych hissed with annoyance. "And only a fool questions his master! If you call a parley, they will think you are weak, and will be tempted to start fighting even sooner. How many times must I remind you? I want this battle over and done before Rhita Gawr arrives! That is why I have spread the rumor among the elves that, if they wait too long, superior forces will come to your aid."

The sorcerer nodded. "That is true, of course. Superior forces *will* come to your aid. But thanks to your new weapon, you will not need them. By the time those forces arrive, the mortals will have been vanquished."

Gradually, the look of uncertainty on Harlech's face shifted to something more malevolent. "There's one person, Master, I'm 'specially hopin' to kill."

"And who is that?"

"An eagleman. Fought me back there on yer dam. Bested me even, but only since he had them blasted wings to fly out o' reach."

"Then I suggest you rid him of his wings, Harlech. Before you rid him of his head."

For the first time in a long while, the warrior smiled. "As you say, Master."

The sorcerer rubbed his smooth hands together. "I share your anticipation, mmmyesss. For there is someone whom I, too, am eager to kill."

His eye narrowed maliciously. "Now go. Rush to the nearest portal, at the gobsken fortress in Rahnawyn, and then on to the Plains of Isenwy. Hurry now, Harlech! And do not return until you have slaughtered them all, every last one."

8 · Voice from the Shadows

ELLI, CHEWING ON HER LATEST HANDFUL OF moss, savored its sharp, peppermintlike flavor. Everything else in this realm of eternal night seemed to dull her senses, not awaken them.

Certainly, there wasn't much to see. The circle of light from her glowing amulet illuminated only herself, the sprite cradled in her arm, the mossy turf under her feet, and the dry streambed on her right—which Nuic believed could lead them from the Vale of Echoes to the Lost City of Light. The only other thing she could see was the utter darkness of Shadowroot.

So thick lay that darkness upon the land, blanketing everything, it seemed to muffle any sounds. Since they had left the Vale—which felt like a full day ago, although Elli found it impossible to keep track of time—the only sounds she had heard were the scrunching of their feet on the stubbly moss. And, of course, Nuic's ongoing grumbles of misery: his way of cheering her up.

Yet he wasn't succeeding. In addition to the gloominess of her surroundings was the memory of their narrow escape from the death dreamer. *How could I have been such an idiot?* she asked herself, staying alert for more trouble as she walked. In that moment of weakness, she had nearly lost her life—as well as her chance to destroy Kulwych's crystal, which was her only hope of helping all the people she cared about.

She had come perilously close to losing that chance forever, letting it wash away with those evil waves. Worst of all, when she was honest with herself, she had to admit that the dream, and those waves, hadn't seemed at all evil. Rather, they had felt comforting, alluring, and supremely tempting.

"You're making fists again, Elliryanna." Nuic's voice, and the reddening tones of his skin, nudged her out of her thoughts.

"Just practicing for Kulwych," she replied, doing her best to sound lighthearted. "I'm fine."

"Hmmmpff. If you're fine, then I'm a pink-eyed cookarella bird."

Elli surprised herself by laughing. And the mere sound of her own laughter made her feel a tiny bit better. *Maybe there's still hope after all,* she mused. Then, glancing down at the little fellow she carried, she felt a strong surge of gratitude. *Thanks to you, my friend. Without you I'd still be wandering around the Drumadian compound, an apprentice priestess third class without a clue.*

She nodded, knowing exactly what Nuic would say to that compliment—that she was *still* just an apprentice without a clue.

Onward she walked, following the dry streambed. Just beyond the amulet's circle of light, shadows seemed to coalesce, shift, and then melt away. What creatures, she wondered, lurked in this gloom? She squeezed Nuic a bit tighter.

Hours passed, or what seemed like hours, as the trek

continued. Her feet began to shuffle across the mossy ground. Would they ever reach the Lost City? And its library that Tamwyn had described? Without that library, and the map they hoped was there, it would be impossible to find Kulwych's hideaway in time.

She scowled. *Even if we do get there in time, I still have no idea how to destroy Kulwych's crystal.*

Suddenly she noticed a strange object on the ground ahead, just at the edge of her crystal's light. As she stepped closer, she could see that, while it was no bigger than the broken bits of rock she'd seen lying amidst the moss, this was something quite different. It was smooth, almost glassy, and perfectly square. Strangest of all, it sparkled with color, a deep emerald green. When she reached it, she stopped to look more closely.

"A piece of tile," she announced in surprise.

Nuic, twisting in her arm so that he could see, harrumphed. "Not just any tile. That, I'll wager, is a piece of the city."

"The Lost City of Light?"

The sprite nodded. "Its original name was Dianarra. Built by some sort of flaming creatures, according to legend—creatures who flew down from the stars."

While Elli had doubts about the legend, she remembered well Tamwyn's description of the city—and the look on his face as he had told her about it. She glanced at the Galator, tied around Nuic's middle, wishing she could look into it again right now.

Following her gaze, Nuic placed his hands over the green crystal. "Thinking about that clumsy friend of yours, aren't you? There will be another time to look in on him, Elliryanna. But not now. We have too much else to do right now."

"What I'd really like to do is talk with him again."

"Hmmmpff. Can't understand why! Besides, you

couldn't do that through the Galator, anyway. You remember what Rhia said, don't you? No matter how much you care for someone, you can only see him, not speak to him, through the crystal."

"I know, I know." She started walking again, keeping close to the streambed. Ready to change the subject, she asked, "What do you recall about the city?"

Nuic's color, an inky brown, brightened just barely. "Not much, really. That was over two hundred years ago. Mostly I remember how beautiful it was, with huge buildings, elegant facades, and colorful sculptures all around. And I also remember how busy it was, bustling with people from every realm. Some of them came through the city's portal, the only one in Shadowroot. Others took a portal to the highlands of Fireroot, then trekked here, following this very streambed through the Vale, past the Evernight Peaks, all the way to the city gates. Of course, in those days the stream flowed with water. Just as the city blazed with light from thousands of torches—so bright they could even be seen, whenever the mists parted, from Fireroot's coast."

Striding on the mossy turf, Elli noticed more scattered tiles. Several were also green, but some were glazed with scarlet and gold. She walked faster.

"Then the dark elves' civil war broke out," Nuic continued. "No one outside Shadowroot knows what really happened, except perhaps a few museos who escaped to other realms. It's all a great mystery! All we know for certain is that suddenly the lights of Dianarra were doused, and its portal closed."

Elli halted. A forbidding shape had appeared at the edge of her crystal's light. Blacker than night itself, it loomed larger than anything else they had encountered on this darkened trek. She caught her breath, realizing what it was.

"A wall," she declared. "A huge wall of stone. And look! There's a gap over there to the left."

"The gates," observed Nuic. "Or what's left of them. Well, what's holding you back? Let's go in."

But she merely shifted her feet on the ground, kicking a broken fragment of tile. "Nuic, what about the dark elves?"

"Terrible people. Vicious fighters. Deadly to intruders—especially since they are able to see in the dark."

Elli groaned. "You're not helping me feel any better."

"I'm just telling you the facts, my fainthearted wench. But there's something else you should know about the dark elves. If what the bards sing is true, all the elves died in the war. Or at least nearly all of them."

Elli relaxed a little. "How do they know?"

"Well, the few bards brave enough to have traveled here (always guided by their museos) say that all the dark elves' towns, schools, farms, and mines are empty now. Even Tressimir and Brionna found no dark elves when they came here—although their trip was cut short when, as Brionna told you, she developed the disease called *dark-death.* Which, fortunately for us, only afflicts elves from other parts of Avalon."

"Fortunately," repeated Elli, though she couldn't help but wonder what other strange ailments existed in this realm.

Nuic's tone turned grave. "But one of their mines, as we have learned, is no longer empty. The one where Kulwych is hiding."

Elli's expression hardened. "He'll soon be having visitors. That is, if we can just find that library with the maps."

The sprite grinned almost imperceptibly. "My memory isn't what it used to be, nowadays. But I seem to remember that the library building had a huge dome and a row of flag-poles out front."

"Nuic, you are amazing."

"Hmmmpff. Amazingly foolish, more like it. Why else would I have followed you into this mess?"

Elli answered by striding resolutely toward the gap in the wall. With every step, though, the truth became clearer: This was no longer a wall, and what it bordered was no longer a city. This was a wasteland.

Toppled stone towers, smashed remains of statues, and scattered tiles lay everywhere. To pass through what was left of the gates, Elli needed to climb over a pair of fallen columns, their intricately decorated surfaces hacked to bits. Then she skirted to one side to avoid a teetering pile of stones and metal—all that remained, she guessed, of a guardhouse.

Inside the gates, the devastation continued. Although many of the city's buildings still stood, several had been completely demolished. And even those still standing had been mutilated, especially those that had once displayed artistic tile work or elegant facades. Holding Nuic securely, she made her way down what had once been broad avenues paved with colorful tiles. Yet now, instead of throngs of people, the streets held only rubble from battered buildings, broken torches, smashed windows—and, she shuddered to find, hundreds of skeletons.

Bones, gray and brittle, lay all around. No matter where she turned, her crystal's light would shine upon someone's cracked skull, twisted leg bones, or contorted hand bones that had been frozen, clutching empty air, in the throes of death. It was hard to avoid stepping on bones, too, as she discovered when her foot landed with a sickening crunch on someone's rib. Skeletons poked out from under toppled stones, lay in heaps on the sides of streets, and draped from open windows.

Down the avenues Elli wandered, alert for crumbling walls that could fall at any moment. Ceaselessly, she looked for any building that might be the library. But she saw no trace of a dome or flags—which made her wonder whether they lay somewhere in the surrounding wreckage.

After taking several turns, they came to an intersection of nine streets; in the center, a ring of pillars had once stood. Although the pillars were now just a mound of rubble, from beneath them came a faint glow of green light.

Before she could even ask, the sprite answered her question. "Yes, that's all that's left of the portal." He clacked his tongue in dismay. "Such imbeciles! To destroy a building is one thing. But to destroy a portal, your realm's best link to the outside world, is quite another."

"Why, though? What made them do it?"

"Hmmmpff. The answers to those questions died with the dark elves. It's part of the mystery of why this city was destroyed, something I'm afraid we will never understand."

Elli moved on, following yet another avenue to yet another junction. She turned down a new street, skirted a heap of skeletons—then spotted something that made her freeze. A row of poles lined one side of the street. Although several of them were broken, and only a few tatters remained of their banners, there could be no mistake that once they had been flagpoles. Nuic gripped her forearm with his tiny hand.

She edged closer. There, in the crystal's penetrating light, she could make out some stone steps behind the poles. They led up to a building, squarish and quite large. Then, as she started to climb the steps, she glimpsed the outline of a great dome.

The library! Despite all the debris, Elli practically bounded up the steps. She swerved to avoid a mass of broken tiles—the remains, perhaps, of a colorful mural—and reached the top. Three steps later, she stood at the building's entrance.

Since the immense iron door had been wrenched off its

hinges and cast aside, she strode right through. Her heart raced with the anticipation of finding the map they needed. But at the instant she placed one foot inside the building, a sharp voice rang out.

"Stop right there! Or die."

She halted, glancing down at Nuic. The sprite's expression, as well as his completely black color, told her what she already sensed. That voice from the shadows belonged to a dark elf.

9 · Always Hungry

ELLI MUSTERED HER COURAGE. SHE PEERED at the toppled shelves of books, smashed statues, and mutilated tile work that lay everywhere in the ancient library. Then, trying her best to keep her voice steady, she called into the darkness beyond her crystal's ring of light.

"We mean no harm," she declared. "Don't attack us."

"Everyone in this city means harm," retorted the harsh, menacing voice. In a still more threatening tone, it added, "Unless you leave this instant, you shall stay here forever."

That final *forever* echoed around the ruined library, repeating for several seconds until at last it died away. For a long moment there was no sound at all within the vast, domed chamber. Elli's mind raced, but she couldn't think of anything to say or do. She just stood there, completely motionless except for the fingers that tugged nervously on her own curls.

It was Nuic's crusty voice that broke the silence. To Elli's astonishment, he said quite casually, "All right then, kill us. But if you do, you'll never find out why we came to this library."

Elli stared down at him in disbelief. But the old sprite merely smirked back at her. Another weighty silence ensued, broken only by the sound of a single piece of tile falling from the ceiling onto a heap of leather-bound books.

Suddenly something stirred. From deep in the recesses of the library, far beyond the crystal's glow, came the sound of slow, trudging steps. It drew nearer and nearer, never pausing, its pace much less hurried than that of Elli's pounding heart.

"What have you done?" she whispered angrily to her maryth.

He continued to smirk, though he also gave her an infuriatingly casual wink.

A shadowy figure reached the edge of the light. Elli took a breath, ready for the worst—then released it in a surprised sigh. For the figure wasn't at all what she had expected.

It was, in fact, just an elderly fellow. *Very* elderly, from the looks of him. White hair, as thick as a bed of ferns, sprang in all directions from his head, almost obscuring his pointed ears. In one hand, he clasped a pair of thin, leather-bound volumes covered with dust. His back was severely bent, making his black tunic billow around his chest. But Elli could see that, like Brionna, he had the slim and wiry frame common to elves. His eyes, though, were much larger than Brionna's, practically the size of a hen's eggs. And Elli could see no malice in those large, silvery gray eyes.

Just intelligence. And something more—something like curiosity. Although he couldn't bear to look directly at Elli's glowing crystal, he didn't seem to fear it, as had the death dreamer. Rather, he seemed genuinely intrigued by its light. And by the strangers who had brought illumination back into this chamber. He edged a bit closer, peering at them curiously with his large eyes.

"If you truly come in peace," he declared, "you are welcome here." His voice, while grinding like a cart wheel on stones, didn't sound malevolent anymore. "I must beg your pardon for the rudeness of my greeting, but I have endured many perilous times."

Glancing down at Nuic, Elli shot him a look that seemed to ask, *How did you ever guess?*

To which the sprite responded with a roll of his liquid purple eyes. She could almost hear his voice: *How did you ever doubt me?*

The elf bobbed his white head, still not looking directly at the source of light. "Grikkolo is my name. I welcome you to my realm."

"And also," Nuic added, "to your library. This *is* your library, isn't it?"

A grin, both ironic and sad, spread over Grikkolo's wrinkled face. He hefted the pair of books in his hand, then tapped one cover as gently as a parent would tap the forehead of a baby. Slowly, he drew a deep breath of the air of this room—air that smelled richly of leather bindings, handmade paper, and centuries of dust.

"As a youth, I was always hungry, deeply hungry—though not for food. For information! I was so curious to learn, I loved no place more than this library. So I studied diligently, worked very hard, and finally won the position of Apprentice Librarian, Linguistics Collection. Yet I realized that even that was not enough." His enormous eyes sparkled. "I yearned to live here all the time, doing nothing but reading these books for the rest of my days."

"And then," finished Nuic, "the war came—and you got your wish."

"Yes," answered the elf gravely, his grin vanishing. "That is true. Now I have lived here, in hiding, for many years. Too many: over one hundred, by my count. Thanks to my elvish sight, I can see in the darkness—well enough to read, and plant my own little garden for food. But I dare not go far from this building, in case any warriors are still lurking in the city."

Elli cocked her head sympathetically. "You must be very lonely."

For the first time, he glanced right at her. Though he quickly turned away again, Elli could see that his expression was one of shock. "Lonely? How could anyone be lonely amidst so many stories, so many languages?" He shook his wild head of hair. "Lonely is the very last thing I am!"

Grikkolo waved both his hands at the library. "I have friends, thousands and thousands of them, in every part of this building. Those ignorant warriors may have destroyed the shelves, the murals, and the display cases. But they left the only thing that really matters." He waved the volumes that he was holding. "The books themselves."

Nuic's color shifted to a thoughtful shade of blue. "Not the only thing. They left something else that matters."

The old elf tilted his head, clearly puzzled.

"A librarian."

Grikkolo's sad grin returned. "They left me plenty of work, organizing and repairing volumes, that is certain. More work than I could accomplish in several lifetimes! Yet perhaps one librarian, even a doddering and forgetful one, is better than none." Then the light of curiosity returned to his eyes. "Would you tell me now why you came here?"

"Yes," Elli answered. "But first, would you tell us something briefly? Just why was your city destroyed?"

Wrinkles seemed to multiply on the old fellow's face. Looking suddenly more frail than ever, he set down his books and leaned back against a pair of shelves that had collapsed together. His weight knocked several more books to the floor, sending up a spiral of dust. He hesitated a long moment before finally starting to speak.

"First you must imagine the city as it was. A center of learning, of art and music and story—that was Dianarra, the City of Light. It was built here by people from the stars, people with bodies of fire, whose very wings were aflame."

Elli lifted her eyebrows in surprise.

"Ayanowyn was their name," the elf explained. "Or, in our Common Tongue, fire angels. They gave us many gifts—more, I fear, than we deserved. They not only built much of this city, they covered its buildings and streets with dazzling tiles of every color, made from the heat of their own flames."

He pushed some stray white hairs off his brow. "And they also gave us the gift of light. Torches flamed everywhere in Dianarra—which, to those people, meant City of Fallen Stars. Their goal, you see, was to bring the brightest of light to the darkest of realms."

The librarian paused, casting his gaze around the room that held uncounted volumes. "That was why they gave to Lastrael the brightest light of all. Stories. Tales from every land, even some from beyond the Seven Realms. Legends and mysteries, mournful ballads and romantic poems— these filled Dianarra, just as storytellers stood on every street corner and mural painters decorated every wall. It was those stories, and the many bards and performers and scribes who came here to learn them, that brought this city its greatest days."

His face turned grim. "And also its downfall."

Glumly, he shook his head. "There were always dark elves who resented the City of Light. They feared its power—and even more, the power of its stories. Suspicious of outside influence, they longed for the bygone times of quiet darkness. Of isolation from all these foreign myths, customs, and ideas. And in our arrogance, those of us who cherished the wider world simply ignored those who disagreed, deriding their foolishness but never trying to help them understand the beauties beyond our borders."

He exhaled a sorrowful breath. "Finally, they attacked Dianarra. The battle raged on, growing more brutal with every atrocity. At the beginning, I fought as best I could with those who defended our city and all it stood for. But in time I could see that Dianarra would fall. When the portal, Lastrael's only one, was destroyed, I fled into the deepest part of the library and hid there."

Hanging his head, he lamented, "I am nothing more than a coward, a terrible coward! I should have given my life to my city. To my realm." He wrung his wrinkled hands. "Yet I just could not bring myself to do that."

His voice now just a raspy whisper, he added, "For this was a war that no one could win. And that was just how it ended. Both armies lost. Dianarra lost. The lovely dark and the inspiring light—both of them also lost."

The lovely dark, Elli repeated to herself. Just what he meant by that phrase, she wasn't sure. Yet she did feel sure that, despite all she had believed, there remained some genuine goodness here in Shadowroot.

She stepped over to Grikkolo, some broken bits of tile cracking under her weight. Gently, she rested her hand against the back of his neck, hoping to comfort him.

In time, the old elf raised his head. Although he couldn't look at her directly, she glimpsed the gratitude in his silvery gray eyes. Then, as his curiosity returned to the fore, he asked, "Now tell me. What brought you here? And what, may I ask, is that light you carry?"

Quickly as she could, Elli explained everything: the darkened stars, the corrupted crystal, and the overwhelming plight of Avalon. As she spoke, Grikkolo listened in rapt attention, his expression graver by the minute. When, at last, she told him about the crystal of élano that she wore, his wide eyes opened even wider.

"All we know," she concluded, "is that Kulwych is hiding underground, in the deepest mine he could find."

"That would be Borvo Lugna," Grikkolo commented. "It is deep, very deep. And also large enough to hold whatever army he might be assembling, with plenty of iron for forging weapons."

Elli traded glances with the sprite in her arm. "How far," she asked, "is it from here?"

"A full day's walk. If you know the way, of course."

"Which is why we came here," she explained. "To find a map."

"That will not be necessary," declared the elf. He pushed away from the shelves where he'd been resting and stood as straight as his back allowed. Facing the doorway to the library, he added with determination: "For I shall take you there myself."

Elli blinked in surprise. Then slowly she smiled, realizing how much this would help them find their way across the realm of darkness. "You would really do that?"

Grikkolo nodded at the doorway. "While many years have passed since I left this place, I still remember well the pathways of my youth." He stood even more erect. "And this time, in this battle, I will be no coward."

10 · Palimyst

THE HUGE, HUNCHBACKED MONSTER STARED down at Tamwyn, who lay helpless on the grass. The creature's tongue licked the lips of his snout, while his immense hairy arms reached toward the young man. Even if Tamwyn had been standing, this monster would have towered over him, much like a tree over a fallen branch.

Indeed, the giant creature did resemble a tree—one covered with shaggy brown hair instead of leaves. His one enormous leg, as thick as an oak, furthered this impression. As did his burly, branchlike arms. Only the two dark eyes above his snout, glinting mysteriously, seemed to belong to a different sort of being.

Just then the monster roared, a wrathful blast of sound that flattened the grass. The pair of drumalings who had been pursuing Tamwyn had already stopped short when they saw the hairy giant. Now they turned and hurried away, their roots slamming against the ground.

Meanwhile, the huge beast's hands, each with seven long fingers, opened toward Tamwyn. He knew that in another instant they would close around his neck or crush his skull. There wasn't time to grab his dagger or his staff, let alone try to escape.

I'm sorry, Elli. So very—

The long fingers reached him. But instead of wrapping around his neck or his skull, they grabbed his shoulders—and lifted him straight up into the air. Tamwyn struggled, trying with all his might to wriggle free before the creature could eat him. From the size of that snout, it would take only a few bites. Yet as hard as he tried to break free, he only felt the fingers' grip tighten.

The hunchbacked giant studied him, dark eyes gleaming. Then, just as Tamwyn expected to see the jaws open wide, he saw instead the creature's lips curl into a quite human expression of puzzlement. At the same time, Tamwyn suddenly heard the creature's thoughts, spoken in a rich bass voice.

Well now, Palimyst. What have you collected today?

Although he had long grown accustomed to hearing the thoughts of other kinds of beings, and understanding their languages, Tamwyn wasn't at all sure that he'd heard correctly. *Collected? What does that mean?*

The creature's puzzlement seemed to deepen. Then, in a deep, rolling growl, it spoke directly to Tamwyn. "You arrrrre an intelligent one, I rrrrrealize that now. Yet neverrrrr have I seen the likes of you beforrrrre."

Without warning, the hairy beast released his grip on Tamwyn's shoulders. The young man dropped back to the ground, landing with a thud on the grass. Tamwyn groaned as the torch pole jammed into his back. But he swiftly rolled to the side and bounced to his feet, ready to run away at any sign of hostility.

"What—I mean, who—are you?" Tamwyn asked, growling in the language of this strange giant.

A deep, bubbling growl filled the air, which Tamwyn sensed was really a kind of laughter. "That is the verrrrry question I have forrrrr you, my little two-leggerrrrr! Yet since you arrrrre, I suspect, a visitorrrrr to this rrrrealm, I shall answerrrrr yourrrrr question firrrrrst."

With a sweep of an immense arm, he declared, "I am Palimyst, of the Taliwonn people. A crrrrraftsman I am— and also a collectorrrrr."

Still a bit nervous about that term, Tamwyn asked, "And just what do you collect?"

"One question at a time, little one." Palimyst bent his broad leg briefly, then straightened up again—what Tamwyn guessed was a bow of greeting. "Welcome to Holosarrrrr, ourrrrr name forrrrr this land. It means *the lowest rrrrrealm,* since we arrrrre the bottommost brrrrranch on the Grrrrreat Trrrrrree."

Tamwyn gave his own version of a bow. "My name is Tamwyn Eopia, a human. And I come from a realm even lower than yours: a root of this very Tree."

Palimyst started at this news, taking a small hop backward. "A rrrrrealm of the rrrrroots? You speak the trrrrruth, Tamwyn Eopia?"

"I do."

"Small as you arrrrre, you have climbed so verrrrrry high?"

"I have." Tamwyn's gaze lifted to the rocky ridge above them, and then higher, to the bright lights in the sky. "And I intend to climb higher still."

The dark eyes of Palimyst stared at him, scrutinizing closely. They showed heightened interest—and also, perhaps, esteem. Finally, he asked, "That tiny blade on yourrrrr belt. Forrrrr what do you use it?"

Tamwyn patted the sheath. "Mostly just whittling. And carving something—a gift for . . . a friend." He tapped the side of his pack, producing a low, quaking note from the wood inside. "A harp."

Tamwyn paused, just listening to the resonant note.

Then, abruptly, his face fell. "Though I don't have the skill. Or even the strings."

Again Palimyst spoke, his growl quieter than before. "I, too, carrrrrve wood, frrrrrom the ancient forrrrrestlands higherrrrr in the rrrrrealm. Like you, I know the turrrrrn of a blade, the contourrrrrr of wood, the language of grrrrrain. And I also know the humility that comes frrrrrom trrrrrrying to masterrrrr a crrrrraft."

The huge, hunched form bent lower. "Tamwyn Eopia, if you would like to visit my lairrrrr, I would welcome you as my guest."

Though he felt touched by the generosity and kindness of those words, Tamwyn shook his head. "I would be honored, Palimyst. But—" He glanced once more at the stars. "I have very far to go, and much too little time."

Palimyst hopped slightly closer, and dropped his voice to a rumbling whisper. "Even if I werrrrre to show you a way to make time stand still?"

"Y-y-you could do that?" stammered Tamwyn, awestruck.

"Forrrrr a fellow wood carrrrrverrrrrr, yes. And yet I must warrrrrn you: I can tell you what I know about the cr-rrrraft. But only you can masterrrrr it."

Still unsure whether anything like this was even possible, the young man nodded slowly. "In that case, I would be glad to come."

"Follow afterrrrr me, then."

With surprising grace for someone so large, Palimyst turned on his leg and hopped into the valley, leaving a trail of compressed grass. Tamwyn hurriedly checked to make sure he hadn't dropped any belongings, then dashed after him. It was all he could do to stay with Palimyst's pace.

Up the gently rising valley they moved, past more steaming pools of hot sap and outcroppings of smooth rock. Tamwyn also spotted, to his dismay, a distant group of drumalings, but the treelike creatures watched them pass in silence. They skirted a thundering waterfall, pouring with billows of mist over a cliff on the ridge. Finally they reached a canyon that joined with the valley.

Here Palimyst turned, hopping higher into the canyon. Although he needed to scramble over a mass of boulders to keep up, Tamwyn couldn't help but notice that the canyon's auburn cliff walls seemed softer than stone—more like some kind of earthen fruit. He also spied a large, coiled snake, as auburn as the rocks, resting on a ledge. Nearby, a pair of green butterflies flitted above a newly opened flower, which smelled as fragrant as honeycomb.

Abruptly, Palimyst veered into a smaller side canyon. A thin stream ran down its center, carrying water from the ridge above. Some of the same bushes with lavender leaves that Tamwyn had found before lined the stream's banks, along with an array of brilliant blue and pink flowers.

Tamwyn hardly noticed, however. For the most striking thing about this canyon was the enormous piece of green fabric, the size of a meadow, that hung from one cliff. The fabric's top was anchored to the rocks above, while its bottom stretched out almost to the edge of the stream in the canyon's center. Great walls of fabric hung from the sides so that, underneath, a huge area was shielded from wind and storm. Palimyst hopped up to one side, lifted a flap, and entered with the ease of a deer bounding into a glade.

A tent, thought Tamwyn in wonder. *He's made himself a tent.*

As he climbed up to the entrance, still panting from his run, he could see that the fabric had actually been woven from thousands of thin, sturdy vines. Each vine had been wound carefully around many, many others, producing a durable yet flexible sheet. Before going inside, Tamwyn paused to run his hand along the weaving's edge. *This fellow really is a craftsman.*

He lifted the flap and entered. It took a few seconds for his eyes to adjust to the dimmer light, but soon he could see very well. And he knew that he had just stepped into a truly extraordinary residence.

On the left side of the well-beaten dirt path that ran down the center of the lair, Tamwyn saw a large open space that held a fire circle. The charred ring, flanked by two great stone benches, rested just below a circular hole in the tent where smoke could escape. Beside the fire circle sat a forge where hot coals glowed bright, a bellows made from the same fabric as the tent, and a wide assortment of handmade tools. This whole area, along with the smoky smell in the air, reminded him of Ethaun's smithy.

Yet Tamwyn could also see one major difference. These tools, unlike Ethaun's, were not intended for gardening. Rather, they were meant for the more delicate work of craftsmanship. There were blades long and short, hammers, wedges, thin needles made of bone and willow shoots, hooks, bowls, spools of thread and twine and even metal wire, a spinning wheel, a turntable with a clay pot, mortars and pestles, stone jars that might have held dyeing powders, several pairs of scissors, files of all sizes, a spiraling metal drill, slats of wood for stretching materials, dozens of iron pots, two sharp axes, a huge loom, tall baskets of bark strips and wood of many kinds, and several devices so bizarre that Tamwyn had no idea at all what they might be.

Opposite this work area, on the right, was a pen of packed straw that must have been Palimyst's sleeping pallet. Nearby sat an immense wooden table bearing half a dozen woven baskets piled high with apples, melons, squashes, and a curling, red-spotted fruit that Tamwyn had never seen before. One especially large basket, on the seat of a vast wooden chair, held only rinds, cores, and clumps of seeds. Bowls, mugs, great stone jars, and other kitchen supplies filled the three tall cabinets behind the table. Next to the wall of the tent, where a row of windows had been cut, rested a gigantic chair hewn from the auburn stone of the cliffs. And in that chair sat Palimyst himself, his leg propped on the thick slab of wood that was the tabletop.

"Welcome to my lairrrrr, Tamwyn Eopia."

The young man glanced at the green fabric that stretched high above his head. "This is the most remarkable home I've ever seen."

Palimyst's growling voice bubbled with laughter. "Perrrrrhaps, my two-legged guest. Yet what I will show you now is farrrrr morrrrre rrrrremarrrrrkable."

11 · The River of Time

PALIMYST SLID HIS ENORMOUS LEG OFF
the tabletop, slamming it down onto the dirt floor of
his lair. Tamwyn, seeing the puff of dirt from the impact,
realized that the leg was even heavier than he'd thought,
more like a stone pillar than a tree trunk. And that made
Palimyst's grace of movement when he hopped all the
more amazing.

Before leaving the table, the hairy fellow grabbed three
apples with the fingers of one hand. In rapid succession, he
popped each one into his mouth, chewed briskly, and then
spat the core into the basket on his wooden chair. His eyes
gleaming, he shot a glance at Tamwyn.

"Come rrrrright along," he growled. Then he turned and
hopped past the forge and all his scattered tools and materials, heading deeper into the tent.

The young man followed. Watching his huge, broad-
shouldered host, he couldn't help but think that the many
objects that he himself carried—pack, dagger, staff, and
torch—really didn't amount to much compared to the immense bulk that Palimyst hauled around everywhere he

went. But the sight of all those craftsman's tools had made Tamwyn realize that the key quality of this creature, and maybe all the Taliwonn people, was not his massive size.

No, it was his fingers. Those long, slender fingers, seven on each hand, were capable of amazingly delicate movement. And, as Tamwyn understood more with every step further into the tent, they were also capable of stunning skill.

Shelves lined both sides of the lair, crammed with crafts of every kind. There were woven baskets, some as small as Tamwyn's thumbnail, others so big he'd have no trouble at all climbing in. There were also painted slabs of wood, engraved metal blades, strangely shaped clay pots and pitchers, sculpted stones, and carefully arranged bouquets of dried grasses, pressed flowers, and even polished snail shells. Tamwyn saw—and couldn't resist touching gently— a colorful sphere made entirely from seeds, a huge mask of iridescent feathers, radiant prisms cut from quartz crystals, carpets woven from dyed threads, beeswax candles, plus (to his surprise) a square of fabric made from the bright wings of beetles.

He found, on those shelves, a miniature landscape carved from the auburn stone of the cliffs. An antler, playfully decorated with beads. A sculpture, made from amethyst and calcite crystals, that looked like a purple mountain draped with glaciers. A huge hat of woven grass, spotted with luminous blue butterfly wings. A tapestry of white lightning stark against a black sky. A pair of rounded shells, painted with exquisite detail so that they resembled the multifaceted eyes of an insect.

Most striking of all, though, were the musical instruments. Palimyst had put so many of them on the shelves that they leaned against each other or sat in jumbled piles, making it difficult sometimes to tell them apart. But Tamwyn had no trouble recognizing several flutes, carved from bone or wood; a set of crystal drums; the largest lute he'd ever seen; and many beautiful harps, whose sound boxes of oak or ash or maple had been intricately carved with flowing designs.

"Well now, my two-legged frrrrriend, what do you think of this collection?"

Tamwyn realized that he'd been so engrossed in viewing the treasures on the shelves, as he strolled slowly down the path, that he had almost walked right into Palimyst. His mammoth host had been waiting for him to catch up. Looking up into Palimyst's face, he fumbled for words.

"It's, it's—well, fabulous. Too much, too big, for description. As you promised, just remarkable."

The enormous eyes studied him. "Rrrrremarrrrrkable, yes. Not because of me, howeverrrrr."

"Not because of you?" Tamwyn stared at him in surprise. "But you made all these things, didn't you?"

"Many of them. And the otherrrrs I have collected overrrrr the yearrrrrs. Yet all I have rrrrreally done is take the naturrrrral gifts of Avalon, alrrrrready so beautiful, and rrrrreshape or rrrrrearrrrrrange them."

Still bewildered, Tamwyn shook his head. "You've put so much work into these things."

"Parrrrrt of theirrrrr virrrrrtue, to be surrrrre. Yet everrrrrrything you see herrrrre—" He paused to wave his arm at the mass of objects on display. "Combines naturrrrrre's infinite gifts with a crrrrrraftsman's finite skills. And the rrrrresult is a special kind of beauty: one that mixes the Trrrrree and the hand, immorrrrrtal and morrrrrtal."

For a long moment, Tamwyn was silent. At last, he said, "I think, maybe, I understand. A carver can do nothing without wood. Or a weaver, without thread. Or a painter, without pigment. But it's even more than that, isn't it? More than just the raw materials that we need. For none of those crafts would even begin to happen without *inspiration*. And that, too, we get from the natural world—from noticing and appreciating its many wonders."

With the fingers of one hand, Palimyst gently drummed

the young man's shoulder, his touch as light as falling rain. "That is the wisdom of a crrrrraftsman, a trrrrrue makerrrrr of arrrrrt."

The word *maker* rang in Tamwyn's mind. He remembered how it had been used by Aelonnia, one of Isenwy's ancient mudmakers. For her, a Maker meant someone with magic in his hands, and humility in his heart. How different was that, really, from Palimyst's view of a craftsman?

"Now," announced Palimyst, "I will show you one thing morrrrre. And then, Tamwyn Eopia, I will tell you what I know about how to stop time."

As Tamwyn watched eagerly, his host swung around and gestured at a large tapestry that hung by itself on the side of the tent. Instantly, the young man recognized its design. It was a map of the stars!

Luminous silver threads marked each star in the sky, while the background colors melted from pitch black to azure blue. Although Tamwyn could identify his favorite constellations—Pegasus, the Twisted Tree, the double rings of the Circles, and of course, the now-darkened Wizard's Staff—they seemed to be in unfamiliar shapes, as if they'd been stretched a bit out of proportion.

Of course! he realized. This was how they looked from Holosarr, the lowest branch of the Tree. All his life, he had seen them from a slightly different angle, down in the root-realms.

Despite this unfamiliarity, though, he gazed with wonder at the tapestry, almost as if he were seeing the stars themselves. For all his life, long before he had ever embarked on this quest, the stars had intrigued him. Called to him, almost. If they had been a text, with mysterious letters blazing on a blackened page, he would have longed to read it; if they had been a field, with radiant flowers blooming underfoot, he would have longed to run through it.

Suddenly he noticed something else that seemed a bit odd. There, running down the middle of the sky, was a vague line of light. The same line that he had seen when he first arrived in Holosarr! Like a subtle crack in a back-lit piece of wood, it glowed ever so slightly, inviting a closer look.

"What is that line?" he asked, pointing.

Palimyst's deep growl bubbled. "That, my frrrrriend, is what I wanted to show you."

Shifting his great bulk, he bent lower—so low that his snout wasn't far above Tamwyn's head. "The Rrrrriverrrrr of Time."

"A river? In the sky?"

"That is rrrrright. It was called, in the Taliwonn's most ancient tongue, Crrrrryll Onnawesh, which means *the seam in the tent of the sky.*"

"Cryll Onnawesh," repeated Tamwyn. "But how is it like a river?"

Palimyst exhaled, growling thoughtfully, as he chose the best words. "The Rrrrriverrrrr," he explained, "divides the two halves of time—past and futurrrrre. So the Rrrrriverrrrr of Time itself is always in the prrrrresent. The now. And yet, even as it stays in the prrrrresent moment, it moves within itself, flowing ceaselessly thrrrrrough all the worrrrrlds that exist. In that way, it connects all the worrrrrlds—not in space, but in time."

He bent the tiniest bit lower, so that Tamwyn felt the warmth of his apple-scented breath. "And herrrrre, Tamwyn Eopia, is the mirrrrracle. If anyone can enterrrrr the Rrrrriverrrrr, he can move acrrrrross the whole rrrrrealm of the sky—but stay in the prrrrresent time."

Tamwyn nodded, his thoughts racing. "In other words, he can stop time."

The craftsman gave a deep, affirmative growl.

"And so," Tamwyn continued, "if the stars are really doorways to other worlds, and if Avalon is the world in be-tween all the others, then someone who enters the River of Time from Avalon can ride to anywhere." He paused, feeling the magnitude of this idea. "And never leave the present moment."

"Now you underrrrrstand." Palimyst straightened up, though not enough to remove his hunchback. "Yet you must rrrrrememberrrrr my warrrrrning: As much as I can tell you about this new crrrrraft, only you can masterrrrr it."

Tamwyn's brow furrowed. "Then you don't know how to enter the River?"

"No, my frrrrriend. As often as I have trrrrried, I have neverrrrr been able to do it myself." His many fingers worked the air, as if they were pulling invisible threads. "Yet I do believe it can be done. Forrrrr the wizarrrrrd Merrrrrlin himself once did that verrrrry thing."

"Really? When?"

"On his final deparrrrrturrrrrre frrrrrom Avalon, when he left forrrrr the worrrrrld called Earrrrrth. He did not rrrrride into the starrrrrs, as he had done beforrrrre, on the back of the grrrrreat grrrrreen drrrrragon Basilgarrrrrad—although no one, not even the drrrrragon himself perrrrrhaps, knew why. That was especially strrrrrange, since he had just rrrrridden the drrrrragon to rrrrrelight seven darrrrrkened starrrrrs—the constellation we call the Staff of Merrrrrlin."

Tempted as he was to say something about his own quest to relight those same seven stars, Tamwyn didn't want to interrupt the tale. "What did he do instead? To enter the River?"

"He climbed to the highest point on the highest rrrrridge of Holosarrrrr, the place we now call Merrrrrlin's Pinnacle, and left frrrrrom therrrrre."

"But how?" The young man ground his foot into the dirt. "Do you know anything more?"

"Only this, I am afrrrrraid. Therrrrre is an old saying among my people:

To swim within the Rrrrriverrrrr of Time
Thy soul must be worrrrrthy, thy motive sublime.

"Perrrrrhaps you possess those two qualities, Tamwyn Eopia."

"And perhaps not!" Frustrated, he swung a punch at the air. "All you really have for me, then, is a legend. And a saying. They could be just one big lie."

"They could be," Palimyst replied. His fingers reached out and picked up one of his harps, carved from the burl of an old cherry tree. He hefted it, feeling its balance of wood, air, and strings. "Orrrrr they could be morrrrrre like this harrrrrp: its surrrrrrface shaped by morrrrrtal hands, but its essence made by immorrrrrtal trrrrruth."

Tamwyn swallowed. "Forgive me, I shouldn't have spoken that way. It's just that . . ." He ran a hand through his long black locks. "I had, for a moment there, such hope."

The mammoth fellow placed three of his fingers, very lightly, on Tamwyn's chest. "I still have hope. Rrrrreal hope. You may be just the one to do what only the wizarrrrrd Merrrrrlin has done—to enterrrrr the Rrrrriverrrrr of Time."

He paused, studying his guest thoughtfully. "And to rrrrrelight, once again, those seven starrrrrs."

Tamwyn started. "How—how did you know?"

Hefting the harp in his great hand, Palimyst replied, "To carrrrrve wood successfully, one must learrrrrn to rrrrread the grrrrrain. And each perrrrrson, like each piece of wood, has a special grrrrrain of his orrrrr herrrrr own."

"Thank you," whispered Tamwyn.

"No," came the response. "It is I who should thank *you*. Forrrrr I neverrrrr expected, when this day began, that I would meet someone who is both so verrrrry small, and so verrrrry larrrrrge, at once."

Tamwyn merely gazed up at him.

Palimyst growled deeply, then continued, "I have some

gifts forrrrr you beforrrrre you deparrrrrt. Dirrrrrections to Merrrrrlin's Pinnacle, forrrrr one. A good meal of frrrrrresh frrrrruits, tuberrrrrs, and rrrrroasted seeds, forrrrr anotherrrrr. And in addition, a chant that I shall teach you, which will help to shield yourrrrr eyes frrrrrom brrrrrightness. I use it to worrrrrk with the hottest coal firrrrres in my forrrrrge, but you can use it when you rrrrreach the starrrrrs."

Tamwyn touched the thick hair of his friend's arm. "I won't forget you."

Palimyst roared with laughter, and with such force that the tapestry of the stars fluttered. "How could you everrrrr forrrrrget me? That is not possible."

Then, using all his fingers, he quickly untied the strings from the harp. Pressing them into his guest's hand, he declared, "One last gift, Tamwyn Eopia—forrrrr that harrrrrp you arrrrre making."

His lips curled in what might have been a grin. "Frrrrrom one crrrrraftsman to anotherrrrr."

Part

II

12 · Song of the Curlew

TO BRIONNA, THE HEAVY WOODEN GATES OF the village of Prosperity seemed like the entrance to a dungeon. A dungeon that no living creature, certainly no elf, should be forced to enter. As they swung open, creaking horribly, she shuddered.

Even so, if she hadn't been marched into the village as a prisoner, surrounded by a ring of green-clad men with bows and arrows ready to shoot, she would have been struck by how little this place resembled a dungeon. As she passed through the gates—along with the tall priest Lleu, the falcon Catha on his shoulder, and the little fellow Shim, who seemed more confused than ever—she entered a realm of greenery.

Not the greenery of the forest, which flourished just outside the gates. Nor even the greenery of emerging spring, which decorated the boughs of every living tree in El Urien. Rather, this was the greenery of a garden—a bountiful, productive garden.

Within the high wooden fences that separated the village from the forestlands, wide cultivated fields were al-

ready sprouting vegetable stalks, vines, and the season's
first leaves of lettuce and spinach. Radishes, cucumbers,
carrots, tomatoes, cabbages, and peppers were not far behind. The earliest squashes, deep green and gold, swelled
in earthen beds. And on many of the houses nearby, window boxes held flowers even more brightly colored than
the houses' own painted walls.

Fruit trees blossomed, giving the air sweet aromas of
apple, plum, and pear. Also in the air were the scents of
budding lilacs, freshly turned soil, and the first hint of juicy
grapes on the arbors. Leafy bushes, draped with new green
leaves, bordered every pathway.

Many men and women, with black earth under their fingernails, worked in the fields. Aided by some strange, clat-
tering machines that spewed fumes far less pleasant than
apple blossoms, these people sowed new seeds, plowed
furrows, and sprayed plants with liquids that Brionna could
not recognize. Just as many people, however, were simply
playing outdoors. Children and adults cavorted on the
swings in front of a pale yellow school building. Others
chased through the village trading center, hurdling newly
made benches and chairs. Meanwhile, plump goats and
sheep, penned in the communal stable, jostled each other
playfully.

As Brionna and the other captives were led through the
settlement toward the large stone building by the central
courtyard, none of the villagers paused to notice them. Indeed, the prisoners' arrival roused no more interest than a
windblown leaf drifting to the forest floor. *What could they
be thinking?* the elf wondered. *Do they see so many prisoners that we're nothing special? Or are the people of Prosperity so blind to their fellow creatures that they really
believe none of this affects their own lives?*

Even as they marched past a row of pear trees, the
young curlew perched in one of the branches went on
singing melodiously. *So he, too, cares nothing about us,*

thought Brionna resignedly. *Or about the war that's going to happen.*

Yet there was something sharp, almost urgent, underneath the bird's spiraling melody. Brionna looked more closely. At once she saw something terribly surprising— and terribly cruel.

"That bird," she cried out, stopping suddenly under the tree. "His foot has been tied to the branch! He can't get away."

"O' course he can't," snapped one of the men as he jabbed her back with his arrow. "This way he's got to keep on singin' fer our people."

"But that's horrible," she protested. "He should be free."

"Know what we do to the ones we keep indoors?" the man asked with a delighted smirk. "We pokes out their eyes! Then they jest keep on singin' and singin', day and night."

Brionna was so stunned by this idea that she couldn't even speak.

"Keep on walkin', elf-girl," barked Morrigon. The malicious old man—if he was, indeed, a man—angrily pushed a low-hanging branch away from his bloodshot eye.

Rudely shoved from behind, Brionna started moving again. Not before she looked back at the imprisoned curlew, though. And made a silent promise that, if she ever found some way to free herself, she would also free him.

She traded glances with Lleu, whose expression showed that he was equally aghast. Catha, meanwhile, continued to flutter her wings and snap her beak angrily. Only the certainty that she would be shot down by one of the archers kept her perched on Lleu's shoulder. And yet her actions made clear that she longed to plunge into battle, seeking bloody revenge—just like the person for whom she was named, the fierce warrior Babd Catha.

Shim, trudging beside the elf maiden, seemed to be in a daze. Yet Brionna could tell by his constant mutterings that he understood something had gone badly wrong. She wished, as she looked over at him, that he were suddenly his giant self again. *As high as the highliest tree,* as he would say.

Just as they arrived at the large stone building, she turned to face Morrigon. He grinned smugly at her—even as he rubbed his unnaturally pink eye. She glared back, thinking, *I know what you are. A changeling! And I will find some way to stop you, if it's the only thing I do before I die.*

"On yer guard, men!" commanded Morrigon. "Whilst I go and report to Olo Belamir, ye can take these bags o' dung to the *guest quarters.*" He chortled at his own choice of words. "And do yer best to make them feel 'specially comfortable."

With a sneer at Brionna, he added, "We'd like them to stay fer a long, long time."

Into the building they shuffled, always surrounded by wary archers. Although the eyes of Brionna, Lleu, and Catha roved constantly, searching for some way to escape, they found nothing. The guards lit a pair of torches, then led them along one darkened hallway after another until they reached a stone stairwell. Down the dank steps, slippery with slime, they marched. Even if she hadn't seen their descent, Brionna could tell, from the chill in her elven bones, that they were deep underground.

When at last they reached the bottom, the men shoved them into a dark, windowless cell. Its only dim light came from a torch, jammed into a niche in the stones outside the cell's barred door. Beneath the torch, one of the men planted himself on a stone bench—after he threw Brionna's longbow and quiver into a dark corner by the stairs.

"Ye won't be needin' them anymore, elf-girl," he said with a loud guffaw.

Before she could even begin to respond, another man slammed the cell door closed. He slid the heavy iron bolt.

The men's crude laughter echoed in the stairwell as they departed, leaving behind the guard on the bench.

"Well, me guests," rasped the guard with a smirk. "Too bad we fergot about yer dinner."

He kicked at the floor, spraying flecks of mud through the bars of their cell door. "Unless o' course ye can eat dirt." With another guffaw, he pulled his own dinner out of his satchel: a large flask of foul-smelling brew. And then, with no further thought of the prisoners, he began to drink.

13 · Pincers and Fangs

WITHIN THE CELL, BRIONNA SPUN AROUND angrily. Moving with the easy agility of her people, she sat down on the dirt floor and crossed her legs. She sighed, her expression shifting from rage to dejection.

As she leaned back against the rough stones, she could feel her old scar from the slave master's whip. *As terrible as that time was,* she thought glumly, *at least I could still see the stars and breathe the open air.*

Far less gracefully, Shim slumped down beside her. Across the cell, Lleu remained standing. The gangly priest rested his shoulder against the wall, as if he could somehow push it aside like an unlocked door. Catha stayed motionless on her customary perch, her eyes unusually dull.

"That Morrigon," grumbled the elf. "He's the changeling, I'm sure of it."

"By the light of Dagda," exclaimed Lleu. "That eye of his! I'm sure you're right."

Shaking his head, Lleu slid down to the floor and folded his arms across his chest. "If only we could somehow break out of here and find Belamir. If he knew the truth, he would be horrified. He'd no sooner tolerate a changeling in his midst than he'd allow himself to be used as a pawn for Kulwych—and Rhita Gawr—at the battle of Isenwy."

Brionna shrugged. "You have more faith in that man than I do. He's the founder of Humanity First, remember?"

"Yes, but he is also wiser than his movement has become. Much due to that changeling, I'll wager. If only I could speak to him! I'm sure he would help us."

"Face the truth, Lleu. We have totally failed! We never should have come here to this village. Now we're just going to rot in this cell while our friends all risk their lives to defend Avalon."

Lleu chewed his lip for a while before answering. When he spoke again, his voice was quiet, yet steady. "As long as we are alive, there's still a chance we can find some way to talk to Belamir. And convince him not to send his followers to Isenwy. Brionna, there's just too much at stake to give up now."

She said nothing.

Hours passed. The sullen group remained silent. Only the snores of the guard, sprawled on the bench in a drunken stupor, broke the stillness.

"Owww," cried Shim suddenly. He rolled aside, grabbing his rump. "I've been stingded!"

Brionna glanced over at the spot where he'd been sitting. Spying a round hole in the dirt floor of the cell, big enough to fit her thumb, she shook her head. "Gouger ants," she said sympathetically. "They bite hard."

"Especially when someone sits on top of their front door," added Lleu.

Shim scrunched his nose as he patted his tender posterior. A trickle of blood stained his torn leggings. "Those antly beasts! Gave me a bigsy bite, they did." He gave Brionna a forlorn look. "And Rowanna, I was just thinking it couldn't get any worse."

"Don't worry, Shim. We'll get out of here somehow." Yet even as Brionna spoke the words, she knew she didn't believe them.

Nor did Shim, apparently. Whether or not he'd heard what she said, he hung his head miserably.

"Well, well, so these are my new guests."

Everyone in the cell turned to see the source of the deep, gracious voice. Standing just outside the barred door, next to the sleeping guard, stood a white-haired man in a gray robe smudged with dirt. A string of garlic bulbs hung around his neck, while trowels, clippers, and other garden tools hung from the hooks and pockets of his robe. Dirt packed every wrinkle of his weathered hands, right down to his broken thumbnail.

"Belamir!" Lleu's delighted cry echoed inside the cell. The priest leaped to his feet, so quickly that Catha barely hung on to his shoulder. "We must speak with you."

The old man smiled, his face creasing like plowed furrows. "I am happy to hear what you have to say." The smile faded. "Although I have been told that you came here to harm me."

"No, that's not true." Lleu wrapped his hands around the bars on the cell door. "We have come only to help you! To keep you from unwittingly serving that warlord of the Otherworld, Rhita Gawr."

The gardener stiffened. "Hanwan Belamir is no servant of Rhita Gawr."

"But your man Morrigon is." Brionna rose and took a step toward the door. Her eyes burning with intensity, she declared, "For he is no man at all. He is a *changeling.*"

Clearly shocked, Belamir faltered, placing his dirt-crusted hand against the door for support. "A . . . what?"

"A changeling," repeated the elf maiden. "He has influenced your followers, and perhaps you as well, to do some terrible things."

"Such as destroying the Drumadian compound," interjected Lleu. "And gravely wounding High Priestess Coer-ria."

Even more taken aback, Belamir's whole face twisted. He looked deeply pained, so much that he seemed about to burst into tears.

Instead, he burst into laughter. Hearty, bellowing laughter.

The captives watched him, aghast. When at last he stopped, he studied them from the other side of the cell door, his eyes dancing with mirth. "You think that Mor-rigon's swollen eye means he is a changeling?"

"Yes," insisted Brionna and Lleu as one.

"Well then," said the gardener in a much quieter voice, "what if I told you that I already know about the changeling in my village? That I already perceive his every move?"

"You do?" asked Lleu, releasing the bars. "Then why haven't you stopped him?"

"And destroyed him," added Brionna.

Hanwan Belamir drew a long, thoughtful breath. "Because, my dear guests, the changeling in my village . . . is *me.*"

As Lleu and Brionna both stumbled back in surprise, he broke into more laughter. Then, waving his badly broken thumbnail before their faces, he whispered, "A swollen eye is not the flaw you should have noticed."

A sudden gasp came from outside the cell. The guard! He had woken up—just in time to hear the most startling news of his life. He started to rise from the stone bench.

Instantly, Belamir shifted shape and pounced on the wretched man. He had no time to cry out. So fast did the changeling move, even keen-eyed Brionna couldn't see more than a blur of claws, fangs, and spurting blood.

Three seconds later, the mutilated body of the guard lay sprawled on the floor. And the gracious old man in the gar-dener's robe stood again outside the cell, panting only slightly. Yet now all traces of kindness had vanished from his face.

"Wretched fools," he hissed. "All of you! Humans, so easily perverted by arrogance and greed. Elves, so oblivious to the world beyond their borders. Eaglefolk, so full of pride and their precious sense of honor."

He spat on the bloodstained floor. "That is what I think of all of you! And soon it won't matter what I think, for Kulwych and I will destroy every last one of you."

He leaned closer, spittle dripping from his lips. "You consider yourselves so intelligent. So very clever. Yet one lone changeling is more clever than all of you put together! How else did I create this entire village? And this movement, this mockery of human superiority? How else, good priest, did I dupe your former colleague Llynia into doing my bidding?"

A smile of satisfaction on his face, he made a gentlemanly bow. "Now, dear guests, I must leave you. I prefer to let you die here, in all your wretchedness, than to kill you straightaway." He wiped his lips on his sleeve. "For I will soon have the pleasure of killing many more of your kinds—on the fields of Isenwy."

With that, the changeling turned and climbed the stone stairs, taking care to hobble like an elderly man. Brionna and Lleu watched, stunned by what they had seen and heard. Eventually, they sank back down to the floor. Shim, who had witnessed enough to understand, merely shook his head morosely.

For quite some time—hours, perhaps—no one spoke. Their dejection swelled, filling the cell like a thick fog. Even the shadows around them seemed to darken.

Finally, Shim raised his voice. He didn't speak about changelings. Or battles. Or cruel turns of fate.

"I is hungrily," he moaned. "Very, very hungrily."

Brionna frowned at him. Out of kindness, though, she dug into her robe and pulled out a small square of elvish waybread. Holding it out to the little fellow, she said, "Here. My last piece."

Shim peered at her gratefully.

Doing her best to grin, Brionna added, "For my favorite uncle."

Although he may not have heard her words, the little fellow certainly understood her gesture. His eyes widened at the sight of food, even such a tiny morsel. Apparently forgetting about his sore rump, he nodded eagerly and stretched out his hand.

Just then Brionna snapped back her arm. She held the waybread to her chest.

Grimacing, Shim sputtered, "Now, now, Rowanna. That's a cruelsy thing to do."

"He's right," grumbled the priest from his place by the wall. "That's not like you, Brionna."

"That's because," she declared with sudden urgency, "I have an idea."

Turning over onto her hands and knees, she placed a tiny crumb of waybread at the edge of the ants' hole. Immediately a large, armored ant with powerful pincers emerged, snatched the crumb, and dropped back into the hole.

As her companions looked on with bewilderment (and, in Shim's case, disappointment), she crumbled more of the waybread. Rising to her feet, she stepped over to the cell door and placed the crumbs all around the iron bolt, taking care to push them into any cracks, however small. She pushed several into the edges of the holes for the spikes that fastened the bolt to the door. Finally, she moved back toward the ants' tunnel in the floor, dropping her last few bits of waybread along the route.

At the instant she placed the very last crumb at the rim of the hole, several ants poured out. Dozens more followed, driven to a frenzy by the prospect of so much food. As Shim squealed in fright and backed away, the aggressive ants quickly crossed the floor and scaled the door, pincers digging out whatever crumbs they could find. As they swarmed over the iron bolt, splinters and chips of stone rained down onto the dirt.

When the ants had finished devouring every last particle of food, they marched back to their hole and plunged inside. Watching them go, Brionna grinned ever so slightly. Then she strode over to the door and struck it with a swift kick.

The bolt burst free of its fastenings and clattered to the floor. At the same time, the door swung open, creaking on its hinges. They were free.

Catha shrieked with delight, ruffling her wingfeathers. Lleu and Shim both gazed at Brionna with gratitude, although the shrunken giant's face also showed a hint of longing for his lost waybread. The elf maiden signaled for everyone to stay quiet, then led them out of the cell.

Gingerly, they stepped over the gory remains of the guard. Then, pausing only long enough for Brionna to retrieve her longbow and arrows, they crept back up the stairs. Because it was now the middle of the night, they saw no one but a sleeping sentry near the building's entrance. With little difficulty, they slipped past him and out into the village, whose buildings gleamed dully from the light of the stars.

Down the pathways they darted, past the houses with window boxes of flowers, the village trading center, and the cultivated fields. As they neared the gates, a pair of sentries suddenly leaped out of the shadows. Surprised, Lleu stopped abruptly. Shim walked right into him from behind.

Their two companions, though, weren't caught off guard. Before one of the sentries could whip out his bow and nock an arrow, Brionna's own arrow plunged right through his chest. The other sentry, seeing this, started to call for help—but his shout ended in a terrified gurgle as Catha's talon slit his throat.

Lleu stepped over to Brionna and placed his hand upon

her shoulder. "That's twice tonight you have saved our lives."

She brushed off his hand, then slid her bow over her back. "I can feel no joy killing another creature. Even one of them."

Lleu studied her grimly in the evening starlight. "Both of us, I fear, will have to do more killing very soon. For now we must travel to Isenwy. To join the rest of your people, and whatever humans are still loyal to the Society of the Whole."

"And to join," she added in a whisper, "the battle for Avalon."

"We must move fast, making no stops at all until we reach the portal that will take us to Isenwy." He cast an uncertain glance at Shim.

"I knows that look," the little fellow declared. "Wherever you is going, I is coming. Certainly, definitely, absolutely."

"All right then," Lleu replied, as Catha settled back on his shoulder. He started to stride to the gates. "Let's go."

"Wait." Brionna abruptly spun around and dashed back toward the village.

Only the fear of arousing more archers kept Lleu from shouting after her. What in the name of Merlin was she doing? He watched as she ran over to the fruit trees and swung herself up onto a branch. A few seconds later, she bounded back, holding something in her hand.

The curlew. Although his leg was badly chafed, he seemed otherwise unharmed. He stood in Brionna's palm, eyeing her gratefully.

As soon as Catha recognized the bird, she piped an appreciative whistle. And Lleu himself nodded with admiration.

"I'll take him back to the forest and set him free," the elf explained. She glanced at the fallen sentries, and at the building where they'd been imprisoned. "That way, at least something good will have happened here tonight."

14 · Loyalty

SCREE RUFFLED HIS POWERFUL WINGS. HE felt ready, even anxious, to depart for the great battle. For he couldn't forget the words that Queen had spoken just before she died in his arms: *Even now, Kulwych gathers his army on the Plains of Isenwy. An army that will conquer Avalon!*

First, though, he paused to look closely at the people of the Bram Kaie clan. They ringed him, a virtual nest of faces old and young, as he stood on the fire-blackened ground outside their fortified village. How many of these people would actually follow him into battle, he wondered, when the only fighting they had done for years was inspired not by high ideals—but by their thirst for plunder? And he could tell that they, too, were uncertain. The villagers watched him warily, their eagle eyes glinting with the red light of Fireroot's sky.

He raised his wide wings and stroked the air, not enough to carry himself aloft, but enough to announce that he was about to speak: Then he made his first command as the leader of these eaglefolk.

"There is one thing we must do before we fly," he declared, his voice echoing across the volcanic ridge. "We shall build a traditional burial mound. For your fallen leader, Quenaykha, and also for the woman she ordered killed."

From the edge of the bubbling lava pit near his feet, he grabbed a bloodied, black-tipped feather. It was all that remained of the clan's other fallen leader, Maulkee. No one else knew that Maulkee had also been Scree's own son—a son he never knew, except in their fight to the death. "And," he added grimly, "we shall bury this feather with them."

Grumbling swelled around him, as the villagers stared at him in surprise—and in some cases, scorn. Even the scarred warrior, Cuttayka, who had just thrown his support behind Scree's leadership, looked at him doubtfully.

But Scree's face remained unmoved. "Why, you ask? Why should we strain our living bodies, hauling stones for these dead ones?" He peered at them, his yellow-rimmed eyes both stern and proud. "Because however wrongly they may have lived, they belonged to our people. And we are, above all else, a people of *honor*."

Many in the crowd shifted uncomfortably. For they knew he was making a point that went beyond a single burial mound. He was urging them to remember who they really were, and the traditions they had shunned for so long. He was, in effect, challenging them to become eaglefolk once more.

The wind gusted, blowing flecks of black ash across the ridge. At the same time, Scree retracted his wings. But instead of folding them behind his back, he shifted into human form, so that the wings became brawny arms, feathers turned to skin, and talons shrank into toenails. Then he stooped and wrenched out of the ground a charred hunk of rock. Turning his back to the villagers' nests, he hurled the rock to an open area. It landed with an explosion of ash, then rolled to a stop next to a sputtering flame vent.

"There," he announced. "We build it there."

Cuttayka clenched his angular jaw for a moment, then also transformed into human shape. He grabbed his spear and pounded its end on the ground. "Well?" he demanded of the crowd. "What are you all waiting for? The sooner we start building this mound, the sooner it's done."

With a glance at Scree that was loyal, perhaps, but certainly not friendly, he grabbed a stone of his own and carried it over to the spot. One by one, other villagers followed. Soon the arduous labor began.

Several people, including Scree and Cuttayka, dug a wide pit. As a sulfurous wind blew over the ridge, they placed in the pit both mauled bodies, arms spread wide in the traditional way of eaglefolk. After Scree added Maulkee's feather, villagers spread a layer of fledgling feathers over the top. Then came hundreds of bucketloads of dirt, pumice, and ash. Finally, the strongest men and women set heavy stones, one after another, upon the mound, arranging them in the shape of an extended wing.

Although no one sang any mournful songs, as the people of Arc-kaya's village had done when their mound was completed, the villagers stood back to see what they had built together. One woman, holding the hand of a silver-haired toddler, bowed her head solemnly, and said, "May our people soar again."

Overhearing her, Scree recalled Arc-kaya's blessing: *Soar high, run free.* His gaze fell to his ankle, and the band of shining gray hair that he wore there. Then, as a new gust of wind rushed across the ridge, he scanned the eaglefolk who stood around him, their shoulders gleaming with perspiration from their shared labor.

Some of them avoided his gaze. Some continued to scowl. Yet others gave him a grim nod or a knowing look. He couldn't be sure, but it seemed that there was now something else in the air besides sulfurous fumes.

Something more like pride.

He was about to speak again when he caught sight of

Hawkeen, the young eagleboy who had followed him all the way here. The lad sat alone under an obsidian statue of an eagle in flight. Hawkeen's knees were drawn up to his chest, and the statue's shadow covered him completely. He was staring blankly at the mound, so much like the one where his mother had recently been buried.

Scree clenched his jaw. He couldn't help but think how different Hawkeen seemed from the merry young fellow who had, just a few days ago, left Scree breathless in a game of catch-the-hare. And how painful it must feel for Hawkeen to be here, among the very people who had murdered his family.

As Scree placed his hand on the lad's small shoulder, Hawkeen stiffened. He looked up, his golden eyes softened by mist. Then, seeing it was Scree, he relaxed a bit. Still, he said nothing. He merely turned back to the burial mound.

"I am glad you came, Hawkeen. Very glad. But you can leave now if you wish."

The eagleboy said nothing.

"Really, I will understand if you decide you must go."

Still nothing.

Scree knelt down in the ashen soil so that he, too, was under the shadow of the statue. He spoke again, this time right into the eagleboy's ear. "I'm leading these people into battle, you know. All of us could die. That means you, too." His voice as soft as a fledgling's wing, he added, "I don't want you to die, Hawkeen."

Still nothing.

Just then heavy footsteps approached. Scree rose, and found himself facing Cuttayka.

The burly warrior jammed the end of his spear into the ground. He stood there, peering straight at Scree's face, as Scree peered back, their shared gaze almost a solid rod between them. The wind lifted, dusting them with ash, but neither of them moved.

Finally, Scree broke the silence. "Do you still want to be first sentry of this clan?"

"I do," the warrior answered gruffly. "But only if we're going to fight to regain our honor, not just make useless piles of rock."

Scree's voice took on the angry edge of an eagle's cry. "You will do as I command, Cuttayka. And if you think about what we just did, you will see that it was about more than a burial mound. It was about honor." Scree waited a moment, dragging his sharp toenails across the soil. "I will keep you on as my first sentry. But only on one condition."

"Which is?"

"That you will always speak honestly with me about your views, just as you have done now. Even when you disagree with me."

Cuttayka shrugged his burly shoulders. "That is the only way I can be."

"Good." Scree's eyes narrowed. "Then gather your warriors. I want them all, men and women, ready to leave for Isenwy in one hour."

"All right." Cuttayka started to turn away, then halted. "Since you want me to speak my mind, you should know this. I don't like being led by an outsider. Not at all. Nor do I like you." His voice lowered so that it rumbled like a distant rock slide. "But I decided to follow you because I think you're right for this clan. We need someone strong to lead us. Very strong. That is what's best for the Bram Kaie, and that is my only real loyalty."

"You have another loyalty, I'll wager."

"What?"

"Avalon."

The warrior merely grunted. He pointed to one of the jagged scars on his chest. "I didn't get this for Avalon," he declared, then strode off.

Scree watched him go, wondering if anyone from this village would really follow him through all the trials to come. That was when the eagleboy beside him finally spoke, in a voice clear and firm.

"Wherever you go, Scree, I am going to be there."

He looked into the lad's face, and knew that it was true.

15 · The Lovely Dark

IN THE LIGHT FROM ELLI'S CRYSTAL, THE OLD elf seemed to grow larger, filling the dusty black tunic that billowed around his body. Grikkolo waved at the ruins of Dianarra's ancient library—collapsed shelves, broken tiles, smashed statues, and uncounted leather volumes that lay in heaps all around them.

"Courage is not my nature," he declared in his grinding voice. "But in the book of my life, this is a page that I truly must write."

"So," Elli asked, "you will take us to Kulwych's mine?"

"Borvo Lugna." He straightened his bent back as much as he could. "I will take you there, yes."

Nuic, shifting his weight in Elli's arm, darkened from blue to black. "There is something you're not telling us." His liquid purple eyes scrutinized the elderly librarian. "Something important."

Grikkolo nodded, making his white mane bounce on his head. "Your eyes are sharper than a feather-quill pen, master sprite, though you are even older than I."

"Hmmmpff. Don't try to flatter me. Now, what is it you haven't told us?"

The elf glanced at the doorway to the library. "Once we step outside this building . . ." His voice fell to a harsh whisper. "We must walk in total darkness."

Elli's hand moved to her amulet of oak, ash, and hawthorn—and the radiant crystal it held. "You mean I must dim this light?"

"No. I mean you must *extinguish* it."

She grimaced. Her hand left the amulet and anxiously twisted some of her hair. "Why?"

"Gobsken lurk everywhere near the mines. Especially, I suspect, the mine where you wish to go." He took a slow, ragged breath. "Some of my own people may also be out there. And if we meet any dark elves outside this library, survivors of the war, they will most likely detest your light—and try to kill you."

Grikkolo frowned, spreading wrinkles across his face like writing on a manuscript page. "The only creatures out there who will run from your light are the death dreamers. And sometimes even light will not be enough to frighten them off. I will watch for them every step of the way, for they possess a terrible power."

"Terrible," whispered Elli, her mind drifting back to her dream of the gentle, soothing waves that very nearly washed away her life.

"No," announced Grikkolo, "if we are to travel there with any hope of surviving, you must trust entirely in my old eyes."

The tiny hand of Nuic reached out and patted Elli's forearm. "Your choice, Priestess."

She shut her eyes, trying to imagine how dark it would be without her glowing crystal. *What insanity! Walk around this realm of eternal night, with no light at all? And yet, if I am ever going to help Avalon—and maybe Tamwyn, too— that's what I must do.*

Opening her eyes, she glanced around the vast domed chamber. Just beyond the edge of what she could see—all those broken shelves and piles of books—were shadows, darker than any she'd ever found before coming to Lastrael. The shadows seemed to thicken, gathering, just waiting for the moment she extinguished her light.

She turned her thoughts to the crystal of élano. *Go dark, my companion. And just hope that I'm not making a terrible mistake.*

All at once, the crystal darkened. Every ray of its light, every glint of its facets, disappeared. It happened with jarring abruptness, as if the world itself had just ended. And perhaps, Elli thought, it soon would.

Darkness. Total, absolute darkness. That was all that she could perceive, other than the continuous canter of her own heartbeat.

"Here," said the old elf, pressing something into her hand. "The belt of my tunic. Hold on to this as we walk. And listen for any changes in my steps, so you will know when I am taking a turn, going uphill, or—"

"Running for your life," interrupted Nuic.

"Or that," Grikkolo replied, his voice suddenly somber. Feeling a new pull on his cloth belt, Elli guessed that he was turning around. "Good-bye, my friends," he said with deep tenderness.

At first, Elli felt a rush of confusion. And fear. *Is he talking to us?* Then she realized what the elf was really doing. *He's saying good-bye to all these books.*

Grikkolo sighed, as only someone who is leaving all the best friends of his life can sigh. And then he started to walk, his steps slow and shuffling, across the library's cracked tiles.

"The doorway is near," he cautioned. "Then remember the steps down to the street. Just do your best to trust in your senses, and this will not be quite so difficult."

"My senses?" sputtered Elli, as she walked haltingly behind him. "I have no senses now."

"Oh, but you do, young woman. Trust in them, and they shall expand."

She snorted in disbelief, shaking her mass of curls.

Through the doorway they moved, which Elli guessed only because she noticed a different texture underfoot. Then down the library's stone steps they crept, Elli feeling each edge with her toes before stepping down. In time, Grikkolo started to lead them through the maze of streets in the ruined City of Light. The turns came so quickly that Elli soon lost track of them, holding tightly to her end of Grikkolo's belt. But for the occasional crunch of bones as they walked, she heard no sounds from the devastation that she knew surrounded them.

Eventually, she perceived a kind of hardening in the darkness ahead. The city wall! Through a gap they strode—though not before Elli tripped on a chunk of stone from a toppled column. She barely caught herself before sprawling, and Nuic was lucky to stay on her arm. But she let go of the belt.

A wave of panic washed over her. Darkness pressed closer on all sides.

No sooner had she gasped, however, than Grikkolo returned the strip of cloth to her hand. He said nothing, and merely patted her wrist gently. Yet she could tell, somehow, through a sense that had nothing to do with sight or sound, that he felt nearly as relieved as she did.

They continued walking, now on the familiar stubbly moss that smelled so much like mint. Up a long, gradual hill they climbed, pausing now and then for the old elf to catch his breath. In these moments, Elli stooped down and grabbed a handful of moss, enough for herself and Nuic to chew.

As the slope started to level off, she heard the unmistakable splatter of a stream. Like an invisible thread woven through the fabric of darkness, it flowed down the side of the hill. Grikkolo led them to a flat rock that they could only feel beneath them. Here they knelt beside the stream and drank deeply, hearing the constant swish and bubble of water.

Onward they walked. The terrain rose and fell in repeated waves, while the ground hardened into packed soil. Soon the mosses disappeared entirely, replaced by some sort of fuzzy-leafed plants that brushed against the travelers' legs. Elli tried to imagine what those plants might look like, attempting to picture many different shapes of leaves. Finally, she gave up, deciding to think of them just as ferns—mainly because she had no better idea.

To her own surprise, she was beginning to stride with greater confidence. Although she still held on to Grikkolo's belt, she didn't squeeze it so tightly as before. The darkness seemed less oppressive somehow. And she found herself hearing more sounds—the distant flutter of a bird's wings, the peeps of a tiny frog, the subtle gnawing of caterpillars on the leaves by her ankles.

As they continued to walk, her breathing grew more calm and regular. Her senses, just as Grikkolo had predicted, slowly expanded. Now she felt less like someone blinded, and more like someone whose abilities to hear and smell stretched out in all directions. Indeed, her sense of smell had become an army of airy hands that reached everywhere, grabbing a hint of huckleberry or a whiff of smoky cinnamon, a scent of discarded snakeskin or an aroma of something almost as tangy as rose hips.

Walking this way, she realized, was itself a form of meditation. Just as she had done back at the Drumadian compound, when she would hide among the pillars of the Great Temple and open herself to the compound's seven concentric rings and the seven sacred Elements they represented, she opened herself to the mysteries of this land.

Listen to Creation's morning, began that wonderful blessing from Rhia. *Waking all around you.*

Was it possible, Elli wondered, for even a land of darkness to know a kind of morning? An awakening that had nothing at all to do with the return of light? After all, this realm was just as much part of Creation as any other. While its mystery and beauty could be quite subtle, and lived alongside terrible danger, was that really any different from the lands bathed in light?

She remembered, in a flash, a phrase that Grikkolo had used: *the lovely dark.* Those words had, at first, puzzled her greatly. Yet now, while they still sounded strange—as if spoken in another language—they also sounded true. She caught at least a hint of their meaning, much as she had caught that faraway scent of rose hips.

Feeling the gentle, rhythmic tug of the cloth that connected her to the elder, she could easily imagine his bent frame trudging along. This was a bold thing for Grikkolo to have done—terribly bold, after living all those years in hiding. She listened to his shuffling steps, and felt deeply grateful to him. For leading them through this realm of darkness, of course. But just as much, for introducing her to another language of the senses.

All at once, Grikkolo veered to the side. He sped up, practically dragging Elli behind him. She was just about to ask him what he was doing, when her newly sensitive ears heard the distant sound of voices. Harsh, grating voices. And the *clump, clump, clump* of boots on the march.

Gobsken!

From the sound, there seemed to be a whole band of them, as many as ten warriors. Now she could also hear the creaking of armor plates and the occasional slap of swords against thighs. Then, just at the edge of her vision, she saw a faint touch of light—the glow of torches behind a ridge.

Grikkolo, panting hard, led them to an area littered with

small, jagged stones. "Duck your head," he whispered, as his pace slowed sharply.

Just as Elli ducked, she felt a sudden change in the air around her. It was a touch warmer; what little breeze there had been now vanished. As she crept forward, her hand on the elf's bent back, she felt the stones underfoot change to damp dirt. She knew at once that they had entered some sort of cavern.

"Here we sit," wheezed Grikkolo. "And wait."

After a moment he added gravely, "They are coming this way, I believe. We could never outrun them, and hiding places are quite scarce. So our only hope is that they will pass by here without discovering us."

Elli crawled a bit deeper into the cavern. She found a slab of rock where she could rest her back, while Nuic rolled aside and propped himself against her leg. As she strained to hear any more sounds of the gobsken, she clasped her darkened crystal.

And wondered at how swiftly tranquility could turn into terror.

16 · Visions

Time passed within the cavern. Minutes, hours, it was hard to tell.

To Elli, this darkened den within the rocks was not much different than a dungeon. For she knew that somewhere out there, just beyond the range of hearing, marched a band of gobsken warriors. They could be drawing nearer by the second.

She shuddered at the thought. Right now, this cavern seemed like the darkest place in the darkest realm.

"You know, Nuic," she whispered, tapping the damp dirt floor with her fingers. "As close as we are now to finding Kulwych's mine, it feels farther away than ever."

"Hmmmpff. That's a cheery thought. I'm so glad you told me."

More time passed. As hard as they listened, they heard nothing besides the anxious breathing of a young woman, a pinnacle sprite, and an old elf.

At last, Nuic raised his voice in a gruff whisper. "Tell me something, master librarian. If you wanted to destroy this corrupted crystal we told you about, before it can do much to help Rhita Gawr, how would you go about it?"

Grikkolo drew an uncertain breath. "I fear I really do not know. Never, in all the texts I have read, have I seen anything of that sort. To serve Rhita Gawr, that crystal must be the absolute opposite of élano—so it can destroy just as irresistibly as élano can create. What could possibly eliminate such a power?"

"That's what I asked you," grumbled the sprite.

Again, time passed in silence. Finally, Grikkolo spoke again. "I believe they must have passed us by. Even as much as gobsken dawdle when they can and often stop to argue among themselves, they should be far away by now."

"Really?" Elli felt as if a heavy gobsken boot, which had been stepping on her chest, had finally lifted. "We can move on?"

"We can."

"Just a minute," said Nuic. "Now that we are safe again, for the moment at least, there is something I want to do. With a crystal."

"You want my amulet?" Elli asked. "Why?"

"Not that crystal, you boneheaded girl. *This* crystal."

With that, the jewel on his chest flashed with a burst of green light. Grikkolo, surprised by the sudden brilliance, winced and covered his large eyes. But seconds later, he was watching the jewel at the edge of his vision. For he had recognized it from the descriptions he'd seen in books.

"The Galator," said the old elf, his voice full of wonder.

"That's right," answered Nuic, bending to look into the glowing green crystal. "It's about time I looked in on somebody."

Nuic peered at the jewel, concentrating hard, his skin color shifting to deepest green. All at once more colors appeared in the crystal, swirling like a whirlpool in the Rainbow Seas. The colors started to coalesce, forming an image in the jewel's center. It was an elderly woman whose silver curls fell to the shawl on her shoulders. Tiny light flyers flew around her, glowing as bright as her gray-blue eyes.

Rhia, thought Elli. She glanced at Nuic, who was gazing at the image of this woman whose maryth he had been so long ago. She could see, in his deep purple eyes, an unmistakable emotion: love. The sight made her smile, for as much as Nuic always tried to hide his feelings under a shield of gruffness, the feelings were certainly there.

Rhia, Elli noticed, looked much frailer than when they had parted in the forest of El Urien. *It's the crystal,* she remembered. *When Rhia gave me the crystal of élano, she also gave away the power that kept her younger than her years.*

She bit her lip. *I only hope that, in the end, I'll have deserved such a precious gift. And such a precious trust.*

An idea struck her, one that brightened her mood a little. When all this was over, if she somehow survived, she would give the crystal back to Rhia! Yes, that would be the perfect way to thank her, and return the trust.

The image shifted, drawing back for a wider view. Rhia was kneeling beside another elderly woman, gently stroking the woman's brow. High Priestess Coerria.

Elli's vision clouded as she studied Coerria's prone form. Light glistened on her long white hair, and on the elegant gown of spider's silk whose beauty took Elli's breath away every time she saw it. But Coerria's eyes, as blue as the bluest alpine tarn, couldn't be seen, for they were closed.

Is she alive? Elli stared hard at the image, but she could not tell.

Abruptly, the image faded. The Galator flashed green again, then went dark. The eternal night of Shadowroot returned, filling their cavern in the rocks just as completely as it filled the realm outside.

Elli felt grim, and she was sure that Nuic shared her mood. But when Grikkolo raised his voice in the dark cavern, she could tell that he was feeling something different: bewilderment.

"I do not understand," said the old elf. "I saw no one there. Yet you, apparently, did. I thought the Galator—"

"Can show you people you love," finished Nuic. "That love allows you to see them, but never to speak to them, since no love is that powerful."

"Ah, I begin to understand. This person you viewed would be someone I do not know, let alone love. But it must be someone *you* love, correct?"

"Hmmmpff. When I don't want to kill her, yes."

Grikkolo sputtered in surprise, momentarily bewildered again. Then his tone changed to curiosity, and he asked, "Do you think, perhaps, I could use the Galator myself? There is someone I long to see, someone who lives in another realm. And although I have never actually met her, I have dearly loved her since the first time I read about her, years and years ago."

"Well," answered Nuic's crusty voice, "if an old sprite can manage, why not an old elf? Just concentrate hard on this person, whoever she is, until her image appears."

Grikkolo peered at the Galator, and it flashed. Colors swirled, with strong shades of blue. But they did not coalesce into an image—at least not one that Elli could see. A moment later, the crystal dimmed. The cavern returned to darkness.

"Well?" asked Elli eagerly. "Did you see her?"

"No," Grikkolo said sadly. "I saw nothing beyond some splashes of blue."

"Who was it," pressed Nuic, "you wanted to see?"

"The Sapphire Unicorn—ancient, wise, and beautiful."

Hearing the name, Elli gasped. But Grikkolo didn't seem to notice, and continued, "She has been called, by many a scribe, *the most elusive beauty in all the lands.* I was hoping," he said glumly, "to see her, even for an instant, through the Galator."

Though her throat was dry, Elli swallowed. She couldn't bear to tell the old elf the truth—that the Sapphire Unicorn, along with the child she was expecting, had been brutally killed by Rhita Gawr's treachery.

"Er, well, perhaps," she fumbled, "you could try again sometime."

"Perhaps," he replied. "Yet I suspect that I will not succeed. Just as courage is not my nature, neither are the mysterious workings of magic." Again he sighed. "Or love."

"Elliryanna," said Nuic quietly, "is there anyone you would like to see before we go?"

"Yes," she answered, not sure whether she felt more annoyed or amused that the sprite knew her so well. He could read her clearly, even in the dark.

She concentrated on Tamwyn. Barely an instant later, the crystal flashed, painting the rock around them with rippling green light. There he was! She bent closer to the Galator, watching intently.

Tamwyn's long black hair streamed behind him. Although she could see only his face, he seemed to be riding something, moving fast. No, not riding—flying. And he looked happy, as happy as she'd ever seen him. A blur of wings obscured him for a second, and then the scene abruptly changed.

Now she was viewing him from afar, at such great distance that he was only a tiny speck amidst bright circles of flame. The stars! He had actually made it all the way to the stars! The place he had always longed to see, the place his father had tried to reach, the place where his quest would be won or lost.

Suddenly she noticed something approaching him from behind—something huge and menacing. Gaining on him rapidly. Whatever it was had wide, dark wings—even darker than the spaces between the stars. Could it be a dragon? Then she sensed, with a surge of panic, that it was something still worse. Her heart froze. That dragon could be Rhita Gawr!

The image jerked sharply back to Tamwyn's face. Elli focused her gaze on him, trying to warn him somehow. But he seemed blissfully unaware of the danger. Only seconds remained, she was sure, before Rhita Gawr attacked.

Warn him! I must warn him somehow. She marshaled all her mind's energy, trying to send him her thoughts. Tears welled in her eyes. Her whole body quaked. She couldn't think any more clearly, or care any more deeply.

But he didn't notice. He looked relaxed and serene—aware, it seemed, only of the beauty of the stars.

"Tamwyn!" she cried aloud, her voice breaking. "Look out!"

For half an instant, his face changed. He looked almost as if he'd heard something—

The image suddenly disappeared, flooded with swirling colors. The Galator, though, continued to vibrate with light—a residue, perhaps, of what had just happened. It glowed dimly, just enough to illuminate the companions' own faces in the dark cavern.

Elli felt wretched. Did he hear her cry? Did she actually warn him in time? She couldn't tell. Most likely, she wouldn't ever know.

Worse, she suspected that she was only indulging in wishful thinking. How could he possibly have heard her? After all, everyone knew that the Galator had never done such a thing before. Rhia herself had declared that speaking through the jewel was impossible. So had Nuic.

She stopped peering solely into the glowing jewel and instead looked at the sprite who wore it. Nuic's skin had turned black with thin veins of red and silver running down both his arms, a pattern she'd never seen on him before. But what surprised her most of all was the expression on his face. He, too, seemed surprised—and, though she couldn't be sure, almost hopeful.

Just then someone spoke. Someone outside the cavern! The voice, practically a snarl, cut through the darkness. "Over here, men. 'At's where I heard the shout."

Gobsken. Even as all the remaining light faded from the

Galator, a new source of light appeared beyond the cavern's entrance. The warriors' torches were drawing swiftly nearer.

Before Elli could move, Grikkolo's hand reached out and grabbed the front of her robe. "Hear me," he whispered urgently. "Do not follow me. Do you understand? *Do not follow.*"

"What are you doing?" she demanded.

The old elf didn't answer. He simply turned away and started crawling out of the cavern. Seconds later came the sound of his feet shuffling over the small stones outside. And then came another sound: Grikkolo's voice.

"No gobsken will ever catch me," he cried boastfully.

Several harsh voices responded. Boots thudded over the ground. The torchlight grew stronger.

"No," moaned Elli. "He's made himself a decoy! He'll get killed."

In the dim, flickering light, she glimpsed Nuic's expression. And she knew that he felt exactly as she did. If there was any chance to save their friend—

Elli scooped up the sprite and scurried out of the cavern. Even as she stood, she saw Grikkolo's peril. A pair of burly gobsken pounded up behind him, one brandishing a broadsword, the other holding a torch. He veered to the side, doing his best to run on the rock-strewn ground. But he was no match for his pursuers.

Elli dashed toward the gobsken, cradling Nuic in one arm. She didn't know what she could do to help, only that she must try. And that she wanted to do more for the elf than she'd been able to do for Tamwyn.

"Stop!" she cried, just a few paces away, as one of the warriors drew back his sword.

Too late. The sword slashed across Grikkolo's back. The old fellow crumpled to the ground as blood poured from his wound, soaking his tunic.

Oblivious to the gobsken who stared at her in surprise, Elli knelt beside the fallen elf. In the wavering light of the gobsken's torch, she held Grikkolo's head, feeling his thick white hair in her hands. Gravely, she peered down at him, then drew his body closer. If this had been Coerria herself dying in her arms, Elli could have felt no more sorrowful.

Suddenly remembering her healing water from the secret spring in Mudroot, she caught her breath. Might there still be time? Hastily she set Grikkolo down on the hard ground and reached for her water gourd. But Nuic grabbed hold of her arm.

"It's too late, Elliryanna."

Turning her gaze back to the elf, she knew that Nuic was right. Although Grikkolo's large eyes were still open, they looked like icy pools, freezing fast.

The old elf blinked at her. "You?" he whispered hoarsely. "You should have . . . stayed safe."

Elli shook her head. "Did you stay safe, my friend?"

"No," he whispered, so weakly she could barely hear. "I am . . . just a fool."

"Not true," she replied. "You are—" She swallowed. "A person of great courage."

The vaguest hint of a smile came to Grikkolo's lips. Then he went limp, and lay still.

"Should I jest kill 'em, too?" rasped the gobsken with the bloody sword.

"No," answered the other. He stared down at Elli and Nuic, rubbing his chin with his three-fingered hand. "Methinks there's something more going on. Why else would these strangers be out here? Let's take 'em back to the mine. Then ol' scarface can question 'em. An' kill 'em hisself."

The first warrior grinned, his greenish tongue dancing around his lips. "Kulwych will like that."

"Right. An' there'll be a goodly reward fer us." The gobsken kicked Elli's back. "C'mon, move! Yer our prisoners now."

17 · The Magical Mist

TAMWYN CONTINUED TO CLIMB THE MIST-
shrouded path, just as he'd done for several hours.
Merlin's Pinnacle was high, all right, just as Palimyst had
warned him. But now it felt more like endless. Part of that
feeling came from the smooth, unchanging slope of this
trail that climbed steadily into the clouds. And part came
from the fact that he could see nothing.

Nothing but mist.

Curling shreds of vapor—some as thick as grass snakes,
others thinner than yarn—wound around his legs and slid
between his toes. More threaded through his hair or curled
around his neck. Unlike any mist he had ever encountered
before, this vapor seemed to rise right out of the ground,
weaving and braiding as it lifted. And stranger still, it
seemed almost intelligent, moving with a will of its own.

Like it's examining me, he said to himself. He brushed
away a curl of mist that had wrapped itself around a lock
of hair, tickling his ear lobe. *Deciding whether or not I'm
acceptable. Or capable.*

Or, he added with a slight frown, *worthy.*

He recalled Palimyst's old Taliwonn saying, making his frown deepen:

> *To swim within the River of Time*
> *Thy soul must be worthy, thy motive sublime.*

At least his motives were good enough! What could be more sublime than to hope to save Avalon? And in the process, to complete his father's journey, taking his torch up to the stars?

He waved away a shred of mist that was dangling from his eyebrow. To be honest, there was one more motive—one not nearly so sublime. He simply wanted to *go* to the stars. To run freely among them, as he loved to run through the meadows and glades of Stoneroot.

Even so, Tamwyn knew that his problem was not whether his motives were truly sublime—but whether he himself was truly worthy. Palimyst had called him a *maker,* the same term Aelonnia of Mudroot had used. But could he make anything really important, really valuable?

His bare feet tramped along the pathway, pushing into the soft, damp grass that never grew any longer than the fur on a rabbit's back. Yet strangely, he never left any footprints. Was that to be the sum of his life? To have walked many places, without ever leaving any mark?

Merlin's Pinnacle kept rising higher and higher. He wondered how much farther it would be to the top. To the place where he'd find out whether he could, in fact, enter the River of Time. But there was no way to tell. All he knew was that this trail kept climbing upward—and that it rose in a steady spiral, always circling the misty mountain.

His thoughts turned to Palimyst, the humble craftsman with such skillful fingers. And also such wisdom, to make his goal shaping nature's immortal gifts with his own mortal hands. The mammoth fellow had convinced Tamwyn to stay the night beneath his tent, despite Tamwyn's sense of urgency that time was fast disappearing. But now, having climbed for so long, he was glad he'd taken a few hours' sleep. Besides, even with his night vision, which seemed stronger than ever, he wouldn't have wanted to walk here after starset. All this thick mist would have made the darkest night he'd ever known.

Not as dark as Shadowroot, though. Worried about Elli, he tugged on the strap of his pack, jostling the harmóna wood within. A soft, melodic hum came from the half-finished harp, someday to be fitted with the strings from Palimyst.

Tamwyn grinned wistfully, despite his worries. It always lifted his spirits to hear that sound. He tapped the sheath of his dagger, whose blade bore those mysterious, ancient words about Rhita Gawr. Someday, when all this was over, he would finish carving the harp. Yes, and give it to Elli at last!

If we survive, that is. His grim mood returned, as he continued to trudge up the trail. *And Avalon, too, must survive.*

His only hope, he knew, was to enter the River somehow. Nothing else would work, given how far he needed to go, and how little time remained. Cryll Onnawesh, Palimyst had called it: the seam in the tent of the sky. If the River really did divide the two halves of time—always moving among the stars but never leaving the present moment—then there really was a chance he could reach the stars before it was too late.

How to enter it, though? Merlin had done it somehow, and without the help of his fabled dragon, Basilgarrad. But that was small comfort. Merlin was, after all, *Merlin*—the greatest wizard of all time. *And yet . . . I have some of his blood in my veins. Just as I have the blood of Krystallus.*

He stopped, as moist tufts of mist pressed against his face. Reaching inside his pack, he pulled out a glass globe held inside a leather strap—his father's compass. Tiny waves of mist rippled across the globe's surface, but Tamwyn could still see inside. The horizontal arrow, as always, pointed westward, while the vertical arrow pointed straight above his head. To the stars.

Krystallus, he remembered, had his own theory of how to ascend to the stars. Whether or not it had anything to do with the River of Time, nobody could say. All that was clear was that it involved some sort of horse, a *great horse on high*.

Tamwyn nodded, reciting to himself the riddle that Krystallus had written in the letter hidden in the Great Hall of the Heartwood:

> *To climb ever starward,*
> *To vault through the sky,*
> *Discover one secret:*
> *The Great Horse on High.*

What did that mean? And did it have anything to do with Rhita Gawr's boast that Avalon would fall *when the great horse dies*? The warlord's boast, Tamwyn now understood, referred to the constellation Pegasus, and the ever-beating star in its center. But a constellation of stars couldn't carry him up into the sky! Could there be more to this riddle, and to the Great Horse, than he had guessed? He scowled, tired of having so many questions, and so few answers.

Stowing the compass, he resumed walking. The path kept on spiraling higher, leading him ever upward. He couldn't begin to guess how high he'd climbed. The mist hid everything around him.

Just as it hid the stars.

Rhita Gawr hid the stars, too, he thought. *But in a totally different way.* He recalled the dreadful sight of those immortal warriors pouring out of the darkened doorways of the stars—the seven stars of the Wizard's Staff constellation. *Even if I make it up to the stars in time, how will I ever relight them? And close those doorways?*

He blew a long sigh, scattering the mist. Figuring out Krystallus' riddle seemed easy compared to figuring out how to do that. He didn't have enough power to light something as small as his father's torch—let alone something as great as a star. This went far beyond the skills of a wilderness guide.

Sure, I may be of Merlin's blood. But I'm also a clumsy buffoon. As well as the Dark child, the person destined to destroy Avalon.

A cool clump of mist slid down his nose. *What I really wish most of all is that Merlin himself were here. Right now. He would know what to do!*

But Merlin wasn't here. The farther Tamwyn strode up the grassy path, the sound of his footsteps magnified by the mist, the more he felt certain of that. And yet he couldn't help wondering why Merlin would choose to stay on the world called Earth when Avalon—the world in between all things mortal and immortal, the world Merlin himself had planted as a seed—faced such terrible peril.

They must be having some serious problems of their own on Earth, he concluded. And then he wondered: When Merlin went through a star doorway to Earth, which star was that?

Almost imperceptibly, the slope of the trail started to flatten. Tamwyn refused to believe it at first, for he'd trekked so far up this mountain without any sign of change. But no, his feet weren't lying to him. The trail was definitely leveling out.

Abruptly, the pathway ended, opening into a flat meadow of the same short grass. Could this be the summit? Since the mist crowded so close that he could barely see past his outstretched arm, he started to explore the area. He quickly discovered that the meadow was circular, about twenty paces across. A group of low, rounded stones ringed its edge. Outside the ring of stones, the slope fell sharply away.

So this was the summit! Feeling expectant, and yet unsure what to expect, Tamwyn sat down on one of the stones. Its surface felt slick from the moisture of the mist. As he rested his tired legs, he studied its smooth contours.

To his surprise, down where the stone met the grass, he spied a flash of color.

An insect. As soon as he picked it up, though, he could tell this was no ordinary insect. Holding it gently in the palm of his hand, he peered at its spiraling antennae, orange wings, jagged blue scales, and enormous, faceted eyes.

He cocked his head, puzzled. For as strange as this creature was, even stranger was his feeling that he had seen it somewhere before. Yet how could that be?

Suddenly he remembered. And burst out laughing. He *had* seen this little fellow before—but from a completely different perspective. When he had used the drop of Dagda's dew, given to him by Gwirion, he had been hoping to catch a glimpse of his lost companion Henni. Instead, he found himself staring at a bizarre, colorful dragon with spiraling tusks. The sight had been so terrifying that it nearly knocked him off his feet. But it was really just this insect, magnified millions of times!

"Some dragon you are," he said to the insect. The tiny creature shook his antennae—or tusks—at him, as if admonishing him for such stupidity.

Amused, Tamwyn set the insect back down in the grass. All of a sudden, he heard the slapping of feet. Someone was coming up the trail! Running fast, from the sound of it.

He stood up and stepped closer to the top of the trail, peering into the impenetrable mist. But he could see nothing beyond the mist itself. He leaned forward, staring hard, when—

A body sprang out of the mist. It slammed right into him, knocking him over backward.

Tamwyn lay on the grass, momentarily stunned. Just as he started to sit up, the same body pounced on top of him, holding his shoulders to the ground and peering down at him with wild eyes.

18 · The One Called Dark Flame

TAMWYN KNEW THOSE WILD EYES.

He swiftly arched his back and rolled sideways, releasing a roar that echoed loudly in the mist. Caught off guard, his attacker flew to the side. He landed with a thud on the damp grass, not far from one of the rounded stones that ringed the summit of Merlin's Pinnacle.

Before the assailant could move, Tamwyn leaped on top of his chest and sat on his ribs. Just to be sure there could be no escape, Tamwyn also grabbed both his wrists and pinned them to the ground. All the attacker could do now was to flap the backs of his oversized hands against the ground.

All, that is, except laugh.

"Eehee, eehee, hoohoohoo ahahaha," came the raucous laughter. "I sure surprised *you,* clumsy man."

"Henni, you old bag of bear turds!" Tamwyn looked at the hoolah's sassy grin and familiar red headband (which was much more tattered than the last time he'd seen it). "I'd kill you a dozen times over, except . . ." His voice softened as a smile spread over his face. "I'm so glad to see you."

Henni's grin vanished and his eyes narrowed in concern.

He peered up at Tamwyn through the gauzy shreds of mist. "Are you all right, clumsy man? You sound almost—"

"Idiotic, I know. But it's true. I *am* glad to see your worthless, wretched, ugly face, even if you've got less sense than a headless troll."

The hoolah's grin suddenly returned, like a fire coal bursting into flame. And within his circular eyebrows, two more fires brightened. "That's better! Oohoo, eehee, I missed you, too."

"What happened to your headband?" asked Tamwyn with sarcasm. He bent closer, so the hoolah couldn't mistake the angry look now back in his eyes. "Did you rip it when you threw us both into the Spiral Cascades? Or later, when the waterfall nearly pounded us to death?"

As if this were just a normal question, Henni showed no sign at all of remorse. Lying there on the ground, he merely shrugged his shoulders. "No, no. It got caught."

"Caught? In what?"

"In the teeth of that dragon-faced boar I met back there on the cliffs. Funny how he didn't seem to like having me pull on his tail."

Despite his anger, Tamwyn couldn't help but smirk. "Still the old Henni, aren't you? Never met a death trap you didn't like."

"Hoohooheeheeha-ha-ha," the hoolah laughed. "You're right about that." He wriggled a bit under Tamwyn's weight. "Say now, eehee, eehee. Would you mind getting off me? You're crushing the old ribs."

But Tamwyn had not heard. For his thoughts had turned to their third companion, who really *had* perished in the Spiral Cascades. Frowning, he said quietly, "I wish we hadn't lost Batty Lad."

A small green object suddenly popped out of the folds of Henni's sacklike tunic. Zipping through the dense mist, it left behind a glowing green trail as it swerved through the vapors.

"Ooee ooee, manny man," the flying object squeaked as it whizzed past Tamwyn's ear. "I thought you'd never, ever remember me! Oh yessa ya ya ya."

"Batty Lad!" Tamwyn leaped to his feet, he was so delighted.

"Hey there, clumsy man," teased Henni as he, too, regained his feet. "You missed your chance again to kill me."

Tamwyn shot him a glance. "Don't worry. I'll get another chance soon enough." He turned back to the creature buzzing around his head. "And you, you little green rascal! How did you ever find me?"

Batty Lad flipped over in the mist, did an erratic loop, then skidded to a landing on Tamwyn's forearm. "Easy, manny man. We justa keeps climbing up and up and up and up, since my most excellently brain remembers where you're so wanting to go."

The young man shook his head, amazed. "You really do have an excellently brain."

Batty Lad's tiny face crinkled into something close to a smile. "The journey was very hard, oh yessa. But the hardest part, absolooteyootly, was keeping this crazy-lazy hoolah from killing us both, ya ya ya."

"I understand, my friend."

Henni, who was happily swatting at shreds of mist, didn't respond.

Tamwyn gazed down at the scrawny little fellow whose mouselike face, cupped ears, and leathery wings made him look so much like a bat. But then there was the strange light that surrounded him, sending rays of glowing green into the vapors. What kind of creature *was* Batty Lad, anyway? Tamwyn was no closer to knowing the answer to that question than he'd been on the day they first met.

Suddenly the wind gusted mightily, scattering the mist on the summit. Vapors parted, drawing aside like rows of undulating curtains. At the same time, the air around the companions lightened, sparkling with new radiance.

Tamwyn gazed at the shimmering mist, unsure whether the sudden light came from the stars above or from something else entirely. Another gust of wind whooshed past, making the mist brighten even more. A third gust blew over them, so strongly that Batty Lad's crumpled little wings flapped on their own and slapped against Tamwyn's forearm.

With a squeak of fright, Batty Lad dived into the nearest pocket in his friend's tunic. Just then the mist opened completely, revealing all the stars of Avalon. Hundreds upon hundreds of them shone down on Merlin's Pinnacle, blazing with such brilliance that Tamwyn and Henni both had to turn aside.

All at once a shadow fell over them. Tamwyn looked straight up to see what had caused the change. Another gust of wind struck his face, with such force that it made his eyes water. Yet he had no trouble seeing what had caused the wind, as well as the shadow.

Wings.

An enormous, winged horse descended from the sky. Announcing her arrival with a rippling neigh, she gave a powerful stroke of her wings, whose silvery white feathers seemed themselves to be made of starlight. Then the great steed landed in the center of the ring of stones, scattering the remaining wisps of mist.

The horse turned her rich brown eyes toward Tamwyn. For an endless moment, they gazed at each other, young man and ageless horse. She was, Tamwyn felt, peering straight into his soul, as a bright shaft of light can reach deep into a murky pool. And he knew that she was deciding whether or not he was truly worthy of a voyage to the stars.

Finally, she swished her graceful tail and spoke directly into his mind. "Are you the one," she asked in a resonant voice, "who is called Dark Flame?"

Hearing her say the first word of his name, he winced. Yet he managed a hesitant nod.

She ruffled her great white wings, folding them tightly against her back. "I am Ahearna, the Star Galloper. Know that I sense much within you, Dark Flame."

The horse whinnied, bobbing her head. "I feel the compassion of your mother, and the courage of your father; the joy of running free, a blessing from your grandmother; and the yearning to be wise, a gift from your grandfather. And I sense much more besides."

Tamwyn straightened, feeling the torch pole against his back. Could it be true? Was she telling him that he was actually worthy—to use Palimyst's word—of a journey to the stars? And was she the Great Horse of the riddle? Who could carry him up to the River of Time, and onward to the darkened stars of the Wizard's Staff?

Ahearna studied him some more, her eyes narrowing slightly. "Yet I must tell you that you are *not* worthy." She lifted her foreleg and stamped the moist grass. "No, definitely not worthy."

Tamwyn reeled, almost stumbling. "But Avalon! The stars! Rhita Gawr is—"

She neighed briskly, cutting him off. "Quiet, young colt." Her ears swiveled, pointing right at him. "I was about to say that your grandfather, Merlin, was *also* unworthy. Yet even so, I chose to carry him to the stars."

He stood rigid.

As smoothly as a shred of mist moves through the air, Ahearna stepped nearer. Now her face was so close that Tamwyn could feel the warmth of her breath against his face. "And so," she declared, "I shall carry you."

"Thank you," he whispered gratefully.

Instead of answering him, she flicked one ear in the direction of Henni, who stood off to the side. Suddenly the hoolah's eyes widened within his circular eyebrows. He stepped back several paces, so hastily that he tripped over one of the rounded stones and tumbled to the ground.

Stifling a laugh, Tamwyn asked, "What did you just do to him?"

The winged horse snorted with amusement. "I merely told him, right to his mind, that if he even so much as *thought* about pulling my tail, I would kick him all the way to the next branch-realm."

"You read him well."

"Just as I read you well, Dark Flame."

Tamwyn swallowed, eager to ask a question—and also to change the subject. "Are you, then, the Great Horse on High?"

Ahearna tossed her head, making her flowing mane ripple in the starlight. "So I have been called. But to me, the greatest horse of all is Pegasus, the constellation that is my home. You see, I fly endlessly around its centermost star, the one called the Heart of Pegasus. That is where I am always circling, ever galloping."

Tamwyn recalled his view of that very star from Merlin's Knothole, and how it had actually seemed to be pulsing with life. In a flash, he realized something. "Your flight around the Heart—the way you keep passing between Avalon and the star—that makes the star look, from down here, like it's beating."

"Rightly so," said Ahearna with a thoughtful tilt of her ears. "For it is my task, you might say, to keep the heart beating. To keep it safe. That is a task I have performed ever since Merlin asked me to do so, when I carried him out of Avalon for the very last time."

"Merlin asked you? Why?"

"Because that star—the Heart—is the doorway to Earth! He asked me to guard it not because he went through it to another world, but because he believed that it was the world, after Avalon, which Rhita Gawr would most want to conquer."

The horse, suddenly agitated, turned a quick circle, her eyes and hooves flashing under the stars. "And he was right! At this very moment, a terrible dragon is attacking the star's flames with dark magic, trying to extinguish them—and thus open the door."

Tamwyn caught his breath. "And that dragon—"

"Is Rhita Gawr, I am certain." She stamped her hooves and flared her nostrils. "I would have stayed to fight him, with all my strength, but Dagda himself came to me in a vision. He told me to cease my flight around the Heart, for the first time in centuries, and to fly as fast as lightning itself to this very mountaintop. Here I would find, he promised, the one called Dark Flame—who, despite his name and his youth, was the only person who could stop Rhita Gawr."

Try as he might, Tamwyn couldn't swallow the lump in his throat. "Why," he asked hoarsely, "doesn't Dagda just come and fight Rhita Gawr himself?"

"Know you so little of Dagda's ways?" The steed raised her magnificent head a bit closer to the stars. "Only the strongest immortal spirits, such as Dagda, Lorilanda, and Rhita Gawr—and the very rare mortal who possesses wizard's powers—can open star doorways. And so only they can move between worlds, and bring their followers with them. Yet Dagda vowed long ago never to use that power, since doing so would violate the basic independence of each world, and its right to choose its own destiny. That is why, whenever Dagda appears in Avalon, it is only as a vision, not as his true self. And that is also why he has now forbidden Merlin to move between the worlds—so that Merlin must remain forever on Earth."

"But this is an emergency!" objected Tamwyn. "Avalon is at risk, more than ever before. As are all the other worlds that Rhita Gawr can reach from here—including Earth."

Ahearna snorted loudly. "Do you think Dagda does not know this? His agony must be excruciating. Either he discards his most fundamental principle, or he leaves Avalon terribly vulnerable. That is a dilemma too great for anyone, even a god."

"Which is part of Rhita Gawr's plan," the young man said bitterly. "How long do we have left?"

"One day, no more."

She reared back on her hind legs, whinnying to the Thousand Groves of the stars. "Even as I flew here to find you, riding the River of Time, I saw immortal warriors emerging through the seven darkened doorways that divide Avalon from the Otherworld. They are gathering up there, waiting for their leader's command. And their leader is Rhita Gawr! They are bound to him, somehow. I could feel it."

"And their signal to attack Avalon," declared Tamwyn, "is when the Heart of Pegasus goes dark."

"Then let us fly!"

The great horse bent down, curling her left foreleg beneath her so that he could reach her back. He climbed on, adjusted his gear, and slid into position on her massive shoulders. Just as he grabbed hold of her mane, he gave Henni a questioning glance. Instantly, the hoolah ran across the grass and leaped onto her back just behind the young man.

"Hold tight to me," Tamwyn told him. Then he patted the small bulge in his tunic pocket and added, "You, too, my little friend."

Ahearna stood and shook her shining mane. With a swoosh of air, she opened her powerful wings and raised them high. All at once she neighed, bent her muscular legs, and leaped into the sky.

It was a leap, Tamwyn knew, that would carry them all the way to the stars.

19 · Star Galloper

AHEARNA, THE STAR GALLOPER, LEAPED skyward, bearing Tamwyn swiftly higher. With each stroke of her silvery white wings, he could feel a sudden tensing of her shoulder muscles beneath him—and a powerful *whooooosh* of air that blew with the force of a giant's breath.

Above, beyond the shredding clouds, the stars burned bright. So bright that Tamwyn couldn't bear to look at them. Instead, he watched the winged horse as she carried them skyward: the forward tilt of her ears, the shimmering light on her mane, the steady pumping of her wings.

Henni sat right behind Tamwyn, his huge hands wrapped around his companion's waist. To Tamwyn's surprise, the hoolah showed no signs of mischief as they gained altitude, not even an irreverent laugh. Whether Henni's good behavior came from the wonder of flight, the seriousness of their quest, or the deadly threat that Ahearna had made, he sat in silence as they climbed through the clouds.

For his part, Batty Lad seemed quite frightened at flying so high. Every so often he stuck his furry little head out of the tunic pocket, so that his cupped ears fluttered like small sails in the wind. But always, within seconds, he would squeak in panic and shrink back inside.

Tamwyn himself felt no fear at all, merely a sense of rising exultation. Whatever perils lay just ahead, both for him and for his world, here and now he was flying. Up to the stars!

I wish Elli could be here now, he thought. *She would love rising through the clouds this way, soaring through the sky. One day, perhaps, we can do this—if we both survive this day.*

The winged horse burst through a bank of clouds. Suddenly the starlight blazed brighter than ever. Tamwyn took one hand off Ahearna's mane to shield his eyes, but even that didn't do much good. He couldn't squint like this forever. And how was he supposed to confront Rhita Gawr, with one hand always on his brow?

In a flash, he remembered the chant that Palimyst had taught him to diminish brightness. But would a simple craftsman's song, designed to dim the light of fire coals, be any help against the far more powerful light of stars?

"No," answered Ahearna, having heard his thoughts. Speaking into his mind, she added, "Yet if you say this little chant, I will pour my own power into it, the same power that I use to live among the stars and not be blinded by their fires."

And so, to the rhythm of her swooshing wings, he recited the words Palimyst had taught him:

> *Bless thee, light of fire coals,*
> *Cinders of a star,*
> *Powers from afar.*

> *Help me seek thy inner soul:*
> *Starlight never bound,*
> *Sacred ever found.*

Let my mortal eyes embrace
Thy immortal flame,
Only in thy name.

Give me power thus to see,
As my spirit lifts—
Thy eternal gifts.

Even as Tamwyn spoke the final phrase, the light all around them suddenly changed. It didn't exactly darken, although the radiance no longer burned his eyes. Rather, the light *deepened* somehow, replacing brightness with richness, just as wood grain will deepen when the wood is washed with oil. Everything he could see—from a single feather on Ahearna's wing to the mist-draped mountain far below—seemed clearer, sharper, and fuller. Details were magnified as never before.

He looked upward—and, for the first time in his life, he truly saw the stars. Perfect circles, flashing with iridescent flames, they didn't look physical so much as spiritual, closer to the realm of ideas than the realm of reality.

Then he caught sight of the rippling line of light that cut across the center of the sky—dividing not just the sky but the two halves of time. The River, always flowing in the present. Like the stars themselves, the River of Time grew steadily more radiant as the travelers approached.

With every wingbeat of Ahearna, Tamwyn drew closer to the realm on high. He spotted many of the constellations that he had studied since childhood—although, as the great horse climbed higher, their shapes began to change. Yet he couldn't mistake the double ring of stars known as the Circles, whose Drumadian name, the Mysteries, had inspired many a ballad and blessing about the seventh sacred Element. Nor could he miss the Twisted Tree, whose star-studded limbs stretched so far across the sky. And then there was Pegasus, Ahearna's home. Exactly in the constellation's center, the Heart shone powerfully.

All of a sudden, Tamwyn noticed a growing stain of darkness that was seeping into the Heart, dimming its radiance. And then, just outside the darkening star's rim, he saw something that made him shudder. It was a tiny black blot, visible only because of his enhanced vision. Although it was much smaller than the Heart, it was clearly on the attack, shooting bolts of blackness into the star. Rhita Gawr, in his dragon form!

Tamwyn's gaze shifted back to the River of Time. Would they reach it soon enough? That was their only hope of getting all the way to the Heart of Pegasus before it was too late to stop Rhita Gawr.

Tamwyn glanced worriedly at the star that would be, if darkened, an open doorway to Earth. Then he turned to another part of the sky and viewed the seven thin circles, completely dark inside, that were the stars of the Wizard's Staff. The doorways to the Otherworld. Blurry shapes—Rhita Gawr's warriors—poured steadily out of them, flowing into Avalon like noxious fumes.

Just then he realized that the warriors already on Avalon's side of the doorways looked darker, more substantial, than those just entering. *Of course! They are forming bodies, just as Rhita Gawr has done, in order to act, and fight, in the mortal world.* Although Tamwyn still couldn't tell exactly what forms those warriors were taking, he felt certain they would be designed for battle.

As if she, too, had seen Rhita Gawr and his warriors, Ahearna flapped her wings even faster. Her flowing mane sparkled with the light of the stars. Watching her, so graceful and strong, Tamwyn felt a touch of hope—and, once again, the simple joy of flight.

Then something new caught his attention: the branches of the Great Tree. He noticed how gracefully they curved. How they stretched like shadowy peninsulas across the sea of stars. And how, on every twig of every branch, a bright star gleamed.

So the branches really *were* pathways to the stars! Struck with wonder, he squeezed Ahearna's mane. Stars, thousands of them, filled the sky—all of them connected to the Tree of Avalon. They hung from its enormous boughs, surrounding its trunk, like celestial fruit whose very essence was light.

Now, at last, I understand. Tamwyn gazed intently at the upper reaches of Avalon. Then, in a burst of inspiration he realized something more.

Since the stars were truly connected to the Great Tree, its sacred élano flowed into them—just as it did into the roots, trunk, and branches. This regular, rhythmic flow of élano, swelling every morning and receding every evening, was the Tree's way of breathing. And because the stars' own fires felt those magical breaths—and were fanned by them—they took that magic into their doorways. Yes—and spread that magic to all the other worlds. To every tree, and every seed, in the Thousand Groves.

Tamwyn smiled with satisfaction. For he knew that he had also finally answered a question that had puzzled Avalon's bards, sages, and sky-watchers for centuries: Why did the stars swell brighter every morning, and grow dimmer every evening after the last rays of starset?

Because of the flows of élano, he said to himself, *so much happens. And so much is connected! The light of the stars on high is actually linked to the élanolight in Gwirion's cavern deep inside the trunk. And to plenty more that I don't even begin to understand.*

He looked downward. Between each stroke of the massive wings, he studied the root-realms far below. There was Stoneroot, jutting out so far from the Tree that it fairly glowed with unobstructed starlight. There was Fireroot, partially masked by reddish smoke; Woodroot, swathed in deep green; and Waterroot, trembling with all the colors of the Rainbow Seas. And there, forever shadowed by the shape of the Tree above, was the darkest realm of all.

Shadowroot. Where Elli was by now. Had she found White Hands? And the corrupted crystal that served both the sorcerer and Rhita Gawr? Her time, like his own, was fast disappearing.

All at once, Ahearna banked sharply to the right. Tamwyn's grip on her mane tightened, as did Henni's grip around his waist. Even as Tamwyn twisted to see why the horse had turned so suddenly, he heard a new rumbling and pounding—endlessly deep, as if it came from a drum that stretched across the entire sky. Then a great wave of light washed over them, foaming like water but sparkling like the stars themselves.

They had entered the River of Time.

The wave of light submerged them completely. All Tamwyn could feel was the horse's muscular back beneath him; all he could see was the luminous foam that bubbled around him. The deep drumming continued at the same steady rhythm, echoing upon itself. Sparks of light burst everywhere, constantly.

Yet strangest of all was Tamwyn's experience of time. Or better, the *lack* of time. Hard as he tried, he couldn't feel sure of any past or future, any yesterday or tomorrow. All he had were his incoherent memories of those concepts. Everything was now, the present moment. Only that existed; all the rest was a dream. And since time did not matter, individuals and the choices they made did not matter.

That's not true, he reminded himself with considerable effort. There really was a yesterday. And there *would* be a tomorrow . . . unless Rhita Gawr destroyed it. Which was why every individual, even a small and clumsy one, could matter.

While he clung to that belief, though, he couldn't begin to guess how long he'd been riding in the River. Radiant foam swirled around him, always moving, but always in the present. However much time might matter to the worlds outside these luminous waves, it simply didn't exist here.

Abruptly, Ahearna's shoulders tensed. With a mighty flap of her powerful wings, she released a neigh that rose above the rumble of the River. Simultaneously, she kicked her legs so hard that the glittering foam exploded in a burst of brilliance.

All at once, the foam vanished. So did the sense of no time—and no meaning. Tamwyn could see Ahearna's wings, pumping hard, as she wheeled above the rippling waves of the River of Time.

He drew a deep breath, savoring the air. For though it was thinner than the air of the realms down below, it still bore the sweetness of Avalon. And of something else, as well—a sense of the future, of choices he could make and times he might change.

Feeling fully alive again, he leaned forward to hug the horse's neck. He felt her mane, wet with sweat, against his cheek. *Whatever is to come, Ahearna, I am grateful for all you have given me. This feeling—and this flight.*

"That is not all I have given you, Dark Flame. For you also have the chance, small as it is, to save many worlds." She spun around, wide wings outstretched, ears cocked forward. "Behold," she declared, "the Heart of Pegasus."

An iridescent circle, enormous beyond anything Tamwyn had ever imagined, glowed before them. They were merely a mote of dust compared to its long, sweeping rim; a speck of ash to its huge, shimmering flames. Its sheer size made it seem immutable, as well as invulnerable.

Yet Tamwyn saw countless jagged cracks, as black as dead fire coals, inside the star. The cracks were spreading, too—growing rapidly larger, extinguishing the flames, like gouges from claws of darkness.

"The work of the dragon," said Ahearna grimly, following Tamwyn's gaze. "It is time we confront him, you and I."

She bent her neck downward, flapping her wings briskly, which turned them toward a lower part of the rim. "He is down there, working his sorcery on the star. Just as he was when I—"

She never finished. For she, like Tamwyn, had suddenly realized that the dragon was nowhere to be seen.

Ahearna flattened her wings, preparing to soar downward for a closer look. At that instant, however, Tamwyn heard something he'd never expected. A voice! *Elli's voice.* It didn't seem possible, yet the voice sounded utterly real. Whether it had come to his mind or his ears, he couldn't tell. But its message was crystal clear.

"Tamwyn! Look out!"

He yanked the horse's mane violently, making her veer sharply to the left. Even as she whinnied angrily, an enormous black tail snapped like a whip at the exact place they had been flying. It missed them by so little that its wind brushed Ahearna's wing, fluttering her feathers.

"Rhita Gawr," shouted Tamwyn. "Behind us!"

20 · Two Armies

WITH A LOUD CRACKLE OF GREEN FLAMES, Brionna fell through the portal. She landed on her hands and knees on the damp brown soil, but bounced to her feet with elven agility. Even as she shifted the position of her quiver of arrows, which had dug into the scar on her back, her deep green eyes scanned the surrounding terrain.

Mudroot's rolling plains stretched in all directions. Under the clear midday starlight, the landscape of Malóch fairly glowed with a uniform brown color, broken only by the flickering green light of the portal, and by the darker shadows of mud-covered boulders. Yet Brionna knew that this land would soon be stained with a new color: the red of blood.

For these were the Plains of Isenwy.

From the portal where she stood, she had no difficulty seeing the two opposing armies that had already gathered. Only an unbroken swath of muddy flats, less than half a league wide, separated the two camps. Yet a gulf immeasurably wider separated their views of the world—which was why this battle would decide that world's fate.

Fortunately, the portal was much closer to the army that included her fellow elves, as well as others who cherished the Avalon she loved—the Avalon of free and magical beings who tried, at least, to live in harmony and mutual respect. Immediately, Brionna recognized some elves she knew from Woodroot, as well as Waterroot. Among them was her childhood friend, Aileen, who was training to become a master woodworker. Catching Aileen's eye, Brionna nodded in greeting. In response, her friend blew a kiss for good luck.

As Brionna blew a kiss in return, she wondered, *Will we ever again drink hazelnut tea together in the boughs of your elm tree home?* She then fingered her braid anxiously, knowing that it was impossible to tell.

She turned from Aileen, eager to view the other warriors in the free people's army. But right away, she felt struck by how little they resembled warriors at all. She could see, milling about, forty or fifty of Lleu's fellow priests and priestesses, all wearing the Drumadians' greenish brown robe with a clasp carved in the shape of an oak tree. Unlike the elves, none of them carried bows and arrows; only a few even held swords or spears. By their sides (or, in some cases, on their shoulders) were their faithful maryths—squirrels, stags, does, hawks, dogs, lizards, owls, sprites, or tree spirits. Seeing all the maryths, who had originally been paired with Drumadians so that humans would never forget their basic connection to other living creatures, Brionna frowned, saddened by the limits of such a worthy ideal. And by the many deaths that those limits would cause.

Joining the elves and Drumadians were over a hundred women and men who had resisted the call of Belamir's Humanity First movement. Although they seemed, for the most part, sturdier than the priests and priestesses, they were clearly not battle-trained soldiers. Many looked as if they had never fought with anything more dangerous than a plow, while struggling to dig furrows in some rocky field. The few weapons they carried seemed flimsy or rusted from lack of use.

With relief, she also spotted some people who could hold their own on the battlefield. These included three or four giants, brandishing uprooted trees that could be used as clubs. At least a score of sturdy-looking dwarves marched nearby, carrying double-bladed axes on their shoulders. And more than a dozen tree spirits, with powerful limbs and roots, stood among the crowd.

Suddenly she glimpsed a group of eaglefolk circling overhead, their broad wings outstretched. Her heart leaped, and not just because those people made such superb warriors. But her excitement faded swiftly, for none of them was the eagleman she most wanted to see.

As she stood next to the crackling flames of the portal, wondering what had become of Scree, a band of mist faeries buzzed past, so close that their whirring blue wings nearly brushed against her cheek. The sight of them instantly knocked her thoughts back to the present moment: *So even the faery folk have come to defend Avalon!* Within seconds, she also noticed a cluster of buttery yellow starflower faeries, and a few green-clad moss faeries who carried miniature slingshots.

Then, off to the side, she saw a group of armored people whose presence here surprised her even more than the faeries. Flamelons. Their orange, upturned eyes glowed wrathfully as they stoked their fires, using specially treated wood that could burn for hours with almost the heat of lava. With the flamelons stood several huge fire oxen— beasts who could easily impale gobsken on their long scarlet horns, or pull heavy loads into battle.

And the flamelons had indeed brought some heavy loads. Brionna couldn't help but gawk when she saw some of their massive (and highly inventive) weaponry, most of which she'd only heard about in her grandfather's tales.

There were gigantic bows that stood on iron braces so they could send burning spears for more than a league, a pair of great catapults, and an enormous wheel that could shoot flaming balls of tar at the enemy. As if those weapons weren't enough, the flamelons also possessed piles of gleaming metal swords, axes, hammers, spears, and spiked maces, all expertly crafted in their famous forges. On top of that, as Brionna had learned from her grandfather, flamelons could hurl firebolts directly from their own hands—although they did so only as a last resort, since the effort left them severely weakened.

The elf maiden watched them, hands on her hips. What amazed her most was not that this warlike people had come all the way from Fireroot to join this battle. No, what struck her more than anything was that they had decided to join this *side* of the battle. After all, many flamelons actually worshiped Rhita Gawr. They viewed him not as a god of war, as did virtually everyone else in Avalon, but as a god of creation, who led their people to new heights of power. Since their bitter defeat, along with the dark elves and fire dragons, in the terrible War of Storms centuries before, the flamelons hadn't attacked any other realms. And yet their fiery, warlike culture still persisted in their homeland—leading to frequent battles between clans. Even their realm's only flower, firebloom, seemed to exemplify their culture: It thrived only on ground recently scorched by flames.

Still, Brionna could guess why the flamelons had decided to join with their former enemies, elves and humans and eaglefolk, to defend the old order. Above all else, flamelons prized their freedom. So they had come here not out of any love for Avalon, or its wondrous diversity of creatures. Rather, they had come to fight for their freedom to live as they had always lived—fiercely and independently.

Just as she started to turn away, to take a look at the other army that they would soon have to fight, she spotted one more figure. A figure that made her catch her breath. It was an elderly bard, with a beard that stuck out on both sides, a silly grin, and a large, lopsided hat. He fit exactly the description Elli had given her of that old bard from Woodroot—the one who had led Elli and the others to Brionna's side just in time to save her life after she'd been mauled by ghoulacas. Now she peered closely at the old fellow, just to make sure she wasn't mistaken. But he ambled off, disappearing into the crowd.

At that instant, the portal crackled loudly. Brionna spun around just as Lleu and Catha arrived. While Lleu spilled out of the green flames, tumbling onto the damp ground, the silver-winged falcon shot into the air. She circled gracefully, eyeing the two armies, before landing back on the gangly priest's shoulder.

Lleu brushed some mud off his cheek, then faced Brionna. "So we're not too late?"

"No," she answered gravely. "We're just in time for all the killing."

"Maybe this war can still be—"

"Avoided? No chance. Just take a look at our allies over there." She waved at the army on the nearby rise. "They've come from all over Avalon to fight. And, if necessary, to die."

Lleu didn't answer. For his attention had been caught by the sight of the opposing force, assembling half a league to the north. Brionna, too, turned that way—and gasped. Not because of the ferocious warriors she could see, but because of their sheer numbers.

Several thousand gobsken, their armored breastplates glinting in the starlight, had gathered on the plains. They stood around carts loaded with weapons, tended dung fires, and scuffled among themselves. Their commander, a burly man with many blades dangling from his belt, strode among them, barking commands and occasionally slapping them with the flat of his broadsword.

Brionna's whole body tensed, for she recognized that man immediately. *Harlech. You murderer! You gave me this scar on my back. And, a thousand times worse, you and that sorcerer you serve killed Granda.*

Her fist tightened around the handle of her cedar longbow. As much as it violated her most basic principles to kill any creature—and worst of all, to kill for pleasure— she desperately *wanted* to kill that man. And surely would, if he came within range of her arrows. That she felt this way sickened her inside, yet she couldn't shake the fact that it was true.

I'm not worthy of elfhood, she thought grimly. *I'm not even worthy of love—not Elli's, not Scree's, not anyone's. But I will have my revenge.*

A blur of motion in the sky above the gobsken warriors caught her eye. Ghoulacas! The mere glimpse of their nearly transparent wings and bodies, and their bloodred talons and beaks as sharp as daggers, made her jaw clench. Bred by the sorcerer White Hands to serve as his spies and assassins, they would be terrible foes indeed.

She lowered her gaze again. Harlech could no longer be seen among the gobsken. But she did pick out someone she hated almost as much: that arrogant human, Morrigon. *He won't be pleased to find me still alive. Or to find an elvish arrow in his heart.*

Then, with a shudder, she glimpsed the man—the changeling—he served. Belamir! Still disguised in the garb of a gentle gardener, he strolled among hundreds of men and women who followed his pernicious teachings. Among them, to her astonishment, was one woman who wore the robe of a Drumadian. And then, spotting a hint of green on the woman's chin, she recognized who it was.

"Llynia," she declared, pointing so that Lleu could see for himself.

The tall priest scowled the instant he spotted her, while the hawk upon his shoulder released an angry whistle.

"How," Lleu asked, "could a priestess of Avalon fall so far? Knowingly or not, she now serves Rhita Gawr."

"Along with hordes of gobsken and ghoulacas." Brionna's sharp eyes roved over the scene. "Plus at least three trolls and half a dozen ogres."

"And don't forget the gnomes! There must be five hundred of them, each carrying a deadly spear."

The elf maiden blew a discouraged breath. "About the only dreadful creatures they *don't* have over there are dragons."

"We've seen enough of those already," Lleu said dryly. "Fortunately, Highlord Hargol can't leave the waters of Brynchilla. Or he'd certainly be here to gobble us up."

Brionna nodded. "The rest of Avalon's dragons—those who can fly, at least—are probably just waiting out the battle to see who wins. And what spoils they can find."

"Count ourselves fortunate. *No one* should be forced to battle a dragon."

"Fortunate?" She kicked at a small clump of mud near the edge of the portal. "That is the very last word I'd use to describe us." She paused, as her brow furrowed. "Lleu, you don't think that maybe the *superior force* we heard rumors about—the force that's supposed to be joining those gobsken soon—could be a dragon?"

The priest's scowl deepened. "Let's hope not! But that possibility is another reason why the elves' plan to attack as soon as possible makes sense."

Brionna shook her head. "*Nothing* about this war makes sense."

Just then the portal sputtered and crackled, sending up a spurt of green fire. Out rolled Shim, landing facedown in the mud. He sat up, wobbling on his wide rump. Grumbling to himself, he wiped a clump off his oversized nose.

"Yucksy mud," he said unhappily, scraping off some more. "This is a disgustingly greeting! Certainly, definitely—"

"Absolutely," finished Brionna, helping him stand. Peering into his sad old eyes, she said, "Really, Shim. You don't need to stay."

Puzzled, he scrunched his nose. "Won't feed who hay? What the queen's beans is you saying, Rowanna?"

She opened her mouth to answer, then closed it and just shook her head.

The little giant frowned, understanding what had happened. "It's me tiny ears again, rightly?" He swung his small fist through the air. "If only I was still bigly, and not so very shrunkelled! Then I could hears you, really and truly."

Brionna began to nod, when a new sound distracted her. Shouts of anger. Coming from the free peoples' army! Some elves and men were arguing, shoving each other roughly. One elf had already grabbed his bow and was about to nock an arrow.

"Wait!" she cried, sprinting over to them. Behind her ran Lleu, with Catha clinging tightly to his shoulder. Far behind them waddled Shim.

Leaping over a pair of seated women, Brionna hurled herself into the fray. She knocked against the elf's bow, deflecting the arrow just as it began to fly. The arrow plunged harmlessly into the mud at her feet.

"What are you doing, Edan?" she demanded, panting. She glared at the elf. "We don't have time to fight among ourselves."

"We do if those hoolahs in men's clothing don't apologize!" he shot back. "You stay out of this, Brionna."

"Who are you calling a hoolah?" A brawny man wearing a leather blacksmith's apron shoved her aside. Grimacing, he faced the male elf. "Take that back."

"Not until you take back what you said about El Urien."

The blacksmith spat on the ground.

"Stop, I say!" cried Brionna. "You two are no better than gobsken."

"She's right," Lleu declared, stepping in between them. "Enough of this, right now." For emphasis, Catha screeched and clacked her beak.

"Go back to where you came from, priest," growled another man. "You, too, elf."

Edan, the wood elf, nocked another arrow.

The blacksmith raised his fist, about to strike him, when—

A lute strummed softly. Whether from the sheer unexpectedness of it, or from some strange quality of the music, all the arguing suddenly ceased.

Apparently unaware of the quarrel that had been just about to explode, the old bard walked right into the middle of the group, swaying jauntily as he strummed. His silly grin seemed wider than ever. The pointed tips of his sideways-growing beard glowed silver in the starlight, making him look like one of the furry-faced monkeys from the jungles of Africqua.

As he passed by, he stopped strumming to raise his hand to the brim of his lopsided hat. With a wink at Brionna, he lifted the hat, revealing the blue, teardrop-shaped museo who sat upon his bald head. Instantly, the museo started to hum—a richly layered sound that reached both high and low at once, thrumming like the deepest river and whistling like the loftiest wind. The hum rolled outward, swelling like a wave that washed over everyone nearby.

How long the bard and museo remained, Brionna couldn't quite remember afterward. She wasn't even sure that she hadn't imagined the whole thing. All she knew for certain was that, like the others around her, she found herself slightly dazed. If there had been an argument, she couldn't remember what it was about. And if the bard and museo had really been there a moment ago, they were now nowhere to be seen.

She turned to Lleu, who looked equally bewildered.

Even as she opened her mouth to ask him what he thought had happened, a voice rang out.

"Parley! The gobsken army wants a parley."

Brionna swung around to face the opposing force across the muddy plain. Sure enough, someone was waving a white flag, tied to the end of a spear. She shook her head, surprised that they would want to talk before the battle. That was a thoroughly ungobskenlike sign of reason—or perhaps even fear.

Then she looked closer, and her puzzlement deepened. For the person holding the white flag was none other than Harlech.

21 · Honor

THE WIND OF MALÓCH GUSTED, BEARING the scent of dung fires, iron weapons, and approaching battle. Meanwhile, the free peoples' army launched into a heated debate—several of them, in fact—over whether and how to respond to the gobsken army's request for a parley. Many suspected a trap, but others felt strongly that the request shouldn't be denied. The tumultuous debates soon led to angry quarrels and scuffles, and would have turned into complete chaos if three natural leaders hadn't emerged.

Kerwin, an eagleman whose feathers shone with the same brown color as the surrounding plains, was the first to bring the unruly allies to order. He succeeded only by swooping just overhead, wings spread wide, screeching his eagle's cry of warning. When, at last, the crowd fell silent, Kerwin vowed that he would use his talons to tear apart anyone who wouldn't speak civilly and in turn. This threat, combined with his reputation as a warrior of very great power (and very little patience), did the trick. Kerwin, hovering above the group, began to call on people to speak, one at a time. And so humans, elves, eaglefolk, giants, maryths, and even faeries spoke their minds—every kind of people except the flamelons, who remained apart from the rest. For to the flamelons, the notion of a parley was a sign of great weakness, too repulsive even to consider.

In time, a second leader emerged: Lleu, the Drumadian priest widely known as the trusted confidant of High Priestess Coerria. Speaking calmly and clearly, with the silver-winged Catha on his shoulder, Lleu argued that it would be a mistake not to send representatives to the parley. Even if this were some sort of trap, canny representatives needn't fall into it. There was even a chance that they could learn something valuable. And finally, Lleu reminded everyone, there was still a possibility—no matter how small—that this parley could lead to peace. That, in some way no one could predict, this meeting might actually avoid needless bloodshed.

"Then let us attack them right after the parley," declared Brionna, who was the next person to speak. She shook her longbow in the air. "And let us stun them with our sheer ferocity as warriors."

She waited, as the many cheers and shouts subsided. "As much as I, too, would much prefer peace, I have abandoned any hope for it. This army we face today has only one goal: to defeat us utterly, so that Avalon can be ruled by the servants of Rhita Gawr—and by Rhita Gawr himself."

Her tone terribly grave, she continued. "And so, good people, let us do one thing more. When this parley ends, give your all to saving our world. Yes, even your last breath! For if we are truly willing to die here today, we might yet prevail, and destroy the army of Rhita Gawr. But even if we do not prevail, we will die in defense of Avalon. And Avalon deserves no less."

"Those are words of great honor," boomed Kerwin, as he circled over Brionna's head.

With that, the matter was settled. Moments later, three

people had been chosen to represent the defenders of Avalon at the parley: Kerwin, Lleu, and Brionna. And so those three marched into the Plains of Isenwy, led by the eagleman—now in his human form, in keeping with the traditional rules of parley. None of them spoke. The only sound they heard, besides the buffeting wind, was the squelch of their feet in the mud.

As soon as they started walking toward the army of gobsken, the representatives of their foes did the same. There were three of them, as well. And in the lead swaggered Harlech himself, bearing the white flag affixed to a spear. But while he carried the emblem of a peaceful parley, his expression looked as hard as the metal of his broadsword. On his wide leather belt hung that sword, along with a hatchet, two daggers, and a spiked club. Something else dangled from the cord around his neck— something shaped like a claw, which glowed eerily.

Yet as Brionna approached him, she noticed none of those things. She was thinking only about another weapon, the iron-tipped whip of a slave master. Rage surged through her, making her temples pound, as she recalled how Harlech had used that whip on her defenseless grandfather, as well as herself, during their captivity. It took every bit of her self-control to resist breaking the first law of parley by shooting him on the spot. Even now, her fingers tapped fitfully against the wood of her longbow.

Close behind Harlech strode another man, someone both Brionna and Lleu had come to despise. Morrigon hobbled along briskly, a bow and quiver slung over his back. His scraggly white hair trembled in the wind that gusted over the mud flats. Yet even though he looked as brittle as a dead tree, the elf maiden and the priest knew that he was surprisingly spry. And that his will remained sturdy, like his loyalty to Belamir.

When Morrigon came close enough to recognize them, however, his step suddenly faltered. The old man's jaw fell open. But his shock quickly turned to wrath. He glared at Brionna, his bloodshot eye darkened by malice.

Beside him marched a woman wearing the greenish brown robe of a Drumadian priestess. At the sight of Llynia, Catha snapped her beak and whistled angrily. But Llynia the Seer, as Belamir had dubbed her, paid no attention. She merely strode ahead, carrying herself with a distinct air of superiority. But the haughty look on her face didn't seem to fit with the triangular mark on her chin, which gave the impression of a shoddy green beard.

They met halfway between the two armies, near a pair of mud-covered boulders. For a long moment, as they stood on the damp ground, no one spoke. The air fairly crackled with animosity as the two groups eyed each other.

Finally, Kerwin broke the silence. Bare-chested in the manner of all eaglemen in human form, he trained his gaze on Harlech and declared, "You need not die if you surrender now."

"Surrender? Us?" The warrior burst into raucous laughter, jamming the base of his spear into the mud. "Yer the ones who'd best surrender, wingboy."

Kerwin's eyes, as deep brown as his skin, narrowed at the insult. Still, true to the rules of parley, he held his temper, though the effort made him tremble. Watching him, Brionna thought of another eagleman who possessed a strong sense of honor—as well as a dangerous temper.

Scree, she thought, *where are you? We could use your help right now.*

Morrigon, still glaring at her, sneered, "So ye escaped, elf-girl? I'm real glad. Now I'll have the pleasure o' killin' ye meself."

Before Brionna could respond, Llynia commanded, "Hush, Morrigon. No one will do any killing until we have exhausted all the possibilities of peace."

"Just as you did with us back there at your temple?" asked Lleu sarcastically. His dark eyebrows lifted. "Or as your people did when they attacked the Society's compound?"

The priestess stiffened, but her voice remained level. "I had nothing whatsoever to do with that attack. I was once the Chosen One, if you remember."

"It's *you* who should remember, Llynia! All your years at the Society of the Whole, and you have forgotten its most basic principles."

With a dismissive wave of her hand, she declared, "I have forgotten nothing. Nothing!"

"Is that so?" Lleu leaned his tall frame toward her. "Then where is your loyal maryth?"

As Llynia's face went pale, the silver falcon on Lleu's shoulder gave a harsh whistle.

"I'll tell you where," continued the priest. Keeping his gaze fixed on Llynia, he stretched out his long arm, pointing at the army of Avalon's defenders.

Despite all her efforts to stay calm, the priestess gasped. For standing silently on the rise, a few steps apart from everyone else, was a tall tree spirit, a lilac elm. Starlight gleamed on the small purple buds that dotted her many arms.

"Fairlyn," whispered the priestess, unable to turn away from those large eyes that had watched over her lovingly for so long. Or from those slender limbs that had given her such sensuous baths, filling the air with sweet aromas.

Llynia swallowed. "I didn't know . . ."

"And there is something else you didn't know." Lleu's expression turned graver still as he leaned closer. "Your master Belamir is really a *changeling.*"

"Wha—what?" Llynia sputtered, backing away.

"It's a lie!" shouted Morrigon. "Ye know it is."

"It's true," insisted Lleu.

"That's right," Brionna declared. "He's fooled all of you! We saw him transform and tear apart one of his guards. This is all—"

"Utter nonsense," Llynia retorted, having regained her composure. Indignantly, she demanded, "How dare you say such a scandalous thing about Olo Belamir? Why, he is the most peaceful person I know! He supported fully the idea that we should offer you a last chance for peace. Under the new order, of course."

"Is that why you called this parley?" the elf demanded heatedly. "So you could offer us your version of peace—which is our version of annihilation?"

"No, no," insisted Llynia. "We called this parley in the true hope that many lives could be spared! From your side as well as ours. And the new order that Olo Belamir and I envision is one where all creatures can live compatibly. Yes, under humanity's wise dominion."

"Wise dominion?" snapped Brionna. "Is that what you call this army of yours? More like a plague! An alliance of murdering gobsken, gnomes, and—" She fixed a frosty gaze on Harlech. "Slave masters."

The big man studied her coldly. Another gust of wind blew past, rattling his weapons and spraying him with flecks of mud. But he didn't move at all.

At last, he snarled, "Why, if it ain't the she-elf from the dam." He chortled savagely. "Ye'll be fun to kill, dearie. Jest like yer old friend wid the white beard."

"My grandfather!" Suddenly all her resolve shattered. As quick as a heartbeat, Brionna drew an arrow from her quiver, nocked it, and aimed straight at Harlech's chest. Blinking the mist from her eyes, she declared, "You will pay for what you did to him."

Harlech merely stood there, rigid. He let go of the spear, allowing it to splat down on the mud. "Ye wouldn't kill me here an' now, would ye? Wid no chance at all to defend meself?"

"That's just how Granda was, before you killed him."

"Wait, Brionna." The strong hand of Kerwin wrapped around her bowstring. "Your rage is justified. And this man deserves no mercy for what he has done." He worked his muscular shoulders, as if lifting powerful wings. "But you remain bound by the honor of parley. You cannot kill him now."

Brionna hesitated, wrath surging through her veins.

"On the battlefield," said Kerwin firmly. "That is the place to slay your foes."

Slowly, reluctantly, she relaxed her bowstring. Kerwin nodded gravely, removing his hand. Just as she lifted the arrow to return it to the quiver, though, a bolt of red light shot out, landing squarely on the arrowhead. The stone exploded in red flames.

Brionna shrieked and jumped backward, dropping the arrow onto the damp ground. As she stared down at it, the flames died away—leaving just the burned shaft. The arrowhead itself had simply *disappeared.*

Aghast, she traded glances with Kerwin and Lleu, both of whom mirrored her own confusion. Then her gaze fell on Harlech. He smirked at her, while twirling the object that he wore around his neck, a claw tied to a leather cord. As it turned, the claw gleamed a malevolent shade of red.

"Did I mention me new weapon?" he sneered. "A gift from yer old friend, master Kulwych." With a shrug, he added, "Kulwych wanted me to save it fer later, after the battle starts. But seein' as how you attacked me, I jest couldn't resist."

Brionna clenched her fist. "I should have killed you when I had the chance, Harlech."

"Right, me dear, ye should've." His expression hardened. "So now yer goin' to die yourself."

"No," protested Lleu, waving his arms urgently. "Whatever is that evil weapon of yours, you can't use it now."

The warrior grunted. He released the claw, so that it fell back against his chest. "Yer smarter than ye know, priest. Garr, I wish this thing didn't need so much time between blasts!"

He seemed to relax—then suddenly whipped out his broadsword. Pointing its glittering blade at Brionna, he crowed, "But nothin' can stop me from usin' a different weapon."

"I can." Kerwin stepped boldly between Harlech and Brionna. His face showed all the battle-hardened severity that had made him famous among his people; his eagle eyes glowed clear and bright. "Since apparently this parley has failed, let us declare it over. I suggest we return to our separate camps."

Harlech heaved a sigh of disappointment. "All right, no more fun. All we can do now is go back to our camps, like ye said." He hesitated, then spoke stiffly, as if his words had been rehearsed. "Too bad this parley ended so soon. I was hopin' to delay ye till our *new recruits* arrive."

Brionna's jaw tightened. She didn't like the way he'd said that, not at all. Was all this just a ruse to lure her side into attacking sooner? Or was there really some new ally of the gobsken on the way? Someone like Kulwych or a powerful dragon—or even Rhita Gawr himself?

"Anyways," continued Harlech, "afore we go, there's jest one more thing I want to do."

"What?" demanded the eagleman who faced him squarely.

"This."

Harlech thrust his blade straight into Kerwin's heart. The eagleman gaped in shock, while his assailant merely grinned. "There's another man o' yer kind I'd much rather kill. But like I said afore, I jest couldn't resist."

Struggling mightily, Kerwin tried to pull free, but could only fall to his knees. With a shudder that racked his whole body, he crumpled to the ground. He made a desperate keening sound, like a dying bird of prey. Then his bright eyes closed forever.

Llynia, standing so close that Kerwin's hand had brushed her shin, went deathly pale.

"Murderer!" shrieked Brionna. She swiftly grabbed another arrow and raised her bow.

But Harlech was ready for her. Swinging his blade through the air, he struck her bow and sliced the wood in two. The longbow collapsed and dropped to the mud at her feet.

Harlech's grin widened. "Well now, looks like this parley really *is* over. An' like me l'il she-elf has no more weapons."

He lifted his sword and lunged at her. Before he could strike, however, Catha flew right at his face. The brave falcon screeched wildly, scratching at his eyes with her talons. Harlech stumbled, falling backward into Morrigon. The two of them slipped in the mud and landed with a splat.

"Come!" cried Lleu. He grabbed Brionna's arm, pulling her back toward their army. "We must run! Before Harlech's claw regains its power."

The priest gave a sharp whistle. "Catha, you must come, too. Fly with us!"

With a piercing screech, the hawk obeyed. She paused only long enough to peck Harlech's brow, drawing blood, as he struggled to rise. Then she winged toward Lleu and Brionna. When she reached them, they were running hard, their feet pounding in the mud. She screeched again—but it couldn't be heard. For a deafening roar suddenly filled the air.

Their entire army, having witnessed Harlech's treachery, charged into battle, shouting and cursing and brandishing weapons. No one could doubt that the great battle for Avalon had begun. Just as no one could doubt that Kerwin, the courageous eagleman, was only the first to die today in this desolate place.

22 · One Problem

ELLI TRUDGED DOWN THE STONE STEPS OF Borvo Lugna, the deepest mine in Shadowroot. Six gobsken marched ahead of her, and almost as many behind, the wavering light of their torches creating bizarre shadows on the walls. Yet she paid no heed. Still numb from the loss of old Grikkolo, she wasn't looking, wasn't listening. She felt only the unyielding rock under her feet, the weight of Nuic against her arm, and the greater weight of hopelessness in her heart.

She had lost any chance that she might have had to defeat Kulwych and destroy his corrupted crystal. She had run out of ways to help Avalon—just as she had run out of time. And to make matters worse, going underground reminded her of her years as a slave to the gnomes, years she had tried very hard to forget.

"Move along, ye filthy spies," barked the gobsken behind her. He jabbed Elli's back with the point of his sword. "Ol' scarface will be awful pleased to see ye."

"An' surprised, too," added another guard. "So surprised he might pop out his only eyeball."

Several gobsken wheezed with laughter at the joke.

Down, down, down they marched, deeper into the mine. The air grew warmer and staler by the minute, and it reeked of something like rotten eggs. Even in the utter darkness of the lands above, Elli could always find good air to breathe. Here, though, she felt an increasing urge to gag. And she was beginning to feel dizzy.

She missed a step and stumbled, crashing into the gobsken in front of her. He whirled around and pushed his face so close to hers that she could see the gleaming drops of sweat on his gray-green skin. Wrapping his three-fingered hand around her throat, he squeezed and shook her angrily.

"Watch out, scum! Or I'll roast yer head wid me torch an' eat it fer supper."

Another gobsken clubbed him hard on the back. "If ye do, Kulwych'll do the same to yer ugly head."

With a grunt, the gobsken released Elli, shoving her backward. She fell onto the steps, coughing uncontrollably. It was all she could do to hold on to Nuic, whose colors had shifted to enraged scarlet.

"Move," commanded the gobsken behind her.

He kicked her and prodded her with his blade, forcing her to stand. She rose, swaying unsteadily. And she couldn't stop coughing, though her lungs ached and her throat stung. Tears filled her eyes.

Yet somehow she kept going, descending deeper into the mine. *Snap out of it,* she told herself sternly. *You're no good to anyone like this.*

Just as her coughing finally subsided, they came to a landing. Someone shoved her into a rough-hewn tunnel, and the group started marching along this level passageway. Although her leg muscles were grateful for the change, this tunnel smelled even more putrid than the stairwell. She clutched Nuic, forcing herself to breathe slowly and stay alert.

For what felt like an endless time, they continued to

trudge. The monotonous rhythm of the gobsken's heavy boots echoed inside the dank tunnel, as well as inside Elli's head. At last, they slowed and came to a halt.

One of the gobsken stepped to the rock wall. With a nervous glance at the others, he raised his fist and rapped against a heavy door set into the stone. Elli noticed an eerie reddish glow seeping through the edges.

Slowly, the door opened, flooding the tunnel with pulsing red light. A harsh, raspy voice came from whatever room lay within. Elli couldn't make out what the voice said, but the mere sound of it chilled her blood.

"It's Kulwych," she whispered to Nuic. "I'm sure of it."

"Hmmmpff. In that case, maybe it's time you started thinking of a plan."

She scowled at him, but knew that he was right. How could she have been so foolish to waste precious time despairing? She should have been thinking of what she still might do for her world!

"At least do your best to hide your crystal," the sprite whispered as he turned the Galator around so that it rested behind his back.

"Right." She patted down the leaves of her amulet so that they fully covered the crystal of élano.

Just then the gobsken finished talking, bowed his head, and quickly backed away. He strode over to Elli, grabbed her by the shoulder, and dragged her roughly to the open door. Without so much as a word, he hurled her inside and turned to go.

Elli stumbled into the room, striking her head against the rock wall. Dazed, she slumped to the floor, vaguely aware of hearing the gobsken's boots clomping down the tunnel. And then she heard another sound: a low, throaty cackle from nearby.

"So, my young priestess, you have come to visit, mm-myesss?" Kulwych stepped closer, peering at them with his lidless eye. "You and your little pet."

Nuic's skin color darkened to black, while veins of scarlet coursed through his chest.

Shaking her head to clear her vision, she cringed at the sight of the sorcerer's mutilated face. The jagged scar that ran from his missing ear down to his chin caught the room's red light, pulsing horrendously. Then, looking beyond him, she saw the source of the light. It was a crystal, throbbing red, placed on a stone pedestal.

The corrupted crystal, she realized. So close! Maybe there *was* still a chance to do what she had come here to do. But how could she possibly destroy the crystal, even if she could somehow get past Kulwych?

The sorcerer rubbed his pale hands together. "You are, I believe, the priestess I was told about. Why else would you be here in Shadowroot? But where, may I ask, is the, er, friend I sent to find you?"

"You mean that murderer, Deth Macoll?" answered Elli, trying to look at Kulwych rather than at the crystal, so he wouldn't suspect her motives. "He's dead."

He drew a sharp breath. "Dead? Are you sure?"

She nodded grimly.

"How unfortunate, mmmyesss." He chortled vengefully. "I was looking forward to the pleasure of killing him myself."

The sorcerer raised one hand to his face and started inspecting his perfectly clipped fingernails. "And what," he asked, still examining his hand, "happened to the crystal of pure élano that he was supposed to steal?"

Elli winced. "It's, um—gone. Lost."

Kulwych turned to her and clacked his tongue. "You are a terrible liar, my priestess. Quite terrible. Yet it hardly matters. I have very little interest in your crystal, having one of my own that is far more powerful—as well as far more useful for my particular purposes."

Thoughtfully, he stroked what remained of his chin. "Now just one question remains. Why did you come all the way here? Surely not for a social engagement, though I am famously good company."

She shifted uncomfortably, her back pressed against the rock wall.

He curled his slit of a mouth into a frightful grin. "Perhaps, then, you came here with a plan. Could it possibly be . . . to destroy my own crystal?"

Watching the color drain from her face, he nodded knowingly. "You cannot fool me, Priestess."

Grandly, he gave Elli a bow. "You were right to try, though. Mmmyesss. There is awesome power in my crystal, more than you can imagine! Why, even now it binds my lord Rhita Gawr to his warriors on high, and me to my warriors on the Plains of Isenwy. And it is capable of much, much more, as Avalon shall soon discover."

Elli fidgeted, her mind racing. She had to think of a way! But what?

Kulwych laughed softly. "There is only one problem with your plan, I am afraid." He bent closer, the crystal's light pulsing in his eye. "My crystal *cannot be destroyed.*"

Her heart froze.

"But you, my priestess, you certainly *can* be destroyed." He rubbed his hands briskly. "So that is what I shall do, this very instant."

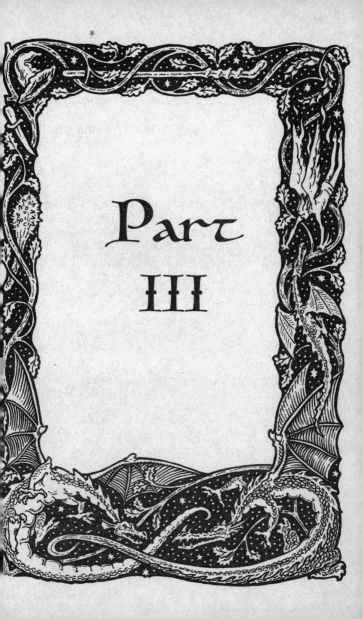

Part
III

23 · Dying Flames

TAMWYN HELD TIGHT TO AHEARNA'S MANE as the great horse whirled around, preparing to confront Rhita Gawr. Light from the enormous star, the Heart of Pegasus, flashed on every feather of her silvery white wings. Yet that light, Tamwyn knew, was fading fast. For jagged cracks of darkness continued to spread rapidly through the Heart.

Ahearna tilted her powerful wings, turning so fast that Tamwyn barely hung on. As she came around, she snorted with wrath, flaring her nostrils. Her angry neigh echoed across the sky, from the nearby star and the branch that held it to the luminous waves of the River of Time.

Then came another sound, a gargantuan roar that completely overwhelmed Ahearna's neigh. So loud was it that the nearest branches of the Great Tree, as well as the sky itself, seemed to shake. Tamwyn winced, while his fellow passenger Henni released his hold around Tamwyn's waist in order to cover his ears. The roar reverberated among the stars, louder than anything they had ever heard.

It was the roar of a dragon.

Ahearna completed her turn—and faced Rhita Gawr. He hovered directly in front of the horse and riders, his massive body a huge dark stain upon the sky. His tongue alone, which flitted hungrily along his lips, was larger than the mortals who dared to challenge him; with his leathery black wings outstretched, he dwarfed them as an eagle would dwarf a moth. Not since the days of the legendary Basilgarrad, long ago, had a dragon so fierce and powerful commanded the skies of Avalon.

The dragon's scales glistened darkly in the starlight, absorbing much more light than they reflected. His claws shone even blacker, as did his many rows of sword-sharp teeth. Yet the darkest parts of this terrible beast were not his wings, scales, claws, or teeth—but his eyes.

They're not only dark, thought Tamwyn, taken aback. *They're empty. Hollow. Bottomless.*

Like two wells of nothingness, as vacant as the void, Rhita Gawr's eyes glared at him. Then suddenly the eyes showed a look of surprise, which swiftly turned into unbounded rage.

"Spawn of Merlin," bellowed the dark dragon. "How is it possible that you are still alive? I thought I had killed you already! Yet now I smell your living blood—and the stench of my old nemesis."

"The only stench you smell is yours, Rhita Gawr!" Tamwyn leaned forward on the steed, his black hair shining. "I've come a long way to find you."

The dragon opened his cavernous mouth, packed with deadly pinnacles, and roared even louder than before. "All you have found is your death, runt wizard."

Faster than thought, Rhita Gawr coiled his massive tail above his outspread wings—and hurled it straight at the challengers. But Ahearna, the Star Galloper, moved even faster. She raised a wing and spun sideways, just as the celestial whip snapped with explosive force.

Before Rhita Gawr could recover, Ahearna beat her wings furiously and dived right at the dragon's head, so fast she was barely a blur of starlight. "Use your wizard's staff," she called to Tamwyn's mind. "Nothing could be more powerful."

In the hands of a real wizard, he answered, suddenly unsure of himself.

Still, he forced aside his doubts and pulled from its sheath the very staff Merlin himself had once wielded, the famed Ohnyalei. As he wrapped his hand around its knotted top, he felt a distinct current of energy, and the seven runes engraved on the shaft began to glow with a subtle blue light.

"The eye!" cried Ahearna. "Strike the eye."

A split second before they reached Rhita Gawr, the dragon realized his danger. Rolling to the side, he slapped at his adversaries with one broad, bony wing. At the same time, Tamwyn raised the staff and swung as hard as he could.

He hit—so hard that the impact rattled every bone in his body. Though Ohnyalei landed just above the dragon's eye, it struck hard enough to crack several scales, each the size of a supper plate. One of them broke off entirely. Moreover, Tamwyn's blow clearly enraged Rhita Gawr even more, for the gargantuan beast released a wild roar that sounded like an exploding star.

Ahearna banked, avoiding the dragon's wing. Meanwhile, Henni released a loud whoop into Tamwyn's ear that was only barely audible above the din. The hoolah squeezed Tamwyn tighter, as if to say, *Nice work, clumsy man.*

As they glided out of reach, Tamwyn glanced at the pocket of his tunic to check on his other companion. While he caught a glimpse of Batty Lad's mouselike face and cupped ears, they were just pulling back down into the pocket. Whatever Batty Lad had seen was enough, apparently, to make him want to hide himself deeper than ever, cowering with fright.

Just then Tamwyn felt something inside his mind. It wasn't a voice, but a *feeling*. Anxiety, concern, worry. But from where?

It came, he realized in a flash, from the warriors who served Rhita Gawr! The place where they were gathering—the seven darkened stars of the Wizard's Staff, now open doorways to the Otherworld—was very far away across the sky, too far for Tamwyn to see what the warriors actually looked like. And yet those warriors could clearly sense their master's distress. They could feel his emotions, and maybe also his will. Just as they could communicate their own feelings to him. Somehow, through a kind of magical connection that Tamwyn didn't understand, the warriors were all bound to their master.

Seconds later, he heard Rhita Gawr's wrathful voice again. "Runt wizard, I shall squash you like an insect! And I shall not need my vast army that gathers even now, awaiting my signal for the greater battle to come. No, this task shall be mine alone!"

The dragon plunged at them, even as he coiled his deadly tail to strike again. But Ahearna, ever alert, saw the attack coming. Anticipating right where the tail would fall, she tilted and swooped downward, passing near the rocky cliffs of a small branch that held no star.

This time, however, Rhita Gawr was one wingbeat ahead. His tail never uncoiled; that had been a feint. The instant Ahearna slowed, confident that the tail would whip past and miss them completely, he attacked in an entirely different way.

From the hollow depths of his eyes came a bolt of black lightning—the same terrible weapon he had hurled at the Heart of Pegasus to destroy the star's flames. The lightning shot across the sky, sizzling as it flew, canceling out any starlight in its path.

Seeing the sudden blast, both Ahearna and Tamwyn realized they'd been tricked. The great horse whinnied and flapped her wings so hard that the muscles of her shoulders and back seemed about to burst. She lifted them higher as the bolt of blackness hurtled toward them.

Too late!

The lightning struck her wing, slicing through layers of feather and bone. While the main thrust of the blast missed the companions and exploded into the cliffs of the branch just behind them, sending countless shards of bark into the air, Ahearna's wound was grave.

She reeled in pain, suddenly unable to fly. She whinnied and kicked her hooves, then tossed her head with such force that Tamwyn lost his grip on her mane. Groping wildly with the hand that wasn't holding the staff, he tried to catch hold again, all the while squeezing her with his thighs. Yet it wasn't enough.

He fell off the steed.

Desperately, Tamwyn twisted to grab the flailing horse. But as he turned, his staff knocked against her haunches and flew from his grasp. Like Tamwyn himself, the precious Ohnyalei plummeted downward. So did Ahearna, along with the hoolah still clinging to her back. Henni shouted something—a cry not of words but of genuine anguish.

All of them spun through the air. Tamwyn glimpsed the staff, flashing as it fell toward the dying fires of the Heart of Pegasus. His last view of Ahearna was the sight of her torn wing, backlit by the radiant River of Time. For a brief moment, the wing glowed so brightly that its feathers seemed to have burst into flames.

Out of nowhere, he saw an immense black shadow. Rhita Gawr! The dragon swooped lower, then arched his wings so that he hovered right beneath his prey.

"Oooff," grunted Tamwyn as he crashed onto a hard, shiny surface. *The dragon's snout.*

He sat up, ignoring his bruises, to find himself staring into one of those bottomless eyes he so dreaded. The enormous, lidless eye glared back at him with malice.

"Well, well, my runt wizard, just look where you've landed. And without your staff! Such a pity."

Beneath Tamwyn, the whole snout shook violently, as

Rhita Gawr released a loud, shuddering roar that could only have been a laugh. It was all the young man could do to hold on to the slippery scales so that he didn't slide off the edge. Or into the dragon's terrible eye, just a few paces away.

"I sense how little is your power," sneered the dragon, his leathery wings flapping slowly to keep himself aloft. "Why, you lack even enough magic to light that torch on your back."

Tamwyn winced, knowing it was true.

"You are a sorry excuse for a wizard," the dragon continued, lowering his voice to a thunderous growl. "Yet I am glad you have somehow survived. For it will be a pleasure to kill you here and now."

Deep within the void of the eye, sparks appeared, coalescing quickly. Tamwyn could tell that only a few seconds remained before a bolt of black lightning would destroy him, as well as any hope to save Avalon.

Had he climbed so high, traveled so far, and endured so much—just to die like this? His mind raced through all the possibilities of what he might do. And yet . . . he saw no way to escape. He lacked the magic to fight. He'd even lost the staff, his best weapon.

Wait. That isn't my only weapon.

Even as the lightning flared within the dragon's eye, just about to strike him, Tamwyn jumped to his feet. In the same instant, he tore his dagger from its sheath. The blade—forged by elven metalsmiths ages ago in the land of Lost Fincayra, infused with power that could serve only the true heir of Merlin, and destined for battle against the tyrant Rhita Gawr—shone with starlight, as well as a deeper light of its own.

With a shout that he knew might be his last, Tamwyn lunged. Just before the bolt of black lightning erupted, he plunged his dagger into the very center of the dragon's eye.

24 · A Surprising Turn

"A AAARRRGGHH!" THE BLACK DRAGON'S mighty roar reverberated across the sky. Partly a shout of rage, partly a shriek of pain, the roar was so powerful that it even affected the Heart of Pegasus. The star's dying flames—all that remained of the magical doorway between Avalon and Earth—wavered like a windblown candle.

Even as he bellowed, Rhita Gawr whirled around with the speed of a celestial maelstrom. Bony wings outstretched, giant tail coiled, he spun in tight circles, reeling from Tamwyn's unexpected attack. His enormous claws dug at his wounded eye, trying without success to remove the poisonous blade now lodged there.

Again he roared, this time entirely in wrath. Because of that treacherous human, he had lost the sight in one eye— and something equally precious, the sweet taste of conquest. Right now, he couldn't even feel the thrill of his plans to control Avalon and the worlds beyond. No, he could feel only endless rage at that miserable young wizard.

Tamwyn, however, was already far away. As soon as his

dagger had plunged into the eye, he'd leaped off the dragon's snout and into the open air. Wind tore at him as he fell, plummeting toward the darkening star. He knew that he would soon die, but at least he'd first inflicted a painful blow.

Not enough, though. Not nearly enough.

He cursed at himself as he spun downward. If only he weren't such a lame excuse for a wizard. He could have done so much more than merely stab an eye. He could have flown on his own power! And fought Rhita Gawr to the death! Yes—and in the process, he could have possibly saved everything and everyone he cared about.

At that very instant, the wind surged. So strongly did it whip him that the whole front of his tunic wrenched sharply, pulling away from his body. Then, in an explosion of threads, his pocket ripped completely apart.

That was when Tamwyn realized that what he'd just felt was not the wind. It was not a force that he'd experienced before. It was not, in fact, anything he'd ever imagined.

It was Batty Lad.

And yet it was *not* Batty Lad. For, as Tamwyn watched in utter amazement, the scrawny little creature with crumpled wings and a curious green glow began to change. To grow. To swell to gargantuan size.

In just a few seconds, his wrinkled face expanded into a large head with teeth-studded jaws; his flappers, as flimsy as dead leaves, into broad and powerful wings. The tiny cupped ears grew to Tamwyn's own height. The mouse's feet became muscular legs with savage claws. His neck lengthened, as did his tail, which now culminated in a massive, bony club. And the splotchy fur that had covered his body transformed into gleaming green scales.

Even as he fell, Tamwyn blinked in astonishment. This creature was no longer anything like the bizarre little bat who had fit so easily in his pocket. He was now a dragon, grand and terrible, more than twenty times the size of

Ahearna. The only similarity to his former self was the eerie green glow that burned within his eyes.

The great green dragon beat his wings and swerved in the air, flying beneath his falling companion. Gently, he raised his head, so that Tamwyn landed just beside one of his long pointy ears. The young man slowly stood, grasping the upright ear for support. He noticed with surprise how soft it felt, thanks to thousands of greenish yellow hairs that grew along its sides.

"You're no longer Batty Lad," said Tamwyn, his voice full of awe. He steadied himself beside the dragon's ear. "But are you still a friend?"

A rich, rumbling laughter bubbled out of the dragon's throat. "A friend I shall always be," he declared in a voice that was the absolute opposite of Batty Lad's squeaky chatter. His new voice sounded so deep and resonant that it made Tamwyn think of harp strings that stretched from one end of the sky to the other. "Just as I was to your grandfather."

Tamwyn squeezed the enormous ear in surprise. "You knew Merlin?"

"Knew him?" bellowed the dragon. He tilted his wings, banking gracefully toward the Heart of Pegasus. The wind blew hard, buffeting them both, but Tamwyn had no trouble hearing the dragon's next words. "Your grandfather and I shared many battles, and many adventures, including his journey to relight the stars after the War of Storms."

The young man caught his breath. "I know who you really are! Not Batty Lad, but—"

"Basilgarrad." The name, spoken with the dragon's remarkable resonance, hovered in the air as if it, too, possessed wings. "And I am glad indeed to have regained my true form."

In a flash, Tamwyn understood. "Merlin! He asked you to stay hidden, didn't he? And used his magic to disguise you?"

The dragon nodded his massive head, making Tamwyn hold tight to the ear for balance. "I agreed so the enemies of Avalon would not suspect I still existed. That was why Merlin did not ride me on his final journey to Earth. And why I remained hidden for so many years, until his true heir appeared at last."

Tamwyn stood erect on the soaring dragon. For the first time in his life, he felt sure that the words *true heir* really did mean him. And he also felt sure of what he must do next.

He glanced at the troubled star, now riven with so many cracks of darkness that its light flickered feebly. Then he looked upward, at the whirling clot of wrath that was Rhita Gawr. So boundless was the warlord's rage, and so wholly consuming, he hadn't yet realized that Tamwyn still survived. The young man glared up at him, thinking of the companions that Rhita Gawr had just killed: Ahearna, the gallant steed, and Henni, the irrepressible hoolah, would never be seen again. They were lost, just like the staff of Merlin. Finally, Tamwyn spoke into the ear of the great green dragon who bore him.

"Basilgarrad, you have faced many foes in battle, always guided by your love of Avalon. Will you join me now, in the greatest battle of all?"

The dragon answered with a powerful flap of his wings that made them swoop suddenly upward. His green eyes aglow, he flapped again, surging higher and higher. As they rose, the wind whistled around Tamwyn, blowing his hair and fluttering his torn tunic. With one arm wrapped around the dragon's upright ear, he felt as if he were riding on the prow of a great ship—the ship of his destiny, perhaps, that had carried him at last to the stars.

As they climbed, dark cracks snaked ever faster across the star. The Heart dimmed abruptly, its fires disappearing. In just another moment, Tamwyn knew, the star would go completely dark.

Above them, the immense black dragon that was Rhita Gawr finally stopped whirling in wrathful circles. Only now did he notice something new, something he'd never expected. Another dragon approached, one who bore the very person who had blinded his eye only minutes before. Rhita Gawr trained his remaining eye on his young foe—and also on an ancient foe he'd presumed long dead.

"Baaasilllgarrrrraaad," he roared, loud enough to make the very sky shudder.

"Rrrrrhitaaa Gaaawwrrrrr," answered the great green dragon, with a mighty flap of his wings.

The two gargantuan creatures flew straight at each other. Black sparks flared in the eye of one; green light glowed within the eyes of the other. They were flying fast, so fast that Tamwyn caught his breath, sure they were going to meet in a shattering collision.

At the last possible instant, both dragons veered aside. They passed so close that their wingtips brushed against each other, knocking loose a few scales that drifted down toward the darkening star. Both roared again, then spun around to face each other, perilous claws extended.

Without warning, a bolt of black lightning shot from Rhita Gawr's eye. Basilgarrad reacted with amazing agility, sweeping sideways so quickly that the lightning passed by, lost on empty sky. In the same maneuver, the green dragon swung around and flew just over his enemy, raking his back with those deadly claws.

Rhita Gawr screeched angrily, arching his back. Before Tamwyn's heart took another beat, the warlord of the Otherworld whipped his terrible tail, slicing across Basilgarrad's wing. The green dragon spun aside, his wing only slightly torn. Tamwyn clung tightly to his friend's ear, certain that the whipping tail had missed him by no more than a pace or two.

On and on the dragons fought: sometimes diving, feinting, and dodging; sometimes slamming together with the crash of wings and the scream of claws drawn over scales. In the fading light of the star, the two titans battled. Black lightning exploded time and again in the air, as wrathful roars erupted. Tamwyn did his best to hang on, wishing that he could do more.

Finally the two dragons pulled back, while they continued to fly around each other warily. Although both had been wounded, neither showed anything but fury in their faces. Their wings, despite being torn in places, beat majestically, ready to plunge into battle again instantaneously.

"You are a fool, Basilgarrad," called Rhita Gawr, panting so hard that his nostrils flared with every breath. "You shall lose to me, in time. But you have already lost the larger battle for this world! For my warriors are now fully assembled, ready to destroy whatever feeble opposition they may face down below. On my signal they shall descend into Avalon, and you can do nothing whatsoever to stop them."

"When I stop you, evil one, that will stop them," roared the green dragon in response. His voice rang out boldly, but Tamwyn detected the vaguest hint of uncertainty beneath his words.

"You shall stop neither!" Rhita Gawr whirled around, spinning in a circle with his wide wings outstretched. "Long as you may live, you are still a mere mortal, destined to die, while I am the greatest of all immortals, destined to triumph."

He flapped his wings again, as if to emphasize the word *triumph*. "And to make your death even more bitter, Basilgarrad, I shall tell you something else. Experienced battler that you are, you might actually find some way to harm my warriors or delay them from their mission, if I were not here to stop you myself." He snarled with satisfaction. "But I *am* here, unfortunately for you. Very much here! And soon I shall destroy both you and your wretched little passenger."

Tamwyn turned toward the seven darkened stars of the

Wizard's Staff, far across the sky. Beneath those seven faintly glowing circles whose centers were completely black, a mass of dark shapes gathered. The deathless warriors of Rhita Gawr were, indeed, poised to strike. And even if they could somehow be routed by Basilgarrad, there was no way to do that from here. So there was no way to stop them. Unless . . .

Leaning his face right into Basilgarrad's ear, Tamwyn whispered, "The last thing he'd ever expect would be for us to leave *him*—and charge *them*."

The whole ear stiffened, quivering slightly, as he continued. "We may well die, my friend—so many of those warriors against just you and me. But we may also do them some harm, as Rhita Gawr said! My guess is that, even though they cannot die, their mortal bodies can still be wounded. And by doing that, we could maybe hamper Rhita Gawr's plans." He drew a deep breath. "At least, by fighting them, we might buy some more time for our friends down below. And, if we die defending Avalon, it would be a glorious death. Don't you agree?"

"I agree!" bellowed Basilgarrad.

Instantly, the dragon spun around to face the darkened constellation. He began beating his wings so fast that they soon became a blur of green, lit by the last embers of the Heart of Pegasus. He shot off toward the immortal warriors, leaving a surprised Rhita Gawr. By the time Tamwyn heard, far behind them, a roar of outrage from the black dragon, they had already covered a good distance.

Nearly as fast as starlight they flew, crossing the sky. All around, hundreds of stars gleamed radiantly, suspended from their branches. For a moment, Tamwyn simply watched the passage of those glowing circles, each of them a flaming doorway that could lead to another world. He gazed at them, awed by the vastness of Avalon's reach and the eternal beauty of its stars.

But they're not eternal, he reminded himself grimly.

Every last one of them could go dark if Rhita Gawr prevailed. Perhaps the glittering River of Time itself would also succumb to his powers.

Shifting his stance by the dragon's ear, he glanced behind. Even now, the Heart star glowed only feebly. Very little time remained before it went completely dark. And when that happened, it would be too late to halt the invasion.

As if he'd heard Tamwyn's thoughts, Basilgarrad's mighty wings beat all the faster. Now they were more than halfway to the Wizard's Staff, and the remaining distance shrank rapidly. At last they were close enough to view clearly the warriors of Rhita Gawr. While what they saw wasn't surprising, it was certainly disturbing.

Dragons. Hundreds of dragons.

Tamwyn shook his head at the sight of them, hovering together under the darkened doorways to the Otherworld. Although much smaller than their master, more the size of wyverns, these dark dragons looked terribly vicious, with spiked tails, jaws of jagged teeth, and claws as sharp as rapiers. Their black wings bore serrated edges, so that a slice from one of them could easily rip apart flesh and bone. And judging from all the violent scuffles going on, their personalities seemed well suited for warfare.

Tamwyn stared at the warriors, thinking how much harm they could do down below. *We must stop them somehow! Chase them back through those doorways. And then lock them out of Avalon.*

First, however, Tamwyn knew that he and Basilgarrad must get to the warriors. And soon! Before they received Rhita Gawr's signal to plunge down to the lower realms. And before they—

His thoughts ended abruptly. For he glanced to the rear just in time to see the Heart of Pegasus, once the brightest light in its constellation, wink one final time, then die. Its fires extinguished, the star loomed now as just a blot of blackness—and an open passageway to mortal Earth.

To make matters worse, between Tamwyn and the dark-ened star, another blot of blackness was drawing nearer. Rhita Gawr. The warlord, though still distant, was flying swiftly. And his anger was unmistakable, seeming to jab at Tamwyn's chest with an icy finger.

Shrill cries from the warriors made Tamwyn turn back around. Having seen their long-awaited signal, the dragons ceased their scuffling and faced the lower realms. In uni-son, they flapped their wings and dived. The invasion of Avalon had begun.

And we're too late to stop it! Tamwyn made a fist and, in frustration, swung at the air by Basilgarrad's ear. Now, he felt certain, he had lost everything. His one chance to save his world. His one chance to be more than just a clumsy buffoon—to be the true son of Krystallus, and the true heir of Merlin. And also his one chance to see Elli ever again.

Suddenly he noticed a change in the invading army. They halted their plunge, scattering in different directions like windblown ashes from a campfire. From their throats came shrieks and roars not of conquest, but of confusion.

Flying up from the trunk of the Great Tree, heading straight toward them, was another group of warriors! Tamwyn shook himself, trembling with disbelief. Yet there could be no doubt. The new warriors glowed with orange light, their very wings aflame.

The fire angels had arrived.

25 · Flight of the Fire Angels

LED BY GWIRION HIMSELF, THE AYANOWYN warriors flew swiftly higher. Their winged bodies flamed bright orange, for with their new leadership had come restored purpose and renewed health. No longer men and women who resembled smoldering charcoal, they burned with *llalowyn*—the fire of the soul. Once again they would add to their people's story, just as, once again, they would deserve their name of old.

Fire angels.

Tamwyn, riding on the head of the great green dragon Basilgarrad, felt as if his own heart had burst into flames of gratitude. He leaned forward while holding tight to the dragon's ear, counting the ascending fire angels. There were sixty, maybe seventy of them, less than a third the number of Rhita Gawr's dragons. On top of that, while the dragons were much smaller than Rhita Gawr himself, they were more than twice as large as their foes. Yet it soon became clear that what Gwirion's forces lacked in number and size, they more than gained in courage, speed—and sheer audacity.

The fire angels flew right into the warrior dragons, attacking with all the ferocity of a horde of angry wasps. Ayanowyn fighters swatted the dragons' faces with burning wings, kicked at their lidless eyes, and even surprised them by landing on top of their scaly necks, so that the added weight made it much more difficult for the invaders to steer—or even to fly. All the while, the fire angels dodged spiked tails, serrated wings, and slashing claws. Although they wore no armor, and no clothes beyond ironwool loincloths, the fire angels' agility in the air spared them from serious injury.

Just as Tamwyn neared the fray, he saw one of the flaming people fly between two dragons, scorch their eyes, then veer away so swiftly that the invaders crashed in midair. The dragons shrieked with anger, then started fighting with each other, bashing fiercely with their tails and wings. Meanwhile, the fire angel who had caused the collision flew away unharmed.

"Gwirion!" shouted Tamwyn. Beneath him, Basilgarrad raised his enormous wings to slow their flight.

Seeing his friend, Gwirion swerved and glided over. With a wary look at the great dragon, the fire angel landed on Basilgarrad's head, right beside Tamwyn. For a few seconds they simply gazed at each other in amazement. Finally, Gwirion placed his hands on his hips and spoke.

"By the Thousand Flames, Tamwyn! You have come a long way from the man who nearly died fighting some giant termites."

Tamwyn raised one hand, feeling the heat that radiated from his friend's body. "And you have come a long way from the child who nearly died swallowing some fire coals, hoping to make your soulfire burn brighter."

Gwirion grinned. With one flaming finger, he touched the Golden Wreath upon his hairless head. "I never truly believed it was possible, until you brought this to my door. Just as I never truly believed that the prophecy would come true—that my people would flame again and fly back to the stars."

"And also," added Tamwyn, "that you would meet Dagda himself, who would give your people its true name."

At that, the fire angel turned aside. He glanced at the battle raging all around them and muttered, "That part of the prophecy is merely a hope."

"And hope, you once told me, is a spark that blows on the wind. All it needs is some kindling to burst into flame."

Slowly, a gleam appeared in Gwirion's eyes, brightening like an ember. "You know, Tamwyn, you have your own inner flames, though they cannot be seen. And the most powerful fires reside in the soul."

A pair of dragon warriors shot past Basilgarrad's wing, pursuing a young fire angel. Deftly, the green dragon flicked his clubbed tail. He struck both invaders at once, so hard that they spun downward, completely dazed.

"Gwirion," said Tamwyn urgently, "this is our only chance. We must drive those evil beasts back through the seven darkened doorways." He pointed at the seven pale circles whose flameless centers led to the Otherworld. "Or we all perish."

The fire angel whistled a few low, wandering notes. "Not so different from battling giant termites."

A deafening roar suddenly shook the air. Rhita Gawr arrived, wrath erupting from his uninjured eye in the form of a bolt of black lightning. Basilgarrad banked swiftly, avoiding the blast. But he turned so abruptly that Tamwyn needed to throw both his arms around the dragon's ear just to keep from falling off. Gwirion leaped into the air, wings aflame, to rejoin his forces.

"Fools!" Rhita Gawr bellowed across the skies to his army of smaller dragons. "Have you forgotten you are immortal and cannot die? And have you also forgotten your bond with me, forged through my crystal of unrivaled power? Do not try to think with your own puny brains.

Merely feel my thoughts, and follow my commands, and we shall triumph in all the ways I have foreseen!"

Rhita Gawr swooped through the air, then stopped to hover directly in front of Tamwyn and Basilgarrad. The warlord turned his working eye toward them. Unlike his other eye, which had been coated with gray film, it shone clearly, a bottomless well of blackness. "Meanwhile," he snarled, "I shall rid this world of a runt wizard and his pet dragon."

Enraged, Basilgarrad flapped his huge wings and shot at the warlord. His ears cocked forward, like spears pointing at his enemy's heart. Tamwyn clung to one of the ears with all his strength so he wouldn't fall. While he knew that no one, not even Dagda himself, could kill Rhita Gawr, he also knew that the bold green dragon intended to try.

Just before impact, the immortal warlord dived underneath Basilgarrad. With a vengeful roar, he whipped his massive tail upward. It flew straight at Basilgarrad's head so fast, it could barely be seen.

Yet the ancient dragon's reflexes were still faster. Basilgarrad dipped one wing, rolling on his side, just in time. The deadly tail flew past, grazing the green scales of his neck and the edge of one ear—the ear that anchored Tamwyn.

The blow, though slight, was strong enough to jolt the young man loose. He flew into the air, crashing his back against the bony edge of Basilgarrad's wing. To his surprise, he didn't feel any of his own bones break, since his pack and torch took most of the impact. He did, however, hear a terrible splintering sound from within his pack, which filled him with the sickening certainty that Elli's harp had been crushed.

He hadn't any time to think about this, though, for he bounced away from the wing and spiraled down into the open air. Sensing his opportunity, Rhita Gawr snorted triumphantly and loosed another blast of lightning. Even as he fell, Tamwyn saw the explosion of black sparks as the bolt leaped toward him. There was no chance to dodge, and Basilgarrad was out of reach, unable to help.

Without warning, a flaming body slammed into Tamwyn's side, throwing him clear of the lightning's path. He somersaulted, but still glimpsed the face of the fire angel who had saved him.

"Fraitha!" he cried, recognizing Gwirion's sister. During his days in Gwirion's village, her laughter had often filled the air.

Before she could answer, the lightning bolt sliced off one of her legs and ripped through a wing. She stared at Tamwyn, as silvery brown blood poured from her thigh and the fire faded from her shaggy, barklike skin.

"Prevail, Tamwyn," she said hoarsely. "By the fires of Ogallad . . . prevail."

With that, her soulfire went dark, just as the fires of a great star had gone dark moments before. As lifeless as a burned-out cinder, her body plunged downward to the realms far below.

Tamwyn blinked to clear his vision, even as he also fell. Suddenly he heard a whoosh of air above the wind. An immense claw, brutally sharp, swung toward him and—

Hooked the strap of his pack. Basilgarrad banked sharply as he swung the young man upward again. With a clatter of his torch pole against the dragon's scales, Tamwyn landed once again on his companion's head. Still shaken from what he'd witnessed, he stood and clasped the dragon's long ear.

"Thanks for saving me," he said into the ear. But down inside there were also unspoken words: *I only wish you could have saved her, too.*

He gazed around at the battle on high. And shuddered. Emboldened by their leader's words, the warriors of Rhita Gawr were fighting with new fury. Perhaps it had been the warlord's reminder that they, unlike the fire angels, couldn't die. Or perhaps it was the tactical intelligence that Rhita Gawr was now providing them through his thoughts.

The result, though, was clear. Gwirion's forces were diminishing. One after another, fire angels lost their lives, spinning downward like smoldering coals. Always they died bravely, fighting to the very last. But nonetheless, they died.

Tamwyn, clinging to Basilgarrad's ear, shook his head. *This can't go on! How can we survive much longer?*

As the green dragon whirled through the sky, Tamwyn's hopes fell even further. For two more questions hit him once again, with the force of black lightning. How could they ever drive the invaders back through the doorways to the Otherworld? And how could Tamwyn even hope to close those doors behind them?

26 · The Battle of Isenwy

E VEN AS TAMWYN AND HIS ALLIES STRUG-
gled to survive the battle in the sky, an equally fierce
battle raged far below, on the Plains of Isenwy. And in that
conflict, Brionna's most gruesome fears proved correct:
The eagleman Kerwin, whose courage and sense of honor
were as famous as his ferocity, had been only the first to
die. Right from the moment the parley had collapsed, the
fighting continued—and only intensified. Now, in the late
afternoon light, the brown mud of Malóch shone with
streaks of red.

Across the treeless plains, warriors from both armies
fought with every weapon they could find. Hundreds of armored gobsken, wielding broadswords and pikes, hacked
away at the alliance of elves, dwarves, humans, flamelons,
tree spirits, and giants. Men and women battled each other,
slashing with swords or grappling with daggers in the mud.
Elves from El Urien and Brynchilla shot precisely aimed
arrows from their longbows, while flamelons used their advanced weaponry to hurl flaming balls of tar, launch burning spears, and throw heavy stones. When the flamelons'

catapults ran out of rocks, they started hurling the bodies of dead or wounded gobsken.

One female giant, wearing a heavy net of river rocks over her robe of woven tree roots, fought two ogres at once—even as she squeezed the neck of a four-eyed troll. Bands of squat gnomes ran just behind the gobsken, wielding their ceramic spears with deadly accuracy. The gnomes shrieked wildly, stabbing at every foe they encountered. And, when their spears broke, these ferocious fighters simply leaped onto their enemies' backs, biting off their ears and throttling them with grimy, three-fingered hands.

Elsewhere on the field now strewn with bodies, a brawny tree spirit swung his oaken arms at a pair of shrieking ghoulacas. While the nearly transparent birds tried to shred his bark and gouge his eyes with their bloodred talons, he bashed at them ruthlessly, swaying like a sapling in a storm.

Nearby, a dense cloud of blue-winged mist faeries flew into the face of a troll, making him stumble and drop his club. Even as he fell, though, he swatted at the faeries, killing many of them. He then knocked a woman off a horse and crushed her underfoot. At last, a trio of elven archers stepped in. They needed to shoot more than a score of arrows into the troll before he finally died.

Standing together on a small rise, a group of mud-splattered men and women strove desperately to hold off a band of gobsken and gnomes. Although Kulwych's forces outnumbered them threefold, the people still held their ground. They were led by Lleu, along with another Drumadian priest, a red-haired man who wielded a saber skillfully, despite his badly wounded leg. His maryth, a sable-eyed doe, also fought bravely, kicking her hooves into the gobsken warriors' breastplates with such force that their armor often cracked—along with their ribs. Meanwhile, Lleu's own maryth, Catha, sailed above the fray until she chose her targets. Then, time and again, the hawk plunged down with an earsplitting screech and scratched out the eyes of surprised soldiers.

When Catha attacked a helmeted gnome, however, the situation changed. She dived, but just before she could strike, the gnome thrust his weapon upward, impaling her. Lleu heard her agonized screech and fought desperately to reach her, slashing with the broadsword he'd taken from a fallen gobsken. While he battled, he silently recited every prayer he knew, begging Dagda and Lorilanda to help keep the silver-winged hawk alive.

Above the battlefield, more fighting raged. Eaglefolk swooped through the air, chasing down the murderous ghoulacas, forcing them into talon-to-talon combat. As the ghoulacas' frenzied shrieks rent the air, echoing across the Plains of Isenwy, so did the cries of the feathered men and women. Although they were outnumbered, and unable to see their foes clearly, the eaglefolk fought with such terrible ferocity that the ghoulacas soon learned to avoid them as much as possible.

Yet among the eaglefolk, the ghoulacas feared most of all the warriors of one particular clan. Marked by brown tailfeathers, black stripes across their wings, and flashing brown eyes, these warriors fought with a fury that knew no bounds. And that was understandable, for they belonged to the Tierrnawyn clan of upper Olanabram—the clan of Kerwin.

Despite their inferior numbers, the defenders of Avalon were, in many places, holding their own against the forces of Kulwych and Belamir. Or even defeating them. They were helped by the fact that Belamir himself was forced to remain disguised as a gentle gardener. For he could not reveal that he was really a changeling without losing his multitudes of human followers. Just the word *changeling* alone made people speak in whispers; the sight of one would produce outright terror and hostility.

Most of all, however, the allies of Avalon were helped by their deep love of their world, its sacred qualities and wondrous places. That devotion gave them all—elves and eaglefolk, men and women, dwarves and giants—a distinct advantage. Call it the power of inspiration, or of love itself, that advantage provided the strength they needed to survive. And, perhaps, to prevail.

But that was not enough. Because of one man, and one weapon, the allies of Avalon were destined to lose.

Harlech swaggered through the melee on the battlefield, a wide grin on his broad slab of a face. Although he wielded a broadsword in one hand and a hatchet in the other, those were not his weapons of choice. His preferred tool of attack was the claw that hung from his neck, a claw that glowed eerily until it suddenly shot out a beam of red light. Anything struck by that beam instantly burst into flames—then utterly disappeared.

Only because the claw required a few moments to regain its power after a deadly blast, drawing more strength from the faraway crystal in Kulwych's cavern, did Harlech need to carry any other weapons at all. Yet he made the most of the claw whenever he could, systematically killing the other side's mightiest warriors. One giant, the black-bearded leader of the dwarves, and some of the elves' best marksmen, all fell to his attacks. Harlech even managed to disable one of the flamelons' catapults, destroying the beam that held its throwing arm to its base.

Virtually unchallenged, Harlech strode through the crowds, pausing now and then to slash people with his sword or bark commands to the gobsken. Even as he scanned the brutal conflict for his claw's next victim, he frequently checked the sky for that eagleman who had humiliated him in the battle atop Kulwych's dam. Now *that* was a target worth finding, he told himself. Severing that eagleman's head from his body would be a true delight.

Just then Harlech saw, standing on a mound of mud, an

elf maiden with a long braid. Brionna. All alone she fought, surrounded by the corpses of gobsken who had fallen to her arrows. Right now, she was firing into the multitudes of angry gobsken trying to reach her.

"Perfect," growled Harlech, his malicious grin expanding. "Since I don't see the eagleman nowhere, that she-elf will do jest fine. She has messed wid me plans fer too long now."

Sweeping his broadsword, he strode toward her. The edges of his eyes gleamed with the same color as the claw that dangled around his neck.

Brionna, meanwhile, was too busy fighting for her life to notice. And too full of grief to care. She had lost so much in a terribly short time. And then, on this field of battle, she had lost one thing more.

Only moments before, a gobsken warrior had savagely cut down her childhood friend Aileen. Before Brionna could do anything to stop it, Aileen—who loved nothing more than brewing a simple cup of hazelnut tea—lost her arm and then her head to the gobsken's ax. At that instant, something inside Brionna snapped. She grabbed Aileen's bow and quiver and then fired the arrows, every single one, into the gobsken. Long after he had died, and fallen on his face in the mud, she continued firing, pouring arrows into his lifeless body.

She felt sickened by her brutal behavior, so unlike an elf of El Urien. And even more sickened by the fact that she felt no regret whatsoever for what she'd done. Worst of all, she wanted to kill more of those gobsken, as many as she could. And she would keep right on doing that until, at last, she herself was killed.

Scurrying across the battlefield, she snatched up a whole armload of quivers from fallen elves. Then, having climbed atop a muddy mound, she started shooting arrows into gobsken. Like a machine, she fired, nocked a new arrow, and fired again. Not even pausing to watch each one die, she had soon killed so many gobsken that the ground all around her was piled high with bodies.

More gobsken came at her, from every side. They were so enraged that they charged headlong, stumbling over the corpses, shouting vengeful war cries as they brandished their blades. Yet Brionna held her position, turning slowly on the mound, firing relentlessly.

More gobsken died. And more. Some of them came so close before they collapsed that Brionna could hear their raspy breaths or smell the sweat on their gray-green skin. Now dozens lay dead at her feet. Glancing down at all the bodies, she realized that, because of her efforts, the lives of many elves and Drumadians might yet be spared.

But that won't make up, she added somberly, *for the lives that have already been lost.*

Finally, she was down to her last quiver. And then, a moment later, her very last arrow. She nocked it, aimed at the nearest gobsken, and fired. He toppled over. But several more warriors were charging, ready to strike her down.

Brionna held her head high, knowing that her time to die had arrived. *I may be just a killer,* she told herself grimly, *and not worthy of elfhood. But at least I'll die defending Avalon, and I guess there's some honor in that.*

The barest hint of amusement shone in her deep green eyes. *Scree would agree.*

That was when she spied Harlech, pushing his way through the fray. She saw the red glow of his claw and the smirk on his face—and realized that he was just about to kill her. His weapon of sorcery would do its work before any of the gobsken's blades could reach her.

"No!" she cried, grasping her empty quiver. "Not like this!"

27 · Strange Sensations

JUST AS A DEADLY BOLT OF LIGHT SHOT FROM Harlech's claw, sturdy talons grabbed Brionna's robe at the shoulders. She was jerked upward and carried aloft, even as the red beam exploded on a pair of gobsken who had been charging at her from behind. The warriors instantly burst into flames, then vanished but for their weapons that fell to the muddy ground.

Shocked as well as grateful, Brionna turned skyward. The face she saw, above the talons and powerful wings that bore her, was the last face she expected to see.

"Scree! It's you."

"You look surprised," he said dryly, pumping his wings as he carried her away from Harlech. Gently, he shifted his talons so that they would pierce only her bark cloth robe and not the skin of her shoulders.

Still trying to comprehend everything that had just happened, she blinked at him and mumbled, "I had shot my last arrow . . ."

"A good thing, too! If you still had any left, you might

have greeted me the way you did the first time we met—and shot me out of the sky."

The elf maiden didn't laugh. Instead, waves of grimness washed over her face. "Scree, I've done some terrible things."

His large, yellow-rimmed eyes glanced down at her. Finally, he spoke, his voice so quiet that it was barely audible over the din of battle beneath them. "So have I, Brionna. So have I."

Their eyes met. For the span of several wingbeats, they spoke only through that shared gaze—a gaze that held all the grief, shame, and loss they had experienced in the recent past. Yet it held, as well, something else: a fragile hope, as slim as a feather, for the future.

Reversing his wing strokes to land softly, Scree set her down by a shallow brown stream, some distance away from the fighting. Even so, as he released his talons from her robe and landed next to her, a ceramic spear splattered on the mud of the stream bank. Scree spun around and glared so wrathfully at the gnome who had thrown it that the squat little warrior turned and fled.

The eagleman turned back to Brionna. "You should—" He caught himself, then started again with a less argumentative tone. "You might consider . . . staying out of the battle now. You've done your share, and more."

She looked at him uncertainly. "What about you?"

Scree dragged his talons through the muddy ground. "Me, I'm going back in there. I have a meeting—with that worm who attacked you. He got away from me once, back at the dam, but it won't happen again." His eagle eyes narrowed. "What can you tell me about that evil bolt of light he shot at you?"

"It came from a claw, born of his master's sorcery." She shuddered at the memory. "Harlech wears it around his neck." She grabbed Scree's feathered shoulder. "And something important! The claw needs some time to re-gain its power. How much time, I don't know. But it gives you—"

"A chance," he finished. "That's all I need." With the feathers of his wing, he brushed her cheek. "Keep safe, now. Please."

Her elven eyes sparkled. "Only if you will."

He nodded. "I'll do my best." Stepping back, he leaped into the air with a mighty downstroke of his wings. As he rose, he released the piercing cry of his people, a cry part eagle, part human, and thoroughly terrifying.

Brionna watched him go, fingering her braid thoughtfully. For the first time in this long afternoon, she felt, to her con-siderable surprise, glad to be alive. Then, viewing the melee on the plains, her expression turned grim. She started walk-ing back toward the fighting, her feet squelching in the mud. Her eyes scanned the terrain, searching for another quiver of arrows. For she, like Scree, had more work left to do.

It took just a few seconds for Scree, flying over the battle-field, to spot Harlech. The burly man stood right where he'd been, near the pile of dead gobsken, whose tangled bodies formed a gruesome burial mound. Harlech was cursing an-grily, swinging his broadsword through the air. *No doubt he's upset at having missed his target,* the eagleman thought as he sailed closer. *Guess I should offer him another one.*

Before swooping down, he scanned the area, looking for the other eaglefolk who had come here with him from Fire-root. To his satisfaction, he saw many Bram Kaie warriors already engaged in battle, aggressively hunting ghoulacas. Led by Cuttayka, the burly captain of the Clan Sentries, they tore into the packs of ghoulacas, slashing with talons and beaks. Their black-tipped wings gleamed like shards of obsidian in the sky. Even young Hawkeen, the golden-eyed lad who had traveled so far to stay at Scree's side, fought viciously, doing more than his share to terrorize Kulwych's killer birds.

Scree smiled slightly, for he could tell that Hawkeen would become, in time, a warrior to be greatly feared. Perhaps he, like Scree, would someday lead his people into battle. And perhaps he, too, would discover that, even amidst life's broken wings of sorrow, there might yet be a single feather of surpassing beauty.

Something else pleased Scree, as well. The Bram Kaie had rejoined the flocks of their fellow eaglefolk. It would take quite some time, no doubt, to regain the respect—let alone the trust—of other clans. But the fact that Bram Kaie warriors were here, fighting alongside the rest of their people, was at least a beginning.

He plunged down to the muddy plains, landing right behind Harlech. Hearing the rustle of wings, the hulking man whirled around. The claw, glinting only slightly, slapped against his chest.

"So," Harlech sneered, "ye finally decided to show yer gutless self, did ye?"

"Sure," answered Scree. "You were just so much fun to play with last time, I couldn't resist."

The man growled, raising his sword and hatchet. "C'mere an' fight, then. Or are ye too afraid?"

Scree circled slowly, keeping his wings open just enough to fly at an instant's notice. The feathers shimmered, bristling as he moved; the veins in his chest and thighs pulsed with power. His talons, as sharp as dagger-points, carved furrows in the muddy ground. Should he attack now, he wondered, hoping that the claw hadn't yet regained its deadly power? Or should he wait until he dodged the next blast, before rushing in for the kill?

Suddenly Harlech tripped on a fallen gobsken, stumbling so badly that he nearly dropped his weapons. Sensing his opportunity, Scree abruptly made his decision. With a whoosh of wings, he leaped into the air and launched himself at his foe, talons extended.

A trick! Harlech, having faked his fall to lure Scree

closer, swung around and hurled his hatchet at the eagleman's head. Scree ducked, barely avoiding the blow. But in that same instant Harlech lunged, slashing his broadsword with terrible ferocity.

Scree jumped backward, flapping his wings to rise out of reach—but not before Harlech's blade sliced his lower leg. Blood ran down the feathers, turning his talons red.

"First blood fer me, wingboy."

Scree hovered above the warrior's head. His eyes gleamed angrily. "Next blood for me, you worm."

Heedless of the risk from Harlech's claw, Scree released a screeching cry and fell on his enemy. Feinting with his uninjured talon, he slammed the bony edge of his wing into Harlech's head. The big man reeled, but somehow kept his balance. He planted his boots on the mud, ignoring the bleeding gash on his temple.

While their battle continued, another warrior was wandering not far away. Despite his best efforts, Shim felt quite useless, unable to assist his army. He was simply too small—or, to use his word, shrunkelled—to assist anyone; too slow, with his lumbering waddle, to chase anyone; and too deaf, with his old ears, to hear anyone. So he wandered the battlefield aimlessly, searching for some way to be helpful.

At last, he found it. There, just beyond the body of a dead fire ox, a giant sat crumpled on the ground. The immense creature was being mauled by no fewer than six ghoulacas, who were trying viciously to peck out their enemy's eyes. Only the size of the giant's hands, wrapped tightly around his or her face, was keeping the attackers from success. But those hands, by now severely shredded by the ghoulaca's talons, wouldn't last much longer. The victim then did something exceedingly rare for any giant: He or she whimpered painfully, trembling under the assault.

Shim stared, aghast. Although he had often been shunned by other giants since being cursed to shrink down to a dwarf's size, that cry of pain from one of his own people brought back all his old loyalties. A frenzy of wrath overwhelmed him. Waving his little arms, he charged forward, shouting, "Away with you, beastly birds! Neverly harm another giant, or Shim will plucker every one of your unsightly feathers! Certainly, I—"

He tripped on one of the fire ox's horns and fell with a splat on the ground. At that same instant, a band of eaglefolk led by Cuttayka swooped down on the ghoulacas, chasing them away. By the time Shim raised his muddy face, all that remained of the killer birds were their frightened shrieks echoing in the distance.

"Hah," chuckled Shim, wiping a glob of mud from his eye. "Guess I'm still a bit giantly yet."

Slowly, the enormous giant he'd saved lowered those bloodied hands and gazed at him with limitless gratitude. It was the sort of look that only a true hero deserves.

Shim, however, stepped backward. His eyes widened with terror; his entire body, right down to the tip of his swollen nose, trembled. For he recognized this giant just as if she had stepped out of his worst nightmare. It was none other than Bonlog Mountain-Mouth—the very giant who had cursed him centuries ago!

He turned to run, waddling as fast as he possibly could. But it wasn't fast enough. Bonlog Mountain-Mouth grabbed him between her thumb and forefinger. She lifted him, legs still churning, into the air, until he was suspended right above her huge, drooling mouth.

Shim nearly passed out. That was the very mouth whose gargantuan, saliva-drenched lips had tried to kiss him at the Battle of the Withered Spring. Even though, in that ancient battle, he had accidentally saved her life, as soon as she tried to thank him with a kiss, he had fled into the mountains. To punish Shim for this humiliation, she had cursed him to lose his giant size. And still not satisfied, she had hunted Shim for many years afterward. The wrath of a spurned giantess knows no bounds.

Now, Shim knew, she would finally have her revenge. "Please, mistress Mountain-Mouth," he begged, "have some mercifully on this poor shrunkelled fellow."

She ignored his pleas. As rivers of spit gushed from her cavernous mouth, she brought him closer. He closed his eyes, certain now that she was going to eat him.

Instead, she puckered her enormous lips and did something that seemed, to Shim, even worse. She kissed him! Her lips smacked so loud that he thought the whole world had exploded.

To his astonishment, it had not. Nor had Bonlog Mountain-Mouth any more punishments in mind, although that one had been horrible enough. She dropped him back on the muddy ground, then stood to depart. Even though it was hard for Shim to see through the mound of sticky saliva that oozed down his face, he thought that, perhaps, she gave him a wink.

As she stomped off, shaking the plains with her weight, Shim felt a strange sensation. All the cries and shouts and clangs of the surrounding battle abruptly halted, making him wonder whether the noise of her kiss had destroyed what little hearing he had left. At the same time, though, he felt a warm breeze, laden with the scent of honey. It stirred his scraggly white hair, even as it entered his body, stirring ancient memories in his bones.

Miraculously, his nose started to swell even larger. His hands, too, grew in size, as did his feet. All across his body, skin expanded. His woolen vest, which for so long had billowed around his chest from being too large, grew tight—and then started to rip into shreds.

Shim, incredulous, rubbed his eyes with his swelling hands. "I is getting big," he cried. "As big as the bigliest tree!"

28 · A Faraway Aroma

ACROSS THE BATTLEFIELD FROM THE AS-tonished Shim, a tall priest fought bravely. He also fought alone, except for the badly wounded falcon who lay cradled in his arm.

Lleu slashed brutally at a line of gobsken warriors. He spun and dodged with agility surprising for someone not trained in swordsmanship, holding the injured Catha in one arm and his broadsword in the other. Several gobsken who confronted him found themselves sliced or skewered. Others, surprised by his ferocity, simply backed away, certain that one lone priest couldn't get very far in their ranks.

Lleu, however, never intended to advance very far. He had only one goal—beyond hoping that Catha might some-how survive, which he knew would take more help than mere mortals could provide. That goal was to break through the line of gobsken to the solitary person standing behind them, a person he meant to challenge.

Belamir. Although he wore the soiled garb of a gar-dener, and carried no weapons beyond spades and shears, the expression on his face didn't fit the image of a thoughtful man of the soil. His eyes spoke of hatred, both for the fools who followed him and the greater fools who dared oppose him. Coldly, he watched the slaughter of the women and men of his village, toying impatiently with his necklace of garlic bulbs.

He was eager for this battle to end. Only then, as Kulwych had instructed, could he reveal his true identity: Neh Gawthrech, feared even among his fellow changelings. And only then could he have the satisfaction of destroying anyone still alive who might pose a threat to the sorcerer's absolute rule. Or to his own role as Kulwych's chief aide. That included Harlech, whose puny brain could fit inside an acorn, and Morrigon, whose simpleminded brutality had been useful to Belamir's Humanity First movement, but who would almost certainly resist serving under a changeling.

He rubbed his chin, using his hand with the broken thumbnail. As he watched the course of the battle, another look slowly came into his eyes. A look of satisfaction. His time had almost arrived. Although the fighting had already lasted beyond what he had anticipated, it wouldn't last much longer, thanks to Harlech's claw—a poor substitute for a changeling, but still reasonably effective.

Suddenly, from the corner of his eye, he saw the glint of a blade. He spun around, so swiftly his feet kicked up flecks of mud. Placing his hands on his hips, he faced Lleu, who now stood only a few paces away. The man's thick eyebrows arched severely, while blood stained his torn robe; he looked much more like a warrior than a priest.

Even so, Belamir shrugged calmly. "I suppose you have the temerity to think you can kill me."

"Yes, I do, by the light of Dagda." Lleu advanced, pointing his broadsword straight at his foe. "Because I know what you really are. And how fast you can move."

"Do you, now? But do you know that, when you saw me

tear out the heart of that guard, I was moving quite slowly, just to savor the experience?"

Lleu kept advancing.

The changeling's gaze flitted across the mayhem of battle. No one was looking his way, so he could safely dispose of this foolish priest. And if there happened to be any witnesses . . . why, it would take just another instant to destroy them, too. Besides, the whole conflict was now almost over, so there was nothing to lose.

Just as Lleu took another step toward him, Neh Gawthrech instantly changed forms. Fangs, curved like the blades of scythes, suddenly appeared on the now-triangular head, along with scarlet eyes that flamed with wrath. Deadly claws sprouted from long, scaly arms. Muscular legs flexed, down to the clawed toes, ready to rip apart their victim. The changeling pounced, leaping right over Lleu's sword, and then—

Crashed to the muddy ground, an arrow buried deep in his chest. The changeling writhed, clawed at the air, then fell completely still.

Lleu was so surprised that he could only stare in disbelief at the motionless body. Finally, he looked up. The archer whose arrow had saved him was just emerging from behind a muddy boulder. Lleu took a sharp breath, for the sight was almost as much of a shock as what had just occurred.

"Morrigon," he said in amazement. "You—"

"Saved yer life, I know." The old man stared at the ground as he stepped closer, examining the scaly, reptilian form of the beast he had unwittingly served for so many years. He ran his hand through the white hair above one ear, his expression a mixture of outrage, confusion, and disgust.

At last, he turned his bloodshot eye toward the priest. "Don't get the wrong idea, now," he snarled. "The ideas he spoke about, the rules he taught us—all that was right an' true."

Lleu glanced down at the bloodied body of Catha, whose eyes were just barely open. "As true as the form of a changeling."

"Don't get smirky, priest! I shot him, yes, but I was jest about to loose me arrow at *you*. Then he changed—I saw him meself—an', well . . . I switched me target." His voice dropped lower. "But don't fool yerself. I don't like ye any better than I did afore."

Turning back to the corpse, Morrigon kicked the changeling's clawed hand. "How could ye do that?" he railed bitterly. "To all o' us who believed."

"Morrigon," said Lleu gently, lowering his sword. "I know this is hard for you. But will you help me now? Will you bring others over here to see the real Belamir, so we can finally stop this war?"

Slowly, the old man lifted his face, distorted by feelings he couldn't begin to describe. "No," he declared. "Belamir, mayhaps, was false. But not his cause."

The lanky priest peered at him sternly. "Are you sure?"

Morrigon averted his eyes. For an instant he seemed to waver. Then, abruptly, he reached for another arrow, nocked it, and aimed at Lleu. "Now, get yerself out o' me sight! Afore I do what I should've done last time."

Before Lleu could answer, a gobsken warrior leaped at him. Still clutching the falcon, Lleu slashed with his sword. Once again, he was fighting for his life.

Morrigon made no effort to help him. In fact, he didn't even bother to watch. For he was staring, once again, at the contorted body of the changeling at his feet.

Not many paces away, someone else who wore a Drumadian robe was fighting for her life. Llynia jumped backward, desperately trying to escape the fire ox eager to impale her on his horns. The ox's nostrils flared as he charged again. Once more, she spun away—but her foot slipped in the mud.

She reeled and crumpled to the ground. Now she was

helpless! The ox lowered his fearsome head for the kill. Starlight glinted on his horns, as red as her own blood.

Just then, at the edge of her vision, she spied a band of gnomes, her allies, raising their spears to attack the vicious beast. But she knew they were too late. Even if their spears struck down the ox, he would have already killed her.

With an angry bellow, the ox lunged forward. His horrible horns shot straight at Llynia. She shut her eyes, too frightened even to utter a final prayer as she died.

But she didn't die. She heard the gnomes' spears pierce the beast's hide; she heard his roar of pain and the thud of his body hitting the ground. Why, though, hadn't she felt his horns plunging into her chest?

She opened her eyes. The sight that greeted her was almost as terrible as the prospect of her own death. For she suddenly realized that someone had thrown herself onto the ox's horns to take the impact, trading Llynia's life for her own.

Fairlyn.

Llynia crawled to the side of the lilac elm, this gentle creature who had taken a maryth's vow of loyalty to her years ago—and had stayed true to that vow until Llynia herself broke their compact by leaving the Society of the Whole. Seeing the horns anchored deep into Fairlyn's trunk, just below her large brown eyes that now stared lifelessly at the sky, Llynia winced painfully. She knew that Fairlyn, like all tree spirits, could live on indefinitely after her host tree had died. Yet she also knew that a tree spirit could still perish, either from grief or from wounds received in battle.

And now, thought Llynia, *you are dying from both.*

Blinking back her tears, she gazed at Fairlyn, whose branches had snapped and whose trunk had split wide open with the force of the blow. Most of the purple buds that dotted Fairlyn's boughs were covered in mud. And, as a sure sign that her life had ended, she emitted no smells at all. The only aroma that surrounded her now was the stench of death.

Llynia, once so proud that she believed the Lady of the Lake would never want to see anyone but her, lowered her head onto Fairlyn's torn trunk. And sobbed.

Suddenly she felt a soft tapping against her back. She sat up, just as the lone branch that had touched her so tenderly fell away. She swallowed, unsure whether it had been just a gust of wind . . . or something more.

Then, so subtly she could not be certain it was real, she smelled the faraway aroma of lilac blossoms.

29 · To Do What Mortals Must

THE BATTLE UPON THE PLAINS OF ISENWY raged on. Mud and blood, in equal proportions, splattered faces, clothing, and weaponry.

Rumors swirled like whirlwinds across the battlefield. Some of them claimed that the warrior Harlech carried a whole slew of terrible, invincible weapons. Others predicted dire events—that the stench of corpses would attract more flesh-eating ghoulacas to the battle, or that the flamelons would soon betray their allies and join with the gobsken. But most of the rumors involved the superior forces that were expected to come soon to the gobsken's aid. While some people guessed that those forces would be another army of gobsken or a company of trolls, most people believed that the new forces would be even more powerful—and even more devastating.

A dragon, perhaps. Or a group of dragons, whose leader would bear the sorcerer Kulwych. Or, worst of all, the spirit warlord Rhita Gawr.

No one, it seemed, knew the truth. But the expectation of such an arrival felt just as tangible as Malóch's muddy terrain. As a result, both sides battled still harder: the soldiers of Kulwych, out of growing hope; the allies of Avalon, out of mounting dread.

All the while, individuals fought and died, cursed and prayed. At the same moment that Lleu slashed away with his sword, and Llynia wept over the body of her friend, another person nearby fought valiantly—but with an unusual weapon.

A lute.

The old bard, surrounded by gnomes, swung at them awkwardly with his musical instrument. All the while, he tried (with mixed results) not to trip over his own cloak. As his lute swept through the air, nearly brushing the gnomes' spear tips, it trembled with deep, whooshing notes.

Whether because they were simply amused, or because they just weren't sure what to make of this bizarre warrior with the lopsided hat and the beard that grew sideways, the gnomes didn't immediately hurl their spears. Instead, they merely watched. They grunted among themselves, keeping just out of reach of the swinging lute.

Finally, one of the gnomes climbed on top of a mud-covered boulder and called out some harsh, guttural commands. Slightly taller than the others, he wore jagged stripes of blue body paint on his chest and arms. On his three-fingered hands, red ceramic rings gleamed in the starlight. Hearing him shout, the rest of the gnomes ceased talking, planted their feet, and lifted their spears higher.

The warriors were just about to hurl their weapons at the bard, ending his songs forever, when an arrow whizzed through the air. It struck one of the gnomes, who lurched backward and splatted on the mud. An instant later, another arrow flew. This one caught a gnome in the thigh, making him crumple in pain.

In the confusion that followed, Brionna sprinted over to the bard, her loose elven robe fluttering as she ran. "Come!" she cried, tugging on his sleeve. "Hurry, old man."

His wrinkled face shone with gratitude. Grasping his lute firmly, he started to follow her.

Too slowly. The gnomes' leader stamped his foot on the boulder and barked some new commands. Quickly, his band of warriors regrouped. They surrounded the elf and the bard, grunting irately among themselves. In unison, they hefted their spears, ready to throw.

Brionna didn't need to glance around to know that they couldn't escape. Too many spears were aimed at them. Even if she was able to get off one final shot at the leader, both she and the bard would surely die.

Gravely, she turned to the elder. What she saw in his dark eyes, though, surprised her. There was none of the despair that she herself was feeling. Rather, the bard looked at her with an expression that seemed inexplicably peaceful.

At that instant, the gnomes' leader released a loud shout. It was not a command—but a shout of rage. For the mud-covered boulder beneath him had suddenly started to swell, expanding on all sides.

Though he waved his arms wildly to keep his balance, the blue-painted gnome fell over backward. He hit the ground with a spray of mud. Two gnomes rushed over to drag him away from the spot, while another dropped his spear and ran, disappearing into the surrounding fray.

Meanwhile, the boulder continued to grow, its surface bubbling like brown lava. Slowly it lengthened, growing taller and taller. At last, when it stood nearly twice the height of Brionna and the bard, it sprouted four slender arms, each with three delicate fingers as long as one of the arrows in Brionna's quiver. Then a rounded head appeared atop its sloping shoulders. Deep-set eyes, as brown as the rest of its body, peered down at everyone.

The elf could only stare back in utter amazement. She knew, from her grandfather's tales, that she was looking at a mudmaker—one of the most elusive creatures in all of Avalon. And also one of the most magical. According to

lore, these strange beings had been given a wondrous power
by the wizard Merlin himself: the power to Make, to form
new creatures out of the mud of Malóch. Creatures as beautiful as the caitlinott bird, whose every feather shone with all
the colors of the rainbow, or as immense as the elephaunt,
whose enormous bodies broke the first trails through the jungles of Africqua, had been crafted by the mudmakers.

The tall brown figure raised her many arms. "Flee,
gnomes!" she commanded. "Or feel you shall the wrath of
Aelonnia of Isenwy."

With a round of guttural shrieks, most of the gnomes
scurried off. Only the leader remained, a scowl carved on
his face. Shakily, he raised his spear. But when Aelonnia
raised one of her flat feet, squelching noisily, and took a
step in his direction, he released a terrified whimper and
fled into the battlefield.

The mudmaker swayed, then turned to the young elf
and the old bard. For a moment she studied Brionna, then
said in a resonant whisper: "A child of Tressimir you are, I
perceive."

The elf maiden swallowed. Nervously, she bowed, feeling the pinch of the scar across her back. "His granddaughter. My name is Brionna."

Aelonnia's round head bobbed slightly. "So it is. Your
name means *strength* in the ancient tongue of Lost Fincayra. And feel sure, I do, that you have needed all your
strength in recent weeks."

Brionna trembled, but managed a nod.

The mudmaker's deep eyes turned to the bard. As she
peered at him, her long fingers moved thoughtfully, as if
they were strumming an invisible lute. "And you," she observed, "a most unusual warrior do seem."

"Olewyn the bard, at your service." He grasped the brim
of his hat, whose crown curled like the petals of a spin-
flower, another of the mudmakers' creations. Then, with a
flourish, he bowed.

Rising again, he declared, "It is an honor to see you, Aelonnia of Isenwy. As it is to visit Malóch, even at this time of terrible conflict."

His hand stroked his silvery beard, which shimmered in the starlight. "For despite all the bloodletting around us, Malóch remains the true soil of Merlin's magical seed, still blessed with the seven sacred Elements of Avalon:

> *"Earth, mud of birth;*
> *Air, free to breathe;*
> *Fire, spark of light;*
> *Water, sap to grow;*
> *Life, fruit of soul;*
> *LightDark, stars and space;*
> *Mystery, now and always."*

Aelonnia drew a deep, slow breath, as if she were inhaling the power of those words. "All the gifts of Dagda and Lorilanda, they are."

Brionna, though, furrowed her brow. With a discouraged wave at the battle raging all around them, she asked, "Where are Dagda and Lorilanda now, when we most need them?"

"Doing what they must, they are." The mudmaker's delicate fingers stirred, weaving mysterious designs in the air. "Just as we mortals ourselves are obliged to do."

Even as Aelonnia's rich whisper filled Brionna's mind, pushing aside briefly the din of battle, the elf maiden thought of another mortal who was doing what he must. *Scree,* she called silently, *I wish I knew where to find you in all this mess! Are you still fighting Harlech? And still alive?*

The answer to both questions, as it happened, was yes.

"C'mere, ye wretched liddle bird," snarled Harlech, panting. His boots clomped heavily on the mud as he circled his enemy.

Scree glared at the big man who stood opposite him. The deadly claw, while shining more brightly by the second, did not yet glow with the same intensity as it had just before it had shot that evil beam at Brionna. Scree guessed that he still had some time before Harlech could use the claw against him. Yet he had no idea how much time.

He gave his wings a shake, trying to rid them of exhaustion. "This battle has gone on long enough," he growled.

"Aye, it has." Harlech wiped the mud off his broadsword by scraping it on the breastplate of a gobsken who lay moaning on the ground. Slowly, he kept circling, watching for an opening. "So c'mere, an' I'll end it."

Abruptly, Scree stepped to the left, causing Harlech to shift his weight. Then, quick as a wingbeat, Scree moved back to the right again, throwing Harlech off balance for just an instant—long enough for the eagleman to spin around, one leg extended. A talon ripped across Harlech's forearm, making him shout and drop his sword. He stumbled, trying to retrieve his weapon.

Wasting no time, Scree flapped his broad wings and leaped onto his foe, just as an eagle would pounce on a rat. Yet despite his injured arm, Harlech recovered with surprising speed. Even as the eagleman's shadow fell over him, he whipped a dagger from his belt and thrust the blade upward.

Scree screeched and reeled backward. He fell hard, as blood poured down his wing, soaking his silver feathers. The soggy soil clung to him, making it hard for him to rise. No sooner had he finally sat up than he found himself staring right at the tip of Harlech's sword.

Scree clacked his jaw, beaklike. Trapped! He couldn't even stand, let alone run or fly.

To his surprise, Harlech slowly lowered the weapon. Scree started to push himself to his feet, ignoring the pain that coursed through his wing. Then he saw Harlech's malicious grin. And he saw something else, even more disturbing.

Hanging under Harlech's chin, the claw now glowed an intense shade of red. Scree knew what that meant, just as he knew that a torn wing was the least of his troubles.

30 · Final Seconds

FOR TAMWYN, THE CONFLICT IN THE SKY rapidly worsened. As he watched many of the brave fire angels perish, his remaining hopes dimmed, until they were almost as dark as the seven stars of the Wizard's Staff. Those stars, now open passageways to the Otherworld, gaped above the aerial battle like so many open wounds.

Tamwyn suffered all the more because he could hear, in his own mind, the tactical commands that Rhita Gawr kept sending to his force of immortal dragons. Unlike the dragons, who heard those commands because of the sorcery that bound them to their master, Tamwyn heard through his own innate power. But that made no difference in the end. Whenever Tamwyn caught one of Rhita Gawr's commands, he pulled with all his strength on Basilgarrad's long ear, steering the great green dragon toward the place where fire angels needed help. Yet time and time again, they arrived too late.

"No!" cried Tamwyn, as he realized that a horde of black dragons was about to swoop down onto some of Gwirion's warriors. Since Gwirion's band was busy fighting against a different group of foes, they would be caught completely unaware.

He leaned his full weight against his ally's ear. Even as Basilgarrad whirled around, banking so sharply that the bones of his wings bent severely under the stress, the black dragons attacked. Their claws raked the fire angels' backs, slashing their flesh so brutally that several of the flaming warriors died immediately. Their fires went out, leaving only charred bodies that spun downward into the realms far below.

Only two of the fire angels escaped through quick maneuvering. One of them, Tamwyn was glad to see, was Gwirion himself. The precious Golden Wreath still sat upon his brow, shining with the light of his flaming wings. Yet Tamwyn knew, as Gwirion surely did, that the Ayanowyn could not long survive. Their numbers were rapidly dwindling.

How, Tamwyn asked himself for the hundredth time, could they ever defeat this army of deathless dragons? By now, that lone goal occupied all his attention. He had given up trying to imagine how they could possibly drive their enemies back through the doorways to the Otherworld—let alone close those doorways forever.

"Hear me now, my warriors," commanded Rhita Gawr, his thoughts echoing inside Tamwyn's head. "It is time to finish off that ragtag group of mortals, to destroy them utterly, so that our invasion can proceed! Listen carefully to my instructions, even as you watch me eliminate my own final obstacle."

Basilgarrad needed no warning from Tamwyn. His own senses, seasoned by many battles, told him of Rhita Gawr's approach from behind. The green dragon veered, turning so fast that his passenger barely clung to his ear. At the instant they came around, Rhita Gawr swept past, close enough that Tamwyn could have reached out and struck his wingtip.

The black dragon roared with such force that the darkened stars themselves seemed to quiver. Then he spun around, even as his winged foe did the same. Wrathfully, the warlord of the Otherworld faced Basilgarrad and the insolent young wizard who rode him.

For a brief moment, the two enormous dragons hovered in the air, surveying each other. Ominous sparks suddenly flared in Rhita Gawr's uninjured eye. Just before he released a bolt of black lightning, he issued final commands to his warriors. At the same time, Basilgarrad flapped his mighty wings and charged forward.

It was a charge, Tamwyn felt sure, that would end this battle at last. One way or the other.

* * *

"Time to end yer miserable liddle life," snarled Harlech as he stared down at Scree.

He grasped the leather cord that held his most terrible weapon, the glowing claw. Its bright radiance touched his fingers, making them seem to be dripping with blood. His hand squeezed tighter with anticipation.

Despite the certainty that he was about to die, Scree lifted his head proudly. His yellow-rimmed eyes glowed with a brightness of their own. "What's keeping you, Harlech? Have you lost your courage?"

The warrior's grin only broadened. "It's not about courage, wingboy."

He raised his boot and kicked a clump of mud onto Scree's torn wing. "It's about a choice, a difficult choice, ye've forced me to make."

"What's that?"

Harlech chortled in satisfaction. "Which part to cut off first! Yer wings—er yer head."

31 · Unexpected Talents

AS TAMWYN AND SCREE, IN TWO DISTANT places, fought for their very lives, Elli did the same in another place. Not in the stars, or on a muddy plain, but deep underground—in the deepest cavern of the darkest realm.

Kulwych laughed softly as he examined her, slumped against the cavern's rock wall. Water trickled down behind her, soaking her curls, but she paid no heed. Her face exuded despair.

Gloating, the sorcerer rubbed his pale hands together. "How inconvenient for you, my priestess! You have come all this way, with great difficulty no doubt, only to learn that your plan was fatally flawed."

He glanced over his shoulder at the vengélano crystal that rested safely on its stone pedestal. Then he bent lower, bringing his mutilated face so close to Elli's that she was forced to look into his empty eye socket. The pulsing red light from the crystal glinted on all the scabs and scar tissue, making the socket seem to crawl with maggots.

"You see," he whispered, "my crystal is indestructible. Mmmyesss, completely indestructible."

Elli shuddered and turned away, as much from this bitter news as from the sorcerer's voice. Yet worst of all was the feeling that Kulwych was, indeed, correct. Her quest *had* been fatally flawed.

She shook her head of thick brown curls, thinking of all the mistakes she had made on this journey—starting with her decision to ignore the Sapphire Unicorn's plea to go straight to the Lady of the Lake. She had led everyone into a pack of gnomes at Llynia's temple. She had welcomed the death dreamer into her arms, almost killing both Nuic and herself. Even when she had tried to do something right, such as call to Tamwyn through the Galator, her very shout had gotten them captured by gobsken. Just as it had gotten old Grikkolo killed.

And now, she told herself grimly, *your single most important task turns out to be impossible.* How could she ever have been so foolish? Kulwych's crystal—whose power, he said, reaches all the way to the stars—simply cannot be destroyed. *At least not by me.*

Nuic stirred in her lap. She gazed down at the pinnacle sprite, her loyal companion, watching his skin vibrate with an angry shade of scarlet as he glared at the sorcerer. Then his liquid eyes turned toward her. Simultaneously, his skin color shifted to orange, his way of signaling impatience. And with it came a ripple of lavender: his simple, quiet statement of affection.

She nodded, guessing his thoughts. *You're right, old friend. What's the point of feeling sorry for myself? There's so little time left! If I'm ever going to do something, it must be now.*

She tried to straighten her back, but even that gesture seemed a challenge. It felt as if she were lifting an enormous weight, as heavy as all the rocks that lay between this deep cavern and the surface of Shadowroot. *What, though, can I possibly do?*

As if in answer, Kulwych spoke again in his grating

whisper. "You can do something for me now, my priestess, mmmyesss. You can die."

"That's right, Kulwych," declared another voice from the cavern's open door. "But first, *you* can die."

Kulwych instantly straightened. His lone eye peered at his new visitor, astonished as well as enraged. For just like Elli and Nuic, he had never expected to see this person again.

"Deth Macoll," breathed Elli in disbelief. Nuic, in her arms, darkened to pitch black.

"Surprised to see me, my gumdrop?" The assassin's sallow face twisted into a spiteful grin. "It would take far more than that little fall you devised to harm the great Deth Macoll. For unlike this amateur magician here, I am full of—shall we say, unexpected talents."

Kulwych bristled, his pale hands squeezing into fists.

Without taking his flinty gray eyes off the sorcerer, Deth Macoll added in a voice that was all the more menacing for its softness, "I shall take care of you soon, gumdrop. You and your treacherous little sprite. And what a pleasure that will be! First, however, I have some plans for my dear friend Kulwych."

Deth Macoll stepped fully into the cavern, the crystal's red glow shining on his bald head. Despite his tattered jester's garb, which had lost all but one of its tiny silver bells, he strode in casually, almost jauntily, swinging his cherry wood cane that held a hidden blade. When he was just three paces from Kulwych, though, he stopped abruptly. He planted the tip of his cane on the stone floor. As its echo reverberated around the dank walls of the cavern, no one moved.

"Kulwych," sneered the assassin. "How lovely to see you. It's been too long."

"Too long that you have annoyed me," rasped the sorcerer. "But that, mmmyesss, will soon end."

Quick as a striking snake, Deth Macoll leaped at his

foe. He thrust his cane, blade extended, at Kulwych's chest. The sorcerer, though, moved with equal speed. He side-stepped the thrust, then locked one of his hands around the assassin's wrist. With revenge blazing in his eyes, Kulwych shot a blast of intense pain into his enemy's arm.

Deth Macoll shrieked in agony, dropping his weapon. The cane clattered on the stone floor. But instead of col-lapsing to his knees, as the sorcerer expected, he did just the opposite. Deth Macoll leaped into the air, flipping over backward to break Kulwych's grip. In the middle of his flip, he kicked one foot into the sorcerer's head, striking the lone eye.

Now Kulwych howled in pain, as the skin under his eye swelled and darkened to blue. Yet even as the assassin landed back on the floor and stood, clutching his sore arm, Kulwych pounced. This time the sorcerer's white hand wrapped around Deth Macoll's neck. Kulwych's slit of a mouth curled in triumph, confident that his next blast would surely kill his adversary.

Just then Deth Macoll flicked his left wrist, popping an-other hidden blade out of his sleeve. Before his foe knew what had happened, the man named Deth slashed his blade across the hand squeezing his neck. Blood spurted from the back of Kulwych's hand, once so perfectly manicured and free of any blemish.

Kulwych screamed, as much in horror as in pain. But his cry was cut short as Deth Macoll threw himself at the sor-cerer, tackling him. They slammed into the rock wall, then tumbled together to the floor.

As soon as the fight had begun, Elli's mind began to race. This was her chance! There would never be another such opportunity. But what could she do? How could she possi-bly put an end to this crystal whose powers were so vast?

She looked at the glowing crystal, and down at Nuic, whose skin was now radiant orange. Then she tried her best to concentrate. What did she know about the crystal? Very little, really. Not even Rhia had understood how it worked. All she could say was, *I suspect that it could be just as destructive as élano is creative.*

Elli scowled, knowing that the conflict in the cavern would not last much longer. She glanced toward the two foes locked in battle. Whoever emerged the victor would swiftly eliminate both her and Nuic—as well as any hope they might have of destroying the crystal.

Who else had told her anything about the crystal? Only Grikkolo, whose erudite words had been no more helpful than Rhia's. *That crystal,* he had said, *must be the absolute opposite of élano. It can destroy just as irresistibly as élano can create.*

Elli's mind fairly sizzled. Destroy. Create. Was there some sort of answer buried in there? Yet what answer could lie in opposites? In *absolute* opposites?

Her eyes opened. That was it! Just as the two combatants fell to the floor together, shrieking and shouting, Elli shot to her feet. Still cradling Nuic in one arm, she dashed over to the pulsing crystal on the pedestal.

"Forgive me," she whispered, as she reached up to the amulet of leaves on her throat and ripped away the crystal that Rhia had given her. Instantly, that crystal brightened, shooting rays of green, blue, and white light around the cavern. As leaves from the sundered amulet twirled to the floor, flashing in the light, Elli placed the crystal of pure élano right on top of its opposite.

All at once, the vengélano crystal darkened. It started to sizzle, like molten rock, even as the other crystal did the same. Locked together, they trembled, tapping on the stone pedestal. Rays of red shot forth, seeming to wrestle with the greens and blues in midair. A strange smell wafted from the spot—more sulfuric than smoky, something like the fumes of a volcano about to erupt.

Elli stood watching, transfixed by the sight, hoping that her gambit might actually succeed in canceling out the corrupted crystal's power. The sulfuric smell grew steadily stronger, as the sizzling sound intensified.

"Er, Elliryanna." Nuic spoke with his usual crustiness, but with an unmistakable edge of urgency. "Time to go, don't you think? Nice as this place is, I wouldn't want to stay down here forever."

She shook herself. Then she glanced at the two long-time foes who were rolling on the floor, utterly absorbed in their battle. "Right, Nuic. Let's go!"

Holding the sprite, she ran out of the cavern. As she turned down the rough-hewn tunnel that dark elves had carved long ago, she almost tripped over the body of a slain gobsken. He had, no doubt, made the mistake of confronting Deth Macoll. Pausing only long enough to grab his sputtering torch, she sprinted down the tunnel.

Her legs pumped, carrying her swiftly. At the landing where the tunnel ended, she found three more dead gobsken, along with another pair slumped on the stone steps. Remembering how stealthily Deth Macoll had entered the dragons' lair in Waterroot, she guessed that they probably hadn't even heard him approach.

Up the stone steps she dashed, climbing higher and higher out of the mine. Her thighs and calves ached, and both legs grew wobbly, but she didn't relent. She ran to the rhythm of her panting breaths, as well as her pounding heart.

Yet she never felt truly fatigued. For she knew that, with all the mistakes she had made along the way, she just might have done one important thing right. Perhaps it was too much to hope that her deed might somehow help Tamwyn. Or Brionna. Or others at the battle of Isenwy. But she hoped so nonetheless.

At last, as she neared the top, cold air wafted down the shaft. It felt so chilly that it practically stung her sweat-drenched skin. That very sting, however, told her that she was, indeed, still alive. And still free.

When finally she emerged from the mine, she was much

too far away to hear Kulwych's cry of victory from the cavern down below, as he weakly raised himself from the motionless form of Deth Macoll. And she was also too far away to hear the sorcerer's sudden wail of anguish when he noticed the changes that had transformed his precious crystal. But she had no trouble at all hearing the muffled explosion from the depths beneath her feet.

Starting with a faraway rumble, the explosion swelled into a rolling boom—like distant thunder, but deeper. At the same time, tremors shook the ground, growing so strong that Elli could barely keep standing. Finally, the vibrations faded away. Then a small puff of smoke, smelling like sulfur, arose from the mine shaft. The smoke hung in the air briefly before it vanished, taking with it the last remnant of Kulwych's terrible crystal.

Elli stood there, panting heavily, in the darkness of Shadowroot. In one hand she held a flaming torch that smelled of oily rags. She raised it high, grateful for its light, even as she missed the light from another source, a light that she had carried all the way to the end of her quest.

"Well, Elliryanna." Nuic's lavender hues flickered along with the torch's flames. "Where do we go now?"

She gave him a sly smile. "Oh, I think you know already, Nuic. We're going back to the Lost City of Light. I can run, so long as this torch holds out—so we can make good time. And when we get there, we'll unbury that portal and use it to transport ourselves to Isenwy. It's our only chance to get there before the battle is over."

He scrunched his little face doubtfully. "What if the portal doesn't work anymore? Or what if it does work, but takes us somewhere else instead?"

"Those are risks," she agreed with a shrug of her shoulders. She gazed into the surrounding darkness that leaned so heavily against the torchlight. Then she spoke again, her voice barely a whisper. "But the greater risk, I fear, is what we'll find at the battlefield."

32 · Magical Fire

WHEN ELLI FELT THOSE TREMORS RISE from the rocky depths of Shadowroot, she knew that the corrupted crystal had finally been destroyed. What she did not know, however, was just how far those tremors might travel. Or just how deeply they might shape the destinies of the people she loved.

Yet far away, indeed, those tremors were felt. For they reached all the way to the stars on high.

Under the darkened stars of the Wizard's Staff, Avalon's greatest mortal dragon charged with all his strength. Basilgarrad beat his powerful wings, focusing every last scale of his gigantic body on the target: Rhita Gawr. In the green dragon's mind was nothing that could be described as hope, but rather a potent brew of outrage, audacity, and love for his world.

Basilgarrad surged forward, as Tamwyn held tight with both arms to the dragon's ear. Wind rushed past, throwing the young man's hair behind his shoulders. Even as black sparks appeared in the one remaining eye of their enemy, something different shone in the eyes of Basilgarrad. He knew well that he could never kill Rhita Gawr, only wound the body that the warlord had assumed. And he also knew that this headlong charge could easily be his last. But he believed, deep in his dragon's heart, that all the flights he had taken over the centuries of his life were preparation for this very moment.

Rhita Gawr hovered in the sky, stretching his leathery wings to the widest. Even as his foe bore down on him, he didn't bother to feint or try to dodge this charge in any way. Why should he? For he felt certain that his moment of triumph had finally arrived, just as he felt certain that he could predict every maneuver of this miserable dragon who carried the spawn of Merlin.

On top of that, the green dragon's allies would soon be eliminated. Thanks to brilliant tactical commands that Rhita Gawr had given his warriors, the flaming creatures who dared to oppose the invasion had lost nearly half their original numbers. They were now almost at the breaking point. With the final instructions he was about to issue to his forces, the fiery creatures would go the way of all mortals—death and dust.

Within his bottomless eye, sparks flared, coalescing into what would surely be the greatest blast of black lightning he had ever produced. He would hurl it straight at the green dragon's head, as soon as he saw the perfect moment. And he would save just enough to throw a second blast at whatever remained of the runt wizard himself.

Rhita Gawr watched the oncoming dragon, ready to knock him out of the sky forever. As the lightning swelled within the warlord's eye, thoughts flashed through his mind—starting with his own entrance into this world just a few weeks ago. He had come into Avalon through the very same star that hung just behind him right now, the central star in the constellation that mortals foolishly called the Wizard's Staff. It would be more accurate, he told himself, to call it the Warlord's Spear! For in the brief time that he had spent here, he had managed to turn himself into a deadly dragon, to give similar but smaller forms to his warriors, and to create a weapon of extraordinary power from Kulwych's crystal. And now, at last, he would destroy his only adversaries—and then drive his immortal spear through the very heart of Avalon.

Foaming saliva rolled down his jaws and scaly neck, for he could already taste the magnitude of his triumph. He had plotted and waited a very long time to reach this moment. First Avalon, then Earth, would belong to him alone. And in time, all the other worlds would follow.

First, though, he needed to eliminate the nuisance of this dragon, this young wizard, and their flaming allies. He started to issue final commands to his warriors—even as he began to release an enormous blast of black lightning.

At just that instant, he felt a sudden stab of pain inside his mind. Like an invisible claw, it ripped away some of his power—tearing a hole in the cosmos, as well as in himself. He reeled, abruptly halting his instructions to his warriors. Meanwhile, the lightning continued to build within his eye, ready to erupt at any second.

But Rhita Gawr was not thinking about that. He felt shocked and confused. And, for the first time in his entire existence, he felt an emotion so strange that its very presence chilled his innermost core.

Fear.

He ground his dragon's jaws, so hard that scores of teeth cracked and broke apart. Something terrible had happened! That was all he knew. He couldn't even tell exactly what it was, or who had done it—though he doubted it was Dagda, his eternal enemy who had foolishly forsworn any interference with the mortal worlds. No, this blow must have come from something small, something he'd overlooked. Perhaps even—

Basilgarrad slammed into him, full force. Both dragons roared as bones crunched, flesh tore open, and scales both green and black splintered into countless shards. Just before the impact, Basilgarrad had whipped his ear backward, throwing Tamwyn clear of the crash. A heartbeat later, the green dragon's massive head plowed straight into Rhita Gawr's chest. This colossal body blow exploded in the sky, sending thunderous echoes around the realm of the stars.

Just then came another explosion. Inside Rhita Gawr's eye, all the pent-up black lightning finally erupted. But with no effort to project it anywhere, the energy exploded upon itself. All the force of the blast struck within the eye of the warlord.

Rhita Gawr screamed, tumbling over backward in the air. Now completely blind as well as hobbled by broken bones throughout his chest and back, he couldn't even fly, let alone guide himself anywhere. His leathery wings fluttered helplessly as he spun downward.

Dazed though he was from the blow, and sore throughout his body, Basilgarrad could still keep himself aloft. And he could also think clearly enough to know what had to happen next. Bending his gargantuan body, he lashed out with his enormous tail. The bony club at its tip crashed into Rhita Gawr's belly, sending the black dragon hurtling into the cavernous hole of the darkened star behind him— and back into the Otherworld.

Tilting his wings, Basilgarrad swooped downward. As he neared Tamwyn, who was falling rapidly through the air, arms flailing, the great dragon careened and deftly hooked one claw through the young man's pack strap. With a sudden lurch that made Tamwyn shout in surprise, Basilgarrad tossed his passenger back onto his huge head.

Landing this time with a thud instead of a clatter, Tamwyn realized how many scales had been ripped from the dragon's head. Green blood congealed in several places; broken scales flapped loosely everywhere. Careful not to step on any open wounds, he regained his feet, straightened the pack as well as his torch, and grabbed hold of Basilgarrad's ear once again.

"Thanks, my friend," he said into the ear, his voice only slightly louder than the whoosh of the wind. "What you just did could only have been done by the mighty Basilgarrad." Then he added with a chuckle, "Or by the clever Batty Lad, so so so famous for his most excellent tricksies."

The dragon laughed heartily. The sound reverberated all around them, as if the Great Tree itself were sharing in the humor.

Tamwyn leaned forward, still clutching the ear. Over Basilgarrad's brow, he could see the dark blot of Rhita Gawr's body, spinning as it fell into the star doorway. A few seconds later, the warlord vanished completely into the black hole.

Just then he noticed something else—other shapes moving toward the darkened doorway. Rhita Gawr's warriors! And behind them, fire angels!

At once, Tamwyn understood. When the violent explosions had struck their master, and his instructions had suddenly ceased, the smaller dragons became disoriented and confused. Gwirion's fire angels had immediately sensed the change and taken full advantage of it. Though much fewer in number, they had flown like skillful herdsmen, driving the dragon warriors into the very same hole as Rhita Gawr. And toward the very same destination.

But for how long? How much time would Rhita Gawr need to extract his spirit from his enfeebled body—so he could return to Avalon, more wrathful than ever?

Not much, Tamwyn guessed. He knew what he needed to do, even though he still didn't know how. *This is it,* he told himself. *My chance. My moment. I must relight the stars! And to do that, I must make magical fire.*

He reached over his shoulder, grasped the wooden pole of the torch, and tugged it free. As he held the torch in his hand, studying the charred, oily rag wrapped around its top, he thought how truly unremarkable it looked. Yet his own staff, which he had carried so far before dropping it into the Heart of Pegasus, had seemed equally unremarkable. And as he knew well, that staff had possessed powers untold, the powers of Merlin's Ohnyalei.

Basilgarrad, perhaps sensing Tamwyn's goal, banked a turn, bringing them closer to the constellation's central star. Meanwhile, the young man continued to ponder the torch. While the wind rushed over his face, he hefted the weathered pole. He could almost feel, upon its surface, the imprint of his own father's hand. Just as he could almost feel, deep within, the call of some elusive magic.

The magic of fire. Of heat and light. Of something far greater than the flames he'd kindled so often as a wilderness guide.

How to bring that fire to life, though? Right now, while there was still a chance to save his world and so many others. Tamwyn's brow creased with anxiety, for he knew that this sort of fire was markedly different from any he'd ever made.

Somewhere from his distant past came a half-remembered voice, asking a question that had haunted him all his life. *So his name means Dark Flame? I wonder, then, which will it be. Will he bring to Avalon the light of flame . . . or the dark of night?*

"Which will it be?" he demanded aloud. "Come on, Tamwyn! Which will it be?"

Fires burned within his brain, scorching his every thought. But those were fires of doubt and uncertainty, not at all what he needed. What did he even know, really, about the fire he had so often coaxed into life when he camped? That it was hot enough to cook by. Bright enough to read by. And also full of opposites: fragile yet strong, useful yet dangerous.

He squeezed the pole, concentrating, so hard his fingers

went white. How was magical fire different from a camp-fire? *Magical fire*, Gwirion had once told him, *must be kindled within.*

But where could he find the power to do that? Where could he find the spark, the flames, that he needed?

Then he recalled something else that the fire angel had said. *You have your own inner flames, Tamwyn, though they cannot be seen. For they reside in the soul.*

"In the soul," Tamwyn repeated. He spoke to himself, to the torch, to the seven darkened stars of the Wizard's Staff. *In the soul.*

All at once, he understood. He turned his thoughts inward, drawing strength from his innermost fires—kindled from passion, hope, and love. For the Great Tree of Avalon, his world of many wonders. For the Thousand Groves connected to its branches. For all the people he loved, who had helped him in countless ways. Gwirion. Basilgarrad. Brave Ahearna—and yes, even Henni. Scree, wherever he might be now. Rhia, who had urged him to create his own destiny. Palimyst, the wise craftsman. Ethaun, who had repaired his broken dagger. Crusty old Nuic.

And, of course, Elli.

He opened himself to those passions, those loves, feeling the warmth of their fires. Stronger they grew, and stronger still.

"Now, my torch," he commanded. "Burn! Burn for Avalon, and for us all."

With a brilliant flash, the torch burst into flames. Tamwyn held it before his face, feeling its heat, watching its glow. At every stroke of the great dragon's wings, a whoosh of air blew across the torch. Yet its fire never wavered.

Turning toward the central star, Tamwyn gazed at its enormous rim—a pale, glowing ring that swept across the sky. It encircled a gigantic well of darkness, a doorway to the world of the spirits. The only darkness deeper than that well was the eye of the warlord who had just fallen into it.

The young wizard drew a deep breath, concentrating on his fires deep within. Then he blew very gently, as if he were coaxing a small, shimmering coal into flame.

A single spark lifted off the torch. As small as it was compared to the star, it glowed with remarkable radiance. Directed by Tamwyn's guiding breath, it floated away from Basilgarrad, dancing over the dragon's outstretched wing. It continued to fly, this tiny dot of light, all the way to the darkened star. At last, it disappeared within the shadowed center.

Nothing happened. Tamwyn held his breath, waiting. Beneath his feet, he felt the vibrations of Basilgarrad's voice emitting a deep, expectant rumble.

Suddenly, with a great *whooooosshhh,* the star burst into flames. Iridescent curtains of flame filled the entire rim, shooting out radiant beams that brightened the sky. Tamwyn's eyes gleamed like smaller stars at this sight, while Basilgarrad raised a wing and spun them around in a celebratory circle.

The doorway had been closed. With Rhita Gawr and his warriors on the other side.

In rapid succession, Tamwyn repeated the process six more times. Blowing on his magical torch with care, he sent a spark into each of the other darkened stars of the constellation. All of them burst into wondrous flames. The barrier between Avalon and the Otherworld had, at last, been fully restored.

With satisfaction, Tamwyn gazed at the seven lustrous stars of the Wizard's Staff. Not since the night he crawled into a heap of dung to stay warm, the night this whole adventure began, had he seen all seven of them alight. And he had never seen them like this—so very near, so very bright.

Only once before, he knew, had these same seven stars been rekindled. That was over three hundred years before, at the end of the Age of Storms. On that memorable day it was Merlin himself, riding this very same dragon, who had brought back the light to the Wizard's Staff.

Today, someone very different had accomplished the same feat. He was much younger, far less experienced, and not skilled at much beyond wood carving. Yet he had somehow succeeded. Despite the ambiguity of his name, and the uncertainty of his destiny, he had finally answered that half-remembered question from long ago.

He had brought to Avalon the light of flame.

33 · Prayers

JUST AS A SUDDEN STAB OF PAIN SURPRISED
Rhita Gawr, a different turn of events surprised the
warrior Harlech. For the tremors from Elli's remarkable
feat had also reached the muddy Plains of Isenwy.

"'Tis a difficult choice," Harlech declared, peering
smugly down at Scree. The eagleman's silver wings were
now drenched with mud and splattered with his own blood.
"But methinks ye'd look even uglier without yer head. So
we'll save that part fer last."

He smirked, toying with the claw that hung from the
leather cord around his neck. The claw twirled slowly,
gleaming an intense shade of red. "So, birdboy, I'll start by
removin' yer wings. Slice them off, I will, one by bleedin'
one. An' then I'll jest take care o' yer head."

Scree's yellow-rimmed eyes flashed proudly. He was
trapped, he knew, and about to die. Even worse, he would
never be able to stop this murderer from harming Brionna.
But despite all that, he wasn't going to add to Harlech's
satisfaction by showing a single feather's worth of fear.

The big man took a step closer, his belt of weapons

clanking as he moved. "Kulwych wants me to hurry an' finish this battle, quick as I can, so I need to get on wid killin' ye." He sniggered maliciously. "But I'm *sure* there'll still be time to play wid that pretty she-elf o' yers, when I find her again. Mmm, that'll be fun."

Although those words made Scree's temples pound with rage, he forced himself not to respond.

Then Harlech bent lower. "Ye know why the hurry? We're expectin' a liddle visit, that's why." He grinned, savoring the chance to reveal this news. "From Rhita Gawr."

Despite himself, Scree stiffened and exclaimed, "Rhita Gawr! Here?"

"That's right, wingboy. But there's no need fer worry. Ye won't be around to see it happen." Slowly, he lifted the glowing object. "All right now, claw. Cut off his puny liddle wing."

Harlech's grin broadened. This was a moment he'd been anticipating for quite some time. He concentrated his thoughts, as he had so many times before in this battle, and waited for the beam of light—the most savage blade he'd ever wielded—to appear.

Nothing happened. He looked down at the claw. The grin suddenly disappeared from his face, just as the red light had suddenly disappeared from his weapon of sorcery.

"Garr . . ." he said, confused. Then, with the swiftness of a seasoned warrior, he changed plans. He reached for the broadsword that he'd dropped on the ground a few minutes before.

Scree, though, moved faster. Leaping to his feet with a spray of mud, he swung his uninjured wing at Harlech. The bony edge of the wing slammed into the man's neck, knocking him sideways with such force that he tripped over a dead gnome and splatted onto the wet soil. As Harlech rose shakily to one knee, Scree tried to rake a bloodied talon across his face.

But this time Harlech moved unexpectedly fast. He fell

back, avoiding the talon, then grabbed the eagleman's leg. Twisting, he threw Scree to the ground.

Even as the warrior reached for one of his daggers, though, Scree deftly rolled over and jabbed the tip of his wing into Harlech's head. The burly man stumbled backward, bleeding from the gash in his jaw. A second later, Scree pounced on him, making him drop the dagger. Its blade plunged into the mud, buried halfway to the hilt.

The two combatants crashed to the ground, wrestling with all their strength. Scree butted with his head and tore with his talons; Harlech punched and pummeled with all four limbs. Curses flew, even when they finally separated and circled each other warily, for both warriors knew that this fight would end only when one of them finally died.

Their brutal struggle continued, stretching into hours that called on their deepest reserves of strength and cunning. Meanwhile, the situation began to shift on the battlefield. Without the help of Harlech's claw, and without Belamir to inspire his loyalists, the allies of Avalon gained momentum. And with no sign of the rumored aid for the gobsken army, the allies began to believe that they might actually prevail.

Courageous eaglefolk assailed the fierce but dim-witted ghoulacas, driving them out of the sky. Drumadians and other men and women, while still outnumbered, slashed away relentlessly at gobsken and gnomes. Increasingly, the Drumadians fought side by side with elvish archers, whose arrows rarely missed their targets. Tall tree spirits, squat dwarves, and maryths of all kinds joined in the fray, swinging their branches, axes, and hooves. Meanwhile, grim-faced flamelons terrorized the enemy by bombarding them with burning spears and flaming balls of tar.

The remnants of the Humanity First movement scattered, as new rumors spread that a changeling had secretly joined their ranks. Swarms of faeries flew into ogres' faces, tormenting them until the archers could move in. The trolls fared no better, because as ferocious as they were, they were no match for the giants—especially one particular giant, who clearly enjoyed his enormous size, almost as if he had lost it for a time and only just regained it.

Unnoticed by anyone except for the tall mudmaker standing nearby, the portal's green flames suddenly crackled. Out from the flames stepped Elli, holding Nuic in her arms. All she needed to do was to glance down at the sprite, whose skin was frosty white, to know that he had found the ride as terrifying as she had.

"Hmmmpff," he grumbled, meeting her gaze. "It's one thing to follow someone—even a bubble-brained priestess—into a portal. But to follow someone into a *damaged* portal, well, that's sheer idiocy."

She smiled at him. "That's why you're my maryth. We're perfect for each other."

"Perfectly insane, you mean, Elliryanna."

She didn't answer. For she had just started to take in the sheer horror that surrounded them on the battlefield. Bodies that had been mutilated, stabbed, and slashed lay everywhere. Whether they belonged to gobsken or gnomes, women or men, dwarves or stags, the brutal reality remained the same, and the poignancy of it struck her like a spear. This place was more dead than alive.

Elli turned herself around, scanning the bloody terrain for any sign of her friends. But she saw nothing of Brionna, even in the band of archers from Woodroot who were pursuing a pair of ogres. Nor of Scree, whom she had hoped would have found his way here with the other eaglefolk. Then, at last, she spotted Lleu.

Looking terribly somber, he was sitting on the corpse of a gobsken warrior he had just felled. By his side lay a bloodied sword. And on his lap rested a small bird, whose head he was tenderly stroking.

"Catha!" she cried. She ran over, carrying Nuic.

Lleu looked up, his expression grave. If he was surprised to see her, he didn't show it. All his thoughts were bound up with his most loyal friend, whose last morsel of life was just about to disappear.

"By the light of Dagda," he said morosely, "there is no way I can save her."

Elli pinched her lips, seeing the deep gash in the falcon's breast. "No," she answered, "but maybe I can."

She knelt by Lleu's side, oblivious to the shouts of battle and cries of anguish that echoed all around them. Pulling out her water gourd, she poured several drops on the wound. The healing water, which Tamwyn had found at the Secret Spring of Halaad not far from this very spot, started to bubble and foam. Next, Elli gently pried open Catha's beak and poured some more drops inside.

Steam began to rise from the wound, as the flesh started to close. Feathers, torn and soiled, sprang back to their normal shape and color. One wing shuddered, then the other. At last, Catha opened her eyes—as Lleu gasped in delight.

The falcon released a joyous whistle, then rolled onto her feet. Standing in Lleu's lap, she peered up at the priest for several seconds, then turned her grateful gaze on Elli. With a vigorous ruffle of her wings, she lifted off and flew back to her customary perch on Lleu's shoulder.

"Thank you," he said to Elli. He paused to reach up and stroke Catha's side. "You came just in time, the answer to my prayers."

She watched the revived falcon, then replied, "Papa used to say that the gods answer prayers of those—"

"Who truly believe," he finished, grinning. "He told me that, too."

Elli was about to respond, when Nuic tugged sharply on her sleeve. "If you'd like to see the answer to another prayer, look up there." His little arm pointed skyward, and his colors shifted to a thankful shade of blue.

"The Wizard's Staff!" exclaimed Elli. "Its stars are shining again."

"Incredible," said Lleu, raising his bushy brows in awe. "They only just changed! The last time I looked up, when I asked Dagda and Lorilanda for help not five minutes ago, they were all still dark." He scratched his chin. "Whatever do you think happened up there?"

"I don't know," declared Nuic, "but my guess is that a certain bumbling wilderness guide does."

Elli, her eyes aglow, turned to the sprite. His color had changed to flashing gold, a sure sign of amazement. Yet whether he was more amazed by the stars themselves or by the possibility that Tamwyn had done such a thing, she couldn't tell.

Suddenly a dark shadow fell over them. Catha screeched, though it sounded more like a cry of astonishment than fear. A pair of enormous hands scooped all of them up, lifting them as easily as if they were just a few blueberries.

Elli, Lleu, Nuic, and Catha, all jumbled together in the middle of the cupped hands, stared at the face above them. It was truly gigantic. Its nose alone was the size of an elephaunt, and a pregnant elephaunt at that. Shaggy white hairs, each as long as the ropes of cloudthread that supported Airroot's Misty Bridge, curled around the massive head.

Shim peered down at them, smiling broadly. He was wearing a huge cloak of woven willows that he'd taken from the giant felled by Harlech's claw. Its leafy collar alone was as large as a whole grove of trees; if he lay down, the cloak would have made him look like a forested hillside.

"Such a sweetly thing has happened to me," he bellowed in a voice as loud as an avalanche. "Certainly, definitely, absolutely."

34 · Starkeepers

TAMWYN STOOD ON THE HEAD OF BASIL-garrad, whose wide green wings rode the winds of Avalon's highest reaches. One of the young man's hands held on to the dragon's ear; one hand grasped the torch, shimmering with magical fire. Feeling wonder, satisfaction, and amazement all at once, he gazed at the seven stars of the Wizard's Staff, flaming brightly once again.

Without even turning, he sensed Gwirion's approach from behind. For before he heard the familiar crackle of the fire angel's wings, he could feel their heat on the back of his neck. He turned around just as Gwirion landed.

The fire angel closed his wings upon his back and stepped toward Tamwyn, careful to place his feet only on the dragon's undamaged scales. He stopped about two paces away, as close as his fires would allow without burning his friend. For a few seconds, he simply observed Tamwyn and the flaming torch, whistling thoughtfully as he gazed.

"Well, human son, you have found your soulfire at last." Gwirion reached up and touched, with a flaming finger, the Golden Wreath on his brow. "Just as you found this."

Tamwyn nodded. "And let me tell you, it was almost as painful as swallowing fire coals."

Gwirion laughed, a sound like wood rich with sap popping on the fire.

That laughter reminded Tamwyn of the fire angel's sister, and her heroism that had saved his life. "I'm sorry about Fraitha."

For an instant, Gwirion's fires dimmed. "She would have been proud to see what you have done."

"What *we* have done. We only prevailed thanks to your warriors." Tamwyn waved at the remaining Ayanowyn, who were flying in joyous loops around them. Then he thought of Ahearna, the Star Galloper, whose wide wings had carried him all the way here. And of Henni, who had never, in all their adventures, really believed that he could die. Feeling as if his own soulfire had dimmed, he said quietly, "And thanks to those who gave their lives today for Avalon."

"Yes," agreed Gwirion.

Tamwyn took a deep breath, then declared, "In addition, we never could have succeeded without one especially great warrior." He leaned into the dragon's ear, and added, "One who pretended to cower in my pocket."

The enormous head beneath them quaked as Basilgarrad rumbled in approval.

Gwirion nodded. "All this is true, my friend. But only you could relight the stars."

Tamwyn grinned slightly, then said, "There is one left to light."

He spoke again into the dragon's ear. Immediately, Basilgarrad raised one immense wing just enough to sail into a turn. As the wind gusted over them, making Gwirion's flames crackle louder, they came around to face a different part of the sky. In the distance, near the glowing ribbon of light that was the River of Time, hung the last of Avalon's darkened stars. The Heart of Pegasus.

Tamwyn drew a full breath, then blew once again upon

his torch. A single radiant spark lifted off and drifted away on a gust of magic. Though it was as small as a mote of dust, Tamwyn knew that it held all the power to rekindle a star. Just as a tiny seed had given birth to his entire world, this spark could give new light to an entire swath of sky.

For you, Ahearna, he thought sadly, as he watched the spark float away. *I only wish you could see your star return to flames.*

To Tamwyn's great surprise, the spark abruptly stopped. It continued to burn brightly, but it hung there in the sky like a miniature star itself, fixed in place. Tamwyn traded puzzled looks with Gwirion, while the dragon who bore them rumbled uncertainly.

Then came a greater surprise. From the central star of the Wizard's Staff, another spark drifted over and merged with Tamwyn's spark, making it glow even brighter. Then sparks from the other stars of the constellation arrived, followed by additional sparks from stars nearby. More sparks came, and more. Stars all across the sky joined in, each sending a tiny bit of their light. Before long, every star on the branches of the Great Tree of Avalon had added to the new point of radiance.

All at once, the collection of sparks exploded. Spots of light flew in all directions. But they did not go far. Instead, they gathered themselves into two new shapes, creating a pair of luminous images in the center of the sky.

Faces.

One face of a man and one of a woman formed in the sky. They grew more defined, and more alive, by the second. Before long, they turned toward Tamwyn and his friends. And the young man knew, right away, exactly whose faces they were.

"Dagda and Lorilanda," he whispered in wonder.

"Our images, not our true selves," said the glowing face of the man. His voice, while deep and resonant, was not loud. Yet Tamwyn could hear it easily, as if Dagda were standing beside him on the head of the dragon. "For we have promised never to enter the mortal worlds, to allow creatures of free will to choose their own destiny."

"Which you have done, Tamwyn, and done beautifully." The woman's face smiled as she spoke. The sound of her rich mellifluous voice made Tamwyn think of a tumbling stream in his favorite alpine meadow, high on the flanks of Hallia's Peak. He shifted his stance, jingling the small quartz bell on his hip, and the bell's voice rippled right along with the stream.

"While we could not come to Avalon ourselves," continued Dagda, "we have watched you and your friends, every step of the way." His radiant eyes filled with gratitude. "And we are deeply, deeply pleased that you have prevailed."

"Much thanks to you, good dragon," said Lorilanda with affection. She waited a moment as Basilgarrad flapped his wings majestically, then added, "You are truly the grandest of your kind ever to have flown."

Basilgarrad gave a small whimper of embarrassment, a sound that seemed impossibly little for someone so gigantic.

"And much thanks to you, as well, Gwirion of the Ayanowyn." Hearing her words, the flaming man stood completely still, although his fires burned brighter than ever before.

"That is true," declared Dagda. "Only because of your courage and faith are we speaking to you now, as your people prophesied. For as you know well, our destinies can take as many shapes as a flame."

Lorilanda's face expanded a bit, as if she were leaning closer. "You have brought your people back into the light, Gwirion. Now you and your descendants shall paint another story, even greater than the one you call Lumaria col Lir. And brighter, as well, for the brushes that you use shall themselves be aflame."

Gwirion's jaw trembled, along with his soulfire. "May I ask you a question that has long burned in my mind?" Seeing the luminous faces nod, he touched his Golden Wreath. "I have heard that this wreath is more than a symbol of leadership, that it also carries a special power. But what that is, I know not."

Dagda and Lorilanda glanced at each other. Then Dagda spoke again.

"It is the power to guide you safely to the Otherworld."

"Your realm of the spirits?" asked Gwirion in disbelief.

"Yes," replied Dagda. "Like Ogallad before you, you may sometimes need to enter one of the seven flaming doorways to our world. If you are wearing the Golden Wreath, you shall survive the journey and find us waiting." He paused, scrutinizing the winged man. "You are wondering why you might ever need to do this."

"I am."

"Because your people's new responsibility, the great story Lorilanda described, shall be to serve as eternal guardians of the stars. To guard all the flaming doorways into Avalon that surround us here and now. To make certain that if Rhita Gawr should ever try again to enter your world, your people will warn all the rest of Avalon."

Gwirion's face shone almost as bright as those of Dagda and Lorilanda on high. "As well as do our best to send him back to the Otherworld."

Lorilanda laughed, turning the sound of the stream into a lilting waterfall. "That attitude is why we have chosen to give you this new role."

"And why we have also chosen," added Dagda, lowering his voice, "to give you something else. Your people's true name."

Gwirion rocked backward, nearly slipping on Basilgarrad's scales. The fulfillment of the prophecy!

"From this day forward," declared Dagda, "you shall no longer be known as Ayanowyn—but as Hie Connedan. Do you know what that means, in the most ancient language of Avalon?"

"Starkeepers," whispered Gwirion. "Guardians of the stars."

Tamwyn nodded. "Fits you, my friend."

Gwirion, first leader of the Starkeepers, said nothing. He merely gazed at Dagda, Lorilanda, and the glittering lights around them.

Slowly, Lorilanda turned, so that she no longer faced Tamwyn, Gwirion, and Basilgarrad. Instead, she faced the uppermost star in the line of seven stars that formed the Wizard's Staff. Whispering quietly, she spoke to that star. Although he couldn't understand any of her words, Tamwyn sensed in his bones that they contained deep magic.

All of a sudden, the uppermost star flashed brilliantly. Then it did something so unexpected that Tamwyn caught his breath. The star began to elongate, stretching downward, until its fires merged with those of the star just below. After a few seconds, the Wizard's Staff had changed dramatically. Now, instead of a row of seven equally bright stars, it consisted of five equal stars topped by one remarkably tall flame.

"A torch," said Tamwyn, astounded. "It looks like a torch."

"Indeed it does," answered Lorilanda. "Long may it burn bright, as a reminder to all of what happened today. And now this constellation, like Gwirion's people, shall gain a new name. Henceforth, it shall be called the Eternal Flame."

Her voice fell to a whisper as she added, "And it has only come into being because of a mortal man who always dreamed of climbing to the stars."

Tamwyn swallowed.

Lorilanda, revered goddess of birth, flowering, and renewal, gazed down at him for a moment. Then she continued, "You have both light and dark within you, as the name Dark Flame suggests. In that way you are no different from

any other human. Much wisdom can come from understanding and balancing those two sides, Tamwyn. But the
balance is essential."

Her image wavered, as if a chill wind had blown across
the sky. "For in these dreadful times for your world, the
darker side of your species has grown powerful. Too powerful. That is why arrogance and greed have flourished,
why some humans have deemed themselves superior to all
other creatures, and why those same humans have nearly
destroyed the fragile bonds that hold this wondrous world
together."

She heaved a sorrowful sigh. "Even now, a fierce battle
is ending in the lands below, on the Plains of Isenwy. The
forces who cherish Avalon have prevailed, I am relieved to
tell you. But their victory has come only at a terrible cost.
And even with that victory, the deeper seeds of disaster—
arrogance and greed—remain. They need only another
season of darkness to flourish once again. For they are
seeds ever present in the human soul."

She paused, peering intently at the young man. "What
makes this danger so terrible is that humans tip the balance
of your world. No other species can make such a difference, for good or ill. If humans can live in harmony with
other forms of life, the world rejoices. If not, the world
suffers—and may not survive."

Tamwyn scowled. "Which means that Avalon will always be at risk, as long as humans live here."

"Or as long," Lorilanda added, "as they have not yet
learned to control their darker side."

"That could be forever!" Tamwyn shook his head, discouraged, sweeping his hair across his shoulders. "Surely
we didn't endure all this just so it could happen all over
again! Too many people have been killed, too many
dreams have been destroyed."

He squeezed the torch. "I wish you could take every last
one of us humans out of Avalon! Bring us somewhere

else—until we can live in harmony with our fellow creatures. That's the only way Avalon will ever be safe, the only way something like this won't be repeated."

"We could not do that," Lorilanda reminded him gently.

"I know, I know! The barriers between the worlds, the right to choose our own course. That's why you and Dagda couldn't help us. Even Merlin couldn't come back to help us. But who *will* help us, if you can't? Who *will* take humanity out of Avalon?"

Neither of the gods responded. A silence as vast and deep as the sky itself fell over the immortals. Beneath them, Basilgarrad continued to ride the winds, soundless but for the flapping of his slightly torn wing and battered scales.

It was Tamwyn who broke the silence, as he answered his own question. "We will do it ourselves," he said with grim resolve. "I will lead humanity out of Avalon! At least, I will try. And if I succeed, we will go through that star doorway that is still open, the one that leads to Earth."

"And after you have gone," added Lorilanda, "we will make good use of that magical spark that you yourself released, for it still burns within us. We will send it into that star to rekindle the flames."

"To close the doorway." Tamwyn's throat tightened so much it hurt. "I just wish that the only way to save Avalon was not to lose it."

Now Dagda's face seemed to draw closer in the sky. His eyes glowed warmly, and when he spoke, his voice sounded so tender that Tamwyn could almost feel a great arm wrapping around his shoulders. So real was this sensation, in fact, that Tamwyn's pack seemed to move in response, jostling the broken pieces of Elli's harp.

"Perhaps, one day, humanity might return to Avalon. That would be possible only after your race has learned how to tame its impulses toward arrogance and greed, which will be extremely difficult. Yet it is possible, nonetheless."

The young man peered up at Dagda—yearning, but afraid, to hope.

"And so, Tamwyn, even though the doorway will close behind you, it remains open just a crack."

"A crack," he whispered. "So our chances are very small."

"As small as a spark," offered Gwirion, rustling his fiery wings.

Tamwyn turned and gazed into the eyes of his flaming friend, grateful for all he saw there.

"You must remember this, however." The voice of Dagda had deepened, sounding both stern and somber. "This task must be done completely or not at all. Those humans who refuse to leave, who will not follow you to mortal Earth, will never be able to have any children of their own. Thus the last traces of humanity in Avalon will disappear."

Somberly, Tamwyn nodded. "So the message I bring my people holds grief as well as hope, loss as well as gain. I may have rekindled the stars, but I will soon darken many people's lives. Maybe I really am, more than anything else, the child of the Dark Prophecy."

Lorilanda's radiant face grew larger and closer than ever before. "No, my dear Tamwyn, you really are, at your core, the true heir of Merlin. The true savior of Avalon. But in order to succeed, you must also bring about Avalon's end—not as a world, or as an ideal, but as a particular kind of place."

"Yes," agreed Dagda. "The one place in the whole universe where humanity and all other creatures live together in harmony."

"It is a place that existed for a time," Lorilanda whispered gently. "And may yet exist again."

Her eyes gleamed anew, with a light that came from somewhere beyond the stars. "That is why, even as you are the child of the Dark Prophecy, you are also the true heir of Merlin."

With that, both her face and Dagda's began to shrink. They compressed farther and farther, until all that remained was a single, glowing spark. It floated in the sky—luminous, lovely, and alone. Tamwyn knew that it would remain there until his task was done.

He turned to Gwirion. "Farewell, my friend. I know you cannot come with me to Earth. But you'll be with me nonetheless."

Gwirion's flames crackled. "You, too, in your own way, are a Starkeeper."

Tamwyn smiled ever so slightly. "May your story be long and glorious."

"As may yours! And, by the fires of Ogallad, may we meet again."

The flaming wings opened, and Gwirion took flight. At the same time, the great dragon tilted his wings and plunged downward, bearing Tamwyn on his final journey home.

35 • Out of Avalon

MOMENTS LATER, TAMWYN AND BASIL-
garrad descended from the sky above the Plains
of Isenwy. When the survivors of the battle saw an enormous green dragon approaching, the last, scattered skir-
mishes abruptly ceased. Battlers froze; weapons fell still.
All eyes turned upward, and the air filled with shouts of
wonder and fear.

At first, the gobsken cheered raspingly, certain that this
was, indeed, Rhita Gawr himself—and that he had arrived
just in time to save them. And to secure the victory that had
nearly been lost. Meanwhile, eaglefolk called among
themselves as they circled the battlefield, preparing to fight
this new foe. The remaining ghoulacas reacted differently:
At the first glimpse of the dragon, they shrieked and tried
to escape from this huge winged predator. Elves and Drumadians raised their swords and bows, grimly ready for a
final battle that they knew they could not win. Yet a few of
the elves, who were most learned in the long history of
Avalon, marveled at the dragon's resemblance to the famous Basilgarrad, hero of the War of Storms and friend of

Merlin. Flamelons, for their part, immediately guessed that a warrior dragon had decided to join the conflict, though none of them knew which side it might favor.

The shouts only grew louder as Tamwyn and the dragon landed on the mud flats just outside the battlefield. Gobsken, gnomes, and ogres, seeing a man standing boldly atop the dragon's head, knew at once that this great beast had not come to help them. Most of them shrieked with fright and ran off, while others fell to their knees and begged for mercy.

At the same time, the surviving allies of Avalon cried out with joy. Then they began to gather around the new arrivals. From the oldest man to the youngest woman, from the tallest giant to the smallest faery, they surrounded Tamwyn and Basilgarrad, jostling each other to look more closely— without getting too near to the immensely powerful dragon.

Tamwyn raised his torch, shimmering with magical fire, high into the air. Beneath him, the scales of Basilgarrad's head and wings shone like emeralds aflame. Almost at once, the crowd fell silent.

He hesitated before speaking, searching the mass of faces before him for the one he most wanted to find. But Elli was nowhere to be seen. Had she, he wondered, perished in her quest? Or was she still alive, but far away from here?

"Avalon is saved," he declared at last, his voice ringing across the battlefield. "But that is true only because of the heroism of everyone here on the ground—and of my brave friend Basilgarrad in the sky."

The great green dragon snorted with approval, as a murmur of wonderment arose from the crowd.

"Rhita Gawr has been banished to the Otherworld," Tamwyn continued. "The doors of flame have been closed behind him. And Dagda and Lorilanda have celebrated this moment by reshaping the very stars of the Wizard's Staff."

He pointed his torch, as if it were the burning arrow of a compass, at the new constellation. Above all the gasps and exclamations, he announced, "Behold! A great torch on high, shining down on Avalon. The gods have named it the Eternal Flame, for it burns as bright as our highest aspirations."

For a moment Tamwyn's face reflected the stars' radiance. Then his expression turned grim. "Yet all is not well in our world. The scourges we have just survived will someday return, unless . . ."

He paused, gathering the strength he needed to finish the sentence. "Unless humanity leaves Avalon."

To the stunned audience, he explained his tragic revelation. He told how the stars were, in truth, doorways to other worlds, and how the Great Tree connected all of them. He described his conversation with Dagda and Lorilanda—about Avalon, its many wonders that came with great fragility; and about humanity, its many gifts that came with great frailty. He explained that humans alone could tip the balance between good and evil, and conveyed the bitter promise that any people who did not choose to leave this world would never bear children. Finally, he revealed the possibility, slim though it was, that one day in the future, humanity might be allowed to return.

"And so it is," he concluded, "that to save our wondrous homeland, we humans must leave it."

He strode across the dragon's massive snout, then nimbly climbed down. Planting his bare feet on the muddy ground, with the torch blazing beside him, he studied the anxious men and women. At last, he raised his voice again.

"Who will join me, for the sake of the world we love?"

For several seconds, no one stirred, let alone responded. Then a lone voice broke the silence, a voice Tamwyn had been longing to hear.

"I will go with you," declared Elli. She pushed her way through a knot of flamelons, emerged from the crowd, and stepped over to Tamwyn's side. In a whisper, she added, "Anywhere you want to go."

He merely gazed at her, his eyes alight.

"What you did up there," she said, "was a miracle."

"No more than what you did, Elli."

"Hmmmpff," grumbled Nuic from his seat on her shoulder. "I'd say you two amateurs are just lucky to be alive." Yet even as he spoke, his color deepened to a proud shade of purple.

Tamwyn, however, was too focused on Elli to notice. Gently, he ran his fingers through her curls. "I missed you."

"And I missed you."

Elli glanced over at Basilgarrad, who was lifting his gigantic wings to fold them upon his back. "Where did this magnificent dragon come from? Did he just appear out of nowhere?"

"Well, you'd be surprised." He turned and winked at the dragon, whose enormous green eye winked back. "Very surprised."

"All right, be mysterious if you like." She shook her head. "What I care about most is that he came in time to help you defeat Rhita Gawr."

"That he did." Tamwyn's face suddenly fell. "I only wish . . ." He swung his pack around and started to open it. "That your harp hadn't been smashed in the battle."

"Smashed?"

"Yes. Rhita Gawr's tail—" He caught himself, awestruck. For within his pack, the slab of harmóna wood gleamed without a single crack anywhere. More than that, the sound box he'd been carving had been finished, and the strings from Palimyst had all been attached. The harp was done!

In a flash, he remembered the feeling of Dagda's arm wrapping around his shoulder. And he guessed that, in that instant, the spirit lord had repaired and completed the instrument. He wondered what musical magic Dagda might have also added to the wood—and knew that he and Elli would enjoy finding out, when the time was right.

He closed his pack again. "Guess I was wrong about that." He smiled playfully. "Just like, when we first met, you were wrong about me."

"Oh, I wasn't wrong," she replied, giving him a nudge. "You *deserved* those black eyes. Both of them."

Before he could answer, another voice rang out. They turned to see someone else emerge from the throng of people.

"I will join you," declared Lleu. As the lanky priest strode toward them, the silver-winged falcon on his shoulder piped a whistle of agreement.

More people followed. Some were old enough to be graying, others looked quite young. Many hobbled weakly or wore bloody bandages from injuries sustained in the battle. Several couples came forward, though most of the survivors were single men and women.

Among them, toward the end of the procession, was Morrigon. Although his thin frame made him look more like a windblown tree than a man, he carried himself proudly. When he approached Lleu, he glared at the priest, angrily squinting his bloodshot eye. Nonetheless, he joined the group around Tamwyn.

Last of all—to the surprise of many, especially Elli— came a young woman wearing the tattered robe of a Drumadian priestess. Llynia, too, tried to walk proudly. In fact, she did her best to look perfectly regal, thrusting out her chin. Yet that very chin glowed green in the starlight, spoiling the effect. And as soon as she neared Elli, she averted her gaze.

At first, Elli couldn't help but feel satisfied at seeing the priestess finally humbled. But her satisfaction soon gave way to sympathy. For she noticed, in Llynia's hand, a small bough studded with purple buds.

Then someone else stepped toward Elli. It was not a human, but an elf, who strode with a graceful air despite her solemn expression.

"Brionna," exclaimed Elli, "I am so glad to see you!" She threw her arms around the elf maiden's neck. "I thought maybe you had—"

"Died," finished Brionna. "For a moment there during the fighting, part of me did die. Then unexpectedly, life returned."

She placed her slender hands on Elli's shoulders. "You and your companions will surely grieve to depart from fair Avalon. But you should know that many of us who stay behind will also grieve. I shall miss you, my good sister."

Elli blinked to clear her vision.

Tamwyn tapped Brionna's shoulder. "Is Scree here? Have you seen him?"

The elf lowered her arms and turned to face him. "He was here," she said grimly. "And he saved my life. But then he left to fight Harlech, that murderer." Her voice dropped to a whisper. "And I haven't seen him since."

Worriedly, Tamwyn scanned the crowd gathered around them. He spotted several eaglefolk who were standing next to Basilgarrad, examining his great wings with open admiration. Scree, though, was not among them. Nor was he anywhere else to be seen, on the ground or in the sky.

As he continued to search, Tamwyn's gaze fell upon the tall, stately form of a mudmaker. He knew, without doubt, that it was Aelonnia of Isenwy. Her brown eyes gazed back at him, while her long fingers drummed against her sides. Then he heard her resonant, lilting whisper, as she spoke directly into his mind.

"Truly a Maker you are, Tamwyn of Stoneroot, as I told you when first we met. Yet believe me you did not."

No, he replied through his thoughts. *I guess I just wasn't ready.* He exhaled slowly. *Which is how I feel right now.*

"Were you ready to climb to the highest reaches of the Great Tree?" she asked in response. "To defeat Rhita Gawr? To rekindle the stars? No, but succeed you did. Earned my trust, you have, and now you must trust in yourself."

With that, Aelonnia bent forward in what Tamwyn knew was a respectful bow. He started to bow in return, when a shadow suddenly fell over him. He looked up—

Into the face of Shim. As enormous as it was, there was no mistaking those wild eyes, that mop of white hair, and that nose which even now seemed too big for its face.

"Shim!" he cried. "You're a giant again."

"Nicely, isn't it?" he bellowed. "And me hearing's come back, laddy. Probably thanks to me old ears getting so bigly! So now I can hears most anything that someone might utterly." He winked at Brionna, who, like Elli, was also peering up at him. "Even the softly voice of me little niece Rowanna."

He thumped his chest triumphantly, rattling his cloak of woven willows. "Bigly I is now, and bigly I will remain foreverly after."

Then a look of anxiety, which seemed most odd for a giant, came across his face. He glanced over his shoulder at a female giant with a mouth that was so huge it was beyond enormous. Seeing that she was standing a good distance away, he breathed a sigh of relief that nearly knocked Tamwyn and the others to the ground. And then he added, as softly as he could manage, "Just so long as I stays away from Bonlog."

Basilgarrad, who had been listening, released a deep, rumbling chuckle.

Shim looked scornfully at the dragon. Scrunching his nose at this creature whose size rivaled his own, he said, "You just don't know what it's like to be smallsy."

The dragon laughed even harder, frightening several of the people gathered nearby.

At last, Shim turned back to Tamwyn. "I is sorry to sees you go, laddy. Really, truly, honestly. I know you is full of madness, like your grandlyfather Merlin. But evenly so, I will miss you."

The young man gave a nod. "I'll miss you, too, Shim."

Just then, Elli grabbed his arm. "Look there! Look who's coming."

An elderly woman strode toward them, her silver curls bouncing with every step. *Rhia.* Even without her suit of woven vines, or the thick shawl that bulged where it covered her delicate wings, Tamwyn and Elli would have recognized her right away. The easy grace of her step, the wrinkles of smiles around her mouth, and the look of unsurpassed wisdom, all spoke of the Lady of the Lake.

"Well, my children," she said as she reached them. "It is lovely, truly lovely, to see you again."

She paused as a pair of tiny light flyers lifted off her wrist. The sparkling creatures circled her once, then nestled themselves in her hair, joining dozens of others whose light set her curls aglow.

Seeing that her small friends were settled, she continued. "You have done well, each in your own way. You, Tamwyn Eopia, have made your great-aunt very proud."

Despite everything, he smiled.

"And you, Elliryanna Lailoken, have done equally well." She reached out and gently touched the young woman's chin. "If I ever had a daughter," she whispered, "I would have wanted one like you."

But Elli didn't smile. "Your crystal," she said hesitantly. "I had to—had to destroy it."

"I know, my child. You did what was necessary for Avalon."

Her gray-blue eyes radiated kindness. "Thanks to you, many remarkable creatures will continue to live with freedom and dignity."

Elli still didn't smile. "Without the power of the crystal, though, you . . . will die."

"True." Rhia bent closer. "But many more beings will live on—including the new Sapphire Unicorn."

Elli gasped. "New unicorn? So the Sapphire Unicorn we saw on Hallia's Peak—"

"Had already given birth. That's right, to a healthy, handsome filly! I haven't seen her myself—she is, after all, the creature whom bards call *the most elusive beauty in all the lands.* But a wandering willow spirit told me that she'd glimpsed the filly scampering through a glade in El Urien."

Rhia's wrinkled face glowed like her silver curls. "So, my child, because of what you have done, Avalon still has one of its most lovely beings, the creature who embodies all that is rare and wondrous in our world."

At last, Elli gave a hint of a smile, though it was a sad one. "I only wish I could be here to see it."

"I know," the elder replied tenderly. "You will miss much about Avalon. And so, after this season of great loss, will I."

Elli stiffened. For she understood exactly what Rhia was telling her. "Coerria! She died?"

"Peacefully. By the time I reached her, I could not help her. Yet we spoke for a few moments. And even at the end, there was much more love than grief in her great heart."

The young priestess stared down at the mud.

"She gave me something, Elli. Something for you." Reaching under her heavy shawl, Rhia pulled out a small bundle. It gleamed with the rich sheen of spider's silk.

As Elli looked up and saw what it was, she covered her mouth in surprise. For she could never mistake the gown of the High Priestess. Woven by the Grand Elusa a thousand years ago, worn by Elen the Founder as well as by Rhia herself, the gown's silken threads held much of the history of Avalon. And much of its beauty, too.

"For—for me?" Elli sputtered.

"Yes, dear one. For you. She wanted you to have it. She made me promise to deliver it to you and no one else."

Standing off to one side, Llynia bit her lip and turned away.

Elli took the bundle. She hefted it, struck by how very light it seemed. Her gaze met Rhia's once again. "Thank you. Both of you."

Then her brow furrowed with a question. "What will happen to Uzzzula? Without Coerria's long white hair to braid, she won't know what to do."

Rhia smiled at just the corner of her mouth. "She will find another way to stay busy, as hive spirits always do. But like you and me, she will miss her friend terribly. That has ever been the way, when priestesses or priests are parted from their maryths."

"Hmmmpff," began the pinnacle sprite on Elli's shoulder. "Rank sentimentalists, the lot of them. Probably enjoy bathing in their own tears! Not me, I tell you. I'll always prefer a cold mountain stream."

Elli turned her head toward him—slowly, for she knew just what Nuic had meant. "You're not coming with me, are you?"

The little fellow tried to speak gruffly, but his tender shade of lavender belied his tone of voice. "Not many sprites where you're going, young wench. And besides, mistress Rhiannon over there needs someone to look after her."

"To keep me out of trouble?" asked the elder playfully.

"Impossible," retorted the sprite. "I'll be satisfied if I can just know where you are some of the time."

As Elli took him from her shoulder and gave him a gentle hug, he wriggled free. "Hmmmpff, mind the ribs, will you?" Then, his color deepening to purple, he said, "But just so you can know where *we* are some of the time, I think you should take this."

He grabbed the leather cord wrapped around his middle, then pulled off the Galator. The green jewel glowed dimly, with the intelligence of a living eye. Carefully, he gave it to her.

"Now, just because you've mastered the art of speaking through this," he warned, "I don't want you bothering me all the time."

Rhia, hearing this, raised an eyebrow in surprise.

Sad as she felt, Elli grinned at him. "No promises, Nuic."

"Hmmmpff. Something tells me I'm going to regret this."

As she handed him to Rhia, she told the sprite, "I'm going to miss your cranky old voice."

"And I suppose, now and then, I'll miss your cranky young voice."

Tamwyn, standing beside Elli, said under his breath, "I wish I could hear Scree's voice again. And what I'd give to hear his eagle's cry, one more time."

Solemnly, she nodded. "We'll miss many other sounds of Avalon, too."

He blew a long breath. "Like the chiming bells of Stoneroot. The crackle of a portal's flames. Or the whispering leaves of Woodroot." He shook his head. "I'll even miss the crazy laugh of that hoolah, Henni."

"Be careful what you wish for," grumbled Nuic.

Basilgarrad snorted in agreement. Then, as Tamwyn turned his way, the dragon rolled his gleaming eyes up toward the sky. Tamwyn followed his gaze, suddenly hopeful that he might find Scree after all.

36 · Wondrous Realms Forsaking

TAMWYN WATCHED AS SOMEONE WITH huge, silvery wings soared out of the sky. His eyes stared with astonishment; his heartbeat quickened with gratitude.

But it wasn't Scree he was watching.

A deep, rippling neigh burst from the throat of the great winged horse, Ahearna. Her cry echoed across the muddy plains now littered with dead and wounded warriors. All the people gathered around Tamwyn looked upward, and even those whose hearts ached from their losses or whose bodies stung from their wounds felt stirred by her triumphant tone. For the steed long known as the Star Galloper had indeed survived.

With a graceful glide, Ahearna landed. She tossed her head, shaking her mane, then folded her wings against her back. So lustrously did those wings glow that they seemed to have been feathered with starlight. As she walked slowly toward Tamwyn, her hooves squelched in the mud, an almost comical sound for such a majestic creature. Then came another sound, even more comical.

"Eehee, hoohoo, heeheeheeyahaha," laughed Henni as he leaped off the horse's back. He hit the ground, splattering his sacklike tunic with mud. But the hoolah didn't care. His circular eyebrows widened as he said breathlessly, "We almost died, so many times I lost count! Hoohoo ee-heeyaha, I'd love another ride like that any old time."

"Not I," answered the winged horse, flicking him with her tail as she strode past. "Be grateful for the miracles that kept you alive! If we had not fallen into the River of Time, where the gallop of hours stands still, and if Lorilanda herself had not come to us and healed my wing, you would not be laughing now."

Henni cocked his head, looking genuinely puzzled, as if he couldn't begin to grasp the concept of not laughing.

Ahearna stopped just a pace away from Tamwyn. She studied him intently, the light from his torch gleaming in her rich brown eyes. "Now, young colt, I can see how very bright your flame burns. You have saved us all. You—and the greatest of all steeds."

She turned, bowing her head toward the dragon whose enormous body rested behind Tamwyn. "Basilgarrad," she declared, "I recognize you from long ago. How you came to this young man's aid after I failed him, I do not know. But I am grateful beyond the stars that you did."

The dragon's long ears trembled. "You did not fail, Star Galloper. You did your part, with courage and grace. And without that part, I could not have done mine."

Bobbing her head, Ahearna turned back to Tamwyn. Her voice much softer now, she said, "Lorilanda told me how it came to pass that you left my star darkened. And how, after you have passed through its doorway, your spark will rekindle its flame. Yet she did not need to tell me how you have suffered by this decision: That much I can see for myself."

His expression grew somber. He gazed at the faces arrayed before him, many of which he would never see again. And he thought of other faces, Scree's in particular, that he would sorely miss. Hoarsely, he said, "Leaving these people, these places, breaks my heart."

It was Rhia who answered him, in a voice quiet yet resonant. "I understand, my child, for in the long years that I have lived apart from my brother Merlin, part of me has hurt so much it seemed to die. Yet that very same death has kept my love for him alive."

Tamwyn shook his head. "I don't understand."

Gently, she took his hand. "Let your heart break, my son. Yes, let it break wide open! For only then can you feel all the truth and beauty that you have lost. Only then can you hope, far in the future, to find it all again."

Hesitantly, he nodded.

All at once, another problem occurred to him, striking him with the force of black lightning. "Wait! How can I ever lead humanity out of Avalon, as I promised?"

He waved at all the men and women crowded around him. "There are far too many people here. Ahearna, you couldn't carry more than a few of us. Even you, my good dragon, couldn't take more than a fraction. And neither Dagda nor Lorilanda is around to help. This whole plan will fail unless I can find someone else who can help us."

"Someone," boomed a voice from over by the dragon's tail, "like me?"

Tamwyn turned to see, striding toward him, a sturdy eagleman, bare-chested in his human form. "Scree!"

The two brothers embraced. When they pulled apart, they continued to peer at each other for a long moment. At last, Scree said, "You've done well, Tam." His yellow-rimmed eyes narrowed. "Though you would have done better if you'd had my help."

"No doubt," Tamwyn replied, grinning. He glanced over at Brionna, whose face positively glowed—with relief, as well as something more. Then he noticed a golden-eyed eagleboy standing nearby. The boy gazed admiringly at Scree, while exuding a mixture of courage, sadness, and dignity that reminded Tamwyn of Scree's younger self.

Turning back to his brother, Tamwyn said, "You may not have been with me. But it's clear you had some other important things to do."

"That I did, little brother." He scratched his hooked nose. "I had to deal with my, er, past. Take charge of a wayward clan. And kill that worm Harlech. But through all that, I never forgot about you. And I'll never forget about you even after you're gone."

Tamwyn scowled. "You may not have to worry about that, Scree. As you heard me say a minute ago, if I'm ever going to go, I'll need the help of someone else—someone who is much more powerful than either of us."

"I know just the person," Scree declared.

"Who?"

"The fellow who healed my wounds from the battle." The eagleman rolled his muscular shoulders, as if opening his wings. "If he hadn't come along, I would have bled to death."

Tamwyn pursed his lips, uncertain. "Who do you mean?"

"Just me, lad."

Tamwyn—like Elli, Rhia, Brionna, and the others nearby—turned to see who had spoken.

Out of the multitudes stepped the old bard. Despite his advanced age and precariously balanced hat, he walked with a jaunty, youthful stride. He paused beside Ahearna, just long enough to stroke her back lightly. Then, twirling one end of his sideways-growing beard, he came closer to Tamwyn. For several seconds he examined the young man from under bushy brows.

"I have come to help you," he declared at last. With a glance over at Rhia, he added more quietly, "And to apologize for not telling you sooner that I was here."

Even as Rhia gasped, Tamwyn demanded, "Who are you?" But his question was drowned out in the roar of recognition that came from Basilgarrad, and the delighted whinny from Ahearna.

For the old bard had already begun to change before their eyes—not into someone younger, but into someone far, far older. Light glowed all about his body, as his garb transformed to an azure blue robe flecked with silver runes. Meanwhile, his beard whitened and lengthened, reaching down below his waist. Wrinkles appeared on his brow, cheeks, and hands. His lopsided hat grew taller, with a pointed tip that leaned drastically. His eyes darkened until they were as black as a raven's wing. Only his bushy brows did not change.

"Merlin," whispered Tamwyn in wonder. "It's you."

"That it is," the wizard replied with a brisk nod of his head. "My, my, young man, how much you have grown! I barely recognize you and your brother now."

"Wait," protested Tamwyn. "I thought Dagda forbade you from ever coming back to Avalon! The independence of each world, and all that."

Merlin's dark eyes sparkled. "True, all true. But we made a little pact, Dagda and I—since Avalon was in, shall we say, *unusual* peril. He agreed to allow me to come back, but only if I promised not to interfere. At least, no more than a little dabble here and there."

Playfully, he toyed with the strands of his beard. "I am, after all, an incurable meddler."

As swiftly as a mountain storm fills the sky, a look of sadness filled his face. "It has been hard, believe me, to interfere no more than that." He gazed around them at the bodies—twisted, torn, and lifeless—that lay upon the muddy fields. "Very, very hard."

He turned back to Tamwyn, and his expression brightened a bit. "Since I am now here, however, I am sure that Dagda would have no problem if I used my power to send you all to mortal Earth."

Tamwyn beamed, as Elli squeezed his arm. Then he asked, "So you won't be coming with us?"

"No," the ancient wizard replied. "For one thing, I want to spend some time searching for human beings who didn't come to Isenwy, to give them the same choice you gave everyone else—and to send them to Earth if they wish. For another thing, I have been wanting to explore a few of Avalon's hidden realms, places that even you have never seen." His mouth curled slightly. "And for another, my good sister would surely kill me if I didn't stay for at least a while." He winked at Rhia, who did her best to suppress a smile.

Tamwyn shifted his weight uneasily, twisting his feet in the mud. "I must tell you something before we go. Your staff, the powerful Ohnyalei. I—er, well . . . lost it."

"Yes, of course," the wizard answered brightly. To Tamwyn's surprise, he didn't seem at all perturbed. "These things happen."

"No, you don't understand. I dropped it during the battle with Rhita Gawr."

Merlin reached out one hand and clasped Tamwyn's shoulder. "I know, my good lad. Ohnyalei and I have spent so many centuries together that we have bonded closely—so closely that we have long been able to tell each other's whereabouts."

He trembled as he spoke, making the runes on his wide sleeve glitter. "That is why I knew you had dropped the staff. And that is also why I am certain that it fell into the partly open doorway of one particular star."

Tamwyn caught his breath. "The Heart of Pegasus. The doorway to Earth!"

"That's right, lad. It is there now, somewhere on Earth, waiting to be found. By you, perhaps—or by someone else, maybe a girl or boy of that world."

He bent closer, so that stray hairs from his beard tickled Tamwyn's chin. "Even if someone else finds the staff, however, they will need help in learning to master its powers. And who could possibly be a better guide than my grandson?" He savored each word as he added, "You are, after all, the true heir of Merlin."

Tamwyn stood a little taller. He gazed at the elder in silence for some time. At last, very slowly, Merlin pulled away.

The wizard took a step backward. "Before you leave, though, I have a gift for you and your companions. A song of Avalon—the last, I fear, you shall ever hear, except in your dreams."

With a dramatic sweep of his arm, he removed his hat. Just as had been true during his days as a bard, a small creature sat upon his head. Teardrop-shaped, with bluish skin flecked with gold, the creature shook itself, making its translucent robe ripple like water. Its expressive face revealed a wide range of emotions—triumph and tragedy, hope and longing, humor and sorrow.

The museo began to hum, a rolling sound whose undertones carried feelings more than sounds, ideas more than melodies. The layered hum expanded, vibrating the very bones of all who could hear. A few seconds later, Merlin reached into his robe and pulled out his little lute. And then, weaving his voice into the hum, he began to sing:

> *To Avalon now cry farewell,*
> *Thy mem'ries only taking;*
> *So many seasons did thee dwell*
> *In wondrous realms forsaking.*
> *Return one day! Thy dearest goal*
> *Keep firm beyond all shaking.*
> *For mist shall ever stir thy soul,*
> *A distant music making.*
>
> *Remember each the sacred realms*
> *Though images glow dimmer—*
> *And steer thy course with homeward helm*
> *Ere time alive grows slimmer:*
> *The Land of Bells shall chime thy loss,*

As lofty summits shimmer;
El Urien, so green with moss,
Shall thrive as dreams still glimmer.

The Rainbow Seas of liquid light
With beauty shall entrance;
While flames atop Volcanoes bright
Shall forever prance;
The fertile Mud shall haunt thee most,
For that gives life a chance;
And Y Swylarna's mist shall host
The maids' eternal dance.

Then lovely dark shall welcome thee
In Shadows' endless night.
The higher realms of Merlin's Tree
Gain wonder with their height:
Their spiral falls and secret stairs
Shall climb beyond thy fright,
And stars on high shall ever shine
To guide thee with their light.

To Avalon now say farewell,
As fires of mem'ry burn;
So many seasons did thee dwell
Where wonders ever turn.
Though destined far away to roam,
Forever shall thee yearn
To find again thy heart's true home:
To Avalon return.

As the song ended, Tamwyn, Elli, and everyone else stood in silence. In their minds, however, they continued to hear the museo's hum. Just as they continued to hear the wizard's final phrase: *To Avalon return.*

Tamwyn ran his fingers along the leather strap of his

pack, thinking of nothing but the song. Then he felt the tooth marks of the gray wolf, from the day he'd met Gwirion. How long ago that seemed! In that time, Gwirion had gained a new identity, as leader of the Starkeepers. Yet to Tamwyn, he would always be a fire angel—and, more importantly, a friend.

Curling his toes in the soft mud, Tamwyn thought of what else his pack contained. So many precious gifts; so many reminders of Avalon. In addition to Elli's harp, whose music would itself be a gift, there was the scroll with his father's last letter, written in the bold blue lettering of Krystallus. The special compass was there, too, pointing ever westward and starward. As was his leathereed flask, still holding some of the sweet water from the Great Hall of the Heartwood. And somewhere near the bottom of his pack was the ironwood vial that contained one last drop of Dagda's dew, which could give magical vision over vast distances.

He nodded, deciding to save that final drop for the day he might journey back to this world. *Meanwhile,* he reminded himself, *you'll just have to rely on the simple eyes of a wilderness guide.*

He hefted the pack, which weighed surprisingly little given how many treasured items it held. Yet his most precious gifts from Avalon, he knew, did not reside in his pack.

Merlin donned his wizard's hat, then raised his arms high. "Journey well, my friends! Though you must go without me, I shall be with you still."

Tamwyn took Elli's hand, squeezing tight, as the air started to shimmer. Suddenly his torch glowed brighter, as did her Galator. Light, green and blue, burst all around them, as if a star had exploded beneath their feet. The whole world fell silent—but for the echoing sound of an eagleman's cry.

The dazzling light intensified, as radiant beams burst everywhere. Tamwyn sensed that he and his companions were being guided by magical flight all the way up the roots, trunk, and branches of the Great Tree of Avalon. But he could see none of that. All he could see, apart from the radiance, was the torch that he carried.

With every second, the torch's flame grew brighter. It reminded him of another flame, one that would burn forever on high.

A Brief History of Avalon

AS ONE WORLD DIES, ANOTHER IS BORN. IT IS a time both dark and bright, a moment of miracles.

In the mist-shrouded land of Fincayra, an isle long forgotten is suddenly found, a small band of children defeats an army of death, and a people disgraced win their wings at last. And in the greatest miracle of all, a young wizard called Merlin earns his true name: Olo Eopia, great man of many worlds, many times. And yet . . . even as Fincayra is saved, it is lost—passing forever into the Otherworld of the Spirits.

But in that very moment, a new world appears. Born of a seed that beats like a heart, a seed won by Merlin on his journey through a magical mirror, this new world is a tree: the Great Tree. It stands as a bridge between Earth and Heaven, between mortal and immortal, between shifting seas and eternal mist.

Its landscape is immense, full of wonders and surprises. Its populace is as far-flung as the stars on high. Its essence is part hope, part tragedy, part mystery.

Its name is Avalon.

—the celebrated opening lines of the bard Willenia's history of Avalon, widely known as "Born of a Seed That Beats Like a Heart"

Year 0:
Merlin plants the seed that beats like a heart. A tree is born:
the Great Tree of Avalon.

THE AGE OF FLOWERING

Year 1:
Creatures of all kinds migrate to the new world, or appear
mysteriously, perhaps from the sacred mud of Malóch. The
first age of Avalon, the Age of Flowering, begins.

Year 1:
Elen of the Sapphire Eyes and her daughter Rhiannon
found a new faith, the Society of the Whole, and become
its first priestesses. The Society is dedicated to promoting
harmony among all living creatures, and to protecting the
Great Tree that supports and sustains all life. The new
faith focuses on seven sacred Elements—what Elen called
"the seven sacred parts that together make the Whole."
They are: Earth, Air, Fire, Water, Life, LightDark, and
Mystery.

Year 2:
The great spirit Dagda, god of wisdom, visits both Elen and
Rhia in a dream. He reveals that there are seven separate
roots of Avalon, each with its own distinct landscapes and
populations—and that their new faith will eventually reach
into all of them. With Dagda's help, Elen, Rhia, and their
original followers (plus several giants, led by Merlin's old
friend, Shim) make a journey to Lost Fincayra, to the great
circle of stones that was the site of the famous Dance of the
Giants. Together, they transport the sacred stones all the way
back to Avalon. The circle is rebuilt deep in the realm of
Stoneroot, and becomes the Great Temple in the center of a
new compound that is dedicated to the Society of the Whole.

Year 18:
The Drumadians—as the Society of the Whole is commonly called, in honor of Lost Fincayra's Druma Wood—ordain their first group of priestesses and priests. They include Lleu of the One Ear; Cwen, last of the treelings; and (to the surprise of many) Babd Catha, the Ogre's Bane.

Year 27:
Merlin returns to Avalon—to explore its mysteries, and more important, to wed the deer woman Hallia. They are married under shining stars in the high peaks of upper Olanabram. This region is the only place in the seven root-realms where the lower part of Avalon's trunk can actually be seen, rising into the ever-swirling mist. (The trunk can also be seen from the Swaying Sea, but this strange place is normally not considered part of the Great Tree's roots.) Here, atop the highest mountain in the Seven Realms, which Merlin names Hallia's Peak, they exchange their vows of loyalty and love. The wedding, announced by canyon eagles soaring on high, includes more varied kinds of creatures than have assembled anywhere since the Great Council of Fincayra after the Dance of Giants long ago. By the grace of Dagda, they are joined by three spirit-beings, as well: the brave hawk, Trouble, who sits on Merlin's shoulder; the wise bard, Cairpré, who stands by Elen's side throughout the entire ceremony; and the deer man, Eremon, who is the devoted brother of Hallia. Even the dwarf ruler, Urnalda, attends—along with the great white spider known as the Grand Elusa; the jester, Bumbelwy; the giant, Shim; the scrubamuck-loving creature, Ballymag; and the dragon queen, Gwynnia; plus several of her fire-breathing children. The ceremonies are conducted by Elen and Rhia, founders of the Society of the Whole, the priest Lleu of

the One Ear, and the priestess Cwen of the treelings. (Babd Catha is also invited, but chooses to battle ogres instead.) According to legend, the great spirits Dagda and Lorilanda also appear, and give the newlyweds their everlasting blessings.

Year 27:
Krystallus Eopia, son of Merlin and Hallia, is born. Celebrations last for years—especially among the fun-loving hoolahs and sprites. Although the newborn is almost crushed when the giant Shim tries to kiss him, Krystallus survives and grows into a healthy child. While he is nonmagical, since wizards' powers often skip generations, his wizard's blood assures him a long life. Even as an infant, he shows an unusual penchant for exploring. Like his mother, he loves to run, though he cannot move with the speed and grace of a deer.

Year 33:
The mysterious Rugged Path, connecting the realms of Stoneroot and Woodroot, is discovered by a young lad named Fergus. Legend tells that Fergus found the path when he followed a strange white doe into the high peaks. Given how mysteriously the white doe appeared, she might really have been the spirit Lorilanda, goddess of birth, flowering, and renewal. The legend also says that the path runs only in one direction, though which direction— and why—remains unclear. Since very few travelers have ever reported finding the path, and since those reports seem unreliable, most people doubt that the path even exists.

Year 37:
Elen dies. She is grateful for her mortal years and yet deeply glad that she can at last rejoin her love, the bard Cairpré, in the land of the spirits. The great spirit Dagda

himself, in the form of an enormous stag, appears in Avalon for the sole purpose of guiding her to the Otherworld. Rhia assumes Elen's responsibilities as High Priestess of the Society of the Whole.

Year 51:
Travel within the Seven Realms, through the use of enchanted portals, is discovered by the wood elf Serella. She becomes the first queen of the wood elves, and over time she learns much about this dangerous art. In her words, "Portalseeking is a difficult way to travel, yet an easy way to die." She leads several expeditions to Waterroot, which culminate in the founding of Caer Serella, the original colony of water elves. However, her first expedition to Shadowroot ends in complete disaster—and her own death.

Year 130:
A terrible blight appears in the upper reaches of Woodroot, killing everything it touches. Rhia, believing this to be the work of the evil spirit Rhita Gawr, seeks help from Merlin.

Year 131:
As the blight spreads, destroying trees and other living creatures in Woodroot's forests, Merlin takes Rhia and her trusted companion, the priest Lleu of the One Ear, on a remarkable journey. Traveling through portals known only to Merlin, they voyage deep inside the Great Tree. There they find a great subterranean lake that holds magical white water. After the lake's water rises to the surface at the White Geyser of Crystallia, in upper Waterroot, it separates into the seven colors of the spectrum (at Prism Gorge) and flows to many places, giving both water and color to everything it meets. Merlin reveals to Rhia and Lleu that this white water gains its magic from its high

concentration of *élano,* the most powerful—and most elusive—magical substance in all of Avalon. Produced as sap deep within the Great Tree's roots, élano combines all seven sacred Elements, and is, in Merlin's words, "the true life-giving force of this world." At the great subterranean lake, Merlin gathers a small crystal of élano with the help of his staff—whose name, Ohnyalei, means *spirit of grace* in the Fincayran Old Tongue. Then he, Rhia, and Lleu return to Woodroot and place the crystal at the origin of the blight. Thanks to the power of élano, the blight recedes and finally disappears. Woodroot's forests are healed.

Year 132:
Rhia, as High Priestess, introduces her followers to élano, the essential life-giving sap of the Great Tree. Soon thereafter, Lleu of the One Ear publishes his masterwork, *Cyclo Avalon.* This book sets down everything that Lleu has learned about the seven sacred Elements, the portals within the Tree, and the lore of élano. It becomes the primary text for Drumadians throughout Avalon.

Year 192:
After a final journey to her ancestral home, the site of the legendary Carpet Caerlochlann, Hallia dies. So profound is Merlin's grief that he climbs high into the jagged mountains of Stoneroot and does not speak with anyone, even his sister Rhia, for several months.

Year 193:
Merlin finally descends from the mountains—but only to depart from Avalon. He must leave, he tells his dearest friends, to devote himself entirely to a new challenge in another world: educating a young man named Arthur in the land of Britannia, part of mortal Earth. He hints, without

revealing any details, that the fates of Earth and Avalon are somehow entwined.

Year 237:
Krystallus, now an accomplished explorer, founds the Eopia College of Mapmakers in Waterroot. As its emblem, he chooses the star within a circle, ancient symbol for the magic of Leaping between places and times.

THE AGE OF STORMS

Year 284:
Without any warning, the stars of one of Avalon's most prominent constellations, the Wizard's Staff, go dark. One by one, the seven stars in the constellation—symbolizing the legendary Seven Songs of Merlin, by which both the wizard and his staff came into their true powers—disappear. The process takes only three weeks. Star watchers agree that this portends something ominous for Avalon. The Age of Storms has begun.

Year 284:
War breaks out between dwarves and dragons in the realm of Fireroot, sparked by disputes over the underground caverns of Flaming Jewels. Although these two peoples have cooperated for centuries in harvesting as well as preserving the jewels, their unity finally crumbles. The skilled dwarves regard the jewels as sacred, and want to harvest them only deliberately over long periods of time. By contrast, the dragons (and their allies, the flamelons) want to take immediate advantage of all the wealth and power that the jewels could provide. The fighting escalates, sweeping up other peoples—even some clans of normally peaceful faeries. Alliances form, pitting dwarves, most elves and humans, giants, and eaglefolk against the dragons, flamel-

ons, dark elves, avaricious humans, and gobsken. Meanwhile, marauding ogres and trolls take advantage of the chaos. In the widening conflict, only the sylphs, mudmakers, and some museos remain neutral . . . while the hoolahs simply enjoy all the excitement.

Year 300:
The war worsens, spreading across the Seven Realms of Avalon. Drumadian Elders debate the true nature of the War of Storms: Is it limited exclusively to Avalon? Or is it really just a skirmish in the greater ongoing battle of the spirits—the clash between the brutal Rhita Gawr, whose goal is to control all the worlds, and the allies Lorilanda and Dagda, who want free peoples to choose for themselves? To most of Avalon's citizens, however, such a question is irrelevant. For them, the War of Storms is simply a time of struggle, hardship, and grief.

Year 413:
Rhia, who has grown deeply disillusioned with the brutality of Avalon's warring peoples—and also with the growing rigidity of the Society of the Whole—resigns as High Priestess. She departs for some remote part of Avalon, and is never heard from again. Some believe that she traveled to mortal Earth to rejoin Merlin; others believe that she merely wandered alone until, at last, she died.

Year 421:
Halaad, child of the mudmakers, is gravely wounded by a band of gnomes. Seeking safety, she crawls to the edge of a bubbling spring. Miraculously, her wounds heal. The Secret Spring of Halaad becomes famous in story and song— but its location remains hidden to all but the elusive mudmakers.

Year 472:
Bendegeit, highlord of the water dragons, presses for peace. On the eve of the first treaty, however, some dragons revolt. In the terrible battle that follows, Bendegeit is killed. The war rages on with renewed ferocity.

Year 498:
In early spring, when the first blossoms have appeared on the trees, an army of flamelons and dragons attacks Stoneroot. In the Battle of the Withered Spring, many villages are destroyed, countless lives are lost, and even the Great Temple of the Drumadians is scorched with flames. Only with the help of the mountain giants, led by Jubolda and her three daughters, are the invaders finally defeated. In the heat of the battle, Jubolda's eldest daughter, Bonlog Mountain-Mouth, is saved when her attackers are crushed by Shim, the old friend of Merlin. But when she tries to thank him with a kiss, he shrieks and flees into the highlands. Bonlog Mountain-Mouth tries to punish Shim for this humiliation, but cannot find him. Shim remains in hiding for many years.

Year 545:
The Lady of the Lake, a mysterious enchantress, first appears in the deepest forests of Woodroot. She issues a call for peace, spread throughout the Seven Realms by the small winged creatures called light flyers, but her words are not heeded.

Year 693:
The great wizard Merlin finally returns from Britannia. He leads the Battle of Fires Unending, which destroys the last alliance of dark elves and fire dragons. The flamelons reluctantly surrender. Gobsken, sensing defeat, scatter to the far reaches of the Seven Realms. Peace is restored at last.

THE AGE OF RIPENING

Year 693:
The great Treaty of the Swaying Sea, crafted by the Lady of the Lake, is signed by representatives of all known peoples except gnomes, ogres, trolls, gobsken, changelings, and death dreamers. The Age of Storms is over; the Age of Ripening begins.

Year 694:
Merlin again vanishes, but not before he announces that he expects never to return to Avalon. He declares solemnly that unless some new wizard appears—which is highly unlikely—the varied peoples of Avalon must look to themselves to find justice and peace. As a final, parting gesture, he travels to the stars with the aid of a great dragon named Basilgarrad—and then magically rekindles the seven stars of the Wizard's Staff, the constellation whose destruction presaged the terrible Age of Storms. At last, he departs for mortal Earth, by entering the mysterious River of Time from the branch-realm of Holosarr.

Year 694:
Soon after Merlin departs, the Lady of the Lake makes a chilling prediction, which comes to be known as the Dark Prophecy: A time will come when all the stars of Avalon will grow steadily darker, until there is a total stellar eclipse that lasts a whole year. And in that year, a child will be born who will bring about the very end of Avalon, the one and only world shared by all creatures alike—human and nonhuman, mortal and immortal. Only Merlin's true heir, the Lady of the Lake adds, might save Avalon. But she says no more about who the wizard's heir might be, or how he or she could defeat the child of the Dark Prophecy. And so throughout the realms, people wonder: *Who will be the child of the Dark Prophecy? And who will be the true heir of Merlin?*

Year 700:
In the eternal darkness of Shadowroot, a new city is founded: Dianarra, the City of Light. Legends say that the city was built by people from the stars, whose very bodies were aflame. Called Ayanowyn, or fire angels, they brought the light of torches and bonfires to Shadowroot. And another kind of light, as well—that of stories from many distant lands.

Year 702:
Le-fen-flaith, greatest architect of the sylphs of Airroot, completes his most ambitious (and useful) project to date: building a bridge, from ropes of spun cloudthread, spanning the misty gap between Airroot and Mudroot. He names it *Trishila o Mageloo,* which means *the air sighs sweetly* in the sylphs' native language. But in time, most travelers come to call it the Misty Bridge. The first people to cross it, other than sylphs, are the Lady of the Lake and her friend Nuic, a pinnacle sprite.

Year 717:
Krystallus, exceptionally long-lived due to his wizard's ancestry, and already the first person to have explored many parts of Avalon's roots, becomes the first ever to reach the Great Hall of the Heartwood. In the Great Hall he finds a single portal that could lead to all Seven Realms—but no way to go higher in the Tree. He vows to return one day, and to find some way to travel upward, perhaps even all the way to the stars.

Year 842:
In the remote realm of Woodroot, the old teacher Hanwan Belamir gains renown for his bold new ideas about agriculture and craftsmanship, which lead to more productive farms as well as more comfort and leisure for villagers. Some even begin to call him Olo Belamir—the first person

to be hailed in that way since the birth of Avalon, when Merlin was proclaimed Olo Eopia. While the man himself humbly scoffs at such praise, his Academy of Prosperity thrives.

Year 894:
In Shadowroot, civil war erupts among the dark elves. When the fighting ends, most—if not all—of the dark elves are dead, the City of Light is destroyed, and Shadowroot's only portal to other realms is closed. What really happened remains a mystery that only the museos may fully comprehend.

Year 900:
Belamir's teachings continue to spread. Although wood elves and others resent his theories about humanity's "special role" in Avalon, more and more humans support him. As Belamir's following grows, his fame reaches into other realms.

Year 985:
As the Dark Prophecy predicted, a creeping eclipse slowly covers the stars of Avalon. So begins the much-feared Year of Darkness. Every realm (except the flamelon stronghold of Fireroot) declares a ban against having any new children during this time, out of fear that one of them could be the child of the Dark Prophecy. Some peoples, such as dwarves and water dragons, take the further step of killing any offspring born this year. Throughout the Seven Realms, Drumadian followers seek to find the dreaded child—as well as the true heir of Merlin.

Year 985:
Despite the pervasive darkness, Krystallus continues his explorations. He voyages to the realm of the flamelons, even though outsiders—especially those with human

blood—have never been welcome there. Soon after he arrives, his party is attacked, and the survivors are captured. Somehow Krystallus escapes, with the help of an unidentified friend. (Some believe it is Halona, princess of the flamelons, who helps him; others point to signs that his ally is an eaglewoman.) Ignoring the danger of the Dark Prophecy, Krystallus and his rescuer are wed and conceive a child. Just after the birth, however, the mother and newborn son disappear.

Year 987:
Beset with grief over the loss of his wife and child, Krystallus sets out on another journey, his most ambitious quest ever: to find a route upward into the very trunk and limbs of the Great Tree. Some believe, however, that his true goal is something even more perilous—to solve at last the great mystery of Avalon's stars. Or is he really just fleeing from his grief? Whatever his goal, he does not succeed, for somewhere on this quest, he perishes. His long life, and many explorations, finally come to an end.

Year 1002:
Seventeen years have now passed since the Year of Darkness. Troubles are mounting across the Seven Realms: fights between humans and other kinds of creatures; severe drought—and a strange graying of colors—in the upper reaches of Stoneroot, Waterroot, and Woodroot; attacks by nearly invisible killer birds called ghoulacas; and a vague sense of growing evil. Many people believe that all this proves that the dreaded child of the Dark Prophecy is alive and coming into power. They pray openly for the true heir of Merlin—or the long-departed wizard himself—to appear at last and save Avalon.

Year 1002:
Late in the year, as the drought worsens, the stars of a ma-

jor constellation—the Wizard's Staff—begin to go out. This has happened only once before, other than in the Year of Darkness: at the start of the Age of Storms in the Year of Avalon 284. No one knows why this is happening, or how to stop it. But most people fear that the vanishing of the Wizard's Staff can mean only one thing: the final ruin of Avalon.

The Many Lives of Avalon
A Guide to Characters and Places

CHARACTERS

Abcahn

This Drumadian Elder is fluent in many languages, including the whispered speech of the mist **faeries** and the exceedingly difficult underwater language of the mer people. (His interest in language began during boyhood when he fell into a den of giant badgers and broke his leg. By the time he left several weeks later, wearing a splint that the badgers had made for him, he was fluent in their form of speech.) As a linguist, he is often asked to travel with the priestesses and priests of the Society of the Whole.

In the Year of Avalon 987, Abcahn accompanied a group of Drumadians to **Waterroot**. When their boat was blown off course in the Rainbow Seas, into a cauldron of bubble-fish, everyone on board became so giddy that they jumped into the water and drowned. Only Abcahn survived, though not because of his wisdom or strength of will. No, he simply slipped and hit his head on the boat's side. He drifted, unconscious, until the bubblefish were gone. Weeks later, he returned to the Drumadian compound with his tale of woe. Among those who heard it was **Lleu**, who later tells it to **Elli**, **Brionna**, **Nuic**, and **Shim**.

Abelawn

The ancestors of Abelawn first settled in **Stoneroot's** land of bells at the end of the Age of Flowering in **Avalon's** third century. Abelawn continues the tradition of farming with Drumadian ethics, always seeking the consent of the goats, horses, and sheep who share his lands and labors. He is a friend of **Tamwyn**, and the young man often helps to harvest melons in the autumn, when there is little work for a wilderness guide.

Aelonnia of Isenwy

Aelonnia is a mudmaker, one of the most mysterious and most magical creatures in **Avalon**. She is the guardian of **Malóch's** southernmost **portal**, near the Secret Spring of **Halaad**, although she rarely shows herself. Normally, when travelers arrive through the portal, she and her fellow mudmakers remain disguised as mud-covered boulders. When they grow to their natural size, as they do for **Tamwyn** and **Elli**, the mudmakers each stand twice as tall as an adult human. They have enormous eyes, as brown as the rest of their bodies, and four slender arms, each with three long and delicate fingers.

Aelonnia's whispering voice carries a lilt more like music than speech. And her words are full of wisdom about magic and its highest uses. For in the earliest days of Avalon, **Merlin** himself gave the mudmakers an extraordinary power—the ability to Make, to form living creatures from the élano-rich mud of this land. In the years since, the mudmakers have used this power judiciously, bringing to life creatures as varied as the giant elephaunts of Africqua to the tiny **light flyers** who accompany the **Lady of the Lake** wherever she goes. As Aelonnia explains to Tamwyn: "To Make, ten things we need: the seven sacred Elements, the mud that combines them, the time to do our work, and one thing more. The magic of Merlin."

Ahearna, the Star Galloper

"The great horse on high" of legend, Ahearna has massive wings, powerful legs, and a strong, rippling neigh. Her wings bear silvery white feathers that gleam as if made of starlight. Her deep brown eyes have seen much—including **Merlin** the wizard, whom she carried into the sky when he departed **Avalon** in the Year 694. Ever since that time, she has flown ceaselessly around a **star** known as the Heart of Pegasus. Just why is a secret known only to her and Merlin.

Aileen

The young elf maiden Aileen is one of **Brionna's** closest friends. Like Brionna, she grew up in eastern **Woodroot**, near to the deepest forest of **El Urien**—and to the rumored lair of the **Lady of the Lake**. Aileen lives in the highest tree house of a settlement built into the boughs of eight enormous elms. Unusually skilled as a carver, she is well on her way to becoming a master woodworker. More important to her friendship with Brionna, however, is Aileen's skill at brewing a tasty cup of hazelnut tea.

Angus Oge

This fire angel showed remarkable courage, as well as kindness, as he explored the farthest reaches of **Avalon**— so remarkable that he is remembered centuries later by **Ayanowyn** storypainters. As **Gwirion** explains to **Tamwyn**, Angus Oge gave so openly to the world that the world gave back to him. Once, when Angus Oge was traveling across a distant realm, he lacked any food and was close to starvation. Weakly, he set his last remaining water to boil, hoping at least to make some thin soup from local plants. But he could not even find any leaves or roots that were edible. Just before he passed out from hunger, however, a wild hare bounded over and leaped right into the pot.

Arbassa

Deep in the Druma Wood of **Lost Fincayra** grew a great oak tree named Arbassa. So wondrous was this tree, and so magical, it became the home as well as the guardian of young **Rhia**. Many years later, in memory of this tree and its surrounding forest, **Elen** adopted the term Drumadians for the members of the Society of the Whole. And for similar reasons, the home of the mysterious **Lady of the Lake** was dubbed New Arbassa.

Arc-kaya

This gray-haired eaglewoman, a member of **Stoneroot's** Iye Kalakya clan, healed **Scree** after he was badly wounded by a deadly shard from **Rhita Gawr**. Despite her fierce yellow eyes, her heart is deeply kind. Scree learns just how kind as he observes her during his recovery. He also learns that she lost a son, named Ayell, when the young eagleman threw himself into the path of an arrow that had been shot at his mother. Irrationally, Arc-kaya blames herself for her son's death. She wishes, above all, that he were still alive to follow her clan's ancient blessing: "Soar high, run free."

Ayanowyn (Fire Angels)

The Ayanowyn people, the fire angels, live deep inside the trunk of the **Great Tree** (a region called the **Middle Realm**). Inhabiting the caverns and tunnels near the upward-flowing **Spiral Cascades**, these people have painted the walls with spectacular murals that tell the story of their lives in **Avalon**. Theirs is a story that is truly glorious: Centuries ago, they traveled far rootward, to the realm of **Shadowroot**, and founded Dianarra, the City of Fallen

Stars (called today the Lost City of Light). Yet their story is also truly tragic: As the fire angel **Gwirion** explains to **Tamwyn**, his people have declined terribly since the Age of Great Light, the Lumia col Lir. And nothing reveals the fire angels' decline more clearly than their own withered forms. When healthy, their winged bodies flame bright orange with llalowyn, the fire of the soul. But when body and soul are ailing, as they are now, the fire angels can no longer fly—and resemble smoldering charcoal.

The last seer of Gwirion's clan, the elderly woman **Mananaun**, prophesied that, one day, the fire angels would return to wisdom and glory. They would regain the power of their wings and the flame of their soulfires. Then, the seer proclaimed, they would fly back to the **stars** from whence they came, long ago, in the time before storypainting began. The fire angels would be greeted by the great spirit **Dagda** himself. At that moment, their story would be renewed, and they would gain, at last, their true name as a people. But Gwirion dismisses this prophecy as wishful thinking. He is convinced that his people have fallen too far; he is sure that any hope they may rise again is merely a spark blown upon the wind.

Babd Catha, the Ogres' Bane
Never have the ogres of **Avalon** met a fiercer foe in battle than Babd Catha. While still a young girl in **Stoneroot**, she lost both her parents as well as her sister to marauding ogres. Although her own leg had been so badly injured in the attack that she would always walk with a limp, Babd Catha vowed to do whatever she could to prevent such tragedies from happening again. By the age of ten, she had become an accomplished swordswoman, and in that very year she fought her first ogre. While she was not able to kill the enemy, she did manage to frighten it so badly that it turned and ran off toward the high peaks of **Olanabram**. What distinguished Babd Catha was not just her ferocity,

but also her tenacity—which is why she tracked that ogre for over two hundred leagues before she finally caught and killed it. Taking a lock of its hair, she wove the lock into her shirt, thus beginning a simple victory tradition that she would continue her whole life.

At thirteen, she had felled more than a score of ogres, usually during their attacks on human settlements. Although broadswords remained her weapon of choice, she also perfected the skills of wielding axes, maces, lances, and pikes. By her sixteenth birthday, she had collected enough locks of hair to weave an entire shirt. That is why it surprised so many that she joined the new Society of the Whole as a follower of **Elen**. The following spring, in the Year of Avalon 18, she became one of the first priestesses ordained. She remained a friend of Elen, **Rhia**, and **Merlin** throughout her life. She was even invited to the wedding of Merlin and **Hallia**, but decided to battle ogres in **Rahnawyn** instead. She died peacefully at the age of 161, and bequeathed her entire collection of ogre hair shirts to the Eopia College of Mapmakers.

Basilgarrad

Considered by most bards and historians the greatest dragon ever to live in **Avalon**, Basilgarrad fought so bravely in the War of Storms that he became a living legend. He angered many of his fellow dragons by siding with elves, humans, and eaglefolk in the centuries-long war. But he swiftly proved himself an extraordinary warrior, often defeating two or three dragons at a time—less through his vast size and strength than through his supreme cleverness. In time, Basilgarrad became a great friend of the wizard **Merlin**, regularly carrying the wizard into dangerous territory. Perhaps Basilgarrad's most famous battle he won without so much as raking the air with his claws: He simply flew right into the lair of his enemies, the fire dragons of the Burnt Hills, and announced that he would destroy anyone who did not immediately cease fighting. So great was his reputation that more than a dozen of his foes that day surrendered.

As a green dragon from the western coast of **Woodroot**, he could not breathe fire. But his sturdy scales shielded him from the flames of attackers. And his unusually broad wings gave him remarkable mobility in flight. His tail, though, was his most powerful weapon. It stretched longer than his entire massive body, and ended in a huge bony club. "Brutal as the tail of Basilgarrad" goes the saying, for good reason.

At the conclusion of the War of Storms, the great dragon carried Merlin all the way to the **stars**, so that Merlin could relight the darkened constellation known as the Wizard's Staff. After that journey, however, Basilgarrad mysteriously disappeared. Although many have pondered the question of where he might have gone, no one is certain. The answer, it seems, lies in the strange green glint in the dragon's eyes.

Batty Lad

Never, in all his travels, has **Tamwyn** met a more bizarre creature than this scrawny little fellow with wings so crumpled that they resemble dead leaves. Because of his batlike appearance, as well as his erratic behavior, he earns the name Batty Lad. But there is also something mysterious about him, hidden behind those glowing green eyes. Tamwyn cannot identify it. All the young man can say with certainty is that this creature makes him smile. Perhaps it is Batty Lad's cupped ears that dwarf his face, or his wacky flying maneuvers, or his peculiar manner of speech—which includes such words as "wetwater," "silwilly," and "absolooteyootly." Or perhaps it is that lingering sense that there is simply more to Batty Lad than can be seen.

Bonlog Mountain-Mouth

The eldest daughter of the giant sorceress Jubolda, Bonlog has long been feared because of her violent temper—and also her huge, drooling mouth that constantly spills rivers of saliva. In the Battle of the Withered Spring, in the Year of Avalon 498, Bonlog was saved by another giant, **Shim**, who accidentally crushed her attackers. Filled with gratitude, she tried to thank him with a kiss. But the mere sight of her puckering lips so terrified him that he shrieked in terror and dashed off into the mountains to hide. Humiliated, Bonlog Mountain-Mouth chased after him. Although she never caught him, a terrible thing did happen to Shim. For no explicable reason, he began to grow smaller and smaller, until he stood no taller than a dwarf. Yet this misfortune did not diminish Bonlog's wrath: She continues to search for him, even to this day.

Brionna

As the granddaughter of **Tressimir**, the revered historian of the wood elves, Brionna grew up learning about the languages, customs, and stories of **Avalon's** diverse peoples. The young elf maiden even voyaged with Tressimir to other realms, including **Shadowroot** (where she nearly died from the sickness elves call darkdeath). Like other elves, she was raised to cherish all life. So she finds herself in a terrible dilemma when she is stolen into slavery and told that she must choose to help the sorcerer **Kulwych**— or watch her beloved Granda die.

Brionna is slim, strong, and an expert archer, carrying a longbow made of springy cedar. She is a natural beauty who wears her honey-colored hair in a long braid. And she is also feisty, with a very sharp tongue. When her deep green eyes flash in anger, anyone nearby should beware, a lesson that **Scree** is slow to learn.

Brionna prefers to wear a loose-fitting robe woven from sturdy barkcloth, whose greenish brown color helps her to blend into the forest. Often, she sits or stands completely motionless, appreciating the many wonders of the woodland realm. She has, in this way, found moments of great joy. Yet she has also experienced times of great sorrow, and those memories are even more painful than her wounds from a slave master's whip.

Catha

This silver-winged falcon is the maryth of the Drumadian priest **Lleu**, great-grandson of **Lleu of the One Ear**. Brave and bold, as well as intensely loyal, she is very similar in spirit to the hawk Trouble who befriended **Merlin** ages ago. Appropriately, she is named for the famous warrior **Babd Catha, the Ogres' Bane**.

Ciann

Ciann belongs to the **Ayanowyn** people, the fire angels. Although he shares the same village with **Gwirion**, they have little else in common. Ciann has forgotten the basic principles of his people, seeking power instead of redemption, ritual instead of meaning. As such, he tries to burn **Tamwyn** as a sacrifice on the clan's holy day.

Coerria (High Priestess Coerria)

Even as a young woman, Coerria struck the Drumadian Elders as wise beyond her years. Her serenity was such that her fellow priestesses dubbed her Quiet Island, since she held within herself a place of profound tranquility. Now, at the age of nearly two hundred years, Coerria has grown frail in body, but that wisdom and serenity are as remarkable as ever.

Even as she strolls through the grounds and gardens of her beloved compound, Coerria's long white hair is continuously straightened and braided by her maryth, a hive spirit named **Uzzzula**. As she moves, Coerria's elegant gown woven of spider's silk glistens, though not as brightly as her eyes. Those eyes are as blue as an alpine tarn. And they are no less observant for their years: Coerria is well aware of **Llynia's** personal ambitions, just as she is quick to notice the potential of an apprentice third class named **Elliryanna**.

Cuttayka

To win the rank of first among the Clan Sentries, the eagleman Cuttayka had to prove his skills as a warrior. And he also needed to prove his loyalty to **Quenaykha**, the ruthless leader of the Bram Kaie clan of **Fireroot**. He did both, many times over, as the battle scars on his chest demonstrate. This burly eagleman with an angular jaw owes his highest allegiance, however, not to Quenaykha—but to the clan itself.

Dagda

Dagda, deeply revered, is the god of supreme knowledge and wisdom. Together with **Lorilanda**, goddess of birth and renewal, he rules the **Otherworld of the Spirits**. As much as they savor the fruits of peace and serenity, they are always working to contain their nemesis, **Rhita Gawr**, who hungers to control all the worlds.

Bards sing that the young wizard **Merlin** once visited Dagda in the Otherworld, at the mist-shrouded Tree of Soul. There the great spirit appeared as an elderly man with a wounded arm. Yet despite his frail appearance, Dagda's brown eyes seemed as bright as a sky full of stars. As he spoke with Merlin, he toyed with shreds of mist, knotting and unknotting them by a sweep of his finger or a mere glance. While Merlin had the distinct feeling that Dagda was doing much more than reshaping the mist, he also knew that the god would never interfere directly with the fate of mortal worlds. For Dagda believes profoundly in the importance of allowing mortals to choose their own futures, to create their own destinies.

That is why, more than a thousand years after that visit

from Merlin, in the great battles for **Avalon**, Dagda resisted the temptation to participate directly. Instead, he chose to rely upon the courage, perseverance, and wisdom of mortals—especially two young people: a wilderness guide named **Tamwyn**, and an apprentice priestess named **Elli**. Joining them were many others, including the solitary eagleman **Scree**, the brave elf **Brionna**, the gruff pinnacle sprite **Nuic**, the irrepressible hoolah **Henni**, the wise craftsman **Palimyst**, the winged steed **Ahearna**, the loyal Drumadian priest **Lleu**, the shrunken giant **Shim**, and the ancient dragon **Basilgarrad**.

Deth Macoll

This master of disguise is **Avalon's** most dangerous assassin—which is why the sorcerer **Kulwych** enlists his services. Although he is human, Deth Macoll can alter his appearance almost as drastically as a changeling. He can appear, at one moment, as an elderly woman who is so hunched over that her head nearly touches her knees. Then, at the next moment, he can become a bumbling jester who wears tiny silver bells all over his clothes, so that he jingles whenever he moves. He can assume many other guises as well, although his true form is that of a bald man with a sallow face and flinty gray eyes.

More than the art of disguise, Deth Macoll enjoys the sense of complete power he feels the instant before he kills someone. He savors that feeling, and often prolongs it by stretching out the death of his prey. As a youth, his parents disappeared just when his health deteriorated; during those years what he most craved was a measure of control. Now, every time he thrusts his hidden blade into another victim, he finds exactly that.

Deth Macoll and Kulwych do not enjoy each other's company, and never have. But they work together occasionally because it is mutually profitable. When Deth is hired to hunt down the young priestess **Elli**, however, the old relationship changes. Now their goal is not merely to eliminate someone, but to gain enormous power in the process—power they are unlikely to share.

Drumalings

Tamwyn first encounters these strange, treelike creatures in **Merlin's Knothole**, and then later in the branch-realm of **Holosarr**. Standing twice a man's height, their woody skin is knobby and weathered, with grassy tufts sprouting from their many limbs. Their faces are found midway up their scraggly forms: Each has a ragged slit for a mouth, a double knob that might be a nose, and a lone, vertical eye that is as tall and narrow as a twig. The eye never blinks. They think not with words, but with emotions. And Tamwyn learns, to his detriment, that those emotions often veer toward fear and violent rage.

Edan

This wood elf is known for his skill as a tracker through the forests of **El Urien**. He is also known, as **Brionna** learned early in her childhood, for his temper. (His name, in the elvish tongue, means "fiery moods.") Like Brionna, however, he would not go to war unless **Avalon** and the elves' way of life were truly threatened.

Elen of the Sapphire Eyes

Elen's life bridged several worlds: mortal **Earth**, **Lost Fincayra**, and **Avalon**. On Earth, in the squalid village of Caer Vedwyd, she was called Branwen; in Fincayra, she was known as Elen of the Sapphire Eyes; and in Avalon, she became Elen the Founder. She embraced the widely varied qualities of her worlds. Perhaps that is why she could love two so very different men: the gentle poet Cairpré, and the ruthless king Stangmar.

Similarly, Elen's spiritual beliefs connected a variety of different faiths. Combining the wisdom of Druids, Christians, and Jews, she became a skilled healer as well as a bard, with a special fondness for Greek myths. As likely to tell a tale about another healer from Galilee as she was to speak of Moses or the Greek goddess Athena, she was respected by the most wise people in her midst—and reviled by the most intolerant. In fact, her son, the young **Merlin**, first called upon his magical powers to save her from being burned at the stake by some of her enemies, a gang of young ruffians led by Dinatius. While Merlin did manage to save Elen's life, he started a terrible fire that caused him to lose forever the use of his eyes. In time, with Elen's help, he learned to see in an entirely different way, a way befitting a wizard: Merlin came to see not with his eyes, but with his heart.

Later, when Merlin's magical seed gave birth to the world of Avalon, Elen and her daughter **Rhia** founded a new spiritual order to govern its many peoples. The Society of the Whole was dedicated to promoting harmony among all living creatures, and to protecting the Great Tree that supports and sustains all life. Elen of the Sapphire Eyes thus became Elen the Founder. Her new faith was built upon seven sacred Elements—Earth, Air, Fire, Water, Life, LightDark, and Mystery—which together comprise the Whole. To give her faith a home, Elen and her followers (including Rhia, **Lleu of the One Ear**, and **Babd Catha**) built a compound in **Stoneroot**. And in the compound's very center stood a Great Temple that was, in fact, the circle of stones from Lost Fincayra known as **Dance of the Giants**.

At the end of Elen's mortal life, in the Year of Avalon 37, the great spirit **Dagda** honored her by guiding her all the way to the **Otherworld**. There she could, at last, rejoin her life's greatest love, the bard Cairpré.

Elliryanna Lailoken (Elli)

Elli was born in **Mudroot**, one year after the Year of Darkness. A playful and resourceful child, she roamed Mudroot with her father, a Drumadian priest who played the harp, and her mother, an herbal healer with extensive knowledge of the medicinal values of plants in the jungles of Africqua. Then, just before her tenth birthday, her life was torn asunder: Gnomes murdered her parents and stole Elli as a slave. For six brutal years, she lived in the gnomes' dark underground caverns, keeping herself alive (as well as sane) by playing her father's harp. Finally, after several failed attempts, she managed to escape. Having heard about the Society of the Whole from her father, she went to the Drumadian compound to learn the ways of **Avalon's** founding spiritual guides, **Elen** and **Rhiannon**. By a mysterious coincidence, an ancient pinnacle sprite by the name of **Nuic** arrived at the compound simultaneously. Despite Elli's penchant for skipping her assigned duties, and her preference for skipping formal prayers in order to meditate quietly at the Great Temple whose origins date back to the **Dance of the Giants**, she was made an apprentice third class priestess. Nuic became her loyal maryth, although he refused to reveal much about his own past.

Despite her childhood losses and the trauma of slavery, Elli's laughter is as lilting as the song of a meadowlark. Her brown hair, with curls as thick as a **faery's** garden, surrounds her face, highlighting her hazel green eyes. While she has no idea that she will one day carry a gourd with magical healing water from the Secret Spring of **Halaad**, she carries something that is, to her, even more precious: her father's harp. The harp accompanies her everywhere—until the day she meets **Tamwyn**.

From the first day she encounters **Coerria**, High Priestess of the Society of the Whole, Elli reveres the elder woman. Coerria's spirit seems every bit as lovely, graceful, and unique as the shimmering gown of spider's silk that she wears. Secretly, Elli admires the gown, even though she is certain that she herself would never deserve to wear something of such remarkable beauty and heritage. Perhaps that is why she is so surprised when Coerria predicts that Elli will play a special role in the future of the Society, as well as Avalon.

Ethaun

This brawny blacksmith looks more like a bear standing upright than a man. His muscular arms are as knotted as tree roots from working the bellows and forging tools; his chest is broad and powerful. Yet despite Ethaun's fearsome size, the gap-toothed grin within his gray beard reveals a friendly disposition. He is partial to expressions such as "tickle me toenails," and enjoys puffing on his pipe as he trades stories.

And he does have some intriguing stories to tell. As **Tamwyn** discovers when he meets Ethaun in **Merlin's Knothole**, high on the trunk of the **Great Tree**, the blacksmith actually traveled with **Krystallus Eopia**, Tamwyn's father, on the fateful expedition to the **stars**. As Ethaun explains, he learned a great deal about the famous explorer on that journey. But did he learn the secret of the magical torch? Or what ultimately happened to Krystallus? The answers to those questions may be elusive, as well as painful.

Faeries

Throughout **Avalon**, travelers will hear the melodious hum of faeries' wings. It is a distinctive sound, common to all faeries. But to determine which variety of these creatures is making the sound, a closer look is required. For the types of faery folk are as varied as the habitats they prefer.

Water faeries have luminous blue wings, as lovely as translucent sapphires. They commonly wear silvery blue tunics, dewdrop-shaped shoes, and belts of dried berries. Parents will often carry their small children in backpacks made from periwinkle shells. Mist faeries also wear blue garb— not tunics, but robes, jerkins, stockings, and sashes. Their clothing is a lighter shade of blue, tinted to match their wings that are always a blur of motion. Their most recognizable feature, however, is the tiny silver bell that adorns each of their antennae. Hedge faeries, by contrast, can be any variety of green, and are covered with prickly fur. These faeries are famous for telling tall tales (and for stealing food from other people's gardens). Starflower faeries have buttery yellow wings. Known for their artistic impulses, they often leave wreaths of brightly colored berries on tree roots and fern fronds. So it is not surprising that the greatest of all faery artisans, **Thule Ultima**, was a starflower faery.

Catnip faeries are recognized not by their coloring or clothing, but by their behavior: They are crazily wild. Watching them buzz about erratically, it is easy to understand the origin of the old saying "crazier than a clan of catnip faeries." Mite faeries are found mainly in **Stoneroot**, and are very small, even for faeries. A whole village of mite faeries could fit on **Tamwyn's** thumbnail. Dog faeries are obedient and hardworking. Some have walnut brown fur, white wings, and dangling pink tongues. (A team of eight of them is trained to pull the rope to ring the Buckle Bell at the Drumadian compound.) Moss faeries look like tiny green humans with translucent wings. They enjoy tending moss, in gardens or in forests, and are often seen carrying water in hollow acorns. Spray faeries, though slightly smaller than most, are easily noticed because of their bright silver wings. These faeries love to congregate at waterfalls or fast-moving streams, glittering like liquid stars on the surface of the water. When they fly away in unison, it looks as if raindrops are rising off the water, raining upward into the sky.

Fairlyn

This tree spirit left her host tree, a lilac elm in the Forest Fairlyn, in order to become the maryth of **Llynia**. That constituted an act of great love, because it meant leaving behind her cherished homeland, a forest famed throughout

Woodroot for its wondrous aromas. Fairlyn's boughs have no leaves, only rows of small, purple buds. But those buds produce a variety of fragrances, depending on her mood: If she smells like freshly picked rose petals, all is well; if she smells like freshly crushed bones, beware.

Fairlyn's special gift is to prepare a sensuous, aromatic bath. She uses her many arms to mix and stir the liquids, powders, and pastes, even while her dark brown eyes scan her surroundings in search of any danger. Often, she enlists the help of **faeries**, who enjoy her fragrances—unless her mood turns to anger or impatience.

Like all tree spirits, Fairlyn can live indefinitely, even after her host tree dies. Yet tree spirits can still die of grief, or of terrible wounds.

Fraitha

Fraitha is the sister of **Gwirion** of the **Ayanowyn** people. Like all fire angels, she is completely hairless. And like the rest of her people, who have lost the use of their wings, her soulfire burns so low that it no longer flames. Even so, as **Tamwyn** discovers, there is still great bravery within her—as well as undiminished hope for her people. Fraitha, like Gwirion's wife **Tulchinne**, often wears a heavy shawl woven from hurlyen, a sturdy red vine. She plays on an amber flute, which makes a deep, resonant sound that is reminiscent of the music of the **Spiral Cascades**.

Ghoulacas

These winged beasts were bred by the sorcerer **Kulwych** for just one purpose: killing his enemies. Although they are not very intelligent, they are dangerous—and are feared throughout **Avalon**, no less than the magic-eating kreelixes were feared in **Lost Fincayra**. The huge birds' wings and bodies are nearly transparent; only their bloodred talons and curved beaks are easily visible. Their screech is loud and terrible enough to freeze the hearts of their prey. Because the ghoulacas' loyalty to Kulwych springs entirely from their fear of his wrath, there is always a chance that they might abandon him in the face of some greater terror. Even so, these killer birds are savage warriors who often battle to the death.

Gobsken

These burly creatures are terribly brutal and quick to anger. More than anything else, they respond to fear, lust, and greed. These qualities make them both exceptionally good warriors and exceptionally bad company. And while gobsken are invariably rude, they are often quite clever, as well as persistent. As such, they are ideal allies for the sorcerer **Kulwych** and his master, the spirit warlord **Rhita Gawr**.

Gobsken, such as those who labor for Kulwych at his lair deep underground in **Shadowroot**, have greenish gray skin and eyes as thin as slits. Their three-fingered hands are most comfortable when curled into fists, or wrapped around the hilts of broadswords.

Grand Elusa

This enormous white spider, larger than a horse, lived in the Misted Hills of **Lost Fincayra**. Her powers, it was said, were exceeded only by her appetite. While she had several important encounters with young **Merlin**, the peoples of **Avalon** remember her primarily for the glistening gown of spider's silk she wove for **Elen of the Sapphire Eyes**, which became the traditional gown of the High Priestess of the Society of the Whole. In time, that gown was worn by Elen's daughter, **Rhiannon**, as well as by **Coerria**. Yet no one, perhaps, loved the sheen and graceful design of that gown more than a young apprentice third class named **Elliryanna**.

Grikkolo

Grikkolo, one of the last survivors of the dark elves' brutal civil war, lives in hiding amid the ruins of the ancient library of Dianarra, the Lost City of Light in **Shadowroot**. Slim and wiry, he resembles a wood elf (such as **Brionna**) in form. But his silvery gray eyes are quite different: They are very large, practically the size of a hen's egg, and allow him to see well in the dark. His back is severely bent, causing his tunic to billow around his chest. From his head sprouts white hair as thick as a bed of ferns.

Grikkolo speaks in an erudite manner, for he is deeply learned. He is, as he explains to **Elli** and **Nuic**, always hungry—not for food but for information. That is why he originally came to the library. And why, although he has lived by himself for many years, he never feels lonely: He has countless friends—all the books that surround him. Yet he also cares deeply for the world outside his library. For that reason, even though he views himself as timid, he decides to do something extraordinarily brave to help Elli's quest.

Gwirion

Like all the **Ayanowyn** people, the fire angels, Gwirion is a winged man with dark brown, shaggy skin that resembles the bark of a burned tree. His eyes, too, are deep brown. He whistles low, wandering notes when he is thinking. His head, like the heads of his sister, **Fraitha**, and his wife, **Tulchinne**, is hairless. And his body temperature when **Tamwyn** meets him—as they are fighting for their lives against giant termites—is so hot that the young man thinks Gwirion is dying of fever. But Gwirion is not actually overheated. He is, instead, far too cold.

For the Ayanowyn people have fallen far. Their soul-fires, called llalowyn, have dimmed so much that they no longer flame. Instead of the bright orange, winged beings they were long ago, when their great leader **Ogallad** led them out of the **stars** and into **Avalon**, they are now flightless creatures who resemble smoldering charcoal.

How did this happen? Greed and intolerance were the causes. As Gwirion explains: "We told ourselves that only we knew what was right and good. At the same time, we started thinking of the **Great Tree** as our land, our possession, to exploit and use however we liked. We grew wasteful, destructive, and shortsighted. We burned forests to clear land for grazing our captive beasts, even if it clogged the air and sullied our streams. Then we moved on to other forests and did the same, over and over again."

Gwirion longs for the return of his people's most wise and glorious days, the time before their decline. That time was known as Lumia col Lir—the Age of Great Light, and is revealed by the storypaintings in the caverns and tunnels of the **Middle Realm**. Even more, he longs for the flames of his own soulfire. As a child, he attempted to make his soulfire burn brighter by trying to swallow hot fire coals. He lost his ability to taste by doing so—but in all the years since, he has never lost his yearning to burn bright.

Hac Yarrow

Hac Yarrow is, along with **Ilyakk**, the most celebrated flyer in the history of the eaglefolk. The story is told that, only a few minutes after she was born in a nest on the ridges of **Olanabram**, this eaglegirl saw a cloud floating high above her. She reached for it, stretching her tiny arms skyward, but could not touch its fluffy form. So upset was she, the story goes, that she cried for several days on end. And the tears finally ceased only when her eagle wings appeared at last, much earlier than usual for eaglefolk. Immediately, she leaped out of her nest, flew up toward the clouds—and rarely stopped riding the winds for the rest of her life. When, in her elder years, someone asked her why she still kept flying, she answered crisply: "I haven't yet found that cloud."

Halaad

A young child of the mudmakers of **Malóch**, Halaad had only begun to learn the ways of her elusive people when she was brutally attacked by gnomes. Gravely wounded, she crawled to the edge of a spring that bubbled out of the élano-rich mud of the plains. The magical qualities of this water immediately healed her wounds. And so, in the Year of Avalon 421, the Secret Spring of Halaad was discovered. Although this spring has long been celebrated in the stories and songs of bards throughout **Avalon**, its exact location is kept secret by the mudmakers. In all the centuries since its discovery, only two other people have been able to find it. They are the great wizard **Merlin**, and a young man whom **Aelonnia of Isenwy** dubbed a Maker: **Tamwyn**.

Hallia

This lovely young deer woman belonged to the Mellwyn-bri-Meath clan of **Lost Fincayra**. In the same season that she lost her beloved brother, she met the man who would become her closest companion for life: **Merlin**. Through Hallia, Merlin learned how to run like a deer, listening not just with his ears but with his very bones. She taught him, as well, the deer people's tradition of circling a story, and the truth about the tapestry of tales called the Carpet Caerlochlann. Most important, she taught him about love. And so Merlin voyaged to **Avalon** in the Year 27 to marry her. They were wed atop the highest peak in the Seven Realms, which the young wizard named Hallia's Peak. Later that year, their son **Krystallus Eopia** was born. Many years later, Krystallus would have a son of his own—a child who, thanks to Hallia, could run with the speed and grace of a deer.

Halona

Although she was born a princess of the flamelons, Halona rejected some of her people's fundamental values: their fierce enthusiasm for battle; their admiration for the war-lord of the spirit world, **Rhita Gawr**; and their disdain for any different races of people, especially humans. When she saw a human explorer, **Krystallus Eopia**, about to be killed, Halona acted boldly. She rescued the man and guided him to safety. Then, unexpectedly, they fell in love. Ignoring the danger of the Dark Prophecy, they married and conceived a child during the Year of Avalon 985—the Year of Darkness. Halona and Krystallus named the child **Tamwyn**, which means Dark Flame in the language of the flamelons. Tragically, the family was attacked soon after Tamwyn's birth. Believing that Krystallus had been killed, Halona escaped with her son into the remote cliffs of the Volcano Lands.

High on those cliffs, a strange and wondrous old man saved both their lives. At the same time, he brought them together with a recently orphaned eagleboy named **Scree**, who became Tamwyn's adopted brother. As full of grief as Halona was about having lost Krystallus, she never told Tamwyn the identity of his father, fearing that the knowledge might put him in danger. Meanwhile, it pleased her deeply to see how well the two brothers bonded, exploring, playing, and wrestling without end. At last, Halona decided that Tamwyn was old enough to learn the truth about his past. But before she could tell him, a band of **ghoulacas** flew out of a **portal** and killed her.

Hanwan Belamir (Olo Belamir)

A simple gardener at heart, Hanwan Belamir has the weathered, dirt-crusted hands of someone who enjoys working with plants. He wears a simple gray robe with long, wide sleeves and many hooks and pockets for garden tools. Around his neck is a string of garlic bulbs; one thumbnail is broken from digging in the soil.

Yet despite his appearance, Belamir is also more than a gardener. He is a charismatic teacher, with a deep voice that is both resonant and comforting. His teachings about improved techniques for farming productively led to the construction of the village of Prosperity in **Woodroot**, a bountiful settlement that is walled off from the surrounding forest. But Belamir's teachings have extended far beyond agriculture. His beliefs in humanity's "special role" as Nature's "benevolent guardians" has led him to develop theories about humanity's rightful "dominion" over other creatures. Those theories, in turn, have spawned the Humanity First movement, which has grown increasingly self-righteous and aggressive. The movement has led to outright scorn for the Society of the Whole's fundamental principle of harmony and mutual respect among all living creatures—just as it has led to violent attacks by humans against other beings.

Although Belamir is reviled by the elves and others, his following among humans continues to grow. Some, in fact, have taken to calling him Olo Belamir, adding the ancient term of honor to his name. No one since **Merlin** himself, who won the name Olo Eopia, has been so revered. Yet Belamir himself scoffs at such attention, preferring to call himself simply "a humble gardener."

Hargol

Hargol, highlord of the water dragons, long ago made his lair in lower **Brynchilla**, amidst the Rainbow Seas. As a direct descendant of Bendegeit, the brave highlord of the water dragons who rallied for peace in the War of Storms, he has a peaceful side. He is also deeply learned, and fluent in many languages; he is given to quoting the ancient adages of diverse **Avalonian** peoples. But he can also be very dangerous (as **Elli** learns). Like all water dragons, when enraged, he breathes ice—vast torrents of blue-tinted ice. And like most of his kind, he hungers always for jewels and crystals of beauty and power. In fact, Hargol possesses a special ability: He can sense the location of crystals, even very far away, and sense their magical powers.

Hargol always wears a bejeweled crown of golden coral on his brow, along with immense earrings made from thousands of black pearls strung on braids of sea kelp. The earrings clink and clatter whenever he moves his head. Barnacles studded with jewels also decorate his enormous snout. Hargol's fiery green eyes are very watchful, and he has ears as large as the sails of elven ships. As is common with water dragons, his massive body is covered with scales that range in color from glacial blue to dark purple. He is, indeed, very large, at least four times the size of his guards, with a head the size of a fortress. When Hargol speaks within the central cavern of his lair, his words rumble like a crashing waterfall. So loud is his voice that the sea stars decorating the ceiling of his cavern often break loose from the vibrations and rain down on his guards.

Harlech
This hulking warrior carries an assortment of weapons on his belt: a broadsword, a rapier, two daggers, and occasionally an ax. He fears only one thing—the wrath of his master, the sorcerer **Kulwych**. On his jaw is a deep scar from an attack by deadly **ghoulacas**. And he harbors a particular hatred for the only person who ever bested him in battle, the eagleman **Scree.**

Harshna
Harshna, ancient warrior-king of the **gobsken**, is remembered for just one quality: his unrelenting viciousness and brutality in battle. Even today, gobsken warriors invoke his name to bring them victory. And young gobsken are threatened with Harshna's ghost, who will gnaw away the brain of any child who shows unworthy traits such as kindness, honesty, or compassion.

Hawkeen

This golden-eyed eagleboy was one of the few survivors of an attack on his village, home of the Iye Kalakya clan of **Stoneroot**. When the attackers descended on his people's nests, built on a remote flank of **Hallia's** Peak, young Hawkeen tried to fight back. But the battle swiftly ended, leaving many dead—including the village healer, **Arckaya**, and Hawkeen's mother, whose heart had been pierced by an arrow. At the clan's burial mound, the eagleboy sang in memory of his mother, in a voice that blended the plaintive call of a child with the screeching cry of an eagle: "O Mother, my ship, my vessel on high! You have flown beyond sight, beyond fears. I miss you beyond any tears."

As he finished, his gaze met that of the eagleman **Scree**, who had once lost his own mother to a murderer's arrow. In Scree's strength, Hawkeen found a touch of hope. And in the eagleboy, Scree found a reflection of his younger self. He recognized this sad but sturdy youth; he knew this mixture of anguish and resolve. The bond between Hawkeen and Scree would grow, so much that they would fight together at the Battle of Isenwy.

Helvin

This bard is beloved by the **Ayanowyn** people, the fire angels. Although he was born blind, his other senses were so acute and his descriptions were so vivid that Helvin's rich, entrancing tales inspired the fire angels' first storypaintings, the spectacular murals that now cover the walls of caverns and tunnels throughout the **Middle Realm** of the **Great Tree**. **Tamwyn's** friend **Gwirion**, himself a storypainter, is most fond of Helvin's tales of **Ogallad the Worthy**. For those tales carry the hope that the fire angels might someday burn bright again—and possibly soar up to the **stars**.

Henni Hoolah

Henni, whose full name is Henniwashinachtifig, stands half the height of **Tamwyn**. But he has more than double the young man's capacity for making mischief. As a hoolah, he has no sense of caution, no sense of honor, and no sense of dignity—basically no sense at all. To Henni, life is just a game. Any mischief is good fun; any danger is irrelevant. As he tells Tamwyn soon after they meet: "I've never met a death trap I didn't like."

Like other hoolahs, Henni has very large hands (good for climbing trees or hurling fruit) and silver eyes surrounded by circular eyebrows. He laughs easily—especially at Tamwyn's clumsiness—and releases a raucous "eehee, eehee, hoohoohoohahaha" that can be heard from one end of a forest to another. In the custom of his people, he dresses simply, wearing only a baggy tunic and a red headband, and carries a slingshot in his belt.

Something about Henni may be changing, however. Gradually, he seems more conscious of his actions, and he may actually be showing signs of concern for others. It may even be true that he is more aware of the value of life (including his own). Yet these changes may not last. And for now, at least, none of this is as meaningful to Henni as the simple fun of pelting Tamwyn with fruit—or pushing him into the **Spiral Cascades**.

Hywel

As the oldest of the Drumadian Elders, Hywel has lived in the compound longer than anyone else—including **High Priestess Coerria**, who is nearly two hundred years old. Hywel was an Elder of the Society of the Whole before some of the current Elders were even born. As such, she takes very seriously her role as the keeper of the Society's traditions, through her responsibilities as the Dean of Timeliness and Decorum.

When Hywel stands beside the clanging Buckle Bell—

which was made from the belt buckle of a giant, melted down by the breath of a fire dragon, molded by dwarves, and decorated by **faery** artisans—she wears woolen earmuffs to protect her hearing. But there is precious little hearing left to protect. Hywel's eyes, however, remain sharp. As she scans the newest crop of young apprentices, who are about to begin their Formal Prayers, she looks for any signs of disarray. What she does not expect is that one apprentice has skipped Formal Prayers altogether—for in all her years, she has never met a young Drumadian quite like **Elli**.

Imbolca

This Drumadian priestess, known for her perpetual scowl, is an ally of **Llynia**. She believes that the Society of the Whole must regain its original purity. As such, she is deeply offended by **Coerria's** decision to admit **Elli** into the order, even as an apprentice third class. Imbolca's normally nasty mood is brightened when her maryth, the ginger cat Mebd, scratches someone annoying.

Ilyakk

No member of the eagle people, except possibly **Hac Yarrow**, ever loved to fly more than Ilyakk. As a young fledgling in **Rahnawyn**, he decided to soar to the top of the highest volcano he could find. When that proved too easy, he rode the swells even higher, sailing over the Burnt Hills of the fire dragons. Finally, when he was too exhausted to fly any longer, he settled down for a rest—not on land, but on the scaly snout of an airborne fire dragon. The dragon, amused by this intrepid youngster, carried Ilyakk higher still, until at last they glimpsed the rumpled ridges of the **Great Tree's** trunk rising upward. This experience merely whetted the eagleboy's appetite. As he grew older, he constantly pushed himself to fly higher and higher, rising to the Swaying Sea and beyond. No creature from the root-realms—save only the great dragon **Basilgarrad**, who once carried **Merlin** to the **stars**—has ever flown so high as Ilyakk.

Kerwin

This eagleman proved himself a warrior of great ability, as well as great honor, in many battles to defend the Tiernawyn clan of upper **Olanabram**. So it was no surprise that he was chosen to represent the allies of **Avalon** at the parley before the Battle of Isenwy. Like the rest of his clan, Kerwin has skin as brown as the muddy plains, flashing eyes, and eaglefeathers marked with black stripes—as well as ferocity that knows no bounds.

Kree-ella

Kree-ella, an eaglewoman of the Bram Kaie clan in **Fireroot**, was bold enough to resist the murderous ways of the clan's leader **Quenaykha**. For this action, Quenaykha ordered her caught, tortured, and killed, then hung from a post as an example to other potential traitors. Such is the gentle temperament of the leaders of the Bram Kaie—leaders whom **Scree** must confront.

Krystallus Eopia

The son of the wizard **Merlin** and the deer woman **Hallia**, Krystallus was born in the Year of Avalon 27. Although he was almost crushed as an infant when the giant **Shim** tried to kiss him, Krystallus survived. While he lacked his mother's ability to run with the grace of a deer, he did demonstrate a strong passion for exploring. Blessed with an exceptionally long life thanks to his wizard's ancestry, he became the first person to explore many remote parts of **Avalon**, including the Great Hall of the Heartwood deep within the trunk of the **Great Tree**. During his many expeditions, he developed considerable expertise in the dangerous art of **portal**seeking. He founded the Eopia College of Mapmakers in **Water-**

root, and chose for its emblem the star within a circle, the symbol for magically Leaping between places and times.

In the Year of Darkness, Krystallus journeyed to **Fire-root**. He was attacked by flamelons, but was subsequently rescued by the flamelon princess **Halona**. Despite the danger of the Dark Prophecy, they married and conceived a child. But soon after Halona gave birth, the family suffered a brutal attack. While Krystallus managed to escape, he concluded that both his wife and their son, **Tamwyn**, had been killed.

Beset with grief, Krystallus embarked on his most ambitious journey ever—to find the secret pathway to the **stars**. Neither he nor any members of his expedition ever returned. No one knows whether he might have left behind any clues about his route upward into the highest realms. And no one can say what might have happened to his magical torch, a gift from Merlin, that continued to burn as long as Krystallus remained alive. All that is certain is that somewhere on his journey to the stars, this great explorer perished.

Kulwych (White Hands)

As he prowls in the dark shadows of a stone wall above Prism Gorge in **High Brynchilla**, nothing can be seen of this cloaked sorcerer but his pale white hands. His fingernails are perfectly clipped; his smooth skin bears not a single callus. The rest of Kulwych, called White Hands by some, remains hidden. But his actions are more easily viewed—whether by finding the disemboweled bodies whose entrails he has read, or by seeing the enslaved creatures whose lives he has destroyed. Those creatures are being forced to build a massive dam across the canyon, a dam whose true purpose is known only to Kulwych and his master: the warlord of the spirit realm, **Rhita Gawr**.

Kulwych pulls the hood of his cloak tight around his head whenever the wind howls through the canyon, as if he detests the wind as much as he does any creatures who dare to oppose him. When, at last, **Tamwyn** causes him to remove his hood, the sorcerer's face looks more dead than alive. A jagged scar runs diagonally from the stub of what was once an ear down to his chin, taking out a chunk of his nose along the way. Where his right eye should be, there is just a hollow pit, full of scabs and swollen veins. His mouth, burned shut on one side, is merely a lipless gash.

Who caused this disfigurement? According to Kulwych, it was **Merlin** himself, at the height of the War of Storms. Kulwych's will to live helped him survive, but brought him centuries of pain. During all that time, he has plotted his ultimate revenge against Merlin—and against Merlin's beloved world of **Avalon**.

Lady of the Lake

Revered and dreaded throughout the realms, the Lady of the Lake first appeared in the deepest forests of **Woodroot** in **Avalon's** sixth century. Where she came from, or how she gained her vast powers, no one can say. Even her precise location has never been confirmed. Of the many brave souls who have tried to find her, only a few have ever returned.

Some people believe that the Lady must be a shape-shifting sorceress; others maintain that she is really the incarnation of the goddess **Lorilanda**. Still others claim that she is just an elderly woman who lives in a tree called New **Arbassa**, who surrounds herself with glowing **light flyers**, and who enjoys eating rivertang berries. Whatever her true identity may be, she remains shrouded in mystery as thick as the mists that swirl around her magical lair.

Le-fen-flaith

Among the vaporous sylphs of **Airroot**, Le-fen-flaith is celebrated as the realm's greatest architect. He designed many structures, including whimsical cloud sculptures viewed by appreciative audiences all across **Y Swylarna** in

the seventh and eighth centuries of **Avalon**. He also perfected the first successful anchors for the strings of aeolian
harps stretched between clouds. His most practical construction project was the Misty Bridge, whose cloudthread
ropes span the narrow gap between **Mudroot** and Airroot.
Although the bridge was finally completed three centuries
ago, in the Year of Avalon 702, it still stands today—albeit
shakily, as **Elli** discovers. The architect named it Trishila o
Mageloo, which means "the air sighs sweetly" in the
sylphs' native language. But in time, travelers came to call
it the Misty Bridge. The first people to cross it, other than
sylphs, were two special guests of Le-fen-flaith himself: the
Lady of the Lake and her friend, the pinnacle sprite **Nuic**.

Light flyers

These tiny, luminous creatures are among the rarest in
Avalon. Made by the mudmakers in imitation of the light
flyers from **Lost Fincayra**, they possess frilled wings that
pulse with golden light, enough to illuminate a room. It is
rumored that dozens of glowing light flyers accompany the
Lady of the Lake wherever she goes, often perching on
her hair.

Lleu

This tall, lanky priest has sharp eyes crowned by thick,
dark eyebrows. He is often accompanied by his maryth,
Catha, a silver-winged falcon who likes to perch on his
shoulder. Lleu was a good friend of **Elli's** father, during
their years together at the Drumadian compound, and is
now one of **High Priestess Coerria's** closest allies. Ac-
cordingly, he is highly suspicious of the priestess **Llynia**,
whose actions are guided more by her personal ambitions
than her Drumadian principles. Lleu's great-grandfather,
Lleu of the One Ear, was one of **Elen's** original disciples
in the earliest days of **Avalon**, and authored the famous
Drumadian text *Cyclo Avalon*.

Lleu of the One Ear

After the world of **Avalon** sprouted from **Merlin's** magical seed, Lleu of the One Ear followed **Elen** and **Rhia** in the founding of the Society of the Whole. He became one of Elen's first disciples, joined by Cwen, last of the treelings, and (to the astonishment of many who had seen her fiercely attack enemies) **Babd Catha, the Ogres' Bane**. Lleu joined Rhia and Merlin in an extraordinary journey inside the **Great Tree**, in the Year of Avalon 131, which led to the Drumadians' discovery of élano—the essential life-giving sap of the Tree, and a source of unfathomable power. Based on this experience, Lleu of the One Ear wrote his masterwork, *Cyclo Avalon*, which describes the workings of élano as well as the seven sacred Elements and the **portals** throughout Avalon. For centuries, this book has remained the primary text for all Drumadians.

Llynia el Mari

Once she became the Drumadians' Chosen One, who would eventually become the High Priestess, Llynia's arrogance and ambition began to overcome her devotion to the underlying principles of the Society of the Whole. Not only was she the youngest Chosen One since **Rhiannon** herself, she possessed the gift of seeing visions of the future. Those visions may have been only occasional, and vague, but they were still enough to win her renown—and also to win her advantage in her political schemes. As Llynia told herself regularly, she should use whatever means were necessary to climb to the highest levels of power. For she alone represented the purity of faith that could bring glory once again to the Society.

Although she resents the efforts of **High Priestess Coerria** to humble her—requiring, for example, that Llynia wear the same simple greenish brown robe as other priestesses and priests—Llynia feels certain that she will prevail in time. She remains convinced of her own superiority even after a strange green mark appears on her chin, the **Lady of the Lake** unexpectedly snubs her, and her maryth **Fairlyn** finally rejects her. Fortunately, the wise teacher **Olo Belamir** appreciates her singular virtues, proclaiming her Llynia the Seer.

Lorilanda

Goddess of birth, flowering, and renewal, Lorilanda is allied with **Dagda** and is equally revered by the many peoples of **Avalon**. Together, Lorilanda and Dagda rule the **Otherworld of the Spirits**. While they greatly prefer times of peace, they must also take time to contain their nemesis, **Rhita Gawr**. For the warlord spirit desires one thing above all else: to control the Otherworld and the rest of the worlds, as well.

In the earliest days of Avalon, the image of Lorilanda often appeared, taking the form of a graceful doe who brought about important discoveries. One such appearance, in the Year of Avalon 33, encouraged a young lad named Fergus to find the only path (other than through **portals**) connecting the realms of **Stoneroot** and **Woodroot**. Perhaps Lorilanda is also watching over **Elli** and **Tamwyn** when they follow that very same path, nearly a thousand years later.

Lott (Master Lott)

The only activity that Lott enjoys more than bossing around his roof-thatching laborers is eating a big, sumptuous meal. Having done much of both activities over the years, he is enormously fat. His eyes, sunk deep into the rolls of flab on his cheeks like a pair of almonds in a mound of dough, study his laborers suspiciously. Especially laborers such as **Tamwyn**—who, in Lott's view, is clumsier than a blind troll. Like many people who live in central **Stoneroot**, he often speaks in alliteration. Thus the terms he uses to describe Tamwyn include "horrible hooligan," "lame-brained lout," and "sluggish scalawag."

Mananaun

The last seer of the **Ayanowyn** people, the fire angels, Mananaun lived a long life. She died only eighty flames before **Tamwyn** arrived at the village of **Gwirion's** clan, located near the upward-flowing **Spiral Cascades** in the trunk of the **Great Tree**. Yet despite the misery of her people, whose soulfires had dimmed almost to the point of going out completely, Mananaun left behind a prophecy of hope. The fire angels, she predicted, would one day regain the power of their wings and the brilliance of their flames. They would fly back to the **stars**, where they had come from long ago in the days of **Ogallad**, and would be greeted by the great spirit **Dagda**. Then, at long last, her people would gain its true name and the story of the Ayanowyn would be renewed.

Maulkee

To **Quenaykha**, the eaglewoman who leads the renegade Bram Kaie clan of **Fireroot**, Maulkee is her most promising lieutenant. But to the eagleman **Scree**, who saw Maulkee murder the healer **Arc-kaya**, he is nothing but a bloody warrior. Maulkee is broad-shouldered and muscular, with a mouth that often twists into a haughty sneer. Though he is no more than seven years old, the eagleman is fully grown, the equivalent of a human in his twenties. And he is very experienced in the ways of warfare—a sport he quite enjoys.

Merlin (Olo Eopia)

Long ago, on a remote and rugged coast, a boy washed ashore. At the very edge of death, the sea had robbed him of everything he had once known. He had no memory, no idea at all who he was. He did not even know his own name. When he first opened his eyes to the sight of the sea, the rocky shore, and the screeching gulls overhead, no one could have possibly convinced him that he would survive that day to become a wizard. Yet he would, in fact, become the person celebrated by many as the greatest wizard of all times. For he would become Merlin—the wise mage of Camelot, the mentor to King Arthur, and the planter of the magical seed destined to become **Avalon**.

During the Lost Years of his youth, Merlin gained much—and also lost much. He witnessed the **Dance of the Giants**, along with his dear friends **Rhia**, the hawk Trouble, and the giant **Shim**. He solved the mystery of the Seven Songs, regained the lost wings of the people of **Fincayra**, and (thanks to **Hallia**) learned to run with the grace and speed of a deer. He encountered the wise and peaceful spirit **Dagda**, as well as the warrior spirit **Rhita Gawr**. Finally, he discovered his mother, **Elen**, his father, Stangmar, and his mentor, the bard Cairpré. And he also learned, through painful struggle, the difference between sight and insight. Along the way, he found that he held within himself both the dark and the light—just as he held other qualities that might seem opposites: youth and age, male and female, mortal and immortal. At last, Merlin won his true name—Olo Eopia, "great man of many worlds, many times." It is a name, as Dagda told him at the moment of Avalon's birth, for someone who is truly complete, just as the cosmos is complete.

That is how Merlin's adventures on the isle of Fincayra ended. And how his adventures in the new world of Avalon began.

Morrigon

Despite his advanced age, Morrigon is spry enough to serve his master, the teacher **Belamir**, quite effectively. And he is also mean-spirited enough to encourage the violent excesses of Belamir's Humanity First movement. Although he looks rather frail, with scraggly white hair sprouting from his chin and both sides of his head, Morrigon is adept at archery. But it is not his skill with the bow and arrow that arouses **Brionna's** curiosity. Rather, it is

Morrigon's irritated eye, which is so bloodshot that it looks pink—unnaturally pink—which could be the sign of a changeling.

Museo

Riding atop the head of the bard **Olewyn**, a museo is concealed by the bard's lopsided hat—until it is time to sing. Then this small teardrop-shaped creature shows itself, and is easily seen, and more importantly, heard. For like the others of its kind, the museo can sing with a rolling, layered hum that can entrance any listener. This rich hum contains many emotions, profoundly affecting those who hear. As the saying goes, nothing is "so deep as the note from a museo's throat."

Although museos can be any shade of blue or green, their skin is always flecked with gold. They are neither male nor female, but both at once. Museos have always been rare, even in their native land of **Shadowroot**. Centuries ago, they were driven out of the realm of eternal night. Since that time, they have wandered **Avalon's** other root-realms with their chosen bards—always searching for the home they cannot find, always singing about the home they cannot forget.

Neh Gawthrech

Feared even among his fellow changelings, Neh Gawthrech is known for the completeness of his disguises and the swiftness of his attacks. He changes so quickly that any witnesses see only a blur of claws, fangs, and his victim's blood. But it is rumored that the changeling's head is triangular in shape, with fangs that curl like scythes and scarlet eyes aflame with wrath. Last seen near the caves of the wyverns near the Wasteland of the Withered Spring in **Stoneroot**, he may have formed an alliance with the sorcerer **Kulwych**.

Nuic

This ancient pinnacle sprite from the high peaks of **Olanabram** is small enough to ride on **Elli's** shoulder. Yet just as his gruff, crusty manner conceals deeper emotions, his diminutive form conceals enormous wisdom and experience. Like all pinnacle sprites, he can produce a net of gleaming silver threads that serves as a parachute to float down cliffs. His favorite pastime, however, is more stationary: Nuic loves nothing more than to bathe relaxedly in a cool mountain stream. An expert herbalist, he often forages for vegetarian foods and herbal remedies. Precisely how old he is remains a mystery, though pinnacle sprites (like giants) can live for over a thousand years. The only mortal creatures who can live longer are wizards. And so it is no surprise that, long before he became Elli's maryth, Nuic was a friend of the **Lady of the Lake**.

While Nuic's liquid purple eyes and green hair are striking, his most remarkable colors are those displayed by his skin, which reveal a wide array of emotions. His skin fairly vibrates with colors, often in combination: orange for impatience, gray for somberness or gravity, red for anger, yellow for hunger, misty blue for contentment, and deep purple for pride. Two colors signify emotions so rare for Nuic that Elli is quite surprised when she notices them— frosty white for terror, and flashing gold for amazement. And then, as she discovers, there is one more color that is even rarer: lavender, for pure affection.

Obba and Ossyn

Combined, the mental capacities of these two brothers equal that of one fully functional adult. And their stupidity is exceeded only by their cruelty. Obba and Ossyn are hired by the sorcerer **Kulwych**, whom they call White Hands, in the long-dreaded Year of Darkness. Their task: to find the child who is the true heir of **Merlin**.

Ogallad the Worthy

Ogallad was the first great leader of the **Ayanowyn** people, the fire angels. Crowned by a golden wreath of mistletoe, a gift from the spirit lord **Dagda** himself, he led the fire angels down from the **stars** long ago, in the days before storypainters began recording the lives of this people. Ogallad led the Ayanowyn to the **Middle Realm** of the **Great Tree of Avalon**—just as he led them to their age of wisdom and glory, the Age of Great Light known as Lumaria col Lir. Today, Ogallad's memory flames bright in the minds of **Gwirion**, **Fraitha**, **Tulchinne**, **Mananaun**, and others. For that memory offers the slightest hint of hope that those days of Great Light might somehow come again.

Ohnyalei, the staff of Merlin

The staff of **Merlin** originally came to him from a magical hemlock tree in the Druma Wood of **Lost Fincayra**. Ever after, even centuries later, the wood bore the fragrance of hemlock, an aroma both sweet and tangy. In the course of its adventures with Merlin, through the help of Tuatha, the staff acquired seven runes—symbolizing the Seven Songs of Wizardry, the greatest ideas that a wizard must master. The runes depict a butterfly, for Changing; a pair of soaring hawks, for Binding; a cracked stone, for Protecting; a sword, for Naming; a star within a circle, for Leaping; a dragon's tail, for Eliminating; and an eye, for Seeing. While the staff was in Fincayra, the runes glowed with an eerie blue light. In **Avalon**, that color shifted to green.

Tall and gnarled, with a knotted top, the staff rarely left Merlin's side. In time, it gained surprising power, even wisdom, of its own. Merlin decided to call it Ohnyalei, which means "spirit of grace" in the Fincayran old tongue. He was counting on its grace, as well as its wisdom, when he entrusted it to a young eagleboy named **Scree**. For there could be no separating the fates of the staff, of Merlin's true heir, and of Avalon itself.

Olewyn the Bard

This strange old bard has a knack for appearing in the most unexpected places. He looks bizarre, even comical, with a sideways-growing beard, a lopsided hat that conceals a genuine **museo**, and dark eyes that seem both very young and very old. Yet despite his appearance, quirky manner, and jaunty walk, there is something hauntingly serious about him. His name, Olewyn, is reminiscent of the legendary mer woman **Olwen**, who dared to leave her people and her ancestral home to wed Tuatha of **Lost Fincayra**. But perhaps that similarity is simply random—defying any explanation, like so much else about the bard.

Palimyst

Palimyst is a member of the Taliwonn people, perhaps the most remarkable creatures on the branch-realm of **Holosarr**. When **Tamwyn** first meets Palimyst, he realizes that he must seem as strange to this creature as the creature seems to him. (In fact, the name Holosarr is the Taliwonn word for "lowest realm," since they have explored higher branches of the **Great Tree** but remain unaware of the existence of the root-realms below.) Like the rest of his people, Palimyst is gigantic in size, standing twice Tamwyn's height. He has two brawny arms, a hunched and hairy back, and a single leg as thick as a tree trunk. By contrast, at the end of each arm is a hand with seven long, delicate fingers, which Palimyst uses for fine craftsmanship. His eyes are dark and intelligent, and he is quick to perceive the hope—as well as the heroic qualities—in Tamwyn. It is he who tells the young man about the fabled **River of Time**, "the seam in the tent of the sky."

As a craftsman and collector, Palimyst lives in a tent of his own making. He displays there objects that he has woven, carved, and sculpted. As varied as they are, these objects share one fundamental virtue: All are made of natural materials shaped by mortal hands. Thus, as Palimyst explains, "they hold both the beauty of nature and the beauty of craftsmanship."

Tamwyn witnesses the strange, silent dance of Palimyst's people. They clasp their slender hands and form a circle, hopping and bowing in unison. Despite their great size and their need to balance on one leg, they move with the fluidity of blowing clouds. And so, like everything else about these creatures, their dance is full of remarkable contrasts.

Pwyll the Younger

Pwyll the Younger followed the path of his father, the poet Pwyll the Elder, and became one of the most famous bards in history. His songs and poems are as beloved by the people of **Avalon** as Cairpré's were by the people of **Fincayra**. Particularly powerful were his ballads about human fallibilities: greed, arrogance, and intolerance. In contrast to his contemporary, **Willenia**, he held a dismal view of humanity, far more tragic than triumphant.

Quenaykha

She is the stern ruler of the Bram Kaie clan of **Fireroot's** Volcano Lands, known by her followers as "Queen." Under her leadership, the clan survived its most difficult time— but it did so only by turning to thievery and murder. Discarding the eaglefolk's longstanding traditions of honor, this renegade group began to attack and pillage other clans. Instead of relying on their speed and talons in battle, the Bram Kaie use heavy wooden bows and arrows. The mere sight of their black-tipped wings and red leg bands is enough to prompt screeches of fear and outrage from other eaglefolk. And those screeches would be louder still if more people knew that Quenaykha has forged an alliance with the sorcerer **Kulwych**, who serves **Rhita Gawr**.

Another side of Queen is known only to one person— the eagleman **Scree**. For he met her long ago, when she still found joy in the sight of firebloom, the realm's only flower, whose orange petals flutter like tiny feathers. Or was that only an act, a ploy to lure Scree into danger? Although he is unsure of the truth, Scree concludes that he must do whatever is necessary to stop the Bram Kaie's murderous ways. And so he decides to travel to their remote nests, and challenge Queen for leadership. But he has no idea what surprises—and trials—await him there.

Rhiannon (Rhia)

Rhia's childhood changed abruptly when, as an infant, she was lost in the Druma Wood of **Lost Fincayra**. Adopted by a great oak tree named **Arbassa**, Rhia learned to speak the languages of trees, rivers, and stones. And she learned, as well, the importance of simply listening. When, at the age of twelve, she met her lost brother, she joined him at the **Dance of the Giants** and ultimately helped him to banish **Rhita Gawr** from their world. She also gave her brother his new name: **Merlin**. In their adventures to come, she would give him something even more important—a kind of wisdom that would enable him to inspire many worlds.

Together with her mother, **Elen**, Rhia created the Society of the Whole to guide the peoples of **Avalon**. The Society (whose priestesses and priests were called Drumadians, in honor of Druma Wood) was founded on two fundamental principles. The first principle was that all living creatures should live together in harmony and mutual respect; the second, that people should work to protect the **Great Tree**, which sustains all forms of life. After Elen's death, Rhia became High Priestess of the Society. After a remarkable voyage with Merlin and **Lleu of the One Ear** into the inner depths of the Great Tree in the Year of Avalon 131, Rhia introduced her followers to élano—the essential life-giving source of unfathomable power.

During the struggles of the War of Storms, Rhia grew disillusioned by the increasing rigidity of the Drumadians.

Finally, after failing to return the Society to its spiritual roots, she resigned as High Priestess. She departed abruptly, to the grief of her closest friends. What ultimately became of her remains a mystery. It is said that not even her loyal maryth, a pinnacle sprite named **Nuic**, knew just where she went. She may have traveled to mortal **Earth** to rejoin Merlin. Or perhaps she simply wandered alone throughout Avalon, unrecognized, and at her death, unmourned.

Rhita Gawr

This powerful warlord of the spirit realm continually battles **Dagda** and **Lorilanda** for control of the **Otherworld**. Yet that is far from the extent of his ambitions. His true desire is to tear apart the fabric of all the worlds and weave them into his own design. Nothing less than controlling every mortal world will satisfy him. That is why **Avalon**, the bridge connecting all the worlds, would be his most highly prized conquest.

Already he has made significant strides. He has won the allegiance of the sorcerer **Kulwych**, who is working to obtain the raw material for a pure crystal of vengélano with unlimited powers of destruction. Meanwhile, Rhita Gawr is rapidly opening the doorways from the Otherworld into Avalon—doorways through which the warlord and his army of immortal warriors can pass. Before long, Rhita Gawr will enter Avalon and assume the form of an enormously powerful dragon. Then, he believes, his triumph will be assured. For no one—certainly not **Tamwyn**, whom he recognizes as the clumsy young spawn of **Merlin**—will be able to stop him.

Ruthyn

This priestess in the Society of the Whole has a passion for the **stars**, and she studies them day and night. No one but **High Priestess Coerria** knows that Ruthyn's mother was one of the brave explorers who joined **Krystallus Eopia** on his ill-fated journey to the uppermost reaches of **Avalon**—a journey from which no survivors returned. Whether she is searching for some sign of her mother, or simply for knowledge, Ruthyn has become one of Avalon's experts on the history and lore of the constellations. But she, like everyone else, remains baffled by the enduring mystery of what the stars of Avalon truly are.

Scree

Bold and decisive are words often used to describe eaglefolk in general, and this young eagleman in particular. Yet down inside, Scree has always felt tormented by doubts about his capabilities and his true purpose in life. Born in a nest on the flaming cliffs of **Fireroot**, he knew only briefly the touch of his mother before she was murdered by men hired by the sorcerer **Kulwych** to find the true heir of **Merlin**. Scree was, on that night, too young to change at will into eagle form. So he could not yet sprout enormous wings from his human arms—wings with row upon row of feathers, entirely silver but for their tips as red as the volcanic fires of that realm. But he was not too young to remember every single word of his conversation with the wondrous old man who rescued him and **Tamwyn**. In the years to come, Scree would often reflect on what the old man had told him about the Dark Prophecy, the future of **Avalon**, and the precious **staff of Merlin**.

When in human form, Scree retains the hooked nose and pointed toenails characteristic of all eaglefolk, as well as the large, yellow-rimmed eyes that can see with amazing clarity over vast distances. Yet his broad, muscular shoulders give only a hint of his potential as a master of the sky. After changing into eagle form, he can swoop down on a foe with ease, wielding his talons as an expert swordsman would wield his blades. When this winged warrior dives downward, he releases a screeching cry, part eagle and part human, that makes most people run and hide. For that reason, he is surprised by the elf maiden **Brionna**. She not only remains in place as he plunges toward her—but releases an arrow that shoots him out of the sky.

For Scree, his future remains as hard to read as the vaguely glowing runes on the staff that he has promised to protect. To find his way—and also to help the young man he calls "little brother"—he must first discover the truth about his own past. Then he must learn to heal wounds deeper than a talon's gash.

Serella

Even as a child near the headwaters of the River Relentless in **El Urien**, the elf Serella showed a strong penchant for exploring. At the age of two, she spent most of a summer stealthily watching a family of wyverns and learning their habits. When she was seven years old, she built a small raft, packed her supplies, and floated down the river for a month-long adventure. As worried as her parents were during her absence, when she finally returned unharmed, they recognized that she had shown remarkable courage and resilience. Rather than try to stop her from making further explorations, they instead found expert tutors who trained her in wilderness traveling, map making, and communicating in diverse languages. Their confidence in Serella proved to be well-founded, for in the Year of Avalon 51, she discovered a magical **portal** in eastern **Woodroot**.

Over time, Serella mastered the dangerous art of portalseeking, becoming the first mortal to survive such journeys through the inner pathways of the **Great Tree**. So strong were her leadership skills that she amassed many followers among the wood elves, who ultimately proclaimed her their queen. After deepening her knowledge of travel by portals, she led several expeditions to other parts of **Avalon**, including repeated journeys to **Waterroot**. These journeys culminated in the founding of Caer Serella, the first colony of elves in Waterroot, at a bay on the Rainbow Seas. Thus the society of water elves was born. In honor of Serella, and in memory of their origins, the water elves made their symbol a rainbow-colored wave encircled in forest green.

Serella continued her travels through portals. Aware as she was of the risks of portalseeking, she still grew increasingly confident. Finally, she organized an expedition to the unexplored realm of **Shadowroot**. Nine brave elves, including Serella, departed—and none ever returned. Whether they were lost within the portals, killed by darkdeath, or destroyed in some other way, no one will ever know.

Shim

One of **Avalon's** oldest mortal beings, Shim was a close companion of the young man who would become **Merlin**. In those Lost Years, Shim helped Merlin destroy the terrible Shrouded Castle and outwit the evil warlord **Rhita Gawr** in the battle known as **Dance of the Giants**. Although Shim was originally smaller than a dwarf, he finally found the secret to growing into his full size as a giant. Thus he became at last, in his famous words, "as tall as the highliest tree." His adventures with Merlin continued, long after the **Fincayran** people won back their lost wings and the world of Avalon was born. Shim the giant became famous in story and song. A hero even among his fellow giants, he was honored without any reservation.

Then everything changed. During the Battle of the Withered Spring, in the Year of Avalon 498, Shim accidentally saved the life of another giant. He fell on top of the warriors who were attacking **Bonlog Mountain-Mouth**, eldest daughter of the giant sorceress Jubolda. Deeply grateful, Bonlog tried to thank him with a kiss. But at the sight of her enormous, slobbery mouth, Shim shrieked in terror and fled into the highlands. The humiliated Bonlog angrily pursued him, searching for Shim over many years without success.

Although he escaped Bonlog Mountain-Mouth, Shim met a new misfortune: For reasons he could not explain, he began to shrink steadily. When at last he emerged from his hiding place in the mountains, he had been reduced again to a dwarf's size—"utterly shrunkelled," as he wailed miserably. Although his bulbous nose still makes him recognizably Shim, few people even notice him now. He seems to be nothing more than an old, white-haired dwarf who is terribly hard of hearing, and whose language is oddly distinctive: "Certainly, definitely, absolutely."

Tamwyn Eopia

Tamwyn was born in **Fireroot**, the son of **Halona** of the flamelons and **Krystallus** the famed explorer, in the Year of Avalon 985—the dreaded Year of Darkness. His name, in the language of the flamelons, means Dark Flame, leading Tamwyn to wonder which would be his true destiny: the dark or the light. Soon after his birth, flamelons attacked the family out of prejudice against mixing races. Krystallus escaped, but believed that his wife and child had died. And so, filled with grief, he embarked upon the most dangerous expedition of his long life—to find a pathway to the **stars**. Halona and Tamwyn had actually escaped, but went into hiding in the Volcano Lands. When a strange encounter with a wondrous old man brought him together with an orphaned eagleboy, **Scree**, Tamwyn gained an adopted brother. Even in the years before Halona died in an attack by **ghoulacas**, the two boys were inseparable—until Tamwyn, at the age of ten, abruptly traveled by **portal** to **Stoneroot**. For seven years he searched for his lost brother, working as a wilderness guide and laborer, always keeping his age a secret because of the rampant fear of anyone who might be the child of the Dark Prophecy.

Although he is quite clumsy, often at inopportune times, Tamwyn still dreams of voyaging all the way to the stars. He longs to run among them, as if they were a radiant field. For ever since he could remember, he has loved to run—sometimes, it seems, with the grace and speed of a deer. Yet until he meets the mysterious **Lady of the Lake**, Tamwyn has no idea that this ability is the gift of his grandmother, **Hallia**, the deer woman of **Lost Fincayra** who married the wizard **Merlin** in the earliest days of **Avalon**. Even then, Tamwyn suspects that he is more likely to be the child of the Dark Prophecy than the true heir of Merlin.

Tamwyn has long black hair, with eyes equally dark. He always goes barefoot. Over his shoulder is slung a simple pack, whose leather strap will one day have its own story to tell. He wears on his hip a small quartz bell; its gentle sound is comforting, for it always reminds him of the land of bells. He carries an old dagger, which he uses mainly for whittling wood. Plowed up in a farmer's field, the dagger is actually "a gift of the land" whose origins are connected, in a surprising way, to **Rhita Gawr**. In his pocket, he carries a pair of iron stones and some dry grass tinder for making campfires in the wilderness. While such fire building has always come easily to Tamwyn, the art of making magical fires has not. In fact, he doubts that he will ever be able to make more than the illusion of magical flames.

Thule Ultima

The greatest of all the **faery** artisans, this starflower faery lived in **Woodroot** during the third century of **Avalon**. He carved, over several years, the ornate oaken doorway to the residence of the High Priestess of the Society of the Whole. He also perfected a technique for carving the nearly invisible bark of the eonia-lalo, **Airroot's** tree of the clouds. But his most famous creations were musical instruments made from harmóna that he and his apprentices gathered from the forests of **El Urien**: That wood is so rich with musical magic that even the slightest breeze will cause it to vibrate harmoniously.

Tressimir

Elder historian of the wood elves, he shares a deep bond with his granddaughter, **Brionna**. She calls him Granda, and they are each other's only family. He also shares Brionna's deep green eyes and pointed ears, as well as her ability to remain utterly motionless in the forest. His robe, woven of green riverthread grass, often smells like lemon-balm, which he uses to ease aching joints.

It is said among the elves that Tressimir could name every living tree in the forests of **El Urien**—and describe all the sights, sounds, and experiences that the tree had known throughout its seasons. He once confided to Brionna that, when it came his time to die, he would want to be buried beneath one of those trees: an ancient beech tree known as Elna Lebram, whose name means "deep roots, long memories." He imagined himself wrapped in several layers of shrouds, woven from silverplume flowers, laurel roots, and leaves of everlasting. And he hoped that, on that day, his life might seem as luminous as the flames of the resinwax candles that elves would set afloat on a nearby stream—flames that, while very small, could still bring light to the darkened boughs above.

Tulchinne

Tulchinne, one of the **Ayanowyn** people, has been the wife of **Gwirion** for thirty-eight years. Like Gwirion and his sister, **Fraitha**, she lacks hair and her soulfire burns low. So she wears a heavy shawl for warmth. Woven from hurlyen, a sturdy red vine, the shawl also covers her wings that are now—like those of all fire angels—too weak to fly.

Tulchinne loves to cook, and regularly serves lauva in ironwood bowls. Although her husband is grateful for the delicious smells, he cannot cook a successful meal himself, as hard as he tries. (This may stem from the fact that he can taste very little, having burned his mouth badly as a child.) Similarly, Gwirion often whistles, and Tulchinne enjoys the music, but has given up trying to master the art. "Whenever I try to whistle," she confesses, "small birds drop dead at our doorstep." Perhaps, **Tamwyn** muses, this arrangement has benefited their marriage: They fill each other's gaps, like two pieces of dovetailed woodwork.

Uzzzula

This hive spirit is **High Priestess Coerria's** devoted maryth. She resembles a bee with purple-tinted wings. Uzzzula is often seen buzzing around Coerria's head, busily braiding the woman's long white strands of hair.

Willenia

Here was a bard who celebrated the wonders of her world with the exuberance of a meadowlark announcing the arrival of dawn. Willenia was revered by the people of **Avalon**, as was her more dismal contemporary, the bard **Pwyll the Younger**. Yet much like Cairpré in the days of **Lost Fincayra**, this bard gave people a renewed sense of hope in themselves and their future. Willenia's cornerstone work was a complete history of Avalon, from the planting of **Merlin's** magical seed through the ages that followed. Its often-quoted opening lines are commonly called "Born of a Seed That Beats Like a Heart."

PLACES

Avalon (The Great Tree of Avalon)

Long ago, on the misty isle of **Fincayra**, the young wizard **Merlin** planted a seed—a seed that beat like a heart. He had won it on a journey through a magical Mirror, but he did not know what it might become. In time, it sprouted into a tree so vast and wondrous that a new world was born: the Great Tree of Avalon.

Avalon is a world in between all other worlds, a bridge between mortal and immortal. It is a place of infinite wonders, with endlessly varied creatures and places. And Avalon is also the only world where humanity and all other creatures live together in harmony—until greed and arrogance grow too powerful. Then, as the **stars** on high begin to vanish, and the sky begins to darken, the future of the Great Tree darkens as well. Whether Avalon will be saved or lost, no one can foresee.

Brynchilla (Waterroot)

Here is the realm of water, where the smallest rivulets gleam with pure élano bubbling up from the depths of the **Great Tree**, and the largest rivers flash with currents of bright color destined for the Rainbow Seas. Everywhere in this realm is the sound of water—from the thunderous White Geyser of Crystillia to the melodious rainfall of the Sea of Spray. Many a bard has sung ballads about the Wellspring of Mist, the watery Willow Lands, or the magical reflections of the Pool of Stars, yet these are but a few drops in an ocean of marvels. Waterroot's creatures range from the joyous bubblefish, who live only as long as a single heartbeat, to the wrathful water dragons—who, when angered, breathe torrents of blue-tinted ice. Phosphorescence sparkles in the waterways, especially in churning currents and in the wakes of elven ships, whose sails are made from woven fronds of elbrankelp. Even the trees of this realm speak of water: Branwenna trees are so fluid that, when their bark is cut open, their liquid wood can be poured.

Dance of the Giants

This climactic battle in the Dark Hills of **Lost Fincayra** finally destroyed the Shrouded Castle and ended the ruthless monarchy of Stangmar. The battle also ensured Fincayra's well-being, thanks to the bravery of the hawk Trouble, by sending the spirit lord **Rhita Gawr** back to the **Otherworld**. Centuries later, bards still sing about the sacrifice of Trouble, the heroism of young **Merlin** and **Rhia**, and the unexpected bravery of a small fellow named **Shim**— who hurled himself into the Cauldron of Death to save the lives of his friends. In doing so, Shim fulfilled Fincayra's most mysterious prophecy and revived Fincayra's most ancient people, while also transforming himself at last into a giant—which proved the truth of the **Grand Elusa's** observation that "bigness means more than the size of your bones."

And so, in this battle, Fincayra was saved, the lost Treasures found, and a young wizard's memory restored. That same young wizard took the name Merlin, in memory of the merlin hawk who had given his all. The crumbled remains of the Shrouded Castle took a new name, as well: Its ring of mammoth stones, standing in a stately circle, became known as Dance of the Giants—Estonahenj, in the giants' ancient tongue. Years later, the great spirit **Dagda** helped the followers of **Elen** transport the great circle of stones to the new world of **Avalon**. Rebuilt in **Stoneroot**, it became the Great Temple in the center of the compound dedicated to the Society of the Whole. Within that circle, a thousand years later, a young apprentice priestess named **Elli** would often meditate.

Earth

Homeland of humanity, Earth is a world of stark and subtle contrasts. It holds sublime beauty as well as horrid ugliness; it contains both mortal and immortal qualities; it knows both the short reach of human memory and the long reach of geologic time. There is war, poverty, and destruction of the very planet that supports all living creatures. And yet there is also natural wonder, diversity of life, and the most lovely expression of the human soul. Throughout history, humanity's qualities of creativity, compassion, generosity, courage, and wisdom have struggled against the darker sides of human nature: arrogance, greed, bigotry, ignorance, and hostility. In the end, the fate of this world rests with humanity's ability to choose its own future, to create its own destiny, through free will.

In all these ways, Earth is perhaps not so different from the worlds of **Fincayra** and **Avalon**—worlds that exist in between mortal and immortal, physical and spiritual. And the fates of these worlds may well be connected in surprising ways. Perhaps that is why the greatest wizard of all times, **Merlin**, chose to make Earth his home. For despite its many troubles, Earth remains a place that inspires our highest hopes.

El Urien (Woodroot)

The forests of El Urien hold trees of every description, along with glades of infinite tranquility, so it is no surprise that the name itself means Deepest Forest in the wood elves' language. Here a traveler can find magical harmóna trees, whose wood vibrates melodiously with every breath of wind; lilac elms, whose boughs produce many sensuous aromas; and the rare Shomorra tree, which grows a different kind of fruit on every branch. This realm's most famous tree, however, is Elna Lebram, an ancient beech tree where the elves have buried their most revered bards and scholars. In addition to the wood elves, who live in elaborate tree houses, the forest is home to billions of **faeries**—mist faeries, moss faeries, starflower faeries, and more. It is also home to innumerable kinds of food, including pears, tangerines, spicy pepperroot, cherries, plums, almonds, and larkon fruit (whose taste, the wizard **Merlin** once declared, is like "liquid sunshine"). Woodroot is the chosen realm of the famous gardener and teacher **Belamir**, who lives in the walled village of Prosperity. Somewhere in the dense woods to the east lives another person, equally famous though far more mysterious: the **Lady of the Lake**.

Fincayra (Lost Fincayra)

The Isle of Fincayra was, like **Avalon**, a world between worlds. Part mortal, part immortal, Fincayra was the first true home of young **Merlin**—and the place he lived during his Lost Years. It was also home to many of the first citizens of Avalon: **Elen of the Sapphire Eyes**, **Rhiannon**, **Lleu of the One Ear**, and the giant **Shim**.

Fincayra was a world of many wonders, of creatures and places of great beauty and surprise. Here one could find the Druma Wood, home of the magical spider, the **Grand Elusa,** and the ancient oak tree, **Arbassa**, who sheltered Rhia during her childhood. The legendary Carpet Caerlochlann, made from the misty threads of story, was woven here, near the dangerous smoking cliffs. Varigal, the original home of the giants, was built here, as was the Town of Bards, where the beloved poet Cairpré often composed. The mysterious **Otherworld** Well, pathway to the spirit realm, lay hidden on Fincayra's northern shores. And the Haunted Marsh held as many treasures as terrors. Perhaps Fincayra's most wondrous place, though, took shape in the very moment when the people of this world regained their lost wings: the place where young Merlin planted a magical seed. It beat like a heart as he gently put it into the ground—and gave birth to another world, the **Great Tree of Avalon**.

Holosarr

This is the lowest branch of the **Great Tree**. The name Holosarr is the Taliwonn people's term for "lowest realm," since they are unaware of the root-realms below. (Hence the Taliwonn craftsman **Palimyst's** astonishment when he first encounters **Tamwyn**.) Much of inner Holosarr, the region nearest the trunk of the Tree, is lined with long, narrow valleys divided by rocky brown ridges. Outer Holosarr, by contrast, is spotted with countless lakes of such clarity that they magnify the images of the **stars**. Because they also act like prisms, these lakes are called Starlight's Palette. In this realm live the Taliwonn people— immense, hunchbacked creatures who move with surprising grace despite the fact that each has only one leg. **Drumalings** also reside here, making any travel dangerous. High above soar colorful birds whose wingfeathers flash in the starlight, while bizarre insects fly nearer to the ground.

Lastrael (Shadowroot)

This is the realm of eternal night. There is no dawn; there are no **stars**. In Shadowroot, any light is an extremely rare phenomenon—to be deeply cherished or greatly despised, depending on one's view. Yet even in the unrelenting darkness, as the old elf **Grikkolo** would hasten to say, there are wonders of richness and subtlety. The **museos**, whose heartrending music touches any listener, originate from this realm. So does ravenvine, which produces intense heat but no flames when it is burned. In the Vale of Echoes, a single footfall can sound like an army on the march; a single drop of rain, like an endless cascade. For a time, there was also a City of Light, Dianarra, which hosted music and stories from many distant realms. The city flourished, adding colors to the night, until a different form of darkness descended—the darkness of intolerance and fear.

Malóch (Mudroot)

The brown plains of lower Mudroot seem dreary and lifeless at first, since they contain mostly vast stretches of mud. Yet this mud, rich with sacred élano, holds extraordinary life-giving qualities. The elusive mudmakers who live in this region include **Aelonnia of Isenwy**. They have long used their magical powers to form new creatures from the mud—and the results range from enormous elephaunts to tiny, glowing **light flyers**. The Secret Spring of **Halaad**, rich with the healing magic of élano, also bubbles out of these plains. But there is danger and brutality nearby, as well, for gnomes reside in underground tunnels. To the north, Mudroot erupts with greenery, in the rich jungles of Africqua. Yet here again, surprising beauty exists alongside stark danger, since the haunts of ghouls are not far away. Perhaps nowhere else in **Avalon** are there contrasts so dramatic as in Mudroot. So perhaps it is fitting that this realm, so rich with new life, is also the scene of terrible slaughter in the climactic Battle of Isenwy.

Merlin's Knothole

When **Gwirion** of the **Ayanowyn** people first told **Tamwyn** about this place, he called it Nuada Ildana, which means "Window to the **Stars**." As Gwirion explained in wonder, "It is an opening in the trunk of the **Great Tree**—where the stars, not élano, are the source of light." The Knothole lies at the highest starward point of the **Middle Realm**. Because it juts out from the trunk of the Tree, people can walk there, just as they do on the root-realms below or the branches above. Most remarkable of all, from this place one can easily view the branches—and all that lies beyond. When Tamwyn finally arrives there, he will view all these things, as well as one more thing that he did not expect to find.

Middle Realm

This is the **Ayanowyn** people's name for the inner landscape of the trunk of the **Great Tree**. Through the center of this realm runs the **Spiral Cascades**, which combine upward-flowing water, downward-moving light, and outward-drifting music. Emanating out from the cascades are countless tunnels carved by water, gnawed by termites, or opened by the workings of élano. The radiance of this life-giving sap provides light to the Middle Realm, making its tunnels and caverns glow subtly. Many sections of the tunnels are decorated with spectacular murals, created by the Ayanowyn storypainters, while others reveal colorful rings that hold the very memories of the Great Tree. High at the starward end of the realm is the Secret Stairway that leads to Nuada Ildana—what the fire angels call "Window to the **Stars**," and what others, such as the famed explorer **Krystallus**, call **Merlin's Knothole**. From that uppermost spot, one can see the branches of the Tree, and beyond, the stars of **Avalon**.

Olanabram (Stoneroot)

Of all the root-realms, Stoneroot has the brightest starlight. No one knows why that is so, just as no one knows why Stoneroot's rocks change color with every season. The high peaks in the north include **Hallia's** Peak, the tallest mountain in the Seven Realms and the only place where a traveler is high enough to see the lower reaches of **Avalon's** trunk. In central Stoneroot's farmlands, bells are everywhere—on barn doors, weather vanes, barrels of ale, and clothing. That is why these farms are often called "the land of bells." The Great Temple of the Society of the Whole is in this realm, in the center of the Drumadian compound. Bards sing that the temple's stones came from the famous stone circle called Dance of the Giants, in **Lost Fincayra**. The realm's plant life ranges from the ancient, twisted spruces of the Dun Tara snowfields to the small, rounded cupwyll plants that grow all year round in rushing streams.

Otherworld of the Spirits

The Otherworld is home to immortal spirits such as **Dagda**, god of supreme wisdom, **Lorilanda**, goddess of birth and renewal, and **Rhita Gawr**, god of war and conquest. It was beyond extraordinary that a mortal man would ever voyage to the Otherworld, especially one so young as the boy **Merlin**—but that was just what he did in the quest of the Seven Songs. To save the lives of the two people he loved most—his mother, **Elen**, and his sister, **Rhia**—Merlin found the secret pathway called the Otherworld Well. His own words, recorded after that journey in *The Seven Songs of Merlin*, provide the best-known description of the mysterious realm of the spirits:

> *The mist of this Well reminded me of the mist surrounding **Fincayra's** shores. Not so much as a boundary, or a barrier, but as a living substance possessing its own mysterious rhythms and patterns. Elen had often spoken about in-between places—places not quite our world and not quite the Otherworld, but truly in between. In the same way that this mist was not really air and not really water, but something of both . . . .*
>
> *As I dropped deeper into the mists, drawing nearer to the Otherworld with every step, I wondered what kind of world it might be. If Fincayra were indeed the bridge, where then did the bridge lead? Spirits lived there, I knew that much. Powerful ones, like Dagda and Rhita Gawr. But what of the simpler, quieter spirits, like my brave friend Trouble? Did they share the same terrain, or did they live elsewhere?*
>
> *Turning endlessly on itself, the spiral stairway led me downward. It struck me that there might be no difference between day and night in this world. There might not even be any time, or what I would call time. I vaguely remembered Elen saying something about two kinds of time: historical time, which runs in a line, where mortal beings march out their lives, and sacred time, which flows in a circle. Could the Otherworld be a place of sacred time? And if so, did that mean that time there turned in on itself, turning in circles like this spiraling stairway? . . .*
>
> *As I followed the Well deeper, something about the*

mist began to change. Instead of hovering close to the stairs as it had near the entrance, the mist pulled farther away, opening into pockets of ever-changing shapes. Before long the pockets expanded into chambers, and the chambers widened into hollows. With each step downward the many vistas broadened, until I found myself in the middle of an immensely varied, constantly shifting landscape.

A landscape of mist.

In wispy traces and billowing hills, wide expanses and sharp pinnacles, the mist swirled about me. At some points I encountered canyons, cutting into the cloudlike terrain, running farther and deeper than I could guess. At other points I glimpsed mountains, towering in the distance, moving higher or lower or both ways at once. I found misty valleys, slopes, cliffs, and caverns. Scattered throughout, though I couldn't be sure, moved shapes, or half shapes, crawling or striding or floating. And through it all, mist curled and billowed, always changing, always the same. . . .

An uneasy feeling swelled in me. That what surrounded me was not mist at all. That it was not even something physical, made from air or water, but something—else. Made from light, or ideas, or feelings. This mist revealed more than it obscured. It would take many lifetimes to comprehend even a little of its true nature.

So this was what the Otherworld was like! Layers upon layers of shifting, wandering worlds. I could plunge endlessly outward among the billows or travel endlessly inward in the mist itself. Timeless. Limitless. Endless.

Portals

Discovered by the wood elf **Serella** in the Year of Avalon 51, magical portals provide a very swift—and very dangerous—

mode of travel throughout the root-realms of **Avalon**. While portals take varied forms, and are found in many different settings, they are always marked by crackling green flames. From the entrance to a portal, a traveler can glimpse what lies behind the flames: pulsing rivers of light that can carry people to any of the Seven Realms (except, in recent times, to **Shadowroot**, whose only portal was destroyed during the civil war of the dark elves). Portals also lead to the mysterious Swaying Sea, which is neither a root nor a branch, and deep into the trunk itself, to the Great Hall of the Heartwood.

Portalseeking requires total concentration. For portals magically disassemble travelers, carrying them through the innermost veins of the **Great Tree**, and then reassemble them as they arrive at their destination. Without clarity of mind, travelers might arrive somewhere else—or, even worse, might disintegrate completely, merging utterly into the Tree's élano. And some portals seem to have minds of their own, choosing random destinations for voyagers. All this makes traveling through portals a delicate and dangerous art. In the words of Serella: "Portalseeking is a difficult way to travel, yet an easy way to die."

Rahnawyn (Fireroot)

Fireroot is a land of flaming ridges and charred rock, erupting volcanoes and plumes of sulfurous smoke. Most of this realm is red or orange; even its water is the color of rust. Ironwood trees, with fiber so hard they are fire resistant, flourish in the valleys. On the ridges of the Volcano Lands grow fire plants, shaped like ghoulish hands that grasp at the feet of passersby. Experienced travelers prize the honey of Fireroot's burning bees, which is always warm. (They work hard, however, to avoid the bees themselves, because their stings burn like hot coals.) Despite the harshness of the terrain, peculiar forms of wildlife abound. Salamanders enjoy lounging in flame vents,

while oxen roam the Burnt Hills, always wary of fire dragons. Only one flower grows in this charred realm—
firebloom, a small orange blossom that thrives on ground
recently scorched by flames. The flamelon people are often, though not always, as fiery and volcanic as their
homeland. They are industrious and inventive, as well,
with particular skill at crafting weapons of warfare. Most
flamelons do not worship **Dagda** and **Lorilanda**, the great
spirits of wisdom and rebirth who inspire many peoples
throughout **Avalon**. Instead, they honor the wrathful spirit
Rhita Gawr, seeing him not as a god of war, but as a
force of creation that scours the land so that firebloom
may flourish.

River of Time
A vague line of light in the sky, the River of Time is visible
only from **Holosarr** or the higher branch-realms. Like a
luminous crack, or a seam in the fabric in the sky, it runs
through the realm of the **stars**. In fact, its name in the language of the Taliwonn people, Cryll Onnawesh, means
"the seam in the tent of the sky."

As the Taliwonn craftsman **Palimyst** explains to **Tamwyn**,
the River actually divides the two halves of time—past and
future. Thus within the River itself, time always remains
fixed in the present. Because of this, anyone who enters the
River can move along its course, which passes near every
star, traveling enormous distances in space while remaining
in the present time. And if **Avalon** indeed lies between all
the other worlds, connecting each of them, the River of
Time may well link these worlds in a surprising fashion:
One could ride to anywhere in the universe—and never
leave the present moment.

Spiral Cascades
Flowing deep within the trunk of the **Great Tree**, this
wondrous place is the union of three cascades. One is made

of water, which spirals higher and higher, connecting the roots far below to the **stars** high above. One is made of light, which floats endlessly downward. And the third, as **Tamwyn** discovers, is made of music. The music vibrates, harplike, while swelling with the fullness of horns and the sweetness of bells.

Stars of Avalon

What, truly, are the stars of **Avalon**? That question has puzzled people through all the ages of Avalon. Many, like the young wilderness guide **Tamwyn**, have often gazed up at them, tracing the shapes of favorite constellations: Pegasus, soaring on high; Twisted Tree, stretching endless branches; the Mysteries, glowing with an aura of lavender blue; and the Wizard's Staff, burning bright for centuries after its stars were lit by the wizard **Merlin**.

Then, without warning, the stars of the Wizard's Staff start to go dark once again. One by one, as Tamwyn and others watch in stunned silence, the light of those stars vanishes. For centuries, people have wondered why the stars dim at the end of every day, after a flash of golden light, just as they have wondered why the stars brighten again every morning. Now, however, they long desperately to know whether the stars—and the world illuminated by them—will ultimately survive.

Y Swylarna (Airroot)

This is the realm of cloudscapes that seem to stretch on forever, and aeolian harps that play haunting music without beginning or end. Mist maidens spiral in their sacred dancing grounds; **faeries** create cloud gardens; and the Air Falls of Silmannon rumble ceaselessly. Across the Misty Bridge, designed three centuries ago by the sylph architect **Le-fenflaith**, the Veils of Illusion conjure images of whatever fears may be riding the wind. Not far to the north, the Harplands' vaporthread strings respond to travelers' deepest emotions, sounding discordant, harmonious, or conflicting mixtures of both. Ghostly forests grow here, because of the eonia-lalo ("tree of the clouds" in the language of the sylphs), whose wood resembles frozen mist and whose bark is nearly invisible. Millions of winged creatures soar through this realm, or rest at the Isles of Birds. Yet their songs are no more sweet, no more lilting, than the sounds of the air itself.